daynight

by Megan Thomason

Dedicated to my muses/twenty-four seven comedic entertainment

Husband: Jon
Children: Ashley, Breanna, Ryan, Alyssa and Christopher

Praise for daynight

"Gripping young adult dystopian novel; compelling conflicts; high stakes; powerful narrative; surprises keep coming; strong writing; page-turner; engaging characters; Readers will be hungry for the sequels."—*BlueInk Review (starred review)*

"Sure to win over YA readers looking for a dangerous, dystopian adventure story... A sci-fi adventure with a sweet YA love story at its center... richly imagined alternate world... distinctive voices and conflicting motivations" —*Kirkus Reviews*

'Thomason's description of Thera's totalitarianism will make fans of Brave New World shiver... SCI, her fantasy corporation, has disturbing parallels to actual companies and regimes that claim to do good while harming people... The author deftly appeals to both romance-loving teens as well as those intrigued by young adults fighting the establishment."—*Foreword Clarion Review,* 4 stars

"The writing is impressive and the story is a real page-turner. So many twists and turns... I'm hooked... I can't wait for the next installment to come out...4.5 out of 5 stars"—*Self-Publishing Review*

'The plot was finely done. It was steady, tidy, and pretty much perfect. I have a feeling this will be one of my favorite 2013 reads, and can't recommend it enough."—*Lust for Stories* blog, 5 stars

"SHE WRITES LIKE THERE'S NO TOMORROW. I really enjoyed Megan Thomason's writing style... I liked that the characters spoke like real people but I especially liked their sense of humor... daynight is definitely a must read. It's the right combination of romance in a dystopia setting written wonderfully in a well-paced, **mindblowing** story."—*Sab The Book Eater* blog, 5 stars

"The story line in Daynight is different than any other novel out there, refreshingly so. The characters are original and you fall for all of them. Daynight by Megan Thomason is better in its 324 pages than all the Twilight Saga books put together. The ending will leave you down on your knees begging for more."—*Castles in the Air Books* blog, 5 stars

"Daynight was definitely a very imaginative and very creative book. It's a Dystopian at it's finest, that is for sure."—*Shortie Says* blog, 4 stars

"daynight is a book for all Dystopian fans. I have never read a world that was created so smoothly and put together. I mean right from the opening line you are hooked."—*A Diary of a Book Addict* blog, 5 stars

"Gorgeous gem of a book... Daynight went from motivation to obsession in three chapters. This book is enthralling, captivating and I just want to devour and then savor everything about it. All three narrators are perfect and beautiful and interesting. This story really captures the unique personalities of the human race; what we will do for love, what we will give up for what's right, what strong morals and unwavering loyalty can do. I am drooling over Thomason's work and I am aching to read the rest of this series."—*Rattle the Stars* blog, 5 stars

"Whether viewed as a modern parable or a thrill ride, Daynight was the most compelling and intense book I've read since Free Souls by Susan Kaye Quinn. I like books with intrigue and puzzles to solve, and daynight provided plenty. I also like books with layered meanings, and daynight had more religious symbolism than The Grapes of Wrath. Wow. 5 Theras."—*Sher A Hart: Written Art* blog, 5 stars

"Delicious humor, intelligence, and sparkling dialogue"—*Amazon reviewer*

"Strangely brilliant and imaginative"—*Amazon reviewer*

"Grips you from the first page and keeps you wanting more"—*Amazon reviewer*

"Plot twists kept me reading till late at night"—*Amazon reviewer*

"Gripping...nothing is as it seems"—*Amazon reviewer*

"love Love LOVE. I really can't say enough about this novel to express my love for it. I am anxiously awaiting the next installment! I would definitely recommend this novel to anyone."—*Amazon reviewer*

PROLOGUE

The moment the perfectly styled, blonde-haired, blue-eyed girl awakens to the sight of her own dead body, she swears and slaps her corpse across the face. The gesture makes no impact. She checks her hands. Not a lick of vomit, despite the fact Dead Her's covered with it.

"Stupid," she yells at her dead-self. "If we were going to go, it should have been in grand fashion. A high speed car chase or skydiving or getting blown to bits by a terrorist. Not by some *fluke*. Not at my own party!" Someone will find us and fix this, she thinks.

She catches a glimpse of her animated self in the mirror. No longer dressed in her tailored Dolce & Gabbana dress or to-die for Prada jeweled satin 5 1/2 inch heel pumps, a simple and quite ugly grey shift hangs loosely from her body. An ear piercing scream leaves her lips. No, no, no. This can't be real. Has to be a nightmare. There's no way she'd ever wear such an insult to the fashion gods. She attempts to remove the shoes from her corpse as they'd easily make her top 100 pairs, but they won't budge. Nor will the Tiffany necklace adorned with a most sentimental ring. Frustrated, she pummels Dead Her with well-placed kicks, but the stiff doesn't flinch an inch.

"This isn't a dream and we generally advise against beating oneself up," a voice booms behind her. A tall man with white hair has appeared next to the girl in her locked parent's master bathroom. His somber tone and white, pristinely pressed suit signal "all business." "Sit down," he invites, gesturing to a small metal table and chairs that weren't there a minute ago. The girl's mother would fall down and die right next to the girl if she saw warehouse quality furniture adorning the special-ordered Italian floor and Louis XVI-era commode.

"Tell me what happened," the man instructs.

"Am I really dead?" the girl asks, ignoring his request and pointing to the

1

lifeless figure on the floor.

"I think that's quite self-explanatory," he says. "Determining the how and why will help me place you."

She rolls her eyes. "Place me? As in Heaven vs. Hell? Let's see. I don't pray or worship anyone other than my personal shopper and tailor. I haven't been to church in more than a decade. So, I'm thinking I'm headed downward. And if that doesn't seal the deal, drinking myself to death at my own party should do it. But maybe you take pity on entitled kids left to their own devices by jet-setting parents?"

He opens a notebook and jots down a few notes, before asking, "You took some pain killers earlier this evening?"

"Yeah. I had some pain," she snorts.

"From the tattoo you got after partying with your friends last night? A single black rose between your shoulder blades?"

"Uh, yeah. How'd you know about that?" she says, wondering if it is still present. The nagging itch and twinge of discomfort that were there yesterday have disappeared.

"Did you know your tattoo was infected?" he asks, not even looking up.

"Serious? No," she gasps, knowing she shouldn't have trusted that grimy Mission Beach tattoo parlor.

"You had fourteen drinks over the past six hours? Six shots, three vodka-tonics, and five glasses of punch?" he says, as he pushes his reading glasses farther up the bridge of his nose.

"Something like that," she sneers. "As I said, it was a party. *My* party."

"Did you know some of your male house guests supplemented the punch with an additive meant to loosen inhibitions?" he asks.

"Nope. Sounds like something the idiots would do though."

"Were you depressed at all? Did you have a desire to die?" he says.

"It was a *mistake*," she says. "It wasn't about depression. It was about fun. Ever heard of it? It's ridiculous I had to die over it. Everyone else seems to get a second chance. Why not me?" The man takes his time reviewing his notes and seems to make some sort of decision as he closes his notebook.

"I know just the place for you, Ms. Goodington," he says. "Follow me."

"Ms. Goodington is my mother," she scoffs. "Call me Bailey."

And God said, Let there be light: and there was light.
And God saw the light, that it was good: and God divided the light from the
darkness. And God called the light Day, and the darkness he called Night.

Genesis 1:3 5

If light is good, what does the dark bring?

CHAPTER ONE

Kira

Escape, I remind myself. That's why I'm here. On a speedboat. With a creepy escort who looks like the human incarnation of Mr. Potatohead. Heading into the open ocean towards an unknown destination. I'd eagerly signed the dotted line of The Second Chance Institute Recruit year-long contract, agreeing to leave all my earthly possessions in San Diego. It seemed easier to run than face my demons. I do regret abandoning my brother, Jared. He's a year younger and it's always been us versus them, and by *them* I mean the judgmental, self-centered beings who gave us life. My parents couldn't shove me out the door fast enough, as my distress infringed upon their illusion of a perfect, carefree existence.

Just the thought of escaping reminds me of the events that led to my decision. I close my eyes and let fragments in, fighting the tears away. The horror-filled incident happened two months ago. My SCI Recruit Test preceded my senior year Winter Formal and after-party, which I attended with my boyfriend, Tristan and best friend, Briella. At the party, they ditched me after having tormented me all evening for considering a "do-gooder stint" with the SCI. I figured they'd drink it off and get over it. In their absence, I met the perfect(ly unattainable) guy, Ethan. Who had me fantasizing about marriage, babies and growing old together. But, we were both taken and, regrettably, parted ways.

The turning point of the fateful evening and reason I'm still alive: catching my boyfriend and best friend groping each other in a steamy make-out session. Refusing to discuss or forgive, I'd fled the posh Rancho Santa Fe estate and out into the darkness. Eerie silence was followed by ear-splitting, bomb-like thunder. Whatever the source, it leveled the house in seconds, raining fire and debris in every direction. I remember being hit by shrapnel and the resulting blood and pain. Being dragged from the wreckage. And then, medical personnel, police and the press all hounding me to know how I escaped the tragedy that left 110 of my classmates—including my boyfriend and all my close friends—dead.

I push the memories aside and lean back on the vinyl cushions of the boat. Listen to the whir of the motor. The spray of the boat's wake cools the effects of the glorious Southern California sun and dampens my long, more-strawberry-than-blonde curls. Cutting through the waves at high speed rocks me into a trance. My SCI Recruiter, Ted Rosenberg—the Mr. Potatohead clone, who I've nicknamed "Spud"—encourages me to "enjoy the nice weather while it lasts," but I don't respond. He yaps about Unit 27, my final destination, warning of "extreme temperature variations." Dump me at the North Pole, I think, if it puts distance between me and my memories.

According to their brochure, The Second Chance Institute places Recruits worldwide, with many prime locations throughout Europe, Asia, Africa and South America. Unfortunately, Recruits don't get to choose where they serve and you can't take anything with you other than the clothes on your back. The SCI provides "everything needed" to adapt to one's assignment. I sincerely doubt they can anticipate my every need, but don't really care. I just want to get there and learn the where/what/whys about this mysterious Unit 27.

My blood apparently contains some random marker called DNT that made me an "excellent candidate" for one of SCI's more "remote" and quite classified locations. So other than knowing that 50,000 residents make their home in Unit 27, I'm going in blind. I'll help "those in need of a second chance at life," but in what capacity I'm clueless. Does it matter what I do? In return for my year of service, the SCI will grant me a full-ride scholarship to the college of my choice. Given I'm shooting for Ivy League or equivalent, I could use the help. My parents firmly believe in "supporting one's self once one turns 18" or in other words, not depleting my mother's jewelry and vacation fund.

The boat slows and my stomach pitches up and down with the waves. I sit up and scan the horizon. What the—? Impossible. A dilapidated warehouse-like building, no larger than a two-car garage sits atop the ocean water. Other than squawking seagulls lining the roof, there's no other sign of life. Spud easily maneuvers the boat up alongside the building and ties it down.

"Where are we?" I ask Spud. "Are we transferring to a larger boat here or something?" I'd spent the morning badgering him about our method of transportation to Unit 27. An airplane, I'd understand. A speedboat, not so much. No land mass off San Diego could house 50,000 people.

Spud bobbles his head and in a harsh tone says, "Ms. Donovan, please follow me. There is no time to waste if you are to adjust properly and start your training on time. We're the last to arrive." He offers me a hand, and helps me to my feet. We both leave the boat, though that does nothing to make me feel like I'm back on solid ground. The building sways with the waves. All directions offer no view of land or ships. Not good. We may be stuck here a while. Perhaps they'll have a comfortable couch and food for the wait. I trail Spud into the dark and musty building. Disappointment strikes. The space we enter has a single, dim lightbulb which illuminates the small room enough to see peeling drywall and dark patches that look and smell like mold. A single arched doorway mirrors the door we entered on the opposite side of the room.

"OK," Spud continues, "Ms. Donovan, go straight ahead to the end of the long corridor and into the large room. I will follow you."

My brain won't accept the thought of the small building containing a long corridor, much less a large room, but I'm eager to exit. I stumble forward through the dark, tunnel-like hallway for the equivalent of a city block before seeing a light ahead. My skin itches from small pinprick-like sensations from head to toe and I am parched beyond comprehension. I feel dizzy and ill, and have to stop to catch my breath as I enter the lighted room, an immense domed space as wide as a school cafeteria with pebbled walls and slate floor. Spud enters the room after me and vomits into a receptacle so violently his body convulses. He motions a small group across the room to join us before collapsing on the floor.

I notice that the wave-like motions have ceased. As I canvass the cavern-like room with my eyes, I'm positive that I am farther than the hundred feet from the boat I should be.

"Mr. Rosenberg, where on God's green earth have you brought me?" I gasp.

"Technically, Ms. Donovan," Spud grunts between spasms, "we are no longer on God's green earth."

"Say what?" I demand. I could have sworn I heard something to the effect of "not on" and "earth" in the same sentence, which isn't possible.

A tall man with wavy hair and glasses smiles widely and says, "Ah, our last Recruit has finally arrived. Ms. Donovan, welcome to Garden City, Thera, otherwise known as Unit 27 of the SCI. And here," he says motioning to the rest of the group with him, "are some of the other SCI Recruits." I immediately recognize the Recruit at the end of the row, arms crossed across his chest, smug look and bright green eyes rolling back in a dismissive fashion. He is the classmate who took the SCI Test with me and saved my life that night —Blake Sundry.

I don't hesitate. Too ill to care about the mind games being played and hyperventilating at the absurd claim we've left earth, I turn to head back into the tunnel and for the boat. Such a seemingly easy task, however, proves impossible. As I reach the tunnel entrance, I'm flung ten feet backwards, head whacking the pebble floor, air expelled from my lungs. In my blacked out state, I fully relive the fateful day that set me on this path.

SCI Test Day. Seven a.m. I'd met Tristan and Briella for breakfast at the bleak iHop within power walk distance of Carmel Valley High. Bri sported a bright blue scalloped sweater that matched her eyes, although her eyes were hard to see behind all her makeup. Even in the wee early hours of the morning she went for the night club look, a look she pulled off beautifully. Her long dark hair fell mid way down her back, although that day she didn't bother to flat iron it, a sure sign she woke up late. Tristan was unusually quiet, his chocolate-colored eyes sullen. I raked my hand through his blonde curls; happy his hair had grown out from his football season buzz cut. Other than the dour expression on his face, he looked amazingly handsome in his yellow long-sleeved tee and jeans.

Our formica-topped table reeked of harsh chemicals from just being wiped, which caused my nose to twitch, and my tummy sloshed over nerves about the Test. Bri, who enjoyed lovingly meddling in my life, railed on me for agreeing to take the Test, given I'd be ditching my senior year if I got chosen. Tristan's grim expression echoed Bri's sentiments. Why was I taking it? Right, the scholarship and a future free of student loans. I tried to assure both Bri and Tristan that I'd never be selected so they shouldn't worry, but no optimistic sentiments on my part could improve the mood.

My body lurched upward as our waitress dropped a hot plate of eggs, sausage, and pancakes all over the floor next to us. The stench of the greasy eggs made me want to retch. So, I excused myself to leave for the testing center early. Tristan gave me a half-hearted peck goodbye. He tasted like mint toothpaste and Coke— which don't mix well. After whispering a monotone, ritual "I love you" in to my ear, he reminded me he'd pick me up at six for dinner and the Winter Formal. I returned the sentiment with more enthusiasm before waving and winking to Bri. She barely managed a smile before turning her attention to Tristan. They appeared to be deeply embroiled in conversation by the time I exited the iHop doors. Ganging up on me I suspect. I felt terrible disappointing them, so disappeared around the corner, head drooped, mood

6

soured.

Seven-thirty a.m. A hooded classmate on a skateboard clipped me as he screeched to a stop in front of the testing center, bruising my shin. He offered no apology, and worse, slammed the door in my face. Blake Sundry from English. What was his hurry, and why did he wear the same hooded black and white flannel every day? I had never seen him hoodless, which made me wonder what he was hiding. Rumor had it, a serious drug problem. I'd been quickly distracted when a fat man who looked like his head was fifty percent too large for his body—and shaped most unfortunately like Mr. Potatohead—droned on about Test instructions for thirty minutes. I imagined sticking different eye-nose-mouth-ear combinations on his face to improve his somber look as an entertaining distraction. His bug eyes and patch of bushy black hair atop his head worked well for the Mr. Potatohead look, but the rest of his features lacked flair.

Noon lunch break. I nibbled on stale goldfish crackers and yogurt for lunch, as we couldn't leave the testing center to get real food. My head throbbed from a migraine that started the third hour during the IQ and Rorschach tests where I had to label more than a hundred ink blobs. The pain worsened during the blood test and physical given the fourth hour. I explained to them that I fear needles and the smell of blood, yet the nurse took several vials with enough force to cause bruising.

The extreme nature of the testing bothered me and I wanted to leave. My conscience plagued me. I couldn't really consider leaving my senior year for their yearlong program, despite the attractive incentives, could I? Wouldn't leaving Tristan and Bri destroy me? Or was I just feeling guilty for agreeing to be tested, knowing how upset they were about it? Had they distanced themselves from me or had I already distanced myself from them, just in case I got offered a position with the SCI? Things had been strained, for sure and neither of them had been kind to me. I begged to step outside for fresh air but the fat lady who stank of cheap perfume guarding the door commanded me to sit down. Entry and exit during testing was prohibited. Period.

Four p.m. The testing room smelled like the boy's locker room after a lost football game—a rancid combination of sweat and fear. All the kids took the Test so seriously, to the point of hyperventilating, like they'd have no future if not offered a spot in the program. Actually, a few of the kids mentioned that their parents as much as told them so. I wished they could see the multitude of options on their horizons. When a door closes, a window opens, right?

The potato-headed man finally summoned me into a cramped, windowed interrogation room off the main room to interview me. "Spud" quickly demanded my attention and rattled off inappropriate question after question about my home, activities, school, friends, personal life, and any obstacles that'd prevent me from participating in their program. My head felt like shards of glass were being thrust inward, fueled by his voice and the harsh fluorescent lights. At first, I answered his questions fully and politely. Until he asked me if I was sexually active. That pushed me over the edge. It wasn't any of his business. And, a very creepy question to be asked by an old guy who smelled like a perspiration and Old Spice cocktail. He acted like he assumed I was, which wasn't the case, much to my boyfriend's dismay.

I hated confrontation, which was the real reason I'd left iHop that morning. Furthermore, my mom taught me to perfect my "fake smile" poker face early on. "Never let them know what you're really thinking," she had implored. But after nine hours of pure nonsense I was done being subjected to a process worse than any college or job application. I stood up, sending my chair flying backwards, and told Mr. Potatohead I didn't give a crap about his Test, his program, or the scholarship, and that he had a room full of kids who did give a crap to choose from, and that they probably didn't care that he's a perverted sexual predator. Or perhaps I didn't say that last part, but I did think it.

Everyone stared at me, the thin walls being no barrier for my raised voice. Regret over my outburst assailed me. Most of the kids had known me for years and never heard my voice rise other than to shout a cheer at a football game. The man's wispy lips curled into a smirk and he dismissed me to return to my seat.

Mr. Potatohead then called in Blake, who chuckled at my tirade. I watched them through the window and doodled unhappy faces on the last test form I'd been asked to complete. Blake looked relaxed, almost chummy with the man, two peas in a pod, but then I noticed his body language change as the conversation progressed. By the end he looked angry, too. Maybe he didn't like discussing his sex life or lack thereof either. He glanced at me every so often as if I was the subject of their conversation, which made me even more eager to escape.

Five p.m. First in line at the door, I bolted towards the bright sun I'd been deprived of all day. The hot Santa Ana winds were stronger than usual. I kicked Blake's skateboard-shaped weapon out of the way as if it could hurt me of its own accord, climbed in my car, and completed the ten minute drive home in seven. I'd hardly have been given an award for good driving, as I nearly hit a student driver in a yellow Beetle when I stretched the length of a yellow light. I entered the house, went straight to my room and scrubbed the effects of the day off in the shower with coconut-infused body wash my parents brought me back from their recent getaway to Hawaii. It took a half hour to fashion my hair into an up-do full of ringlets. Then, I pulled on a light green and gold gown that complemented my like-colored eyes.

Six p.m. Tristan, Bri and Bri's boyfriend, Lucas, pulled up in a stretch Hummer limo, complete overkill for our small group. Thrilled to see friendly faces, I ran to give Tristan a hug. He looked nice in his black tux with green and gold cummerbund and tie to match my dress. Unfortunately, his breath stank of vodka, which did not bode well for a happy ending to my day. I smiled anyway and refrained from criticizing him. He placed an orchid on my wrist and I pinned a rose on his tux lapel. The limo ride provided my friends with further opportunity to party, while I abstained and enjoyed the scenery as the limo driver took "the long way" to the restaurant.

At dinner, Tristan ordered me steak and lobster—his favorite—but I could only eat a few bites. He ate the rest. I felt like I was on trial and my friends were playing part of judge, juror and prosecutor. They interrogated, criticized, and berated me for taking the Test and considering ditching senior year. Besides, the Test was over. I'm the one who had time I wanted back, a backlog of homework, and a lingering headache. My friends continued to taunt me until I left to use the restroom to adjust my makeup, take a few deep breaths, plaster back on my happy face, and return to shift the conversation to a more pleasant topic.

Nine-thirty p.m. The tacky "love makes the world go round" dance decorations disappeared from view as I was pushed deeper into the mosh pit. Tristan was grinding his drunken body against mine and thrusting his garlic-butter-alcohol infused tongue down my throat, deep enough that I could feel vomit rise. It disturbed me that he picked that day to journey to the bottom of the bottle. I bet my taking the cursed Test drove him to do it, and wondered if the possibility of me leaving him or besting him had him tweaked, but I didn't ask.

Ten-thirty p.m. The dance got too crowded, so we headed to an after party at Bailey Goodington's, a spoiled, wild, fellow cheerleader who lived in a ten thousand plus square foot castle in the Ranch. The spread of food and alcohol could've beat out most wedding receptions. Tristan and Lucas dove into a game of beer pong, while Bri hit the champagne in earnest. I grabbed a closed soda bottle and avoided any alcoholic additives. My bloodletting earlier had me still feeling queasy. I didn't trust I'd be able to keep my cool under the influence. No one else did. Plus, I'd promised my parents to stay sober and be a good girl. They'd check compliance by home breathalyzer. Failure meant consequences. Painful ones.

The other girls on my cheer squad performed a new number in dresses and heels, which I captured on phone video and uploaded while waiting for the bathroom. Tristan was so wasted he attempted to undress me in front of the entire line. "Ha ha, sweetheart, you wish," I told him. He signed me "no worries, forgive me," one of the many endearing things we'd learned in the sign language class we took together, and then he left with Lucas to find another drink.

Eleven-thirty p.m. I found Bri and a dozen other girls fighting over who'd make the best vampire bait. Back and forth, they shouted out ridiculous lures for hot-bodied bloodsuckers before downing shots of tequila. Bailey, our party host, mocked me for saying I didn't find the thought of being with a cold, hard, dead guy the least bit interesting, since apparently if the guy's a cold, hard, *hot*, dead guy it's worth it. She'd never been very discriminating, so I left in search for a higher concentration of working brain cells.

Twelve forty a.m. Classmate after classmate accosted me with slurred speech, inappropriate advances, and unstable drinks. What had been amusing at stage one of their inebriation—the flirty, uninhibited conversations—quickly got old by stage three or four when my friends started making some poor choices. Anna and Sadie stripped Gina Barton down to her underwear and body-painted her with sundae toppings on what was clearly a Goodington family heirloom Oriental carpet. Brooke, poster child for teen abstinence, hooked up with Ben, class sexual indiscriminate, and made haste to the master. Naive freshman Leila Sundry, Blake's sister, ended her table dance early as she puked the supposed non-alcoholic punch all over the male audience that fed it to her.

Stale beer, Doritos-filled vomit, and a nasty mixture of perfume and extreme body odor made for a seriously repelling combination. OK, it was time for me to leave. Past time to leave. City curfew had been in force for hours and the Rancho Santa Fe cops would be trolling for inebriated teens, with a long history of deaths recorded on the dangerous, windy roads.

Despite my determination to exit, I couldn't find Tristan, Bri, or Lucas. Our limo had left an hour prior, our reserved time depleted. In my search for my friends I avoided the upstairs and the soft porn displays I'd find there. Drunken girls filled the kitchen, forcing food down in a feeble effort to sober up before they got in their cars. Hookups abounded in the pool house, and similarly, the family room, rec room, dining room, office, library, craft room, media room had couples paired in every dark nook and cranny.

I started asking everyone I encountered. "Have you seen Tristan or Briella?" Dozens of shrugs and negative responses from people who likely didn't remember their own names, so I gave up and sat down on the plush hall carpet. Perhaps if I stayed put, they'd find me. I admired the impressionist artwork on the brown faux-painted walls for a while. That got old and I buried my head in my knees. Couldn't someone, anyone, help me?

When I finally looked up I saw a startlingly striking face with dark hair, blue eyes, and a five o'clock shadow sitting across from me. He wore a black suit, white on white pinstriped shirt, and a yellow power tie. Man he was drop-dead gorgeous. Why hadn't someone lured him into a dark corner?

"Hey, I'm Ethan," he said. "You look kind of bummed. Can I help?" he said in a deep, alluring voice. I liked him already, just for reading my mind and knowing I needed assistance. He loosened his tie and unbuttoned the top button of his shirt. He shifted uncomfortably, as if he wasn't quite certain he wanted to be there.

It took me a moment to compose myself, disarmed by his out-of-context presence and stunningly unique and quite beautiful eyes. They were a deep sapphire blue, but sparkled with topaz-colored specks and framed by dark, curly lashes. His dark-brown hair was cut above the ear, but on the long side, disheveled, and had a slight wave. That combined with the stubble along his perfectly carved jaw line made for sheer perfection.

"It's just this entire day. I'm done with it," I said.

"I don't blame you. It's pretty late," he said. "So why are you still here?"

"I can't find my boyfriend, Tristan. Or my best friend, Briella. And everyone's had so much to drink that I'm not getting a lot of help locating them," I said.

"Your best friend and boyfriend—they ditched you?" he asked.

"Yeah, Bri's been my best friend for ten years. And, Tristan and I have been dating for a year. But, I did something that really upset him today, so he was drunk by the time he picked me up for the dance and it's gone downhill from there," I said.

"Do tell," he'd said, his smile spreading from the right side of his mouth to his left. "I love a story about a rotten day."

"Why's that?" I said, returning his smile. "You like to see strange girls miserable?"

"Hardly. It's a matter of perspective. If your day sucked enough, it'll make mine seem tolerable," he said, laughing, although his laugh had a nervous twitch to it. Hot guy with a sense of humor and a tinge of shyness. As if he needed more appeal.

"Why was your day sucky?" I asked.

"Hmmm. My parents and uncle want to control every aspect of my life, including who I date. I got forced to do a ridiculous job that I didn't want to do. And, then I saw some stuff tonight that I never wanted to see. Your turn," he said. I wonder what he saw tonight that bugged him? Maybe he toured the upstairs by mistake. Or maybe he got a glimpse of the whole body painting on the Oriental carpet incident.

I needed to talk things through with someone, so I unloaded about the SCI

Test and how terrible I felt for letting down my friends. Given how well he listened and how supportive he was, it was the one time I'd regretted being tied down to Tristan. But, I'd have never acted on it. Despite how much I wanted to. If I had to rate how attractive Ethan was on a scale of one to a hundred, I'd give him a billion. No guy's ever had such a strong effect on me, and it wasn't just because of his looks. The only way I could describe it is that he felt right—as if he were the finishing touch on my masterpiece I didn't know was missing.

Ethan was sweet. Flirty. Sober. Soft-spoken. Shy. Kind. Smart. And he gave me a serious case of the butterflies. Talking to him was effortless and made me happier than I'd been in months. He asked me about my life and interests for what seemed like hours, even though the conversation lasted less than forty minutes.

Mid-way through our discussion he shifted over to sit directly next to me. So close that we rubbed shoulders. "Let me see your hands," he said. "I'm a bit of an expert on life lines."

"Are you? Where do you pick up such a skill? Did they cover that in Bad Pickup Lines 101?" I asked with a chuckle. He took my hands in his and ran his fingers along my palms, which sent shock waves through my body and made my heart race. His fingers were long and soft, silky almost.

"I must have missed that class. To be honest, I've never had occasion to, uh, use a pickup line," he said, looking embarrassed. "I learned palm reading from my mom. She's a little quirky. I don't believe in any of this life line stuff, of course, but if I did, this would show that you'll have a long and happy life full of passion with the man of your dreams, and that you'll have a whole host of children." He pointed out the various lines that were supposed to validate his theory. So, if I considered Ethan to be dreamy, did that mean I got to have his host of children?

"You've never used a pickup line?" I asked. He gave me a puzzled look. "No, you wouldn't, would you? You probably have to fight girls off with a stick." I cringed and then blushed, not having meant to say that last bit aloud.

"Something like that," he chuckled.

In an effort to change the subject, I grabbed his hand and turned it over. "And what do your lines say?"

"That my mom taught me how to get a pretty girl to hold my hand?" he joked, the nervous twitch in his laugh appearing again. I bit my lip as he looked up at me through his impossibly long lashes. Why couldn't I have met this guy a year ago? Of course, Tristan had been sweet and kind at first, too.

"I thought you were beating girls off with a stick, not having to get pointers from your mom," I said with a flirty smirk. He grinned from the right side of his mouth again. Wow. Sexy.

He took a deep breath before saying, "Sorry, I hope I didn't offend you in my lame effort to continue to make conversation." He paused a long moment. I watched as he rubbed his fingers along his thumb in a fidgety manner and then said, "So, is it a forever kind of thing with your boyfriend?"

"Uh, well, I mean, I don't know," I'd replied, tripping over my words. "I'm seventeen. I'm not thinking about forever quite yet."

"Really? I'm surprised. I guess that I think you just know if you're meant to be with someone. Or that a person should after a year," he said, a sober look on his face, as he did the whole hand fidgeting thing again. He was right and I knew the answer, but didn't feel comfortable dissing Tristan with a guy I was so attracted to.

"So you're telling me that you can tell off the bat if a girl you meet is perfect enough to spend a lifetime with? You believe in the whole love at first sight thing?" I asked, turning his question back at him, a little curious if he had a "forever someone" since I was starting to think there was something to the whole love at first meet thing myself.

"Definitely. I mean, I'm pretty sure I've found my better half," he said, looking up at the ceiling. "I'm not sure I'll ever recover after meeting her. Over the course of our very first conversation I went from being an avowed bachelor to wanting marriage, kids, growing old together, the works..." Not fair. Of course. The good ones are always taken.

"So, are you going to marry her? Did she feel the same way when she met you? The whole thing's so romantic," I said. And so unfair, I thought to myself. Because over the course of my conversation with Ethan, I went from being Tristan's girlfriend and not thinking about forever, to imagining marrying Ethan, having his kids, and growing old together. But, Ethan was already planning that life with someone else.

"Hmmm," he said as he stared into my eyes in such close proximity that I could smell the hint of cinnamon on his breath. "I surely hope so on both fronts, but I guess I'll have to wait and find out."

"Lucky girl," I said, meaning to say it under my breath, but he obviously heard it and I turned crimson.

"On the contrary. I'd be the lucky one," he said before taking another deep breath. I watched as his eyelashes fluttered as he thought about the girl. Then he checked his watch, the moment having turned quite awkward. "Perhaps I better help you find your friends. What do they look like?" To be honest, I'd completely forgotten that I was at a party, had come with my boyfriend, and had been searching for him. I flushed an embarrassed red and then gave him detailed descriptions of Bri and Tristan. His face went dark as I finished.

"Maybe it'd be better if I gave you a ride home. I think I saw them and they were in pretty bad shape. You might want to let them sleep it off and talk to them tomorrow," he said. I paused because I was tempted to accept the ride and avoid dealing with my drunken friends. Plus, I'd have loved to spend more time with Ethan.

"Where were they?" I said, jumping up and realizing that I'd never leave Tristan and Bri behind without making sure they were okay. Ethan hesitated and then stood. Stuck his hands in his pockets and rocked back and forth for a while. Stared at his feet. He mumbled his response.

"Last I saw they were in the game room down the hall and to the left… back of the basement," he said, biting the side of his lip and giving me a look of sheer pity.

"Thanks. I should go deal with them… mop up their puke or whatever," I'd said, but hesitated when Ethan spoke again. I wasn't ready for our conversation to end, but felt guilty about talking to him, especially after I'd been thinking of having his babies after just meeting him.

"Yeah, of course. I shouldn't have kept you so long. It was selfish of me, but I can't help it. It was really, really nice to meet you. Would you mind if I took your picture to remember you by?" he said. "You look… out of this world." Me, otherworldly? Hardly. Him? Definitely.

"Sure," I'd said, blushing at his compliment. He came close to brush my hair out of my eyes with his hand and my knees buckled at his touch. He hesitated as he stared into my eyes and then trailed his gaze to my lips. In that moment, I lost my senses and wanted him to kiss me. Or perhaps it's now that I want that, given what I saw after, but instead he was a perfect gentleman; perfectly loyal to his girlfriend as he should be. My cheeks burned when he took a quick picture with his phone. After, I wished I'd taken a shot of him, but at the time I didn't want to have to explain to Tristan why I had a picture of a hot college guy on my phone.

"Kira, I hope to see you again soon. Good luck with your friends." He waved goodbye and slowly walked away, turning back a couple times to look at me. I paused to watch him leave, taking note that he looked as good from the back as he did from the front. Should have gotten a last name to make it easier to stalk him online and scout out the lucky girl that scored big time. All that conversation and I realized I knew almost nothing about him.

Oh well. Time to locate and detox my friends. I followed the directions Ethan had given me and opened the door to the game room. The sight sickened me.

Tristan and Bri were making out smack dab center of a large circle of kids and they seemed to be enjoying it, because my mental clock clanged thirty notches of no-holds-barred tongue action, groping, and body grinding before they stopped. Lucas had rolled to his side he was laughing so hard over the spectacle.

Tristan caught my eye and panicked. "It's not what you think. It's just a stupid game of truth or dare. Lucas dared us. Go ahead and kiss Lucas if you want to get even," he said. He signed another "forgive me." Reflexively, I shook my head to the side. Not cool, not cool at all, I thought. Tristan and I supposedly loved each other, despite the recent awkwardness. Bri was my best friend. I couldn't handle it, so I bolted. I figured I'd deal with them when they were sober and I hurt less. Neither followed me. Were they too drunk to walk or understand what they'd done? Too ashamed? Or waiting for me to cool off? Who was I to talk anyway given I'd just spent a chunk of the last hour flirting with a guy who embodied everything I'd ever wanted in one single, gorgeous package? But I didn't act. That's the difference. Loyal me. And, apparently, stupid me.

One thirty-three a.m. With the front door behind me, I ran down the long driveway into complete blackness. My cell phone had zero bars in the house, so I kept moving in an effort to get a signal to call and beg my brother or parents to rescue me. The only sober soul I'd encountered—and thus only candidate to drive me home—was College Boy and I couldn't find him after he pointed me in Tristan and Bri's location.

No bars on my cell. I started pleading with my phone to behave and make the call. Then I thought I heard someone call my name. I looked around to see the source, hoping my brain properly registered it as Ethan's. He'd have made a perfect knight in shining armor come to rescue me.

Suddenly lights blinded me. A pickup truck turned into the driveway, coming inches from hitting me, swerving just in time. I stood shaking from the near miss. A boy jumped out of the truck to make sure I was okay. I'd been shocked to see it was Blake Sundry. I hadn't seen him at the dance, nor was he dressed for it. He wore the same flannel and jeans as earlier. Why was he there then? Right, his drunken sister was inside and she'd probably asked him to bring her home. At least she'd had the sense to call him. Maybe they could drop me off on their way back?

"Trying to get yourself killed? You about gave me a heart attack!" he said without apology for almost running me over.

"Not at all. I'm so sorry. I couldn't get a signal on my cell phone to call my parents for a ride and wasn't paying attention to where I was standing," I said, although he made that turn at a pretty high speed.

"Well, I didn't see you until the last second. You were right in the middle of the..." He didn't finish. His eyes went wide.

A gush of hot air blasted me into Blake, followed by a sonic boom so loud my ears rang in pain. Subsequent explosions sent us flying alongside missiles of glass from his truck and a fiery rain of shrapnel. We both turned towards the house to see the source of the explosion, but where the house once stood looked like an apocalyptic graveyard, with walls of fire descending the hills in every direction. Panic paralyzed me.

I could see their faces. Tristan. Bri. Lucas. Ethan. What happened? Were they still alive? I wanted to help but my muscles failed me. Moments passed before my brain registered physical pain radiating throughout my body. Glass fragments embedded in my arms and legs, burns from flying debris, my dress shredded, blood everywhere. How could we help our friends escape as the fires of hell bore down upon us with no visible path through?

Blake scooped me up and shoved me into the truck, ratcheting it into reverse and accelerating to beat the fire. I choked on smoke that smelled of burning oranges, while trying to stop the worst of my bleeds without driving the glass farther beneath my skin.

One forty-three a.m. Firefighters had surrounded the scene in an attempt to battle the blaze. They evacuated Blake and me by force to a "safe" zone—a neighborhood grocery store parking lot a couple miles from the Goodington estate. Paramedics patched our cuts and burns while police officers tried to take a statement. I nearly passed out when they removed a chunk of shrapnel from Blake's wrist. I stared at the swirling lights of the police cars, and growing fire in the background with periodic bouts of fireworks-like displays. "How many kids were in that house?", I heard the police officer ask. "A lot," I'd eked out before my sobbing prevented me from further communication. In an attempt to calm me, the paramedic drew a needle, the second I'd seen in twenty-four hours. I became hysterical and it took three people to hold me down.

The bottom line—Tristan never showed. Nor did Bri or Lucas or Blake's sister. And the other fifty? Seventy-five? One hundred? More? I struggled to get a handle on the magnitude of the tragedy. The firefighters confirmed our worst fears. No one survived other than Blake and me. Every one of my friends died in an instant. And I couldn't bear the thought of life without them.

The only mystery that remains is the fate of Ethan. He wasn't on the list of "confirmed deceased," but then again, there were dozens at the party who never showed up back home and whose remains were never found. In my fantasies, I imagine he's still alive and we meet again. I remember him stuffing his hands in his pockets and rocking on his feet, running his fingers across his thumbs, taking deep breaths before answering my questions, and nervously laughing. And his smile that spread from right to left. Sometimes I think I see him and my stomach flutters as it did the first time I met him, but then the image disappears. The glimmer of hope's too minuscule to compete against the mass of loss and despair. And guilt. Tristan and Bri, my two best friends in the world died and I still can't get Ethan out of my mind. Despite two solid months of therapy. No wonder the universe hates me.

My eyes and limbs feel like concrete as I feel myself being gently set onto a soft surface. "Where am I?" I mumble. I vaguely remember trying to leave SCI's Unit 27 and being knocked to the floor.

"Shhh, Kira," I hear. The voice sounds eerily familiar and I swear I smell a hint of cinnamon. "You were given a sedative to allow you to adjust to the schedule here. But you're in your room."

I try to open my eyes. My vision is hazy and the room is dark, and the shadow leaning over me fits the voice. But I've been prone the last two months to attributing every shadow, every voice, and every face to him. "Ethan? Is that you?"

"I'm sorry. So sorry. I wish things were different. Sleep well," my benefactor says before leaning over and giving me a kiss on my forehead. I feel the drugs pull me under and I succumb to an imagined deep sleep in Ethan's arms.

CHAPTER TWO

Ethan

I receive the call I never expected.

"Ted found a pure-bred Light... not too far from you. Carmel Valley High," the familiar voice purrs. "Her blood work was a work of art. I suggest you high tail it over there and check her out."

"*A female pure Light?* Impossible. Even if that's true, what's the hurry? Why not wait until she's there? I assume she's headed your way at least," I say, hardly jumping for joy. There's nothing less romantic than a blood panel preceding every date. Thus, I've resisted my father's archaic Cleaving process my entire life and don't see any reason to succumb now, just because he's finally dredged up a suitable candidate two years post-deadline.

"Two reasons. One, she's reluctant to go—has a boyfriend tying her down or something. She's going to need some *motivation*, which I've already got in motion. And two, you have competition. Ted *also* found a pure-bred Dark male with a cleaner medical history than you have. A classmate of hers." I hear worry in his voice. Despite my father's immense power in my hometown's political climate, the rules are pretty clear. It's unlikely I have a shot with her, even if I want one.

"I don't see any reason to bother if there's another heir apparent," I say. "If I wasn't suitable for anyone there, why would I be trusted with a pure-bred Light, the likes of which haven't been seen in centuries?"

"*I* have yet to be convinced that either is suitable for our needs. You are the only eyes and ears there I fully trust. Watch them," he says, following with very specific instructions as to my assignment. His tone belies his mistruth. He doesn't trust anyone, much less me.

Disappointment looms. Either she'll be dreadful and forced my way or spectacular and forced the other guy's way. There's yet to be a situation that clearly weighs in my favor.

The moment I see her my faulty heart swells with misplaced hope. Why couldn't *the other Dark* have been born with a defective heart? My childhood was nothing less than pathetic. I spent my first dozen years locked in a one hundred-fifty square foot, sterile room to "protect my health," or realistically to hide the extent of my abnormality from the rest of my parents' colleagues. As a result, I'm horribly claustrophobic.

Most of the human contact I had during my youth was with my parents and the medical staff. I spent a hundred times more time with Doctor Christo, my heart specialist, than my father. A wise, white-haired man, Dr. Christo augmented my standard-fare "home studies" schooling with curriculum designed "for the very elite." My parents wanted me well versed in the family business and Dr. Christo wanted me well versed in "the great universal truths." This filled 8-10 hours a day.

My early years conspicuously lacked affection, playtime, supervision, or fun. From the age of twelve to fifteen my interactions with other kids were sparse, leaving me shy and awkward. My one consistent "friend" aka forced playmate and classmate has been Jax, Dr. Christo's son, a know-it-all boy with a superiority complex. As a kid, he forced me to call him King Jax and bossed me around incessantly. Still does. He's infuriating, but all I have.

Eventually, after a dozen-odd surgeries, my health improved and my parents chose to foist me on my Uncle Henry, to "further my education and prepare me for my destiny." Forget free will. Forget personal choice. My parents assume their agenda trumps my agenda. Today's the first and only day I've seen our agendas so much as overlapping, much less aligning. Every memory serves as a reminder of this important truth.

I vividly recall waking up post surgery number 9 at the age of eight to the rare sight of my parents and an all too familiar heavily sanitized hospital smell. My dad flanked my left and appeared to be frazzled with worry. My mother sat on the edge to my right, looking weary, with dark smudges detracting from her typically bright green eyes.

"Ethan, it's about time," my father said, tapping on his watch. "You took 37 minutes longer than anticipated to come out of the anesthesia." I felt guilty for causing them such consternation. They'd surely been stressed that I wouldn't wake up at all.

"I…I…I'm sorry, Father," I whisper. "It hurts," I said, referring to the incision in my chest. Dozens of tubes protruded from my frail body and machines whirred in the background.

"That's what pain killers are for, Ethan," he said, rising and rounding the end of my bed to grab my mother's hand. "You've made us late for a Council meeting. We expect you to follow every order from the doctors and nurses and recover in a more timely fashion than your waking," as if I'd had control over either.

"Dr. Christo's the very best," my mother said, patting me on my arm before standing. "We are investing in you. You are important. If we can just get past these little medical hiccups, you'll be a major player in the future of our civilization. The doctors will keep us posted on your progress and time permitting, we'll check in on you later this week."

They never did check on me. Time rarely permitted where my parents were concerned. My doctors assured me that my parents were intimately involved in my medical decisions. I'm sure they considered it a medical necessity to keep me alive, lest their political aspirations suffer.

My father gave me crystal clear instructions about the girl, none of which involved speaking to her, but I choose to selectively ignore the mandate to keep my distance. A pretty girl does not necessarily a suitable match make, and if she's at all deficient on the personality front, I'll happily let the medically sanctioned boy pursue her. I'm determined to undermine my father and manipulate the situation to my benefit, if only in some small way. Plus, the beauty has the whole damsel in distress thing going on and as a frequent victim myself, I can't keep from offering her the compassion I was never afforded in my youth.

"Hey, I'm Ethan. You look kind of bummed. Can I help?"

CHAPTER THREE

Blake

"She's the one." The words and her face ripple through my head. My life, and the life of my family, depends on some shallow cheerleader who isn't even interested in the program. She refuses to ditch her senior year because she's in love with a boneheaded jock whose future is sure to be closely tied to AA meeting schedules. Why am I worrying? They'll never persuade her to go. Thank goodness for that, because the chick hates me just like everyone else. After all, I almost ran her over with my skateboard this morning in my hurry to get to the Test and I don't think I even apologized, not out loud anyway.

Why am I so nervous anyway? I've been preparing for this forever and with my dad's connections I'm a shoo-in. It's not the Test, but the pressure of what's coming and that I have to go back. My dad's words haunt me, "We're counting on you, son. All of us are counting on you." Getting in isn't the hard part anyway. Getting what they need and back out alive, that's another story.

Kira Donovan. As much as I can't stand Kira on paper, I have to admit that I loved watching Miss Goodie Two-Shoes go off on Ted Rosenberg. I mean wow —she told him she didn't give a crap about his Test in front of everyone. Classic. Maybe she does have it in her. Man though, I wish I didn't have to depend on her, wish I could do it alone.

Kira's probably right where I'm headed, partying it up with the rest of the losers from Carmel Valley High. Or worse, hooking up with her jerk boyfriend somewhere in the Bailey Goodington's freakishly big house. I'd vowed to *never* enter Bailey's hallowed grounds again. When I first started at Carmel Valley High Bailey lured me over to her house for a "study date" and I temporarily (well, in secret, for weeks) fell prey to her ice blue eyes, stick straight platinum blonde hair, and modelesque figure. She particularly liked to "study" by her pool in a very tiny bikini that probably cost enough to feed a small country, and to my benefit her suit often "accidentally" dislodged when she entered the pool. She gave me my first kiss (or two or hundred, I lost count) and a real education in baseball. I was head over heels. In a young love bout of insanity, I even gave her a promise ring. There weren't just sparks with Bailey, it was a full-blown atomic detonation when we were together.

When my dear daddy caught wind that I had a girlfriend, however, he forced me to end things. I tried to fight him on it, but he used his fists to persuade me. The relationship-ending "why" I gave to Bailey was lame, so I came across as a real dick. No one breaks up with Bailey Goodington. To gain vengeance, she spread every possible rumor to turn me into a social pariah. Worked for me, allowing me to drop off the radar and avoid my dad's ire. Through the Baileyvine, I found out I'm currently a meth addict who prostitutes myself to kinky old men to support my habit. Ironic, given she liberally partakes of mind-altering substances and has a reputation for being easier than a first grade math test. First love or not, I hear Karma's real vindictive and coming for you, Bailey, and I just hope I'm there to witness your downfall.

My thoughts revert to my current predicament. I'm pissed. I can't believe my sister, Leila, agreed to go to the dance, much less this particular after-party. Now she's tanked and I have to come pick up the pieces. If only she could better remember our previous circumstances and the sacrifice made to bring her into the world. Even though I was only three, I'll never forget Leila's birth.

We moved seaside when Mom bellied to make it more comfortable for her as it was so freaking hot inland that she couldn't function. We'd traded caves with an Interceptor who'd been injured trying to procure supplies from an Industrial City ship. I missed playing in the canyons and resented the confinement of the cliff residences, accessible one to another solely by rope ladders.

My dad taught me how to climb the ladders for safety, but playing on them was strictly forbidden. Even my father panicked at the thought of maneuvering them at night and no one could get far during the day without getting fried. I'd have hardly had the energy anyway, given kids in third world countries likely ate more often, and I had the protruded belly and skeletal figure to prove it. Well, perhaps that's a bit of an exaggeration. We either had plenty or none based on the pirating success-rate. Fresh food didn't last long without refrigeration and even the non-perishables perished in the heat.

I awoke to my mother's screams and my father's panicked pleas for help from our neighbors. Unfortunately, they'd all left on a supply run as it was shipment night and the community rations would be lucky to last another week. From the light streaming through the makeshift sunscreen woven of canyon brush I could tell it was mid-afternoon.

"What's wrong, Mama?" I'd asked.

"The baby's coming," she'd replied, sweat streaming down her face, and blood covering her garments. Even though I had little sense of time, I knew it was too early for the baby to arrive. Scared, I'd climbed upon her matting and burrowed up to her, caring little that her long black hair was slippery with perspiration, and that the water my dad had sponged over her steamed into a stinky mist. I picked bed bugs from her face, squeezing them to their death before they could get to her mouth. Meanwhile, my dad paced furiously and cursed loudly as he'd tried to figure out how to handle our predicament.

"Blakie," he said finally, bowing his head in defeat. "I need you to go get Doc Daryn." It took a lot for my dad to admit he needed help. He looked more exhausted than usual. I could tell because his hazel eyes usually sparkled, but looked cloudy and dull. I wondered if he had dared to swim in the ocean or if his bushy brown hair and beard were wet from sweat.

"But Daddy," I said. "Sun's out." I knew the way to Doc's, but had never attempted it without my parents or during the heat of the midday sun. The thought of the ascent up the rope ladders alone scared the crap out of me.

"You're big now. You can do it. I have to stay with your mom and we need Doc to help your mommy with the baby," he said. My mom pulled me closer to her, knowing the risk of me never returning to be high. But after my dad whispered something in her ear she'd reached over to retrieve a rare piece of cloth she'd been saving for the baby and wrapped it around my head.

"This will protect you," she said, kissing my forehead. I nodded, believing her words because the alternative was unthinkable. My oversized shoes couldn't be used on the ropes, but my long sleeves and pants would cover my body. Only my hands and feet would be exposed. "I love you, little one."

"I love you too, Mama. I'll get Doc Daryn, don't worry," I'd said.

"Be careful and be fast, my good boy," my dad encouraged. He draped a satchel of water over my shoulder before lifting my small body onto the ropes directly outside our cave. I choked on the heat, but spray from the waves below cooled me and gave me courage to press upward.

I'd climbed as fast as my tiny muscles could, the ropes and sun singeing my hands and feet. My dad told me later I'd ascended more than two hundred feet to reach the top of the cliffs. The one time I glanced down and saw the dizzying distance between me and the rocky shore of the ocean below, I lost my footing. As I hung by one hand from the ropes, something kept me from releasing my grip. Whether it was love for my mother and baby sister, survival instinct, divine intervention, or the wind, I somehow swung my feet back towards the cliffs, looped them into a rung, and grabbed hold of the ropes with my other hand. The contact ripped open the blisters on my hands and watery fluid and blood dripped downward, but I kept going with renewed energy and focus.

Once atop the cliffs, I'd collapsed from exhaustion face down into the dirt and rocks, making myself an instant target for fire ants. After several minutes of being stung, inhaling dust into my lungs and coughing it back up, I remembered my water satchel and thirstily drained it. I rose, batting away the ants, and ran as fast as I could across the rocky path towards the canyon. The ground was hot as coals on my feet, my back ablaze from the sun. Then it had been down another ladder and across a thin ledge to the doctor's comparatively lush accommodations in the canyon.

"Doc Daryn," I'd yelled. "My mama's having the baby. She needs help!" Doc's Cleave, Linda, snatched me from the ledge, letting out a cry at the sight of me. The Doc knew it must have been bad for my dad to have sent me and quickly gathered his supply bag, tying it around his waist. He tried to leave me with his Cleave, but I'd kept screaming that I wanted my mama and daddy, so he'd slathered an ointment on my hands and feet before wrapping them with gauze. A minty cream I recognized as toothpaste—a rarity in our community— was caked on my face in effort to ease the burning sensation and swelling from the ant stings. At his urging, I clutched to his neck and twisted my legs above his belly bag. His Cleave secured me to him with a belt, doused us both with water, and then we reversed the path I'd just taken, passing several men guiding mules packed with newly procured supplies for our community.

By the time we'd descended to our cave, the sun looked like a giant orange resting upon the water, the sparse clouds glowing crimson. The heat had subsided slightly making the air more breathable. Poor Doc was panting from the extra weight of his supplies and me. My daddy broke down with tears of relief to see the two of us. Mom looked so pale and weak that I wondered if she was dead. But within moments she screamed bloody murder as she tried to eject the baby with a long contraction.

"She's been pushing for an hour, but something's wrong. The baby's not coming," my dad had said. Doc put me down and dug into his bag. My dad attempted to shield me from seeing the events of the next hour as the doctor used tools to remove the baby and try to stop my mom's bleeding. Doc tied the baby's cord, cut her from my mom, and then swaddled her in an old rag from his bag. He handed me the crying, writhing little girl, so my dad could help him save my mom. Ten tiny fingers and toes, a black patch of hair and creamy skin, and facial expressions that shifted continually finally helped distract me.

Thanks to the Gads, my mom lived for eight months following Leila's birth.

Long enough to nurse the life out of her, saving her baby girl, a gift she'd willingly given. Doc didn't think she'd make it through that night, so the extra time was a blessing. She'd been too weak to leave the cave, so we'd made do in space smaller than my current bedroom. My dad filled the time with stories of a fantastical place of plentiful food, beautiful trees and flowers, luxurious homes, and daylight play without being scorched or burned. On her deathbed my mom had my dad promise to deliver us safely to the place of his stories and never let us return.

My dad honored half that promise, but by forcing my participation in his plans of revenge, we're both about to dishonor the other half. As I remember my mom's blazing eyes as she demanded this of my father, I shudder and whisper for her forgiveness. No, my sister will never understand the sacrifices, including the one I'll be undertaking shortly to avenge my mother's death. Leila remembers living in a "really hot place," but that's the extent of it. She adapted quickly to life in San Diego, and our favorable circumstances here.

I have too much to do to deal with her crap, too much to prepare, but I wind my truck through the Ranch, at ease in the darkness of the hour.

I wonder if I'm the only Carmel Valley High student who didn't attend the Winter Formal. Bailey-branded losers like me don't get dates. When we first moved to the area, I tried to fit in, to blend in more. But I don't blend. I can't stand to make attachments, to care about people who have no place in my future. So after the Bailey fiasco, I withdrew from the pack, hiding behind the protection of my hood and a skateboard, despite—or perhaps because of—the inherent negative stereotypes associated with skaters, and made peace with my solitude. Boarding's as natural as walking to me, so the subterfuge worked its magic.

I slow as I approach my destination and turn into the Goodington's driveway. My brain catches sight of someone in my path, reacting before I can fully process, and I swerve out of the way and slam on the brakes to avoid hitting a eucalyptus tree. Shaking from the near hit, I yank my hood up over my head and get out of the car. My averted victim is none other than Kira Donovan, who appears sober, dateless, and is yelling at her cell phone. She looks like a freaking Disney princess with her hair up in curly-qs and body perfectly shaped in a long green dress.

"Trying to get yourself killed? You about gave me a heart attack!" I say.

"Not at all. I'm so sorry. I couldn't get a signal on my cell phone to call my parents for a ride and wasn't paying attention to where I was standing," she says. Then pay attention. You're no good to me dead.

"Well, I didn't see you until the last second. You were right in the middle of the..."

I stop mid-lecture, as I see a series of bright flashes and then watch the Goodington house explode into flames—there one second and completely gone the next. The force of the blasts knocks Kira into me, and then both of us to the ground. My first thought, wrongfully so, is "Bye-bye Bailey. Karma found you after all." But then I realize that it's not as satisfying as I thought it'd be and that I'm a victim to Karma's whims myself. Painful hunks of crap have penetrated my skin, some of them burning. I know all about burns, my mind reverting to the weeks of treatment I required after my journey to fetch Doc Daryn. It takes a couple days for the burns to "set," the skin still cooking like a Thanksgiving turkey removed from the oven. The ointments, the searing pain, the oozing of the wounds. Is this what my sister will have to experience if she makes it out?

I want to go in and save my little sister from the fiery inferno, but my survival instinct tells me that's not an option, as the winds push the fire directly towards us. I can tell Kira's in shock, so I load her thin body into the truck and snap the gears into reverse while dialing 911. Once back on the main road I hit the accelerator, retracing the path from whence I came, begging for help from the 911 operator. I pull into a parking lot and suck in a deep mouthful of air.

As I look at Kira and the overwhelming grief I see on her face, a single thought races through my mind: "What has the SCI done?"

I often think that the night is more alive and more richly colored than the day.

Vincent Van Gogh

CHAPTER FOUR

Kira

An unfamiliar female voice urges me to wake up and be ready in 30 minutes, and I startle, searching for the source to no avail. There must be some sort of built-in speaker system. Barely conscious, I look around my room, something I wasn't able to properly do in my drugged state last night. It's larger than the average dorm room and has a twin bed, desk, dresser, closet, and private bathroom. I undress, locate what I assume to be my Recruit uniform and get in the shower. The hot water helps pull me out of my sleepy haze and I reflexively reach for my travel shower pack before realizing that I didn't bring it, or anything else for that matter. Thankfully a corner shelf in the shower has shampoo, conditioner, body wash and a razor. I note that each product has an "Industrial City" label, and the shampoo, conditioner and body wash have an unfamiliar "Theranberry" scent, which reminds me of a lemon-strawberry-passion fruit combination, a suitable replacement for my Hawaiian products.

After drying off and dressing in the white, short-sleeved, tight-fitting, silky top, and shimmery yet soft silver-toned pants provided, I stare at myself in the mirror to see that the dark circles under my eyes have Saturn-like rings. "Awful. There had better be makeup!" I say to myself. I survey the drawers and find lotions, makeup, and everything I might need, all with the telltale Industrial City markings I found in the shower. Everything sparkles as I apply it, making me feel like I'm preparing for a night at a disco, not an evening in the training center. I don't bother to dry or straighten the curls from my hair, and instead pull it back into a ponytail, not wanting to be late.

A knock at my door makes me think I'm tardy, but I check the clock and have fifteen minutes to spare. If I could just find my shoes, that is. The clothing

I'd arrived in, including my shoes, has disappeared. This in itself would be fine if it didn't imply someone had entered my room to remove the items. Creepy. Really creepy. I shudder at the thought of a stranger watching me sleep or climb into the shower. With some effort, I finally find the standard issue socks and shoes, put them on, and answer the second knock on my door.

"What are you doing here?" I grumble at a surprisingly hoodless Blake Sundry. The last time I saw him I'd swear his hair was long, or did I just assume that? Maybe he did have long hair and cut it recently? In any case, his face is framed with dark, straight hair that has streaks of platinum highlights. His green eyes are flanked by dark eyelashes. He looks better hoodless and well groomed. But he's not quite normal, his shimmery ivory skin being an anomaly, given we both came from such a sunny climate. Not that my slightly freckled skin tans easily, but his skin appears porcelain. I watch as he runs his hands through his hair. His hands are marred, as if they were transplanted off a burn victim. Abruptly, he pulls them into his long sleeved shirt and I realize I must have been staring.

"I'm your flatmate," he says as he motions for me to step into a small living and kitchen area. "We each have our own room, but share the kitchen and living room."

"*We* are sharing this place? This is where we'll be spending a year?" I ask in a harsh tone. I don't mean to sound snotty, given it's pretty nice, but I'm just surprised and somewhat horrified that they have me sharing a suite with a guy. Particularly this guy. I hope the SCI drug-tested him and checked his background to make sure he's not dangerous. Sure, he saved my life, but I hardly need a constant reminder of that night and I can't see Blake without seeing fire, flying debris, and dead bodies.

I must have allowed a nasty look onto my face, because Blake grimaces at my reaction and says, "Just the first week, apparently, while we are in training. They plan to transfer us to our long-term residences Saturnight."

"Saturnight?" I ask. "You mean Saturday night?"

"Whatever, uh yeah, just repeating what they said while you were passed out," he responds, looking at me like I must have missed a couple-hour briefing that he doesn't intend to fill me in on. "Anyway, I made some breakfast if you are hungry."

"Awesome," I say, figuring he must have popped some pre-made waffles in a toaster or something. "How long have you been up?"

"Our wake-up call was at the same time, but I'm a guy so it only took *me* 5 minutes to get ready. And I was starving, so yeah, I made eggs."

"Cool, thanks. I'm hungry, too, though honestly it feels like we should be eating dinner, not breakfast."

"Maybe because it is 1850 hours? 6:50pm," he says, reminding me that for some reason our training is happening in the evening.

"What's up with evening schedule, anyway?" I ask. "And what else did they mention while I was passed out?"

He shrugs and says, "Nothing they won't cover again in training, I'd assume," and then walks over to the small table to eat his own breakfast.

"They didn't mention anything about interplanetary travel?" I say. He rolls his eyes and I join him and marvel at the simply executed ham and cheese omelet before me. It's a little rubbery, but I quickly inhale it. In the last 24 hours I've only had a stale bagel and cup of juice.

"Do you also do dishes, cleaning and laundry?" I joke when I'm done.

"Don't push your luck, gorgeous," he says. I grimace. The compliment makes me feel uncomfortable, since the last person to call me gorgeous was Tristan. I don't like being stuck in a suite with Blake or being around any guy for that matter. It makes me feel like I'm cheating on Tristan, even though I can't cheat on a dead boyfriend. Not that he was a great boyfriend in the end, but it's not like I got to resolve the whole cheating issue before he died.

Blake must see the displeasure on my face and adds, "Give me a break. It's not like I'm trying to hit on you, Kira. I don't even know you. We've been assigned partners for training, that's it. But don't ask me to pretend like you aren't beautiful and probably used to having everyone bend over backwards to cater to you—which, by the way, I was not trying to do by making your stupid breakfast."

Pompous much? I plaster on a fake smile, get up from the table and without response to his insult, take his plate and mine, and hand wash them in the sink with some Industrial City dish soap. That insult was so uncalled for, but I'm going to ignore it. Once done with the dishes I slip past Blake and try to leave through the door to our suite, which won't budge, and has no easily apparent way to unlock it. They locked us in. I wonder why? Don't want the new Recruits exploring? That sucks since exploring seems appropriate for our arrival on supposed alien land.

"It's locked," Blake says. I continue to smile, but in my head roll my eyes and give a sarcastic "thanks." Couldn't have figured that out on my own. Still upset by Blake's inflammatory comments, I retreat to my room to look for my watch, which I swear I was wearing when I went to sleep. Mine has vanished, but an "Industrial City" issue has been placed atop the dresser. I put it on and notice it is 18:59. As the time changes to 1900 hours I hear a click and our escort arrives to release us from captivity.

We follow the man—who doesn't even bother to introduce himself, exchange pleasantries, or respond to questions—through a winding maze of hallways painted different bright neon colors to a door marked UNIT 27 TRAINING CLINIC. We're ushered inside and greeted by two nurses who separate Blake and me into separate white-walled examination rooms.

The nurse asks me a series of questions about any unusual symptoms or issues I might have had since our arrival. Other than feeling ill and parched when I first entered, and the lump on my head I got while trying to leave, I haven't had much time to experience any issues, as I was drugged and forced to sleep for hours, I tell them. Yes, I was able to get breakfast down. No, I never vomited. Yes, I feel fine now. No breathing issues, no rapid heartbeat, no intestinal distress, no seizures or convulsions, no skin lesions, no dizziness, seeing spots, or fainting. Seriously people, what were you expecting?

Once they're done with the invasive interrogation, they check my eyes, ears, nose, heart, lungs, skin, and palpate my abdomen to make sure I'm not lying. Then the parasites drain my blood. I ask why, but they claim it is "standard procedure and will occur often," like I should know what their standard procedure is. Making sure my high DNT levels are still intact? The nurses then leave us be for a few minutes to confer with the doctor before returning to give both Blake and me shots "to help us further acclimate to our surroundings." The needle hurts going in and the sting lasts for several minutes after. When the nurse tells me she'll see me tomorrow I am too upset to speak.

To reach our training room we head out a set of double doors to a dimly lit outdoor walkway, illuminated by soft up-lights in the path and the occasional wall light. I lean over the walkway railing and it takes a few moments for my eyes to adjust to the darkness. Once I do adapt to the new lighting my senses overload.

I am indeed in an unknown place, albeit not enough different from Earth to think I've left it. Although it's late evening the temperature is hotter than any record setting San Diego day, but very arid, desert-like heat. Despite it being dry, sweat immediately beads and starts to drip down my back. It won't take long outdoors to be drenched in a sticky stench, but I try to ignore the fact my bra strap is uncomfortably soaking up all the mess and focus on what little I can see in the poor lighting.

The walkway runs along the top edge of a very steep and deep canyon that is lit with the full spectrum of colors, making it look both eerie and majestic, if that's possible. Sparse, dry, treeless vegetation in form of cacti and brush is scattered between what appears to be paved paths and a concrete floor. I look up at the sky, but the lights of the canyon obscure any view of a moon or stars. Long cables crisscross the canyons between platforms and I swear I see someone zipping across by pulley. Two enclosed bridges are in view and from the whooshing noise emanating from them—some sort of train, perhaps?

As we approach one of the spotlights shining into the canyon I see it is covered with a variety of large, nasty looking bugs. Beetles with long antennae, jumbo cockroaches, and fuzzy spiders. Remind me to stay away from the lights. Or maybe it'd be safer to know where and what the creatures are. I wonder what's hiding in the brush, thinking of all the fun stuff I'd encountered or could've encountered on canyon hikes in San Diego. Snakes? Lizards? Scorpions? Coyotes and mountain lions? Hopefully most of the wildlife has chosen to live outside the city borders.

I screech when a cockroach at least four inches long lands on my shirt. It is no use to try to shake it off, as it has no intention of relocating without encouragement. "Please get it off me," I say to our escort with urgency. "I hate bugs. Especially really large ones." The escort keeps walking, but Blake plucks it off my shirt and flicks it a few feet away.

"That was a waste of some good protein," he jokes. The multi-colored lights and shadows make him look like a maniacal clown or an extra in a purposefully deranged music video.

"Disgusting. The moment we're expected to eat bugs will be the moment I head home," I mumble, speeding up my walk to catch up with our escort. I can hear Blake laughing behind me, likely remembering my last attempt to jump ship.

The sight of several men herding a pack of mules up the canyon, all loaded with boxes reminds me of my parents' pictures of their trip to Santorini, Greece. My parents had ridden donkeys up a switchback trail cut into the cliffs and told us the donkeys were used to not only transport people, but supplies. I'd always envied their trips, but it's my turn for an adventure.

Blake appears to also be taking in the new landscape with awe, particularly when he sees a figure whooshing along one of the paths at high speeds by skateboard.

"Suh-weet!" he says. "Can I try?" he signals to our escort.

"Later. It's time to move along. Your training room is up ahead on the right," our escort says, first words spoken, in a low rumbly tone.

"Where are all the people and the city center?" I ask. From my count, I've seen a few dozen people at most.

"This is a restricted area solely used for training," he explains. "And since you showed up off-season you won't encounter the masses until you transfer to Garden City High."

"How many Recruits come during the peak season?" I ask.

"More," he says. Helpful.

"What about the other Recruits who greeted me when I arrived yesterday?" I ask.

"They already finished their training and are en-route to their final destination assignments." He then rushes ahead, signaling our conversation is over.

Blake and I walk as slowly as allowed, until we're pushed into a large room the size of a school gymnasium with its ceiling several stories high. The room's walls are a sunny yellow, except for the one hundred-eighty degree curved screen directly ahead of us. We're motioned to sit in two front-row chairs, center of a row containing what looks like massage chairs on steroids. Each row of chairs is suspended from the ceiling by heavy cables. Twenty seats per row times five rows equals a hundred seats. Do they really usually have that many Recruits?

"This is sick," Blake says to signify his approval of our training room, even though upon sitting down, we're both strapped into the chairs like death row inmates. My chair is attached to Blake's, our armrests shared. The seats are so close together I can't help but brush my arm and shoulder against Blake's, much like you'd experience on an airplane, though I lean away from him since I'm still irked that he called me the equivalent of a pampered princess. Why couldn't he be a perfect gentleman like Ethan was? I sigh just thinking about Ethan and my fantasy that he carried me to my room and tucked me in upon my arrival.

We're each given a tablet computer device and simple instructions how to use it. Although it seems powerful, the function has been limited to serve for training purposes. We can type or record notes by voice annotation, as well as ask questions about each subject, and the answers are immediately pasted into the notes program. We're warned, however, that we can only ask questions relevant to the subject being taught, as it is being taught. I test the claim by typing in "Where is Thera?" and I get a standard response saying, "Please post your inquiries during training sessions relevant to the subject at hand," which isn't very helpful.

I'm less interested in the functions of the simple computer and more interested in the fact it has the now familiar "Industrial City" logo on it. I haven't met a product or device yet that didn't have those markings—a telltale sign that capitalism isn't alive and well here, and thus I'm betting democracy isn't either. When I'd signed the SCI paperwork, Spud had mentioned that I'd be subject to the rules and regulations of the Institute. Well, get on with it then. I want to know what the rules are, folks. How stupid was I to sign those papers without knowing anything other than the fact the SCI is a philanthropic organization on Earth? My bet—off-the-charts.

"Have you noticed that everything is manufactured in Industrial City?" I whisper to Blake.

"Yeah, hard to miss the logos," he says with a smirk. "So, are you talking to me now?" His eyes brighten. While my eyes are gold-rimmed green, his are a bright emerald color that are so pure they look manufactured.

"I'm sorry. I wasn't not talking to you. I just wasn't talking while I dealt with some… bad memories… about the night of the explosion," I say. Might as well be honest with him, so he realizes that he's not to blame for my mood. He did say some things that were pretty nasty, but I decide to forgive, forget and give him my patented "all is right" smile.

"Of course," he says. "I'm sorry, too. For the things I said. They were rude." He maintains his gaze and I imagine him thinking, "but probably justified." What can I expect given how people *perceive* I was raised? My parents have money. They just choose not to spend it on or share it with their children, in an overblown effort to make sure we are anything but pampered. "You need to earn your own way in this world, not leech off us," my father always says.

I continue to stare at Blake's eyes. The last time I saw eyes this pretty was when I met Ethan. Ethan's sparkly sapphire eyes had blown me away. Blake's eyes have a similar brightness and glimmer. "Do you wear contacts?" I ask. Maybe they have some new line of contacts that give cute guys an alien, jeweled feel.

"Nope. These," he says, pointing at his eyes, "are all natural. I've got perfect vision, even at night. I'm like a cat," he jokes.

Predatory cats come to mind. Lions, tigers, panthers, cheetahs… Blake simply does not give off the warm and fuzzy vibe of your average house cat. He radiates the bad boy vibe. Best to be wary of my flatmate. I sink back in my chair, trying to remember where the conversation started anyway. Oh yeah, Industrial City products and lack of democratic process here.

"Think our training will cover the uh, expectations or rules of wherever the heck we are? Garden City? Thera was it? Do you really believe we're no longer on Earth?" I ask.

"We were in the middle of the ocean one minute," he responds, raising his eyebrows. "And then the next, we were on solid ground. So unless they figured out how to hide a giant island behind a floating barge, I'm thinking they're onto something about the having left Earth thing."

"I guess," I grumble, his condescending tone annoying me.

Could it really be that easy? Our government spends billions of dollars on space programs and all it really takes is a short boat ride followed by an uncomfortable stroll down the hall of an abandoned building to hit intergalactic soil? If someone had discovered a way to leave Earth so easily why wouldn't it be publicized? People cash in on lesser exploits everyday and this one would be akin to winning the lottery a thousand times over. Forget finding new Egyptian treasure, Biblical documents, or a new species of monkey, proof of human life beyond Earth? Now that's huge. Front-page headlines and preempt-all-your-scheduled-TV-programming kind of huge.

As I ponder, the screen lights up and the image of the tall man who'd greeted us this morning appears.

"Welcome to Thera, Recruits. I'm sure you have many questions, and I'm confident we'll get them answered for you. Our first unit will describe Thera and its city and unit structure. The second will describe the rules and regulations each inhabitant need know for their assigned unit."

To the contrary, I doubt they'll make a dent in my questions.

Mandatory exercise time is enforced at 2230 hours. Wouldn't want the Recruits going soft. I'm happy to get out of that chair, though. As comfortable as they are, especially during the periodic messages, I was going insane. At the content of the training sessions and at the proximity to Blake, who despite the strong declaration of platonic intentions couldn't help but brush his hand and arm against mine. And also because I nodded off and woke to my head on his shoulder. He looked all too amused at my unconscious attempt to be cozy. Ugh.

I change into standard issue workout clothes in the ladies' changing area, and get on the treadmill, working up to a light jog. Skimpy I think, about the clothes, which consist of a "barely there" tank and short shorts. Wonder what they have the guys wear?

Any questions I'd had about Blake's relative strength to Tristan are answered when he enters, shirtless, into the gym and gets on the treadmill next to me. He barely glances my way before doubling my speed. The boy is slender but muscular, like a marathon runner or triathlete. Stunned that his physique is not of an emaciated meth addict, I awkwardly stumble and have to catch myself on the treadmill's sidebars, lower my speed, and start up again. If he reacts to my blunder he doesn't show it.

I want and need to digest the material presented this evening and the terrifyingly cool way they presented some of it, but I'm too distracted by the figure next to me. All he would have had to do at Carmel Valley High was take off that flannel, flash his smile and join the track or swim team, and he could have had the pick of most any girl in our school. But instead he chose, and that's what intrigues me—that he chose—to become invisible, hiding beneath the façade of a delinquent board-loving loser. I scour my memories of English class, searching for a single time he spoke up to participate and can't think of one. Most of us thought he was probably strung out, too dumb to form a coherent comment, or asleep. But instead, not only does he score top two percent of California test takers and get selected to take the Second Chance Institute Test, but he snags the coveted spot. The boy is a mystery, and apparently a genius.

After a half hour of jogging I can't take it anymore. I've been watching beads of sweat careen down his muscular back like a pinball game and the effect destabilizes me. Thankfully, his personality repels me, since his body surely doesn't seem to. I turn off the treadmill and go practice some meditative yoga moves I learned in gym class on the mat, facing the mirror. Blake, too, leaves the treadmill and heads to the corner behind me to lift weights. Needing to concentrate, I close my eyes. I left everything behind to become an SCI Recruit and need to understand what my next year will entail. My parents' belief that my life will always revolve around a man will only become a self-fulfilling prophecy if I let it. And I refuse to let them be right. So, I block my past and present men from my mind and focus on Thera.

The entire first training session focused on the planet we'd purportedly traveled to in less than five minutes time. Our host described Thera as an "inverse" or "polar" Earth. Due to lack of satellite technology they've had to explore it by "old-fashioned" methods, but believe Thera is the exact size and shape of Earth. However, as our instructor described, it would be like viewing a negative in a dark room. Where land exists on Earth, there is sea on Thera; and vice versa for sea on Earth and land for Thera. That's why we left Earth by sea and arrived on land. Even days and nights and the direction of the sun are supposedly inverted between Earth and Thera. The whole thing makes zero sense.

How'd it work? We went through a "magic" portal. Uh huh, because those exist. If I'm to drink their hopped-up Kool-Aid, Thera is largely unpopulated, with exception of SCI unit-built cities in various habitable locations near Earth's portals. We entered a Pacific Ocean portal, one of a couple dozen or so access points. There are far fewer exit points than entry points, something I wanted to understand further, so I'd enquired as to the reason on my tablet computer, and found out that no one knows; that perhaps they haven't discovered all the portals yet. Or they have no explanation because it is all a bunch of bull? We could be on a sound stage with cameras trained on us for all I know.

I started to barrage my tablet with questions. Where's the closest exit portal and can you please provide directions? Why does no one on Earth know about the portals? If it's true we're on a different planet, why's it being kept a big secret? How many earthlings have randomly wandered into a portal and ended up on Thera? Do you feel guilty about the overpopulation problems in India and elsewhere, when you've found a perfectly habitable world that has plenty of room? I pounded on the worthless piece of electronic garbage when it offered up crap like, "only select people can pass through the portals, limiting entry numbers." Blake pried the device out of my hands, and refused to return it until I'd promised not to break it.

Apparently, the Bermuda Triangle is the largest of the portals and has both entry and exit points, and is the locale of Import/Export City. They'd rattled off the names of dozens of cities too fast to write down, but I did catch Industrial City, Military City, Farm City, Food City, and Power City. I wonder why the naming conventions are so provincial. Must be that the same not-so-enterprising guy who discovered Thera and decided not to cash in named everything out of his simpleton vocabulary.

As the session continued I got more upset, at one point demanding that they "prove it." Particularly about the claim that on Thera the sun rises in the West, and settles in the East. I'd asked as nicely as possible, "Give me a compass then," but neither the guy on the screen or my tablet complied with the request. How can they possibly expect us to believe such extreme statements just because they claim it to be true?

After the substandard geography lesson, we'd moved onto meteorology. Our resident expert on all things alien explained that the weather is much more extreme on Thera, and "more suitable to exchanging days and nights." Thus, all activity on Thera happens at night with sleeping done during the day. Extreme temperature variations dictate the shift, with the high reaching upwards of 150 degrees during the day and down to eighty or ninety degrees at night. It had to have been at least a hundred, if not a hundred ten when we were out there, so I finally find something I can believe. That does explain the wacky schedule they've got us on with the twenty-four hour clocks, but the thought of life in darkness terrifies me, even if the artificial lights they use are beautiful. Special "color spectrum" lighting is used in the canyons and all public areas. Purportedly unique to Thera, the lights stay cool and like a prism can reflect out a full rainbow's array of colors, creating the light show we'd seen.

Garden City dates back to ancient times and is believed to be the original city on Thera. Excavations done to build modern residences have found old murals thousands of years old, which depict small residences surrounded by lush gardens, thus the name. Hmmm, can you say global warming? Because all I saw was some serious desert landscape, certainly nothing that'd be worthy of painting. Despite the lack of greenery now, the residents of the city have continued the tradition and painted life-sized murals of gardens throughout the city's buildings and homes.

Thera headquarters is located in Garden City, as are all scientific studies related to the phenomenon behind Earth's sister world. And although the "management" for the SCI resides here, locally instituted "governing bodies" oversee the night-to-night operation of each city. Thousands of scientists and doctors reside in the city and manage hundreds of research projects, including "Cleaving," although most are considered classified.

"What's Cleaving?" I'd asked my censored device and was informed that "Cleaving will be covered in a future training session." Don't encourage super achievers. Seriously people—you send me to training but don't want me to learn? I take a few deep breaths to calm myself and re-focus. I'm sure they'll explain everything in their own due time.

Two things I did find fascinating were the fact that there is no monetary system and no paper in Garden City. Citizens are issued "everything needed," so money is "not required." This means no stores, no shopping, and, most disturbingly, no choices. All jobs merit identical benefits, apparently. The trainer cites "lack of usable trees" as the reason behind a paperless system. The government issues each resident a portable tablet like the ones given to us for training to be used to list-make, note-take, and journal-write. I wonder though, despite applauding the lack of waste and destroying natural resources, whether the impetus centers back to central control. I bet every tablet device is connected, perhaps monitored? Should I ask my device, "Do Therans worship George Orwell?" Ha ha, probably not. It might be wise to make only mental notes of things that could be construed as contrary to whatever political body runs Thera. I'm sure I've pissed them off enough for one night.

Solar energy fuels most of Thera and given the temperatures most of the water is processed at desalinization plants close to the oceans, one of which is in Garden City, and through purification plants that recycle used water. It was during the very detailed explanation of the water collection process that I nodded off. I'm hoping Blake can fill me in on the missing details, but prefer to ask him when we're alone in our suite.

My nap had ended abruptly as our chairs were hurtled upward, and the screen filled with an aerial view of Garden City by day. Our chairs moved with the scenery to create the impression that we were flying overhead, reminding me of Soarin' Over California at California Adventures Theme Park, though more lifelike. I felt like I was outside, feeling wind rush against my face. We first flew the city boundaries, seeing the entire dead man's land border surrounding it. Then we soared low through the miles of canyons stretching towards the East coast of the unnamed continent. Snaking paths weave through the canyons, while the basins of the canyons have been paved and treated to be able to collect rainwater into large cisterns beneath the earth—that explains what appeared to be a concrete floor.

Our instructor narrated our journey, pointing out everything from government buildings to the solar power fields, to water purification facilities, to the school we will attend. I mentally recorded the layout of the sprawling city as best as possible, but struggle to remember the details now, particularly since everything appeared to be built to blend into the landscape. The cables and platforms I saw suddenly made sense. Zip lines. I once did that in Mexico on my one out-of-the country experience. My grandparents hosted a family reunion on a short cruise. We all zip lined in Puerto Vallarta, each getting harnessed and then attached to a pulley that allowed us to ride from platform to platform. It's fun and exciting, if not a little scary, but appears to be a quick and relatively efficient form of travel here.

Once we'd explored the nooks and crannies by day, the sky darkened and we viewed the city by night, swirling lights whirring by. The effect was exhilarating, and like Icarus, my desire to fly overwhelmed me. But then, our night journey completed, the chairs lowered back to floor level, and our first session ended.

A crashing sound yanks me back to the present. I open my eyes to see that the interruption was just the sound of clanking of weights. I catch Blake's reflection in the mirror. He's doing bicep curls with some free weights I'd be lucky to be able to pick up with both hands, but his eyes are transfixed on me. Perhaps switching planets brought out his predatory side, since I never saw him show an interest in the female race back on Earth. I shift my yoga position to better stretch and re-close my eyes, trying to edge out his image.

It takes a few minutes to refocus and remember what the training video said about Theran inhabitants. I typed in the exact words, but the mostly useless device is back in the training room. However, I do believe they said two very interesting things. First that, "There are two types of residents: Second Chancers, and those who have the ability to pass between Earth and Thera." Second, they said, "That which exists on one planet cannot exist on the other, with some exceptions," which they chose not to expand upon. I'm guessing those that can pass between Earth and Thera have everything to do with those high DNT levels. My device refused to confirm or deny my suspicion, but I'm positive that's what Spud Rosenberg meant when he said DNT would allow me to adapt to SCI's "remote" locations. And if we're really on a different planet, that's about as remote as one could get. But, what I don't understand is how the Second Chancers get here and who they are.

The conundrum eats away at the fringes of my consciousness until I feel a tap on my shoulder. It's Blake and he offers me a hand and a towel, both of which I accept.

"Sorry to interrupt that sweet display of flexibility," he smiles, "but we've got to go learn the rules of the place."

"Our hour is already up?" I say, my eyes scanning him up and down. I still can't get over the fact that he hid a near perfect physique underneath that nasty flannel, docking him only for his scarred hands, a few small scars on his back, and a barely noticeable bump on his nose as if it was once broken. His body actually gives his eyes a run for a lottery-sized jackpot of beauty. Despite the good looks, he doesn't make my heart flutter the way Ethan did and still does when I think of him.

"Over an hour... they give us some time to shower. We're due back at midnight," he says. Focus Kira. Who cares if he's good looking? He's a jerk and I'm hardly ready to start dating again. "Showers are in the locker rooms," he adds, pointing to mine. "Something wrong?"

"I'm having difficulty adjusting to our new wardrobes," I say, blood rushing to my cheeks, and immediately wishing I hadn't said it out loud. He laughs and strokes my chin with his fingers. I recoil a bit from his touch, surprised that he's capable of making a kind gesture. This is the same guy who insulted my upbringing mere hours ago. And there's something about him that I just don't trust, though I haven't been able to pinpoint why I feel that way.

"Likewise, my lovely friend and partner," he says, with emphasis on the friend and partner. "See you back in there?" He winks and starts to walk towards the men's locker room.

"Can't wait," I say, but then realize he might take it the wrong way, so I add, "I'm awfully curious about all those rules."

CHAPTER FIVE

Blake

"Crap, crap, crap," I think, pounding my head on the side of the shower.
I don't know how to do this, and am quite sure I'm going about it all wrong.
Kira seems to be intrigued by me, which I need her to be. This is exactly what
the powers that be want—they want us to hook up and make the Cleaving
automatic. I need them to think that it's going to happen so I can cover my
tracks on my real mission here.

I was a complete dick to Kira at breakfast, because I just know that she's
been waited on hand and foot, and that trend's got to stop, so I tell her I'm not
after her. Guys always get accused of going after the challenge, but chicks can't
resist the unattainable either.

The medical pit stop went fine and I think I managed to act surprised at the
outdoor landscape, but then we go to training, and I can tell right off the chairs
are biometric. This means the powers that be will be tracking every single
heartbeat, so they can observe how we're responding to the smelly load of crap
they're feeding us. They want to make sure the info is new and fresh coming in,
and that we're not plants. Kira aces her reaction, pummeling them with
questions and pounding on her tablet when the answers aren't to her
satisfaction.

I'm trying to figure out how *I'm* going to pull it off and then it occurs to me
that if I can get them to think that any abnormalities in my feed are because
they stuffed me in close quarters to this incredibly hot chick, then I'll pass with
flying colors. She's all up in my face and asking me about my eyes, staring at me
all lovey-dovey, so then I start "accidentally" brushing her with my hands and
arms, and next thing I know she's asleep on my shoulder. My mind starts
wandering places it shouldn't go, but there's only so much involvement I'm

willing to have with this girl. Maybe Kira's not the airhead cheerleader I originally thought, but not really relationship material either. As if I could allow anyone to become relationship material. Been there, been burned.

The workout was physically great, mentally brutal. I've been trained to focus, so that's the only thing that got me through. Because when I walked in and saw her dressed in the standard issue close-to-naked workout fare, I started thinking maybe I can mix a little pleasure with business. But then I think, no way, I'm not her type anyway. She likes big, burly, stupid dudes who pretend to respect her by burying themselves in a bottle. Then she sees me shirtless, about falls off her treadmill, and I think she just may be able to adapt to someone slimmer and smarter. I don't react though. I've been taught well and that gives me the upper hand.

Now what do I do? I pound my head a few more times, letting the cold water wash over me, trying to figure out my next play. What I need to do is dial it down a few notches. I know what's coming when training finishes and she's going to lose it, that's a certainty. And when she finds out I knew about it ahead of time and didn't warn her, she's going to hate me. But she'd want me dead if I started something with her now and then found out. Didn't I learn my lesson about how psychotic girls get when you betray them? Kira could turn me in for revenge. And I have too many people counting on me to die over what is realistically a hormonal reaction to a hot chick. I back off or come clean with her, the latter being pretty impossible when we're being watched 24/7 and I still don't know if I can trust her. Plus, I'm counting on her reaction to what's on deck to be genuine and if I give her a heads-up we could both end up dead by week's end.

I decide dialing it back is my best bet, get out of the shower, and wrap myself in a towel. As I walk to my locker, I hear a familiar voice coming from the steam room and think maybe Ted has some info I need. As I approach I see he's not alone, so stop in my tracks and strain to listen instead. The man speaking with Ted has his back to me, so all I can see is the remains of his thinning dark hair and a few extra rolls of fat. I crouch down to stay unseen, creating a pool of water below me as I drip onto the floor.

"What brings you to the Recruit gym, Ted? I thought you'd still be recovering from your entry."

"I came to see how my new Recruits are faring—to make sure they're adjusting well to things," he says. "But then I started to feel some heaves coming on and decided to step into the steamer for a bit."

"Getting the girl was a major coup. Promotion material. We'd all thought pure Lights were extinct. And to get both Light and Dark Originals, a perfectly Cleavable set even, is nothing short of miraculous. They came through without a scratch, too, which has the geneticists celebrating. Amazing. The specifics are above my pay grade, but rumor has it we're witnessing history in the making." My father didn't instruct me about any "Originals," although the term does sound familiar. I can't retrieve the memory, so focus on what I do know, which is that I don't like hearing that Kira and I are central to the future of the Second Chance Institute.

"It's confirmed, then? I hadn't heard the final DNA tests were back." I wish I could look at his face, because Ted told me that he didn't know what they wanted us for and I'd like to know if he's bluffing to get the information or if he's known all along.

"Confirmed, though with DNT levels that high they had to be. They are very special, those two. And there seems to be chemistry there, as least that's what their feeds are showing. Think they'll Cleave on their own, or will they need help?" he asks.

"I'd guess that will depend on how they react to meeting the Second Chancers," Ted says. "The girl may not take it well."

"I don't think that will be an issue. He'll likely be Cleaved before their training is complete. And if not, we'll force the issue by showing her the footage." He thinks we'll be Cleaved before training is complete? Or is he even talking about me? I'm not sure. Not after that reference to Second Chancers, which may mean they're playing with some serious fire. And what "footage" will they show Kira?

"That sounds like a solid plan."

"It will be if we can get Brad Darcton to agree. He has other ideas for the girl that are resonating with several members of the Ten." What ideas?

"I thought this whole thing was his plan?" Ted says.

"Getting the girl was his idea, but not the duo. He doesn't think the boy's right for her, even though he's got a cleaner health record than the alternative," the stranger says, confusing me further about what boy he's referencing. He pauses before adding, "But, I'm here because I have a more pressing concern. The girl has been asking a lot of questions through her tablet, some of them pretty derogatory. We tallied over seventy-five this evening alone. Should we be worried? Her Test results didn't paint her as rebellious."

"Nothing to fret over. Everything is a puzzle to her and this one is incomplete. Just give her some pieces that'll fit. Be creative." Great, Ted. Encourage them to tell us more lies, because I haven't heard enough already.

I want to stay to hear the rest, but can't risk being caught eavesdropping or late to the next training session. Things can go downhill quickly here if you start skirting the rules. I momentarily unhitch my towel to sop up the puddle of water below before heading to get dressed, committing the conversation to memory.

The two men sounded like my father with all the talk of Kira and I being "special." The last I time I heard those words was the day I passed through the Exiler-controlled exit portal from Thera to Earth. After my mother's death, my father obsessed over finding a way to get my sister and me off Thera. He couldn't be sure we'd have the ability even if a portal were found, but he'd promised my mother, so he joined every search party for nearly four years before the Exilers located and secured one. The problem with discovering new portals was that any portal exiting on land in Thera would enter in water on Earth and vice versa, making the passage extremely dangerous.

A couple Exiled Daynighter men lost their lives as they happened on a portal by accident, landing in ocean water with no boats in sight to provide rescue. Usually, Second Chancers led search parties, as they'd bounce if they hit a portal, not being able to go through. After the Daynighters disappeared from view, but didn't return by way of the entrance portal later, the Exilers decided to send the next men through with crudely made rafts. The plan worked, and these men then arranged to have a more permanent, albeit primitive structure erected, anchored to the ocean floor.

My father dumped us in Doc Daryn's care for six months after the find while he went to secure us a new home and identities on Earth. He hooked up with my "Aunt Jennifer," a childless distant relative of another Daynighter who'd been Exiled. She owned (and still owns) a modest house in a pleasant area of San Diego with good schools, a beautiful garden, and had inherited enough from her grandfather to support our family. Her location proved strategic for my father, being equidistant between the Exiler-controlled entrance and exit portals to the Garden City area of Thera.

The four-night journey to the exit portal on foot sucked for my father with a five and eight year old in tow. He carried my sister most of the fifteen-mile hike each night. We scrambled to reach Exiler-hosted shelters by sunrise, but the inland heat made sleep during the day uncomfortable. My sister begged to return to Doc Daryn's house. I whimpered with every step, my undersized shoes blistering and bloodying my feet.

The first night we passed the Eco barrier of Garden City, the canyon lights aglow in the distance. I'd only seen them once prior. Leila squealed and clapped at the spectacle, the only lights she'd previously seen being flashlights, cooking fires, and the sun. Upon visiting the outskirts of the city before, I'd envied the lights and seeming comfort of city life, but my dad and a near death experience soured my opinion. That day bad dreams haunted my sleep, making me slow and weary the following evening.

Two bands of gypsies shared shelter with us on our trip. The first had been workers in Farm City and had been Exiled for resisting the extreme work conditions that included daytime harvests. Their leathery skin cracked and scaled like a desert lizard's. I'd been shocked to see the unhealthy looking collection of "escaped" farm animals that accompanied the party, including a horse, milk cow, goat, and mule. Since their Exile, the workers had traveled south in search of Exiler communities, trying to rally support for a full-scale external revolt against the Theran cities. My dad pointed them in the direction of the other extremists in our home community.

The second group hailed from Military City, twenty-five men and women marching in perfect unison. Their tales of the dictatorship regime, blind obedience expected, and execution of unwanted Second Chance citizens made my father's description of Garden City sound like paradise. Well organized, they had a plan to train an army and overthrow Garden City headquarters that piqued my father's interest, but they'd been Exiled without their weapons. Without the right arsenal any attack would be fruitless. They'd either have to bring munitions from Earth, or gain access to Military City's vast supply. The latter would require crossing the Eco barrier, an impossible feat without insider information. At nightfall, the Militants were sent along to join my father's band of Exilers, with promises that my father would return soon to hear more of their plans to shift the balance of power on Thera.

I see how that chance encounter with the Militants turned my father towards extremism. Had we taken an alternate route to the portal, left a different night, or slept in different caves, my father may never have gotten on the Militants' bandwagon of revolt. Sure, the Exilers had always looked for ways to improve their situation or make changes in the status quo on Thera, but their ideas and methods were tame compared to the Military City men and women's brute force approach. But, my father readily drank their poison and sent them to infect the rest of the Exilers. They were received with open arms by my father's cohorts who'd resorted to extreme measures to protect our band of misfits in the past.

On our final night's travel to the portal we got a late start. Leila staged a dramatic temper tantrum. I dragged, slowing us further. The bugs swarmed more than usual and as I required more oxygen and had to suck in air by mouth, I'd ended up consuming bug chunks all night. My dad welcomed the "extra protein," but chewing on the crunchy creatures made me gag. I forced myself to swallow, knowing the roots we'd had for breakfast couldn't provide the sustenance to take me the distance.

At sunrise we had five miles left to go, and my dad chose to press on. Two and a half hours later we'd arrived, dehydrated and severely sunburned, at a small hut. An aged lady, horrified by our condition, insisted she minister to our wounds before allowing us to attempt passage. She covered us with a silvery-green paste and poured water into us until we felt bloated. The delay irritated my father, as our boat ride on the other side could decide we'd failed to pass through and return to shore, leaving us stranded.

"We must leave now," he'd said, pulling Leila from the lady's arms.

"How can you be sure they won't bounce?" the woman responded.

"They are special," he'd said.

"Originals?" she'd asked. *That's* where I'd heard it.

"It'd be hard to prove that without a DNA test out here, wouldn't it?" he'd quipped. Why didn't he ever mention it to me? Years of training and he fails to note something so critical to the motivations of the SCI?

"Blake, you go first. Just walk down that dark corridor. Leila you'll follow your brother, and I'll follow you." Energized by the water, ointment, and visions of food and bounties in the "promised land," I bounded forth. The shock-like sensations I felt couldn't touch the pain of my burns and blisters, so they barely registered.

Once through, the motion of the uncovered barge amplified an already queasy stomach, and I vomited what little water remained in my system. My sister did the same, although her reaction was more violent than mine. My father convulsed and heaved more heavily than Leila and me combined. I sat on the platform and let the ocean breeze wash over me. In two minutes time the temperature had dropped more than fifty degrees. The fact that the sun shone brightly but the air felt cool floored me. I shivered as my body adjusted.

A shiny object on the horizon grew in size as it neared, eventually revealing a man and a woman aboard a small boat.

"Hank," the woman exclaimed to my father. "Thank goodness you're back. And these must be Blake and Leila. They are beautiful, just beautiful. You were right. They made it through. They are special!"

"Leila, Blake, meet your new mom, Jennifer," he'd said, a sad look washing across his face. Too young to understand then, I now know that although Jennifer took on the role of main parental caretaker, she never replaced my mother as my father's Cleave, nor became my true mom. Just Aunt Jen.

The other man aboard the boat that day was Ted Rosenberg. It was on the trip back to shore that my father and Ted hatched the plans to send me back to Thera. The Militants knew we'd need "insiders" to pull off their plan. Ted procured Recruits for the West Coast, and after seeing how easily we'd come through, he knew we'd be assets the Second Chance Institute would desire. My father refused to subject Leila, but he'd willingly agreed to transform me into a trained mole. This new plan of revenge was something my father could really sink his teeth into. In deciding this, he ceased to be a father to me altogether—instructor, trainer, dictator, yes, but loving father, no. My only real family left was Leila and now she's gone, too.

Yes, the Second Chance Institute has taken everyone I'd ever cared about and will continue to wreak havoc unless stopped. There's no reason I can't do a little digging about the Originals while proceeding with daddy's plan. He knew and kept it from me. I need to understand why. Forget backing off. I need Kira to sort this mess out with me and I do believe I know a safe way to suck her in.

Most glorious night! Thou wert not sent for slumber!

Lord Byron

CHAPTER SIX

Kira

Embarrassed to the brink of humiliation, I decide to avoid acting like a twelve-year-old desperate for attention and focus on staying awake for the next session. Rules are rules regardless of what planet I'm on. Since a swift exit isn't possible, I'm forced to be a law abiding citizen. A jet lag-like fog has descended and my body fights the graveyard shift with vigor. The box "lunch" they served raised my blood sugar a hair, but not enough to keep me lucid for long. It would help if our instructor was actually in the room with us and not a pre-recorded video, or used inflection in his voice. This dude could bore another bore to death.

The SCI encourages strict adherence to rules, or as they call them "Canons" through a merit/demerit system called the "Circle of Compliance," though the system is linear, not circular in the slightest. Everyone starts at neutral and ascends towards inclusion in the "Grand Council" through compliance, and descends towards Exile through disobedience, a typical carrot and stick system. The Grand Council is the governing body of the city, composed of the most obedient citizens, and are able to add new rules to the Canon for everyone else to abide by.

Exile, from what I can read between the lines, is akin to a death sentence, or at least that's what they want you to think. When exiled, a citizen is forced to leave Garden City wearing Exile-identifying orange clothing, no possessions, and a night's worth of food. They are placed outside the "Eco Barrier" that surrounds the city and left to fend for themselves against the harsh elements of Thera. The barrier, a 50-foot strip of barren land surrounding the city, emits plague-like biological elements strong enough to melt the skin off a person's body, preventing re-entry. And escape, I infer.

The most serious offense in Garden City is treason. Those guilty face Exile or execution, with the decision as to the offender's fate left to the presiding Ten of the Grand Council. Several offenses lead to immediate Exile, including murder, aggravated assault, grand theft, inciting rebellion, discussing the past with Second Chancers, and "violating the terms of Cleaving." Huh? Those last two seem a little extreme.

The man drones for ten minutes about the sanctity of life for Second Chancers; the importance of having the opportunity to live without re-experiencing mistakes or painful instances from the past. He says there is a high probability Recruits will encounter Second Chancers we know—but that under no circumstances can we reveal that we know them. Nor can we discuss the Second Chancer's past acquaintances, relationships, or the situations that brought them to becoming a Second Chancer.

I can't imagine I'd ever run into someone I knew here on Thera. It's not like I know many people who have majorly screwed up. Maybe some of the kids from school who ended up in rehab and never returned? And there were those three girls that had some sort of pregnancy pact and went off the deep end when they couldn't handle being moms. They ended up foisting their kids on the foster care system. Sure, I can totally understand why they wouldn't want to be reminded of stuff like that. But none of that really meshes with what Spud told me about the people "accidentally" happening upon their misery.

Then the man starts to talk about Cleaving. Despite my exhaustion I perk up for this, sitting up straight in my seat. I sense Blake does too, but don't look his way. Our trainer begins by explaining that Second Chancers arrive at Garden City at all different ages, and that SCI's goal is to make sure everyone has a loving support system. The population of each Theran city has population limits, due to housing and resource constraints. These parameters (at least in Garden City) led to the institution of Cleaving. He posts a list of Cleaving "rules" which I furiously type into my tablet.

At the age of eighteen each male Theran Cleaves to a suitable mate, if they have not already Cleaved.

Cleaving is for life and cannot be undone under any circumstances.

Cleaved couples must apply to be Endowed with a Theran child entrant under the age of fifteen OR to enter the lottery for an Assisted Pregnancy.

Maximum children per household through Endowment or Assisted Pregnancy is two.

Non-Assisted Pregnancies are not allowed; violators subject to Exile. All women sixteen and older are required to take birth control.

New Theran entrants over sixteen and prior to their eighteenth birthnight will be placed in monitored student housing to allow opportunities for self

Cleaving.

Young adults over sixteen and prior to eighteen who engage in sexual activity are automatically Cleaved and Cleaved for life.

The last point makes me start laughing so hard tears spring from my eyes. The video halts, as if it knows I need a moment.

"What is so funny?" Blake finally asks me.

"Sorry. I'm just thinking about how many people in our high school would be married off by sixteen with that rule. And how pissed the guys would be to be limited to the first girl they snagged. Just think of how much time we spent in health class hearing about all of it, when the solution was so freaking simple."

"So, you think it's a good idea?" he asks, looking at me like I'm insane. I don't know. An arranged marriage at eighteen—or before—is more than a little sketchy, but I do like that it's for life. The thought of ever being with more than one guy disgusts me. Something does bug me about it and then it finally occurs to me.

"We don't have to do it, do we? Be Cleaved? They can't make us do that, can they? I turn eighteen in December. Hey, when's your birthday—or I guess it's birthnight here?" I joke.

"In sixty-five nights," he responds, sounding a little panicked. "That would be seriously messed up if we signed up for a year gig and they forced us to get hitched. My parents would freak. No, I'd freak." I'm jealous at how quickly he's picked up the "nighttime" lingo. I constantly mix up my day and night terms, although I'm starting to get the hang of it.

"Really? It's not appealing to get married at eighteen and be handed a fifteen year old to parent?" I say, trying to get a rise out of him. It works too, as he has to wipe the sweat from his forehead onto his sleeve.

"So. Funny. Keep talking like that and I'm gonna root for you to get sexed up by some Second Chancer and get your own gaggle of rugrats." If he thinks his parents would freak, he hasn't met my parents. My dad and his buddies would hunt down Spud Rosenberg without mercy.

"Yeah right. If I didn't go there with Tristan, I can assure you I'm not going there with some random dude who made a bad enough mistake to land here." I roll my eyes at him and sit back in my seat, waiting for the video to resume. Within moments it does.

The man finishes out the list.

Recruits who engage in sexual activity—with other Recruits, or with Second Chancers—will be Cleaved and become automatic citizens of Thera.

Special circumstances may allow additional Cleaving to occur, subject to direction by the Senior Ten of the Grand Council.

Blake and I both become rigid. As if I needed new reasons to stay celibate, my resolve cements instantly. Any physical appeal Blake had in that gym has disappeared. The consequences for letting things "go a little too far" on Thera are too severe to ignore: a lifetime sentence of darkness and bizarre rules with someone with whom you may or may not actually be compatible. If they manage to rustle up Ethan and bring him to Thera I might reconsider, but short of that, consider me unavailable.

The rest of the session covers hundreds of rules, from major to menial. A few stand out and I type them into my tablet while I share my impressions out loud with Blake. I figure that if I keep talking I'll stay awake.

Don't leave the city without Official permission. "How could we with the Eco barrier blocking our way?"

"I don't know," Blake says.

Never speak about the possibility of a Supreme Being. Native Therans use the term "Gads" frequently, but it is a slang expression for power and authority, not an acknowledgment of deity. "So, how do they enforce that? Are all the Second Chancers atheists?"

"How would I know?" Blake asks.

No more than twenty minutes during daylight hours in direct sunlight. "When they thought that Unit 27 was the 'perfect fit' for me did they not realize that I require hours of sunlight a day to function?"

"Did you tell them that or did you expect them to be psychic?" Blake asks, rolling his eyes.

Keep off the board tracks during storms. "Does this place even get rain? I didn't see a single thing that was green."

"Neither did I," Blake says. "Although I did see some variations of brown."

All zip line runs must be logged. "So much for the zip lines being an efficient form of travel. Why would they care if we zipped instead of walked?"

"No clue," Blake says. I can tell by the inflection in his voice that he's starting to get a bit annoyed by my questions.

Stay in your residence during curfew hours from 10:00 to 18:00. "That's pretty easy to enforce when they lock us in. I guess it's a good thing I need eight hours sleep, although I'd really prefer my eight hours of lockdown to be when it is dark."

"Our place has no windows, so does it matter?" Blake says. "Do you have questions about everything?"

"Well, yeah, duh," I say. "Aren't you the least bit curious about the how's and why's? I like to know how everything works."

"Clearly. Just don't expect me to be your resident expert when your tablet can't even answer all your questions," he says, definitely irritated now.

"Geez," I say. "I wasn't expecting you to answer. Haven't you ever heard about rhetorical questions?"

"No, I lived such a sheltered life that I'm afraid not. What is a rhetorical question? And what is the meaning of life? My parents never told me that, either," he says. I give him a little shove, which may or may not have come across as more violent than playful.

"Sarcastic much?" I ask.

"Inquisitive much?" he responds with a smirk.

"Fine, I'll keep my questions up here," I say, pointing to my head. "I will figure it all out. That's the benefit of inquisitive minds."

"I just bet you will," he says with a laugh.

I return my focus to the rules and try hard to stay awake. Water conservation is a big deal, so we need to stick to the rules about shower length, turning off water while brushing teeth, and limiting our toilet flushing. Canons for garbage disposal, recycling, garden maintenance, regular doctor visits, and transportation all run together as I become more and more tired. My head starts bobbing and I'm thrilled to catch that the full set of rules are now available on my tablet because it's nap time.

I close my eyes, lean back deep into my chair, and wonder if there are consequences for sleeping during dull training sessions before I drift into frightening images of darkness, menacing computers that arrange Cleavings, and being dumped into Exile for throwing something into the trash rather than a recycle receptacle.

"Have a nice nap?" Blake says. "You missed all the juicy stuff about the proper way to wear your uniform and lather yourself with sunscreen nightly. They even showed some disgusting clips of a dude with leathery skin and some lady with skin cancer on her face." Nasty, I think, wiping my mouth to check for drool and rubbing underneath my eyes to remove my mascara bleed-out.

"Sorry. I tried to stay awake, I really did, but that guy's voice could be used as a safer alternative to sleep drugs anytime," I respond.

"You're in luck then, because we are done for the day, or night or whatever it is. We have free time and they said we could explore the canyon and watch the sunrise. Up for it? Or you want to head back to our digs for another nap?" I avoid looking directly at him, not wanting to give him any further impression that I'm a bit infatuated.

"Sure," I say. Despite my continued exhaustion, he had me at the mention of "explore" and "sun." I realize it's only been a day without the sun, but it seems like an eternity and I'm having major withdrawal. Somehow the thought of blistering in 150-degree heat is preferable to no sun at all.

"They even gave us boards," he says, pointing at two identical Industrial City issue skateboards. I grimace at the sight, hoping that I didn't miss some rule about being required to travel by one, given there are no cars here.

"No thanks. I choose life," I say.

"I can teach you," he offers, raising his eyebrows. "Boarding is killer."

"Exactly. You said it yourself—boarding is a killer," I say, revising his words slightly. "I look at that thing and I see cuts, bruises, broken bones, more trips to the evil doctors, needles, comas, being buried in soil that would cook me and turn me to dust in seconds because it's so hot here... I'm sorry. It just isn't happening. You go. I'll watch."

"Wimp," he teases. "OK, fine, prepare to be blown away. Those skate tracks are calling my name."

"Whatever, showoff," I mumble. I take up residence on a bench overlooking the canyon, pulling my knees to discourage any creepy crawlers or fliers from hiking up to or landing on my shirt.

Blake's right—I am blown away. I alternate between watching Blake's unreal ability to maneuver the narrow tracks provided and marveling at the bizarre landscape and lighting of the canyon. While Blake's board seems a natural attachment of his legs, I'm the polar opposite. I never made it past the bunny ski slopes, my first surf lesson, or showed any promise on skates, street or ice. Landing a dozen back handsprings or doing a flip on cement is my domain and the aspect of cheer I've enjoyed the most all these years.

It finally hits me what the glowing colors of the canyon remind me of—the Northern Lights—from the pictures I've seen anyway. Our journey "by air" during the earlier session went too fast to get the full experience, but looking at it from a stationary position is hypnotic. The temperature, while still hot, is much more comfortable than earlier and I prefer hot fresh air to the stale, over air-conditioned air of the training room that was present the entire time, with exception of the warm air blown in for our "flight."

Without warning, the light show disappears and I can see the sky for the first time due to the quickening brightness of the dawn. Blake joins me to watch the sky change colors from a dark blue, to lighter blue, to shades of pink, and then finally orange and red as the sun rises above the horizon. I have to shield my eyes for a few minutes until they adjust to the influx of light. We ooh and ah as an intricate patchwork of clouds makes the colors particularly intense and spectacular, but otherwise remain silent.

By the time the sun visibly appears in the sky the temperature has notched up at least ten to fifteen degrees. I have to brush the sweat beading on my forehead. It's then I notice a line of nasty-looking red ants marching inches from the bench and jump up, shaking myself of any potential intruders. Blake chuckles at my ants-on-the-pants dance.

"Now that sun's up we get twenty minutes to get our nightly dose of vitamin D," Blake says, also standing up and offering me his hand. "Want to take a walk down the canyon and back up?"

"If I can stand to be out here that long," I respond, trying to pull my hand away from him. Instead, he intertwines his fingers with mine and pulls me alongside him and down a windy trail unsuitable for skateboards, and from the sticky piles of stench, I'd guess one frequented by mules. "I promise I can handle the trail myself," I say, trying to pull away my hand again. Why's he being so pushy when we barely know each other?

"Kira, I don't know what you think," he says quietly, almost whispering in my ear, "but I'd swear that we're being watched and listened to. I figure, the canyon is probably safe to really talk, you know. So pretend you're into me and let's take a walk and chat. Given how obsessed they all seem to be with people hooking up, it's a great cover." I laugh about the way he suggests to I pretend I'm into him, as if he doesn't think I already am. While I may have given that impression, I'm hardly sold on his hot/cold routine.

"Ha ha, yeah sure, sounds good," I say, watching the corner of his mouth curl upward in response. We debate about whether we're actually on a different planet or stuck out in the middle of some earthly desert, and then discuss all the oddities of Thera, including the lack of money and paper, weird chairs we've been strapped into, and censored information. I share my fear of Exile, and how I don't get the SCI's obsession with the Second Chancers and keeping their pasts from them. We agree to keep mental notes of everything we hear and compare concerns, all the while being completely cooperative with SCI direction outside the canyon. As we approach our twenty-minute limit, I ask him about a comment he'd made about the SCI purposefully pairing males and females.

He gives me his theory. "They pair up members of the opposite sex, because they want them to Cleave and become permanent members of their happy-go-lucky society. If I'm right that means they want us to hook up. We give them the illusion we're heading down that path, and they'll want us to have some private time to move things along." I stop, yanking him backwards.

"So, that's what all the flirting has been about tonight?" I ask. His eyes sparkle and his lips form into a smile.

"What flirting?" he says, running each hand down his opposite arm as if to deflect the accusation. "You were the one flirting with me and that started before they told us about Cleaving, which is what gave me the idea." I roll my eyes and shake my head. Barraging him with questions equals flirting? Maybe it was the falling asleep on his shoulder? If anything, *he's* been doing the flirting.

Not me. Though I can tell no amount of discussion would be sufficient for him to admit the effort was lopsided in his direction.

"Whatever," I respond. "Fine, I'll go along with your little *charade*, but only because I want answers and you're the only person I can talk to about it. But I don't care how much they want it to happen, I'm not Cleaving anyone, much less someone as clearly full of themselves as you are." He chuckles, and then looks at his watch before tapping on it.

"Five minutes," he says. "Race you. Last one to the top has to initiate the first kiss." Kiss? Dream on, buddy. He then sprints up the hill, leaving me behind. I march slowly and steadily, reaching the top with a minute to spare, amazed at the number of lizards that appear to sunbathe in the morning light.

"You lose," he quips.

"Works for me. That way a kiss will never happen," I whisper in his ear, and then skip to the double doors where our escort awaits, probably to return us to our suite and lock us in. I say to the man, "Thanks for the free time. The nighttime lights and the sunrise were just incredible. What's next?"

"Ms. Donovan, here's a compass, as requested." I look at him incredulously given I'd only asked the tablet and video-man for proof. "Go ahead, check for yourself," he says. I grimace, but return to the railing and look at the sun in relation to the direction noted on the compass. Indeed, I'm facing south and the sun just rose to my right, which is west. No way. Maybe they rigged the compass?

"It's not rigged. You are no longer on Earth, Ms. Donovan," the man says, walking up behind me, reading my thoughts. "So perhaps you can focus less on disproving the assertion that you've left Earth and more on learning about Thera?" If I had any question my device was monitored, I no longer do.

"OK, fine," I say. "We're not on Earth. We're on Thera. We traveled here through a magic portal."

"It's not magic," he refutes. "There's just not an explanation that can be explained by conventional science."

"I'll take your word for it. Thanks for the compass," I say, not wanting to discuss it any further.

"Let me show you back to your suite and the two of you can have dinner before retiring to bed," he says. "We've left a bottle of sleep aids for you in the kitchen. I can't emphasize how crucial it is for you to adjust to the new timing and avoid napping during training sessions." I recoil slightly, wondering if his chastisement is sufficient, or if I'll face more extreme consequences.

"I'm sorry. I really did try to stay awake because I didn't want to miss any material. Hopefully after a good night's—or I guess good day's—sleep I should be good." Blake is by my side, but letting me do all the chitchatting.

"Adjustment is difficult," the man agrees. "You'll both go to the clinic again in the evening. Your doctors may be able to help." I'd already suppressed the memories of our clinic visit, but they come gushing back and I shudder.

"Super," I say. "Do we just visit the clinic every evening this week, or every night that we're here?" I ask, trying to sound merely inquisitive and not horribly annoyed. It's not the man's fault that I have to be poked and prodded.

"As often as the doctors determine is needed for you to adjust and prevent future difficulties," he says.

"So, does that mean bad stuff can happen to us from being here on Thera?" I ask, this time not being able to hide my fear, truly not remembering fine print about possible medical side effects.

"Our doctors are exceptional," he responds "As long as you submit to their regimen without complaint you shouldn't have anything to worry about." His message is clear. Do as I am told or I'll have a whole heck of a lot to stress over.

"Uh, ok, yeah, will do," I mumble, remembering Blake's admonition to be cooperative.

"Here you are," the man says. "Suite Six. Your wakeup call will be at 18:00, and an escort will be here precisely at 19:00. Enjoy your dinner."

"Thank you," I say, entering in, the door snapping shut and lock engaging as soon as Blake passed the threshold.

"Suck-up," he whispers, close enough for his lips to brush my ear. I turn to him and put my hands on his shoulders, gently but firmly pushing him away.

"Well, someone has to be," I say, "given you have no social skills, loner boy. And besides, everyone here is so nice and helpful," I say with no inflection in my voice to indicate I'm not serious. He leans in to me, his eyes dizzyingly close to me. This makes me nervous and I step back.

"So, princess," he says, I'm sure as payback for calling him loner boy, "you making dinner?"

"Happy to," I say, since despite his ridiculous impression I'm incapable of manual labor, I took a year of cooking and typically made dinner for my family. I turn to hide the hurt I feel from his comment and check out the contents of the refrigerator, trying to decide what I can make without a recipe given what's in there. "You like teriyaki chicken?" I ask without looking at him.

"Sounds perfect," he says, his voice coming from the living area. He's relaxing, I'm sure.

"Anything for my fake boyfriend," I mumble incoherently under my breath. Where's that gorgeous, sweet, humble, gracious guy, Ethan, I met at the party again? Dead, missing, gone, who knows. I sigh and get to work.

As the week progresses the training sessions blur together. Every night starts with a trip to the clinic, where we're invaded in every possible way, physically and mentally. The nurses claim my nightly shot will help me adjust better, but I swear it's just making me crankier and more hormonal than usual. And bloated if that's possible, or maybe it's just the food here that's a little off taste and digestion-wise. They take my blood every other night and even have the gall to do an ultrasound of my entire abdomen, this purportedly to ensure my digestive system is functioning and no "lesions" are forming on my reproductive organs. The doctor claims a fraction of previous Recruits have had abdominal and reproductive issues and that he's just trying to "stay ahead of any problems."

In class we review the Canon of rules to really hammer them in, and then learn about exciting new topics, like "Befriending Your Second Chance Classmates," "How to Deal with Stress Appropriately," and "Focusing On The Future." All of them emphasize the same thing: don't you dare screw up and mention anything from the past to a Second Chancer, even if you have issues, because you'll ruin their "second" life and, in consequence, will be Exiled. Let me just meet them already and maybe all your dumb rules will make sense.

After our workouts Blake and I hike the few canyon trails that are well-lit and well-marked, traveling as far as possible in attempt to explore our surroundings better. Each time we approach the perimeter of the "Recruit" facilities we are nicely, but firmly, encouraged to immediately turn back. Feeling a little claustrophobic, I try to escape our Recruit quarters a few times, but the locks proved impenetrable. Why won't they let us explore the city? The simulated tour by air was cool, but insufficient to really get to know the place.

Two field trips promise to break up the monotony and even provide some excitement. On the first we're told we can tour two Garden City "model homes" across the canyon from our training room. It's a thirteen hundred foot zip across—the longest zip of the city, and one that I've avoided. The high-speed ride through darkness terrifies me and I do a poor job braking and come into the platform going a little fast, knocking Blake over. I apologize profusely for using him as a human domino, but part of me thinks he deserves it for his constant jabbing and inconsistent behavior towards me.

Once he shakes off my assault, my fake boyfriend grabs my hand and escorts me to the first house, which is roughly a hundred yards towards the ocean from the zip-line platform. We pass several others homes on the way. They all look disturbingly similar. Our guide informs us that, in fact, Garden City residences are constructed cookie cutter—the only difference being that Cleaved Couples get an extra bedroom to house their children, as well as an extra bathroom. They build each house of cement and into the top of one of the dozens of canyons in the city, with a porch overlooking the canyon area. The layouts are identical, with the rooms of each home circling a "sun room" and "filtered garden." Residents can get their twenty minutes of sun in the sunroom without having to venture into the canyon. The garden room, while outdoors, has some special ultraviolet ray and heat filters to allow certain fruits and vegetables to grow. Each resident is required to maintain their garden and even the garden layout and crops are prescribed.

The interior rooms consist of a kitchen, dining room, living room, bedroom and full bathroom, and powder room for guests—all stocked with "everything needed." Besides the bedroom variation of the houses we visit, the murals depicted on the walls differ, though each one is spectacular. I ask my tablet device who does the murals and am told that each resident has options: take a class at the school to learn how to do it yourself, or an artist will be provided free of charge. Of course it's free of charge since you can't pay them without money, there is no money on Thera, and workers don't earn wages anyway. They mention that fifty percent of residents choose to do their own art so they can depict garden views to their likings. Not sure where on Thera anyone could get decent inspiration.

Blake and I flit through the houses, being complete goofballs as we pretend to be an old Cleaved couple, ordering kids around and doing chores. We invite trouble as we do a little "gardening" at one of the homes. Blake "accidentally" throws a tomato to me without warning—claiming poor visibility—and it splatters across my white shirt. I return the favor and then it's all out fruit and veggie war, and I smell like "citrus surprise" by the end. Our escort informs us that lunch is served and that if we are hungry we can suck the pulp off our clothing. I about pass out working out on an empty stomach after that, but seeing Blake so covered with fruit that he had to take off his shirt made it worthwhile.

After our behavior during our first field trip, they nearly cancel the next, but I sweet-talk our escort, promising that we'll be on our very best behavior. Our escort takes us by private train, only accessible by key card, to an unlabeled destination. We exit our train cars, and the man uses his access card again to enter an extremely long, but well lit tunnel with doors on either side, each located at least fifty to a hundred feet apart. We travel the great length by moving sidewalk, and after having counted five doors on each side we dismount the sidewalk, and our escort punches a long code into a keypad to grant us access. As the door opens, both Blake and I say, "Wow" simultaneously.

A perfect scale model of Garden City lays before us—residences, canyons, plants, headquarters and all. Despite being completely indoors, even the nighttime lighting has been recreated. Very cool, but again, why not let us explore the real thing? A bridge takes us over the simulated "Eco barrier" and into the city. Dozens of representatives from the city's industries are on hand to discuss career options in Garden City. I find it crazy they went to the expense of modeling the entire city just to host a career fair. But, it is better than watching training videos, so I keep my mouth shut. Even if it is a little disconcerting to try to find our way around in the dim lighting, relying on path lights and the hundreds of workers on site to point us in the right direction. Thankfully our "target destinations" are well lit with spotlights illuminating outdoor classroom seating areas.

Solar technicians show us the vast fields of panels and how they convert the sun's energy to raw power for the city. The small-scale desalination plant magically transforms salt water to drinkable water, and we taste the before and after to confirm it, the salt water reminding me of swimming and snorkeling at the beautiful San Diego beaches with my brother, Jared. We view hundreds of minerals and other natural resources excavated from Garden City canyons and learn they are used to improve life on Thera. Artists share mural technique and styles, and let us try our hand at sponge painting a tulip patch using stencils. One of the artists reminds me of a guy who used to live in our neighborhood, the resemblance striking, but I dismiss it as coincidence and faulty memory, not having seen him for years after his family moved.

Teachers show off the latest technology for interactive online classes. Doctors expound upon their advanced screening techniques that allow them to catch problems, including cancer and other diseases, in early stages. Members of the Grand Council, Garden City's politicians, vaguely discuss how rules and regulations are proposed and passed using a simple majority. Business Importers handle trade with other Theran cities to insure Garden City residents are provided with everything needed.

I tarry with the DNT scientists, who let me see "native" DNT under a microscope—fish-like organisms—and then their attempts at "artificial" DNT, which looked like finless fish. Despite the fact I despise having my blood taken, I allow them to prick my finger so that I can see my own blood under the microscope and confirm that my DNT is indeed "native." The scientists hem and haw about the reason for their focus on DNT, but do confirm that the higher the levels, the easier travel between Thera and Earth becomes.

I search for Blake, who lost interest in the scientists' spiel quickly. Given the poor lighting I scan for a white and silver Recruit uniform amongst the sea of blue and tan city employee uniforms. While being unsuccessful on my hunt, I happen upon the dockworkers. They're unloading food and supplies off boats at the fake ocean mouth of the center canyon, and onto distribution trains, which run through tunnels to warehouse delivery locations. From there, distributors manually deliver to residences and workplaces with the help of pack mules. It's weird to imagine a world without FedEx or UPS, semi-trucks, and cross-country trains, but Thera has no equivalents to any of these. I'm glad it all gets delivered in a timely fashion and they do give out samples, which quell my appetite, but given I have zero interest in the supply chain, I move on.

After wandering past the waste and recycling and cistern management centers without stopping—careers equally as dull as food distribution—I finally find Blake, who is embroiled in conversation with a "Foreign Relations" specialist, dubbed a "Daynighter." The man handles relations between the Second Chance Institute offices on Earth and Garden City. Blake asks seemingly innocent questions like, "So how far do you have to travel to get to the exit portal?", "Do you get to work directly with the Grand Council?", and "How much time do you spend on either side?" He feigns great interest in the man's work and likely learns more than he was supposed to, such as the fact the man works within the Council headquarters building, presents to them once a month, and splits his time equally between the two sides. The guy grandstands his job like it's the second coming for both worlds' political landscape. I listen to the exchange while enjoying the view out past the Eco barrier and towards the "ocean."

Once burned out on foreign affairs, Blake drags me past the City Center Medical Clinic and directly to the Grand Council Headquarters' building at the far end of a huge plaza. Unlike any other building in town, it stands apart with its stone edifice and multistory height. Tiny lights, embedded into the mortar, wash the building with stunning color and brightness that would win any Christmas light competition. If its scaled-down counterpart is any indication, the real Headquarters building must be spectacular. Given that it was built on the highest point of the highest canyon top, I'd have to imagine it can be seen for miles in every direction.

The same man who greeted us upon entry to Thera does so again. This time, he introduces himself as Brad Darcton, a member of the presiding Ten of the Grand Council. Or, in other terms, Theran bigwig.

Whereas we'd been allowed to question the other representatives, Brad grills *us* for twenty minutes about our experiences to date and areas of career interest based on what we've seen so far. He then explains in broad generalities about the work done within the headquarters building, including Cleave contracts, Council sessions, additions of new Canon to the Circle of Compliance, and rulings on adjustment to resident status on the Circle. When I dare ask how the government structure differs between Garden City and the other Theran cities he suddenly has an urgent meeting to attend and directs us towards the Weather Center for final instruction. Blake takes me by my hand, ready to move on.

I hesitate, dragging as I watch Brad Darcton enter the model Headquarter's building and see a young man with dark hair and a five o'clock shadow greet Brad. I freeze in my tracks and yank my hand away from Blake. The guy looks a whole lot like Ethan, but I can't get a good enough look. So, I briskly walk towards the building. Brad sees me and motions the man away.

Blake follows me and asks, "What are you doing, Kira?"

"That guy that Brad Darcton was talking to in there. I swear I know him," I say. Perhaps I need psychiatric help. Every single time I see a dark haired guy I think it's Ethan and my stomach goes haywire, I want it to be the case so much.

"Doubtful," Blake says. "Come on, we're due at the Weather Center."

"Yeah," I say. "I'm coming." I stare back at the Headquarters building. It's the not knowing that gets to me, I think. Ethan was never confirmed dead. The continual "what ifs" are a killer. Brad steps back out of the building.

"Ms. Donovan, can I help you with something?" he asks. "Mr. Sundry, go ahead to the Weather Center. I'll send her along shortly." Blake looks concerned, but slowly walks away.

I ignore Blake and turn to Brad Darcton. "That guy you were talking to. Is his name Ethan? He looks so much like a guy I met on Earth."

"Under what circumstances did you meet this… Ethan?" he asks.

"Oh, I met him at a party and we talked for a long time. But then he disappeared and I've been wondering what happened to him," I say. I don't bring up the explosion or the fact that Ethan may very well be dead, not wanting to sound crazy and all.

"I believe that you were warned in your training that you'd likely run into people on Thera that you'd known previously," he says. "Need I remind you about our Rules concerning discussing past relationships or acknowledging you know them with Second Chancers? It's important not to run up to every person you think you might know and try to figure out if you have some sort of shared past."

"Was that man a Second Chancer?" I ask. Ethan didn't seem to be the kind of guy who would do something where he'd need a second chance.

"We really try to make every citizen of Garden City feel important and not thrust labels on them," he says. "Now run along and I'll expect you to be more careful in the future." I shiver, as his stern warning sounds more like a threat. Discussing the past with a Second Chancer is cause for immediate Exile, I remind myself. It's a five minute walk to the Weather Center and I chastise myself the entire way for irking a member of the Ten.

"What was that about?" Blake asks.

"Brad was just refreshing me on the rules concerning Second Chancers. I really don't get what it would hurt to acknowledge you knew someone before, but I'd definitely prefer to avoid making a member of the Ten angry again," I say.

"No kidding. Don't beat yourself up about it, though. I'm sure he was just trying to protect you from getting into trouble," Blake says. "Let's go learn about weather and get your mind off of it."

"Let's," I say, although my attention is still back at what I saw transpire at Headquarters.

The Weather Center sits atop an ocean cliff and monitors incoming storms, as hurricane-level rains and flash floods threaten the community every few months. Ah, so there is rain here. They tell us they're going to run us through a training drill that simulates the experience of being in the canyons during a storm, the description of which terrifies me and will likely give me nightmares for years. I'm so busy trying to decide whether it was Ethan I saw or not and what reason he could have to be on Thera that I completely miss the whole part about "how to survive a flash flood in the canyons." Mental note to avoid it so that my non-existent skills will be never be put to the test.

We hike down the mini canyon towards the cement floor, as directed, with some difficulty. Although the canyon lights create a spectacular show from afar, they don't provide the best lighting to keep steady footing, alternating between blinding when close to the lights and barely visible away from them. Once close to the bottom of the canyon we hear a warning siren. Torrents of water and mud attack us from every angle. I immediately regret being inattentive during the survival lecture. Blake grabs a rope ladder, and then me, pulling us up toward safety as if he is some sort of pro. I can't see or hear, much less climb. Blake works for both of us, saving my life. They wouldn't have let us die in a training exercise, would they? Thankfully, Blake only had to pull me up a fraction of the way he'd have had to if we'd been out in a real canyon. A guy hanging from a zip line gives us a hand at the end and explains that he uses the lines during real emergencies to do rescues.

Mud covering every inch of our bodies, our escort arrives to shuttle us to the gym to shower and exercise. As we mount the moving sidewalk to return to the train, both Blake and I notice another door open and get a glimpse inward before our escort shields our view. From the slice I saw, it had to be a scaled down version of Farm City and although neither of us comments, we both know that behind each door lays each of the settled Theran cities and a wealth of knowledge only obtainable by reaching the Grand Council inner circles. Our escort attempts a cover up by saying, "That's a test farm to see if Garden City soil will work for growing food."

Even he knows his explanation falls short.

CHAPTER SEVEN

Ethan

"So I talked to her that night. What's the big deal? She couldn't find her slimeball boyfriend or best friend and I helped her out," I say as I pace the floor of the scaled down administration building. She'd been less than fifty feet away and *recognized* me and my father refused to let me talk to her. He ushered me away and then went out to scare her off. For two months I've felt like a freaking peeping Tom, watching her from afar, banned from getting anywhere near her. The only time I'd been allowed in spitting distance was upon her arrival when they'd drugged her and I'd been used to transport her to her room.

"Your orders were clear. Observe only," my father says. "She says the two of you talked 'for a long time.' That's a far cry from observation."

"For years you searched for the perfect female specimen to Cleave to me. You find a pure Light, send me to watch her and expect me not to see for myself whether she's cleavable material?" I say incredulously. "What better way to observe than to have a conversation? I don't specifically remember you specifying that I *couldn't* talk to her." What does he expect from a law student? I'm hard-wired to find loopholes.

"I told you there was competition," he says. "The Grand Council voted to partner the two of them and see how things progressed, given the boy Blake's clean health record."

I run my hands through my hair. All my life, I've listened to my parents complain ad nauseum about my heart defect. Even though I have a completely clean bill of health now, it still haunts me, and if Kira ends up with Blake, it always will. "I'm not okay with this. I plan to talk to Dr. Christo and see what the real odds are for my heart defect being passed along. All I want is a shot...

to date her and see where things go."

"Patience... I have a plan. And you're an integral part. I've got a way to satisfy the Ten's desires for the girl *and* make sure you fulfill your destiny. If you go screw it up by pursuing the girl, then the Grand Council will think we're making a play. We are, but can't let them know we are."

"I don't want anything forced on her. Not Blake. Not me," I say.

"It's not up to you. Or even up to me. Remember that we all answer to someone. Even the Council. And a purebred Light Original... well, she's a game changer, Son. You're going to just have to let it all play out. And, well, if it doesn't work, your Uncle Henry can find you a suitable mate on Earth."

My Uncle Henry's a well known, well liked politician with a bright future. Law degree. Wealthy. Extensive social circle. His life is one giant fundraiser. And Uncle Henry likes to show off his family. There's a lot of people who want to be in Uncle Henry's good graces. A lot of campaign-donating, obnoxious men with agendas. And they have sons and daughters. The sons get foisted on my cousins (Uncle Henry has two daughters, both older than me). The donors' daughters, however, get flung my way. Uncle Henry brokers dates like he would business deals. If he wants Joe CEO to be his Next Big Donor, then Joe's daughter is my next date to Critical Fundraiser.

FBD (Fundraiser Blind Date) usually boils down to the following... on the physical side we've got bleach blonde, nose job, boob job, expensive clothes, even more expensive shoes and corresponding purse. She's usually fairly attractive if you go for the half human/half plastic thing, which I don't. On the personality side we have entitled, whiny, slutty, lazy, pushy, and downright annoying because they talk incessantly about absolutely nothing of importance. Once we go on our date to Critical Fundraiser, FBD tries to blackmail me into a MBR (Mutually Beneficial Relationship) e.g. her daddy will make a huge donation to my Uncle if I agree to become her sex slave (or make her my sex slave, depending on the girl and her particular set of preferences).

When Jax visits, Uncle Henry arranges for the Ultimate Bimbo double dates. These I actually enjoy. As annoying and meddling as I find Jax, he's pure entertainment when placed around Dumb and Dumber Barbies. They're so charmed by his dimpled smile and double speak that they leave me alone and don't even realize he's insulting and demeaning them in every possible way. "You are *so* charitable, Mandy. The fabric saved on making your dress could clothe an entire orphanage. And as an added bonus, all the hard-up men here tonight won't even have to spend money on porn tonight." "Vivs, you're a shoo-in for Miss America *and* for our future Secretary of State. Your idea to drop signed love notes and chocolate hearts instead of bombs throughout the

Middle East and Africa would *definitely* get the attention of every misguided soul. I'm sure they'd want to become your BFF online and maybe even pay you a most personal visit." Unfortunately, Jax pops by infrequently and thus, I have to endure most of my dates without his help.

Sarah was the most recent Uncle Henry Setup and she won the award for Owning Most Raincoats to Show Up at Door With Nothing On Under. And it hardly ever rained in San Diego. My Uncle forced me to take her to two separate events and she assumed that meant a marriage proposal was on the horizon. Holy freaking psycho, this girl made it her mission to try to seduce me. If I saw one more of her artificially enhanced body parts on display by text, email or in person, I would have gouged out my eyes with her high priced stilettos. I heard her talking once to a friend on the phone about "when he gets me pregnant, he'll have to marry me." For the first time in ages, I looked forward to leaving for a summer on Thera just to escape her.

Beth had a rare attribute that most of the others didn't—a brain. She'd been studying to get her MBA and planned to be a CEO like her daddy (who was honestly named Joe). She thought we would make the perfect Power Couple. I didn't hate her, but wasn't the least bit attracted to her and man, she bored me to death. Sure, it's great you can use calculus to price stock options, but a decent dinner conversation that does not make.

Courtney creeped me out big time. She paid the photographer at Bigwig Local Fundraiser for all pictures taken of us separately and together and had a book made and delivered to me. She even used one of those photomerge baby makers to show me how lovely our 2.5 children would be (yes, she had a half a baby in our "family photo.") Enough said.

Aliya believed in mixing alcohol and pharmaceutical drugs. She had major daddy issues and felt the best way to address said issues was to embarrass the heck out of daddy in public. And I do say found great success in this endeavor. Stripped down to a sheer corset, thong and heels, and then table danced... very memorable for all in attendance, including the San Diego Police Department.

I'm sure there are lots of guys who'd have been thrilled to have girls throwing themselves at them. But nothing interested me less than abject desperation. And given that my father threatened early on to put a bullet in my brain if I had sex with any girl before he found me a "proper Cleave"... well, there wasn't a whole lot these girls could offer.

That's why meeting Kira felt so different. She was naturally beautiful without any plastic parts. She was brilliant. Funny. Caring. Loyal. Flirty, but not pushy. Sweet. I know that I did not imagine the connection with her. But there was no way I was going to act on it at the time. She had a boyfriend and I was on assignment. She clearly didn't have a great impression about the SCI after taking the Test, so I didn't point out my ties to the SCI.

Loopholes... there has to be a way around my father and the rest of the Ten on this. It's just so unfair that this Blake guy's been given unlimited access to her. The Ten even has them as partners and roommates. The Ten wants the two of them to Cleave? I wonder how Blake feels about permanent cohabitation with a girl he barely knows on this nightmare rock called Thera? Given I haven't been banned from spending time with Blake, perhaps I should remind him about the consequences of getting too close to my Cleave interest?

It's time to put myself back in the game.

CHAPTER EIGHT

Blake

My head will freaking explode if they shove any more crap in it. There's the propaganda, the Canon, the questions, stuff I learned about the city's layout, and then there's the plans—mine to help my father, and the Theran rulers' plans for Kira and me. I use my workouts to sort the data into the appropriate list and file it away, because I know I'm going to need it all at some point to get out of this mess.

Masterminding the bogus relationship was genius and has given Kira and me time to try to sort the truths from the used car salesman spiel. Kira's often able to spot the missing pixels from the picture better than I can, so I process data twice as fast with her around. The problem with my grand plan is that I sometimes find it hard to remember that our "relationship" is all for show. Touching her face and holding her hand has me feeling stuff I haven't felt in a long time, distracting stuff that could lead to mistakes.

Kira's been staring at me the entire workout like I'm the sole food supply on a deserted island. It helps our cover I guess, but kills my concentration. It's not like we can act on the physical attraction to get it out of our system. We'd end up Cleaved and there's no way I'm being saddled down with that baggage. So, I pretend to pull a muscle lifting and make the excuse that I'm going to go soak it off in the locker room whirlpool. Once settled into the whirlpool's water, I hike the jet and bubble action to max and relax for the first time in a week, though the feel of the water reminds me of our flash flood training. We'd only had ten minutes training before the exercise and yet I'd gotten us out of danger as if I'd had years' training. I hope they assumed my survival instinct kicked in and not guessed the truth, which is that I experienced a horrifying and quite real flash flood when I was six.

My dad's sulking took a lot of time, so after Doc Daryn's Cleave gave us nightly school lessons, Leila and I would play in the canyon until sunup, when the heat would force us back into the cave. Leila liked to run up and down the hill, giggling wildly, until her legs would give out. Or she'd roll down barren patches of canyon I'd helped my dad clear. By the age of three, Leila had long dark hair like my mother, but she had my father's hazel eyes. I must have gotten my bright green eyes from a more distant relative. We both had pale ivory skin, which Leila tanned by way of a good dirt covering. This infuriated my father as baths wasted precious water reserves, so we often went weeks without a good washing. "You rolled in it, so you can sleep in it," he would say to us.

Living in Exile with little access to information, we had no idea a storm was brewing in the East and headed our way. It had been months since the last one, so I'd forgotten about the risk and we'd ventured farther into the canyon than normal. Looking back, I'm surprised no one noticed the obscured stars and sounded the warning. We had headlamps strapped to our heads so our view was limited to the twenty-odd feet in front of us.

Dry one moment, and torrential downpour the next, the hills turned to mud, sliding us towards a raging river at the bottom of the canyon. I yelled to Leila to grab my ankles, and I reached for the branch of a bush, but it broke and we kept sliding, thankfully into some larger brush and cacti that stopped our forward motion twenty feet above the river. Sharp thorns embedded into my back, but I'd have taken that over drowning any night.

As the rain continued with the force of a waterfall, I pulled away from the cacti and searched for the familiar rope ladders that litter the canyons, hoping to find one nearby. I yelled for help but the clatter of the storm overpowered my voice. The rain and mud obscured my view, so I buried my hands into the nasty slop and dug around, starting to my left a few feet and working to the right. I continued to shift our location, staying in front of the brush until I located the familiar twined feel of the ladder.

Climbing the ladders at any time proved difficult, but that night I thought it'd be impossible. Leila mounted my back, gripping my neck so tightly I could hardly breathe, and I struggled to make progress, one rung at a time. The rain abated for a time, which slowed the rush of mud and water. We managed to ascend to a wide plateau, still well below and west of the caves that served as our home. I found us shelter below a rock outcropping where I intended to stay until the deluge ended. Wet, muddy, and exhausted from the climb, I clutched Leila in my arms and we waited it out. For what seemed like hours the downpour resumed, even past sunrise. And then, as quickly as it had started, it ended, and we dared step out into the sunlight to view the carnage.

Carcasses of dead lizards, bugs, and animals blanketed the landscape, including the one community milk cow. I circled the area to get my bearings, watching as the canyon fossilized into its new dried form. Everything looked different. The heat of the sun instantly caked the mud to our skin, providing a decent, albeit itchy sun block. Knowing my father would be panicked, I used the sun to get a fix on our location and we traversed the plateau. Somehow we'd ended up more than a mile west of our caves. Finally, we scrambled up the hill to our home. The lookout team exclaimed shouts of relief upon seeing us. As Doc Daryn scrubbed us, removing thorns and hunting for wounds, my father gave his men instructions to round up the search party.

Later that morning, unable to sleep, I watched from the mouth of my cave as two lifeless bodies were carried up the hill, blue, bloated, and ravaged by fire ants and scorpions. The bodies belonged to men I'd known since birth and who had wives and children of their own. The entire community of Exilers mourned their loss. Both had been found in the riverbed, drowned. No one ever said as much, but I'm certain those men died trying to find and save Leila and me during the storm. Whenever I question my loyalty to my father and his plan to save the Exilers and free the Second Chancers from oppression, I think of those two good men and how they willingly put themselves in harms way for me.

"Mr. Sundry," I hear from a familiar voice, yanking me back to my more comfortable spa-like surroundings. "So good to see you. I've wanted to catch up with you and Ms. Donovan to see how you're enjoying training. Mind if I join you?" It's about time Ted made an appearance. He has some explaining to do, as I struggle to reengage and leave the memories of my childhood behind.

"It's pretty awesome," I lie. "This place is incredible. I mean, we're still trying to take it all in—being somewhere other than Earth. That's huge." Ted plops his bulging body into the water and we talk training sessions, skate tracks, and upcoming school and sports for a few minutes.

"You and Kira are really lucky to be able to experience it. Not many people can make the journey, you know. It's taken me all week to recover. But since you're so young and adaptable, I hear you've had no issues." I try to read between the lines to see what he's getting at. With the noise of the jets it's very unlikely our conversation can be heard, but I know to be careful anyway.

"Well, the doctors and nurses have been all over us trying to manage any side effects. They seem pretty invested in making sure we're a hundred percent healthy." I can tell by his expression I've hit the jackpot.

"Of course they are. How often are you seeing them?" he asks.

"Nightly. They've been pretty worried about abdominal issues and some sort of lesions that muck with our reproductive systems so have checked our blood and given us vitamin shots. They even gave Kira a full abdominal ultrasound because she was complaining… about female stuff probably. I think she said bloating or something. They, uh, made me do some awkward tests too to make sure my fertility's intact, but I guess the doctors don't want my future wife showing up here one night accusing them of making me sterile, eh?" I laugh for effect.

"That's assuming you don't fall in love with someone here on Thera," he says. "You and Kira have been pretty cozy, I understand. I just knew you'd like her once you got to know her."

"What's not to like? She is smart, hotter than hot, and actually pretty sweet to me. I mean, she wouldn't have given me the time of night back home, but I don't have a lot of competition here," I say. "If it wasn't for the whole Cleaving weirdness I think we could really be an item. But we're both a little freaked about being stuck here and never being able to see our families again." It would be only natural for us to feel this way, so I don't stress over saying it. He knows I have no family back home except "Aunt Jennifer" and I'm sure she's relieved to have me far away. I'd heard her label me "Unabomber clone" more than once when I'd chosen to be anti-social with the family.

Ted addresses my Cleaving comment with, "You guys shouldn't be worrying about that! Of course you'll see your families again." Under his breath he adds, without moving his lips, "They do not plan to ever let you go. You both are pure descendants of the Original Theran settlers. I don't know how this makes you so important yet, but I'm going to try to find out. They're saying you are the 'future of Thera' and that scares me." Ted's words send chills up my spine, despite being immersed in hot water. We're stuck here on Thera, with our only out of Garden City being Exile. He adds, in a regular voice, "The only way you stay is if you Cleave Kira or any other girl here."

"Uh, yeah, I don't think Cleaving is on my near term to-do list," I say in an irritated tone. "What's the whole Assisted Pregnancy thing anyway? Did people forget how to get pregnant the old-fashioned way?"

"All pregnancies are done in-vitro here to ensure only healthy babies are born," he says. I wish I knew more about in-vitro, but reproductive technologies never hit my list of things to become an expert on.

"So, when are you heading back to Earth?" I ask, my implication being, "when will I be on my own?"

"Actually, change of plans," he says. "The Grand Council promoted me, so I'll be working right here at the SCI headquarters in Garden City. I'm excited. I love it here. I really think the place will grow on you and Ms. Donovan, too."

"Wow, congratulations," I say. He gives me a wide grin. This has been his hope—to get stationed here so that he can help me succeed from the inside.

"Well, I have to be getting back," Ted says. "I'm so glad you and Ms. Donovan are enjoying your stay. I think you'll really enjoy working alongside the Second Chancers. Give my best to Ms. Donovan and I'll keep in touch."

I wave goodbye, and sink back into the bubbles for a few minutes. Future of Thera? There's something I'm missing, but it's eluding me. All that focus on Kira has really messed up my concentration.

As I'm about to get up, another guy joins me in the hot tub. He looks a couple years older than me. Dark hair. Blue eyes. The kind of guy that girls would kill their best friend to get near and the kind of guy I want nowhere near Kira. Unless he's a total oaf he could get a girl to Cleave him just by smiling her way. His only flaw's a shimmery scar on his chest, but I'm sure the war story to go with it would just endear him to the ladies even more. I wonder what he's doing here and why he went under the knife.

"I didn't know there were any other Recruits right now," I say to him. "I'm Blake Sundry." I offer my hand, which he shakes.

"My name's Ethan. And, technically, I'm not a Recruit. I'm an Intern," he says.

"What's the difference?" I ask. "Between a Recruit and an Intern?"

"Probably not much," he says with a laugh. "Except, I don't work with the Second Chancers. Instead I'm bogged down in tabletwork hundreds of files long. Consider yourself lucky."

"Are you from here?" I ask, interested to know whether he's an Earthling or Theran.

"That's a long and complicated story. Let's just say that my parents live in the city and I spend my summers here," he says with a tone that leads me to believe he doesn't love the arrangement. He takes a couple deep breaths and adds, "How are you enjoying the program? Being treated well? Did you get a decent partner?"

"So far, so good," I say. "It's a lot to take in. And I got a fabulous partner— Kira. She's amazing. Smart, organized, fun—and beautiful." Have to keep up the illusion that Kira and I are an item for anyone who might be listening in. I blush and I stop myself from bragging too much. He looks unhappy, seems to be clenching his teeth. Maybe he got a not-so-perfect partner.

"It wouldn't be the first time that a guy has fallen in love with his female counterpart," he says. And then in a hushed tone he adds, "Just be careful. If you Cleave her, your placement here becomes permanent."

"I know that and I never said I was in love with her," I object, grimacing at the "L" word that I decided never to use again after my Bailey ordeal. Gads. Why would he assume that? So I occasionally have unclean thoughts about her.

Who wouldn't? The girl's gorgeous. Her strawberry blond hair falls into curls without electronic help, although she's equally pretty when she straightens her hair. Her green and gold eyes are large and widespread. She has lush, full lips. Distinct cheekbones with a sprinkling of freckles that give her a touch of the "all-American girl" image. Her body is fabulous, with plenty of curve and muscle, but zero fat. She's neither too short nor too tall. And that's just her looks. Her personality's even better with an incredible combination of smart, flirty, fun, and nice. Almost too nice, in fact. She gets more upset at her tablet than any person. With people she seems to have an automatic filter that keeps her from saying an unkind word, except where Ted Rosenberg is concerned.

"There's some girls that just have that effect on guys," he says. "I should know. I fell for a girl like that myself. I met her at a party and knew she was the perfect girl for me. Now I'm ruined for life. I don't even want to ever look at another girl." I hear the men of Thera collectively rejoicing, myself included.

I size him up. The men of Thera, Earth and every other planet in the universe would feel even safer if this boy was Cleaved and off-limits for the eternities. "Shouldn't you already be Cleaved? You sure look older than eighteen."

"I fall under a different jurisdiction, although my parents would love to have me Cleave anyway," he says, getting a little fidgety. He's staring at his hands and running his fingers across his thumbs in a nervous manner.

"So why not Cleave this girl you are so madly in love with?" I ask. Maybe he just needs a little push in the right direction. "Does she feel the same way?"

He chokes out the words. "I thought she did... feel the same way, but my parents have forbidden me from seeing her—for now at least—so it's not like I can even ask her."

"Why would they do that?" I ask. Perhaps I should have a little chit-chat with his parental units. After I barricade the guy in the locker room so that he doesn't have a chance to come out and meet Kira. I realize I'm being ridiculously territorial over a girl I'll never have a future with, but I can't seem to help myself.

"My parents think she has had too much going on and that I'd just be a distraction," he says. "Plus, they're not sure I'm worthy of her." Let me get this straight. He's plenty old enough to make his own decisions, but is letting his parents keep him from his one true love? Seriously, dude, grow a backbone.

"Not worthy? That sounds like a bunch of crap," I say.

"I was born with a heart defect and the doctors didn't think I'd make it. It took a bunch of surgeries to fix the problem. Now my parents have a bunch of people trying to convince them that I'll saddle my future mate with bad genes and that all our babies will be born defective like me," he says. I think back to what Ted said about Assisted Pregnancies being all about making sure only healthy babies get born. Was Ethan the impetus for this rule or an exception to it, I wonder.

"That's ridiculous," I say. "Why do you listen to them?"

"The punishments my parents dish out aren't worth the rebellion," he says with a shudder, as if he's picturing being waterboarded or having toes chopped off or something. He's an adult and his parents still punish him? Uh, he really needs to get a life. Of course, I'm only two months away from being eighteen and I'm doing my father's bidding, so who am I to judge?

"Your parents know her? The girl?" I ask.

"My dad does," he says. "She, uh, kind of works for him. So he thinks he knows what's best for both of us." Well, there was your first mistake—falling for one of daddy's employees.

"I hear you on the father front. My dad's super controlling, too," I say, trying to make him feel like less of a wimp than he clearly is. "Aren't you worried that the girl might fall for someone else while your parents have their moratorium going on?"

"That's exactly what keeps me up at day," he says. "It would kill me if I lost her to another guy." I nod at him. Poor guy. I feel for him. Kind of. He definitely got himself into a crappy situation.

"So you're ready for the whole deal—commitment, kids, the works?" I ask.

"I never thought I'd be saying it and certainly wasn't before I met her, but yes. For this girl, definitely. I'd do anything. Unless I'd felt that mind-blowing, world-altering connection with her, I wouldn't have even considered it. If I'm going to be with someone forever, she's got to be the one and only, you know. And I'm pretty sure this girl is it for me," he says. "She's all I can think about." What a sap. But he's right, if you're going to be forced to be with someone for freaking decades, that person would have to be pretty perfect.

"Wow. I'm so not there yet. Just the thought scares the crap out of me," I say. Now it's my turn to shudder.

"All the more reason to keep your impulses in check then," he says with a half-cocked grin. "All it takes is one slip-up here and there's no do-overs."

"Well, hey. I've got to go meet back up with Kira. We get to go walk the canyons and it's my favorite time of the night," I say.

"I bet. You take care of her—your partner. She sounds pretty incredible," he says. I can't help but give him a slightly evil glare, as I don't want this guy to even be thinking of Kira at all, much less to think she's incredible.

"Sure," I say as I get out and shake off the water before grabbing a towel. "Good luck with your girl. I hope it works out between the two of you."

"Me, too. I've just got to be patient and trust that it will," he says, though his head and shoulders are slumped, body language that screams defeat.

Man, I hope I'm never in a situation like his. What if I did fall for Kira? What if I couldn't be with her and she fell for another guy? I wince at the thought of being so smitten that I'd lose sight of the important things in life. Like winning freedom for the Exilers.

The grave is but a covered bridge leading from light to light, through a brief darkness.

Henry Wadsworth Longfellow

CHAPTER NINE

Kira

I am so frustrated. This whole fake relationship with Blake is getting to me. Right now, I don't know what to think.

Blake makes me breakfast every night. I make dinner. He flirts constantly. I pretend to pretend to love it, since I actually do relish the idea of someone liking me. And he's very interesting—well versed in many topics so that we never run out of things to talk about. We walk every night in the canyon, starting well before dawn. All the hand holding, brushing of my cheek with his fingers, kisses on the cheek, and longingly looking into my eyes while discussing our conspiracy theories is making me a little psycho. I have no idea if it's really all for show or if he actually has feelings for me. I get the strong impression he hasn't made up his mind either way. Attraction wise, he falls short of Ethan, but he's grown on me. Personality wise, I'm less sold. He avoids personal topics to the extent that I feel he's hiding something and his temper's volatile. Sweet one minute and snippy the next, although he snaps out of it quickly—as if he's been trained to maintain the illusion of stability. This makes me wary. I'm not sure I can trust him.

We take a walk in the canyons at sunrise the morning before our evening transfer to student housing. Things seem particularly awkward between us. Tonight we'll be meeting the infamous Second Chancers. We have no idea who we'll be rooming with or what classes we'll be taking. Despite a full week's training I have little idea of what working with the Second Chancers entails. Blake's super tense and I'm uber-hormonal and a little too attracted to him after watching him run and lift weights, the yoga and meditation not working for me tonight.

We stop near the bottom of the canyon and to breach the awkward silence, I pipe up with "I'm dying to know who the Second Chancers are." My thoughts turn to my conversation with Brad Darcton and potential sighting of Ethan. Could he really be one of them? "I mean, do you really think we'll know some of them."

"How would I know?" Blake says in a nasty tone, and then as per the usual, catches himself and adds, "Sorry. I…uh…am just a little stressed out. I wish I could answer all your questions and put your mind at case, but I think we just need to let it play out." He turns his head and looks like he's in physical pain. I lean in to whisper that it's okay, I don't expect him to answer all my questions, when his head snaps back and our lips meet.

What's worse than a kiss with someone you aren't quite sure if you like? An accidental kiss between two people, both of whom aren't sold. As soon as the sensation registers in his brain he takes a full step back and buries his head in his hands. I step back the other way leaving an uncomfortable four foot distance between us. What can I say that will case the tension? Not much. That unplanned first kiss rates a one on a scale of one to ten.

Before I can get a word in Blake chimes a "Crap, crap, crap. That should not have happened."

I fold my arms defensively and spit out my response. "Crap? That's what you have to say about accidentally kissing me? I thought that was next step for our *fake* relationship. Won't the watchers be expecting it?"

"Crap, Kira, yeah I'm sure they're expecting it, wanting it, but I am just pretty worried that you're going to regret doing it."

"I already do," I snap. "But wait a sec. Me? You think I kissed you? Hardly. But whatever. You can pretend like you don't like me. I'll pretend like I don't like you—which will be easy given that I don't a big chunk of the time. Forget that it ever happened. I already have. It was completely, freaking forgettable."

He ignores my poor review of the non-kiss and says, "Yeah, Kira, sure you like me in the 'we've been thrown together and I'm the only one you can really talk to' sense. But you love Tristan, not me, and well, I just don't know if the whole thing is kosher. I can't compete with your perfect dead boyfriend." This upsets me and I raise my voice to respond. He's going to blame it on my dead boyfriend now? And when did we go from fake relationship to implying it could be real? I swear this guy's brain damaged.

"Tristan is dead! How I feel or felt about him doesn't really matter does it? And he was far… no, miles away from perfect. I've only met one guy I thought was perfect—ironically the night of the Goodington party. He was some college guy. We instantly clicked, but I stupidly blew him off because of Tristan, who was busy kissing my best friend, Bri, at the time."

Blake grimaces at my mention of Tristan's indiscretion. He says, "That sucks what Tristan and Bri did. That still doesn't mean that we're right for each other and should even contemplate making this whole deal anything other than a cover. I don't hear you calling me perfect." Perhaps I shouldn't have mentioned Ethan, even if I didn't do so by name. He adds, "Why are people always meeting the perfect people at parties, anyway? Gads. That's the second time tonight I heard that."

I cock my head and give him a puzzled look, imagining which of the few people we've run across would be the type to be at a party. Not seeing it. "Well, with any luck you'll be rid of me come tonight and will only have to see me at school," I snarl.

"I'm not trying to avoid you, Kira. We won't stop being partners just because we're relocating. Just promise me that no matter what happens you aren't going to hate me... that you'll still have my back?" he says.

He's right. Given he's the only person I know here from home, I'm stuck with him. "Sure. I still have your back."

I arise before my wakeup call for the first time, reeling from Blake's psychotic reaction to our happenstance kiss, and longing for Bri who listened to me overanalyze every aspect of my relationship with Tristan for more than a year without complaint. She would have some useful advice or witty thing to say about my situation that would calm my nerves and make me think that there's still hope. My attempts to imagine what she'd say fall flat and even her image in my memory is faded ever so slightly. I sob for the remainder of my shower as I realize I've let my training and confused feelings about Blake crowd out my memories of Tristan and Bri. And even though I came here to do just that, I hate myself for allowing it to happen so fast.

Today, or I guess tonight—I'm still working on the terminology shift—I get back some sense of normalcy with the return to school. Even though the format will be different and the kids will be strangers, I'll still be surrounded by teens and have a routine of homework and activities to keep me grounded. It won't just be Blake and me, and that alone will help me figure out if my "crush" is just situational or something real.

Blake must not have slept well either, because he's already making breakfast when I leave my room. I'm fidgety since I feel like I should be packing, given we are moving, but there's nothing to take. Our notes from our training sessions have already been transferred to our new tablets and everything will be provided at our new residences. We both pick at our food and keep conversation to a minimum as we wait to be fetched by our escort. Any lighthearted, joking atmosphere Blake and I had disappeared post accidental kiss, so figure I'm in for a whole lot of awkward.

Our escort arrives promptly at 1900 hours. I was hoping to avoid an evening pit stop at the clinic, but have no such luck. In fact, they do a longer workup than usual, including another full abdominal ultrasound. The technician looks a little worried as he scans my belly, and calls in the doctor to confer, who informs me I have a small lesion that will need surgical correction. I freak at the mention of surgery, but the doctor assures me that it's a very minor procedure done with a local anesthetic and that I'll be in and out in an hour. He schedules the procedure to be done at the school clinic a couple evenings from now, and sends me on my way. Thank goodness I didn't eat a big breakfast or I would've lost it all over him.

Our escort takes us on an amusement park-ride style train, traveling eight or nine stops before exiting through a set of tall glass doors at the GARDEN CITY HIGH stop. Two rights and three lefts later, we're through a set of double doors and at an outdoor walkway similar to the one at the training center, though this one has periodic ramps and staircases up to another level above. I lean over the rail and note that this canyon looks the same as the last one. We walk the equivalent of three city blocks and are motioned up a ramp to our right onto a lovely porch overlooking the canyon below, which at this hour is a sea of dazzling lights.

"This is your new home," our escort informs us.

"Wait a second," I say, confused. "Mine or Blake's?"

"You are partners, so of course you will be sharing housing."

"Who are our roommates? A couple other students?" I say hopefully.

"Just the two of you, as you are the only two Recruits serving at Garden City High right now, and we never mix Recruits with Second Chancers," he says. "But you are surrounded by other students who you'll meet shortly." I shove a finger in my mouth and start chewing my nail as I contemplate a year of unsupervised cohabitation. Now I'm positive they want us to Cleave and be stuck here forever.

"Sweet," Blake says, trying to diffuse the tension and maintain our cover. "Let's take a look," he says, grabbing my hand and pulling me inside, and then whispering in my ear, "Chill. It'll be fine." I nod at him and we proceed to walk through the rooms of our new home. Inwardly I think, "No way it will be fine. A whole year of awkward? You've got to be kidding me."

The house is identical to the Cleaved housing residence we'd toured and in immaculate condition. Elaborate tromp l'oeil three-dimensional garden paintings cover every wall and like the other paintings we'd seen, do not resemble the landscape of Garden City. Where on Thera do they get their inspiration?

"The previous occupants had the murals commissioned. If you prefer to paint your own, we'll have them painted over immediately," our escort advises.

"No, no. Don't do that," I say, running my fingers across to feel the uneven surface. "I love them."

"Me, too, and I'm definitely no artist," Blake adds.

I'm surprised to find we have two bedrooms and bathrooms, since the Cleaved training implied the only way to get one of these was to be a Cleaved couple with children. The man senses my surprise.

"Uncleaved, dissimilar sex recruit partners are given two bedroom homes. Obviously, if the situation ever changes for either of you housing would be reevaluated." Well, I guess the powers that be do have some semblance of morality. Not much, but at least enough not to want Recruits to get word back home that they're sharing a bedroom with a member of the opposite sex. That'd be a quick way to destroy the SCI's unfathomably stellar reputation.

"Thank you. I appreciate that. And my parents will appreciate it, too," I say, smiling, though unfortunately the man looks as if I've just threatened him. "So, when do our classes begin?" I ask to change the subject.

"Tomorrow, I believe," he says. "You'll meet with an administrator here shortly to schedule your courses, and then will meet the other Garden City High students during free time a little later. After exercise time and dinner, you'll each meet with your assigned Handler to discuss your night." Mr. Rosenberg had told me way back I'd have to do nightly reports, but I'd forgotten until the mention.

"Sounds good," I say pleasantly, hoping to sound as amenable as possible. He continues by explaining most of our schooling will be done online from our home and that the administrator would provide more details.

I'm no expert on square footage, but I'd guess the house is about a third the size of my family home, so somewhere around 2,000 square feet. But because of the layout, central garden and outdoor sunroom, and the lack of all the junk my parents have accumulated, it feels plenty big for a family of four, and complete overkill for just Blake and me. At the time we'd visited the model homes I'd had no idea we'd be living in one. Somehow I'd assumed students would be housed in dorms of some sort.

The living area opens to the dining room and kitchen, which I like, but the sunroom is my favorite. With the lights off inside, I can sprawl out on the lounge chairs and look up at the night sky, seeing the stars for the first time. The edges of the sky are blurred from the lights of the canyon, but not enough to completely obscure the feeling of being in a planetarium.

Blake gets the bedroom with two twins and I'm appointed the one with the queen. He scores two closets, but when we are forced to wear a uniform at all times—even Industrial City issue pajamas—I guess closet space means nothing. Our new clothes are similar fabrics to our training uniforms, but are green and gold shimmer, the school colors, rather than white and silver. Thank goodness they picked colors I can pull off. The maroon and gold I had to wear for Carmel Valley High cheer was bad enough, but I didn't have to wear it 24/7. Several alternative outfits fill my dresser drawers, but I'm clueless as to their purpose. Swimming? Prostitution? There's some seriously skimpy stuff in there.

The man finally leaves us to change and prepare for our administrative guest. I quickly throw on the new uniform, check the contents of the bathroom to make sure everything needed is present, and freshen up. Then I head back out to the sunroom to do more stargazing. It's too hot to stay for long, but enjoyable nonetheless. I'm starting to get used to the dry heat. I search the skies for the familiar constellations my father taught me such as Orion's Belt and the Big Dipper, but don't see them. Oddly enough the moon looks roughly the same, although has a definite blue-green tinge to it, rather than the white or slightly yellow or orange tints I'm used to.

"You going to be OK with this?" Blake says, taking up the lounge chair next to mine. "You and me for a year?"

"Sure," I lie. "You?"

"I'm good," he says, avoiding my gaze. "Cool place. I can't believe they give students their own houses. It's all seriously crazy, but hey, I can't complain. Well, except for the fact there is no TV, games or music that I can find."

"It is creepy quiet here. I miss my music, especially while working out," I say.

"Seriously," he says. He looks ready to add some sort of insult, but is interrupted by the chime of the doorbell, which Blake jumps up to answer. The school administrator, a frumpy lady with frizzy gray hair who'd be lucky to top five feet in height, urges our prompt attention to her business.

The next hour and a half is spent going over transcripts, discussing class options, and configuring our new tablets for our class schedules. Our desk area in the living room has headphones, two large monitors to view our lessons on, and our tablets, which will be used for note and test taking. We'll be taking the same core classes we were taking at CVH, but will have electives "more suited to Garden City Living," like psychology to help us work with Second Chancers, gardening, and art. Turns out you can cover a lot more curriculum when it's just you and the computer, so we have eight classes instead of six; four each night for an hour and a half each; 1-3-5-7 on M-W-F and 2-4-6-8 on T-Th-Sat. School on Saturnight? I groan at the thought.

Free time doesn't start until 0200 hours, and it takes us only ten minutes to eat lunch, so I wonder what we're going to do with two hours of free time. I'm thinking nap? I'd read a book, but the options on my tablet look less than interesting. Alas, the same voice that wakes us up each evening appears out of nowhere and urges us to watch the prepared video on our monitors, which will recap our instructions for working with Second Chancers. Boring. I guess I'll get my nap in, though at a desk instead of my nice new queen bed.

At two o'clock sharp, we receive a knock on our door, which serves as an instant wake up call. I jump up to answer and am surprised to see it's my buddy Spud Rosenberg.

"Ms. Donovan, I hope Mr. Sundry shared with you the news that I'll be staying on Thera. In addition to some new responsibilities at headquarters, I've been assigned to be your Handler, which I'm very excited about." I look at Blake. When did he talk with Spud? He certainly never mentioned it and I wonder what else he's kept hidden.

"Oh, man, I'm really sorry, Kira. I totally spaced. Mr. Rosenberg ran into me in the locker room yesternight and he told me to say, 'hi,' but by the time I was out of there, poof, totally gone." Blake never forgets anything, he's said so himself, but I don't dare push anything more than a glare in front of our new "Handler."

"Anyhoo," Spud says. "It's an exciting night. You finally get to meet some of our Second Chancers—your fellow classmates. I assume you brushed up on etiquette by watching the video."

"Uh yeah," I say, not wanting to admit I was out cold, drooling on the desk for most of it.

"Really educational," Blake says, rolling his eyes. "So, let's go do this."

"We can walk or zip," Spud says. "It's actually faster to walk, though, as it takes four zips to get there."

"Walking's fine," I say. The zip lines would be more fun, but I'm eager to get there and see what the big deal is with the Second Chancers. See if Ethan's one of them.

"And safer," Blake adds, needling me in my side. I've figured out how to brake properly on the zip lines, but Blake still hasn't let me forget that I ambushed him the one time.

Spud leads us out the door, down the ramp, and then down a walking path in the canyon that leads around a bend to the right. Since the path is new to me, I'm extra careful with my foot placement, as the lights seem more sporadic here than back in the training canyon. We get delayed waiting for some workers and pack mules to cross the path on their way up to a group of residences. Close up I can see they carry boxes of Industrial City supplies. Wonder what goodies we're getting? New soap? Towels? Kitchen supplies? Given the boring nature of the authorized resident belongings, I doubt it'll feel like Christmas, whatever the boxes include. I wonder if they even celebrate Christmas or any other holiday here? Another question for my tablet that I doubt will get sufficiently answered.

I can see the large flat area ahead we saw by air in our "flyover" and in the scaled city, with dozens of skate paths and trails leading to it. There are tables and chairs, an outdoor basketball court, and a large opening into the side of the canyon. Students are everywhere, gathered under large flood lights, but we're still too far to get a good look, so I imagine them being animated Ken and Barbie dolls in green and gold casual wear.

"There is an indoor soccer/football field, as well as specialty classrooms for science labs, art clinics and such inside," Spud says. "The medical clinic is also there."

"How many students are there?" I ask, trying to get a sense of how the environment will compare to what I'm used to.

"Fifteen hundred, give or take," Spud responds. Not as big as Carmel Valley High, but still a big high school.

The Second Chancers see us coming their way and herd toward the path entrance to greet us. About twenty-five feet out I start to identify some faces. Most I don't know, but a few too many are impossibly familiar. I try to scream, but it gets stuck in my throat and the last thing I hear is Blake saying, "Holy crap" before I stumble headfirst into a thorny bush to the side of the path.

"Gads, the new girl tanked into a Theranberry bush," I hear a familiar voice say. "She better not have damaged it."

"Shut up and give her a break," I hear Blake say. "She tripped."

"Oh, hey, look, she's waking up," the boy says. I open my eyes to confirm what I'd seen wasn't something out of a horrible nightmare, scramble off the table they'd put me on, and run to a nearby garbage can to vomit up my lunch, a tuna fish sandwich, something I'll never eat again after re-tasting it upon exit. Blake rushes to my side and caresses my back, whispering in my ear.

"Kira, I know you are seriously tripping. I am too. But, we have to be really careful. We screw this up and we're Exiled and likely dead within twenty-four hours." He hands me a towel to wipe my mouth. What I really need is a toothbrush to dislodge the fishy morsels from my teeth. And some tweezers to dislodge Theranberry thorns from my arms.

"I can't do this," I respond. I sit down on a bench, hyperventilating, and start to dig the thorns out of my flesh with my fingernails. "I can't pretend like I don't know some of these people. I don't know what kind of sick, twisted trick they're playing on us or how the heck they pulled it off, but they crossed the line big time."

"Yeah they did," he says, keeping his eyes peeled for eavesdroppers, but the hordes seem staying away to allow me time to fully recover, and to stay clear of my vomit repellant.

"I mean—how many times did I hear the term Second Chancers, and not once, not one freaking time did I ever entertain the thought—because it is so not possible," I say, although it does shed some light on many things that Spud said.

"Hey, you can't keep the new chick all to yourself, buddy." The boy and a band of do-gooders have joined us, despite the smell, and I take him in, head to toe, looking for something, anything to prove I'm insane. But he looks exactly the same as the last time I saw him, save a change of attire.

"My name's not buddy. It's Blake. And this is Kira," Blake offers, as if it should be news. The two shake hands briefly, but the boy quickly shrugs off Blake and moves forward to address me.

"Hey Kira, good to meet you, gorgeous. I'm Tristan, and we Garden City High kids aren't all that bad, certainly nothing to puke over. Come meet my girl, Briella, and the others." He puts his hand out to shake mine. His big brown teddy bear eyes are as entrancing as ever, even if I last saw him kissing "his girl, Briella" a.k.a. my (supposedly dead) best friend.

"Yeah, just a minute. I need a word with Mr. Rosenberg first," I say, pointing towards Spud and ignoring Blake's warning head shaking. "Excuse me." I turn and walk across to the tabled area where Spud is taking in the scene.

"Please explain," I insist. "What are my dead boyfriend, best friend, and classmates doing here? I witnessed the explosion and saw the heaps of incinerated bodies after the fact. So, again, please explain. Now." Blake has joined me and is listening intently.

"Everything has been explained to you already, dear," he says. "Your friends are being given a second chance here on Thera. Remember that you were told that 'what can exist on Earth can't exist on Thera' and vice versa? Well, for certain people—those as I told you before that were victims of circumstances not of their own making, such as the accident your friends perished in—they are allowed to live out the remainder of what their natural life would have been on Earth here on Thera. I even do recall telling you that my own daughters were happily living out their lives in the next world. The next world has a name. It's Thera." He'd told me the story of his daughters' drowning when he came to my house to offer me a spot with the SCI and have my parents sign the paperwork.

"Yeah sure, you said all those things, but you left out just enough information for me to be able to put it together. You deceived me," I say.

He shakes his blubbery chin and asks, "Do you not want your friends to have the opportunity to live out their lives?"

"That's not it. They don't even recognize me. How is that? And why did Tristan call Briella his 'girl'?"

He puts a patronizing hand on my shoulder and in a hushed tone says, "You have to realize that you and Blake and me being here is the anomaly—we've been given a gift to travel between Earth and Thera. All others who come here must die first, but I can assure you that Second Chancers arrive here in a state of comfort and happiness. They have zero memory of their life on Earth, but their personalities and talents remain intact. They often do become attached to the person they were last with on Earth." His intimation is clear. How does he know, though, that Tristan and Bri were together?

After allowing a bit of a smile to peek through in recognition that he tweaked me, Spud continues, "The Second Chancers' welfare is our primary concern, which is why we like to bring in people who know them and can report on their progress from an insider's perspective. Think of it as an advanced psychology experiment." My body burns with fury at his arrogance, at the arrogance of the Second Chance Institute. They're using my friends as lab rats and I'm the mad scientist who gets to push the buttons.

"Mr. Rosenberg," I say. "You are a first class psychopath." Blake grabs my arms to keep me from physically attacking him.

"We can discuss your concerns at our debriefing later. But now I insist you join you friends and get reacquainted, without discussing the past, of course. The areas beyond Garden City are not very habitable from what I hear," he says, threatening tone present. Perhaps he'll do something worthy of Exile and happen upon the Eco Barrier, which if there is any justice on Thera, will turn Spud into potato soup.

"Fine," I respond, gritting my teeth. Despite the Second Chance Institute's philanthropic claims, I'm not convinced that their primary concern is for my friends or any of the other Second Chancers, but for much more selfish reasons. And even though I'm no afterlife believer, if there is a God and a heavenly place we go after death I'm pretty sure this isn't it.

I drag my feet as Blake and I head back towards the crowd, jabbing Blake in the side as we do. "Why didn't you say anything?"

He stumbles over his words. "Uh, well, uh, because I'm a little tongue tied and somewhere between being thrilled to see my sister alive, and freaked that the love of your life is standing fifteen feet away from us after you kissed me." I want to deck him. What's his obsession with that sucky, accidental kiss anyway? Forget that. Tristan is alive? Tristan and Bri are boyfriend and girlfriend? I have them back, but I don't, since they're just shells of their former selves. The pain I feel is unbearable, but I'm going to have to wait a couple hours to have the breakdown that must happen. Until then, I'm going to plaster on my cheer smile and make friends with my friends.

As we rejoin Tristan, I say, "Sorry about that. I just needed to talk to Mr. Rosenberg about the medications the doctor shot into me this evening. Clearly they had some major side effects that no one told me about." They all nod as if they can relate, although I doubt they get the pleasure of nightly clinic visits. Or maybe they do if they're really lab rats. "Anyway, let's start over. I'm Kira Donovan. This is Blake Sundry, and we're obviously new to the school."

"Where'd they house you?" Tristan asks.

"Around the bend. Nice place. How about you guys? Where are you at?" I ask. I point in the general direction of our house, but realize all I can see is swirling lights.

"Bri and I are sharing a place that way, too. That'll be sweet. We can skate over together after classes," he says. Several others point in the general direction of our house, as well.

"Blake's an awesome skater, but I can't quite get the hang of it," I say, a lie given I've never tried, but it is a certainty that I'd suck.

"You guys have a thing going?" Tristan asks as he gestures between Blake and me. I don't know quite how to answer that. The powers that be assume we have a relationship going. Given the situation now, am I prepared to keep that up? Blake is looking to me to respond, as I can tell there's no way he's going there.

"Uh yeah, some sort of thing," I say with enough finality to make it clear I don't intend to share more. "And you are with—was it Bri or Briella?"

"Yeah, Bri and I are pretty tight. We haven't Cleaved, but we're seriously thinking about it. We just had this instant connection, you know?" he says, motioning Bri over. She's as stunning as ever, her athletic figure adapting well to Theran attire. She seems to be checking out Tristan's reaction to me before determining whether I'm friend or foe-worthy.

Bailey Goodington joins us, too, but ignores me completely. She seems to be in shock at the sight of Blake, looking him and up and down like he's a melting popsicle that she wants to lick. Blake, on the other hand, is looking at Bailey like she's a popsicle that he'd like to take a blow-torch to. I can see Bailey going after fresh meat, but what Blake's deal with Bailey? I have to snicker at seeing Bailey, the former queen of fashion, in a standard issue Garden City High uniform, even if she does manage to rock it. Back on Earth Bailey's wardrobe seemed to self-propagate and I always imagined her closet to be complete with a personal tailor (actually, I know she had a standing Tuesday afternoon appointment with her tailor so that her weekend wardrobe could be finished by Friday. He, however, worked offsite at his Goodington-funded studio).

"Kira and Blake. Meet Bri and Bailey," Tristan says. I bite my nail again, still not being able to get my head around Tristan and Bri together. Flashes of that night fill my head, which aren't helped as Tristan shoves some tongue down Bri's throat right in front of us. It's him all right, hasn't changed a bit.

"So," Blake says, finally finding his voice, "why don't you guys show us around?" Thank you Blake for getting us off the topic of relationships and Cleaving or I'd be doing a lot more heaving. Tristan drags Blake off to show him the sports facilities and I'm left with Bri and Bailey.

"Kira, is it?" Bri asks. Bailey's busy watching Blake walk away and muttering "unfreakingbelievable." I guess he made quite the impression on her. I feel a small pang of jealousy over her open gawking at my fake boyfriend.

"Yeah," I answer Bri as I stare at her. She looks the same. Still tall. Hair's still dark and wavy. Eyes are still bright blue and surrounded by heavy eyeliner and eyeshadow. But her demeanor has changed a bit. She looks happier, less jaded. The last year before her death she'd been a little withdrawn, always wanting to talk about and meddle in my business, but never willing to open up about her own.

She can spew out words faster than anyone I know. "Ignore Tristan. He's a super competitive showoff. I swear he thinks the next couple to self-Cleave is going to get some sort of prize or something." I can't respond to that one without saying something I shouldn't, so just nod.

"Your boyfriend is hot," Bailey pipes up, making conversation. "His name's Blake? He's got gorgeous eyes and a smokin' body."

"Yes, his name's Blake Sundry. But, we aren't quite at the whole boyfriend/girlfriend thing," I respond. Bailey shoots me one of her well known "I'm better than you" smiles. I can already see the scheme forming in her head. She's nothing if not one of the most calculated and manipulative people I know. We always got along as fellow cheer squad members, but those who weren't on her good side were targeted and tortured. She was particularly vindictive while wasted and she rarely abstained. If she's got her sights set on Blake and she thinks I'm in her way it could get ugly.

Briella pipes in. "Kira, I bet you and Blake will Cleave. You look right together. There's no hurry though unless his eighteenth is coming up like Tristan's," she says, presumably to irk Bailey. Bailey looks at Briella like she wants to stab her.

Bailey says, "I have to disagree. Kira here looks all 'what you see, you can't touch' and well, Blake looks like the real touchy-feely sort. And I just know he feels real fine. Someone's gonna Cleave that and I'm willing to bet my teebs that it'll be someone who knows what to do with such exquisite merchandise."

"I don't think either of us are thinking about Cleaving," I say, trying not to let Bailey know she's hit a nerve or three.

Bri says, "Knock it off, Bailey. You've been anti-Cleaving all along. Don't pretend like you're suddenly a fan."

"That's because I've been surrounded by uninteresting dolts… until now," Bailey says, flashing her most wicked grin. Yeah, in your past life you seem to have found most of these guys quite interesting at one time or another. "Besides, a girl has a right to change her mind. Cleaving may just be for me after all."

Bri ignores Bailey, rolls her eyes and addresses me. "We've already seen a couple of our guy friends not Cleave and then be Cleaved to random people they barely know. Maybe it'll work out, but I prefer to choose my Cleave myself." Gah. They look the same, talk the same, but they're dead and I'm having a hard time getting past that critical piece of data. And their obsession with Cleaving? Shut up already about it. I so do not want to be even thinking about it, much less talking about it all the time.

"Yeah, I definitely think choice is a good thing," I say. So's freedom and governmental checks and balances. But, those seem to be missing in Garden City, too.

"We're going to get along, you and me," Bri says. "I'm glad you're here. I can tell we're like-minded." I used to think we were on the same page until I found her groping my boyfriend.

"Thanks," I say. "So, what's there to do around here?" And with that, they show me around what is actually an enormous complex, serving children from preschool through high school depending on the area. Several areas are so crowded, it's almost claustrophobic, but everyone seems to have friends and be generally happy, so I guess that's good. It all feels old school to me, like it must have been for my parents before everyone got obsessed with TV, the internet, texting, music and games. The focus appears to be on getting out and staying active, or on exploring one's artistic talents. Had I come here cold turkey without having my self-imposed mourning period of inactivity I would have gone nuts, but by now I'm plenty used to not being attached to my phone, computer, and music at all times.

We stop by the school clinic to clean and bandage my Theranberry bush wounds before continuing our tour. While walking I ask Bri and Bailey all kinds of generic questions, like where to get my hair done (they come to you), and whether they get to take any trips into the city (they take at least one a week to see various Career options). I'm careful not to ask about anything that they probably don't have like restaurants or shopping, keeping it to inquiries about free time and school classes.

I want to find out when they got here, how they got here and where they were prior, but know better. How can they deal with being seventeen, almost daynight

eighteen, and not knowing what they did for the first seventeen years? I suspect that's why the past can never be mentioned. If the seed isn't planted then they don't even worry about the existence of the seed. Briella does most of the educating me about the way of things, while Bailey peppers me with questions about me and Blake and where we were before we arrived. For someone with no memory of what happened, she seems oddly inquisitive. I was wary of alive-Bailey and surely don't trust dead-Bailey.

We meet up again with the boys on the interior football field where Tristan is tossing the ball to Blake with the force of a bullet. Tristan's posse is cheering him on and laughing at Blake's comparatively inept ball handling skills. Blake looks less than happy about it. Tristan's got his shirt off and is calling plays as if Blake should know the entire high school playbook. Blake sees me and bolts off the field to my side, skirting Bailey who tries to grab him.

"Save me," he whispers. "You promised to have my back."

"Then save me," I whisper back. "Because I'm having a seriously bad nightmare that involves zombies."

"What are you two whispering about?" Tristan says, getting his sweaty body a little too close for comfort. "You already see some other guys you like better and want to ditch Blakey boy here? You probably never saw him try to catch a football before, eh?" he says—I'm sure as a joke—but it just sounds conceited and makes Bri even more uncomfortable than it does Blake and me.

I roll my eyes at Tristan's dig at Blake. High school antics really are universal and I guess boys will be boys no matter what planet they are on. To Tristan I say, "Blake and I want to go take a walk in the canyon and check it out."

"I can show you the best paths," Tristan offers.

"I think that they're looking for a little alone time, Tristan," Bri says, and when I see Tristan sign "Forgive me" to her, I can barely squeak out a response.

"Thanks, but another time," I say. "See you guys in a bit," I add, before grabbing Blake by the hand and heading to the first path I see once leaving the interior. I walk carefully, but purposefully, paranoid about tripping into another thorny bush or happening upon some creepy critters. The path I chose isn't as well lit as most. Every sound makes me jump and I don't want to stray so far from the school, but I need distance from the dead kids. So, I wait until we're at least a hundred yards away from anyone before I speak again.

"Can I scream now?"

CHAPTER TEN

Blake

"I'm not sure screaming is going to help," I say to her. "It'd just echo through the canyon and then you'd have to go back and explain why you're having a meltdown over meeting some kids—who we aren't supposed to know —and, who tried to be nice and show us around." She's pacing back and forth and flailing her arms like a deranged chicken and I know I need to get her to chill quickly.

"OK, so those freaking SCI psychopaths stick us in a school with all our dead friends and want us to watch them like a bunch of mice in a cage and report on them nightly. Am I missing anything? What is the punishment for blowing the lid on all of it? Exile? How bad can it be? Maybe I could find shelter, food, and an exit portal out of here. That Daynighter dude implied the exit portal was close," she says in a hushed, but clearly upset voice.

"Or we can both calm down and work on a plan that doesn't involve immediate Exile. I mean I have ideas about what to do." That was a slip. I can't tell her now, can I? No, no I can't. Then she'd distrust me as much as she does Ted. I need her to stay on my side.

"Like what?" she asks. I move in close to her, staring into her wide set green and gold eyes that are definitely high on the "Things I find attractive about Kira, despite my attempts not to" list. My body betrays me at every possible junction.

"I'm going to hug you now," I say, putting my arms tightly around her, which sends an electric sensation through my more sensitive areas. I don't want to let go. "You're just going to have to trust me. You've had enough crud dumped on you tonight and don't need all my baggage as well. So why don't we get through this first and then I can have sharing time, and you can hate me for dragging you into it."

"That does sound like a plan," she says. "How much longer before we get locked in our house and I can have my meltdown?"

"We've got a half hour until our mandatory workout time. Afterwards, we can go back for dinner and meltdown," I respond.

"Where do we workout exactly?" she asks. "Please tell me we don't have to work out with the dead kids, please, please, please?!" I grimace, knowing she's not going to like my answer.

"Sorry. Didn't you see that monster gym off the back of the fields?" I ask.

"Yeah, I saw it," she says.

"Well, that's where we're required to work out with the zombies," I say, chuckling in a feeble attempt to lighten the mood. "I don't think they're exactly zombies though. They're a bit too lively."

"I think I'd be better with zombies," she says. "Because it's one thing to imagine decaying bodies digging themselves out of a grave, and quite another to have completely blown to bits bodies suddenly reappear in perfect form. I mean, Humpty Dumpty never got put back together again and he was just a freaking egg."

"Come on, you seriously never contemplated any sort of life after death? Billions of people in the world believe in it and we've just seen proof. That's actually pretty cool if you think about it," I say. Of course, there's some people who don't really deserve life after death, mainly Ms. Bailey Goodington. Since she can't remember squat about our history, I think I may have to make an effort to ensure her "afterlife" is as close to the hell she deserves as possible. The way she looked at me though… eerily like she used to back when we were steaming up her pool (and the pool house). It was hot then and, to be honest, it's still kind of hot. Scary, but wow. Thank goodness for that "Cleave-axe" positioned over my neck or I might be tempted to refill my drink so to speak.

Kira answers my life-after death question with, "I mean I thought it'd be nice, but it's not like I was raised by born-agains or anything, so God and I aren't really on a first name basis. And if there is a God I really doubt he's only going to give a fraction of the people who die every year a second chance, and send them to some sort of autocratic world where no one's allowed to mention him."

"Everything has to make perfect sense to you, doesn't it?" I respond. "Do you ever take a leap of faith on anything?"

"Ha ha," she says with a weak smile. "I'm trusting you aren't I? I want to crawl in a hole and die right now, but I'm giving it a go because you asked me to."

I want to comfort her, or somehow say the exact right thing. "How are you about Tristan? And Tristan and Bri?" I ask. That wasn't the right thing. I can tell by the look on her face. My eyes have adjusted to the low light enough to catch the glare. Her mental wheels are spinning as she tries to place all her feelings in cookie cutter pieces to get the solution to the puzzle.

"I don't know. I mean it's them, but all that shared history we have is gone. Dead Bri and I clicked, but I can tell she's pretty defensive about Tristan. And they're supposedly dating but Tristan was kind of flirty with me, yet saying and signing things to her that he usually did with me. But it doesn't matter, since they're dead and can never exist again on Earth."

Kira rambles about her confused feelings. The only nugget I pick up on is that she thinks Bailey Goodington has a thing for me. No way I'm telling Kira about my history with Bailey. Kira's tirade continues for a few minutes and my brain hurts from her psychoanalysis. Man I'm so happy I'm not a chick. They think way too much and overcomplicate everything.

"And how do you feel about keeping up our little charade? Or do you want to make a play for Tristan? I mean, you can't do both and I know his Cleave date is coming up." I hate to push on this stuff so soon, but I can trust her unedited thoughts better than the contrived ones she might give me later once she sorts her strains of paranoia.

She pauses before answering, avoiding my gaze and taking a few deep breaths. I brace myself for the inevitable blow to my ego. How could she ever choose to continue with our fake relationship—a guy she's only known a couple weeks—over her long time boyfriend? It's going to royally screw up my plan, though, if she bails on me. She's my cover. Finally, she speaks, "As long as you can deal with one overly hormonal, really messed up girl as your pretend girlfriend I'm good to leave things the way they are for now. In the meantime, I have a lot to work through so I'm probably not going to be so great to be around. Can we just say I'm cranky about my upcoming surgery?"

What the hell? "Surgery? What surgery? You didn't mention that," I say.

"Sorry, the doctor told me this evening that I do have one of those reproductive organ lesions, but the surgery's apparently just an hour-long deal and they'll give me a local for it… though I wish they'd knock me out since I think it involves a really big needle," she says.

"I don't want to freak you out any worse, but do you believe them? Could it be something else? Extracting your DNT like you were worried about or something?" I ask. I grab her when the blood drains from her face, because she looks like she's going to keel over again.

She fixates her eyes on me, glaring. "I hadn't thought about that, but I was needing some more fodder for my nightmares, so thanks."

"Technically, here they're called daymares—or I'd think they would be. But sorry. I'm an admitted paranoid," I say, shrugging my shoulders.

"The doctor seemed sincere, but it's not like I know how to read an ultrasound. They gave me an extra couple shots and some meds to take to get ready for the surgery and help prevent infection," she says. I wish I knew for sure what they were doing was legit, but I have absolutely no reason to think they'd be messing with "the future of Thera" unless it was necessary.

"I'm sure I'm just overreacting after everything that's happened tonight. DNT is in the blood, so if they wanted that they wouldn't stick a needle in your tummy. There may well be medical consequences to passing from Earth to Thera. After all didn't—" I pause because I was about to say Ted, but I quickly change because Kira isn't quite on a first name basis with him, "—Mr. Rosenberg tell you that we are anomalies to be able to be here? It probably does muck with our systems and the doctors are probably trying to help. But, don't let them put you under, Kira. Watch what they do so we can talk about it and make sure it adds up, OK?"

She looks terrified, my attempt at comforting her being an epic fail. "Yeah, sure, I guess. Or maybe I can beg to have you there since I'm really not positive I can look at that needle."

"That'd be even better." I'm not certain they will go for it, but what teenage girl wouldn't want her boyfriend at her side holding her hand through something uncomfortable? It's worth a shot.

"Thanks, Blake. You're the only thing getting me through this," she says, with such a sweet look that I'm tempted to brush up on my making out skills. Kira's just as gorgeous as Bailey. With less venom for sure. But, I know I need to remain in control. I've kept my hormones tamped down for a long time and need to continue to do so. My one and only job here is to combat evil in its purest form.

My mind reverts to memories of my dad, and my years of no-holds-barred training. He worked me for hours after school and every weekend he was in town. Some of it required mental prowess, the rest physical strength and acuity. I didn't beat him in hand-to-hand combat until my fourteenth birthday, but he had no issue with starting my training at the age of eight. Day after day of having the crap beat out of you takes its toll. So when I finally won celebration was in order, but the only celebration I got was mental triumph.

On that particular day we were doing combat in a dumpy shack located an hour into Death Valley. During the fight my dad made a crucial mistake, as I'd faked a hit to the abdomen, but whirled around and chopped him in the kidney from behind. His recovery was quick, but his stamina suffered, and the strength of his blows to my knees and left shoulder weren't enough to keep me from a blunt kick to his shins, buckling his body and allowing me to pin him to the ground.

My dad never once showed pride in my efforts, that day being no exception. Instead, he pointed out my flaws and weaknesses, each posing a risk to my life, and by extension everyone important to him.

"I beat you," I said.

"Your hits were weak, and I'd have been able to break your grip before you'd disabled me," he responded. Sure, I thought, as I watched him wipe the sweat off his receding hairline. He'd long since shaved his beard and wore his hair military style—a stark contrast from the bushy mess he'd kept in my youth, probably due to lack of shears or razors. Although my father had aged as all parents do, he kept a youthful glow about him, or what I like to call the "fire of revenge" within.

"Well then, perhaps you should get someone else to go back to that hellhole," I turned to storm out of the sauna he'd chosen for our match.

"Don't you dare walk out on me! We have hours of work left. Once you get past the Eco barrier sim and across miles of desert you can rest. Until then, stop whining and focus, or I'll leave you here and you can try to get back to civilization intact," he said, voice raised so high it cracked.

All kind feelings he'd once displayed vanished the day my mother died, every pore of his body and soul having been devoted to getting us to safety, and then taking down the SCI. I blame the Militants for my dad's changed demeanor. They took his seeds of disillusionment and blossomed them into a full-out obsession with revenge on the SCI that splintered the Exilers into two factions. Fanatical and practical. Guess where my Dad sided?

"Will I get birthday cake?" I said with a glare, not expecting an answer or the cake. "Happy birthday to me."

"Just be happy you're even able to have a birthday. Your mother's not so lucky," he responded, as if I needed the reminder. I followed him out of the shack. We walked a hundred yards where my "obstacle course" awaited me. Rather than waste time with further argument, I slipped into a thin white reflective suit and protective mask, and squeezed my toes into the grips of the handmade stilts I'd fashioned from desert brush.

Placement of the stilts through the simulated dead man's land was crucial. I blocked out everything but the pattern of chemical detonators. This pattern resembled the Milky Way. Any pressure applied on an actual Eco barrier sensor would fog the area with deadly gas. If the gas didn't kill you immediately, the prolonged reaction to the acid released with the gas would melt the clothes from your body and disintegrate your flesh.

My dad could only simulate the experience. To live once back in my homeland, I'd try to figure out a way to disable all Eco barriers. Short of that, I need to locate and mentally store each city's Eco barrier pattern, along with all the other data my father and his cohorts need. Had I not been blessed with a photographic memory, the task would be impossible. But I'd inherited my parents' brilliant minds, and so the memorization was easy. I just had to master the physical execution.

Failure had plagued me the first couple dozen times I attempted the Eco barrier sim exercise. I'd set off my father's fake chemical "smoke bombs," choking on the cloud of fumes generated and having to be dragged off the field. However, I refused defeat on my birthday, and so that day I'd used extra care to maneuver the grid, completing my mission in record time, despite the heat and dry brush littering the desert landscape. Twelve inches left, eight up, nine kitty corner to the right, back four, sideways to the right fourteen, and so on, three hundred sixty-four steps total. My legs had ached. Thirst consumed me, not having been allowed water in over twelve hours. But I removed my suit, wrapped it around my head in a makeshift sun hood, and ran the final five miles averaging seven minutes per mile to my destination, a small camp. There I'd coughed bloody mucous until my father had offered me a meager amount of water and dry biscuits.

"Your form was terrible," he said. "You came within inches of the pressure points more than twenty times."

"Whatever. I'd like to see you try," I'd said, as I attempted to dislodge hot sand from my sweaty clothes. "I finished and I want to go home now."

"Survive the night without being killed by scorpions or rattlers, and you can return to your cushy life at Aunt Jennifer's," he'd said.

Why has my father bemoaned me the life he'd promised my mother I'd have? But, ultimately he's not really responsible, is he? The Second Chance Institute and their benefactors shoulder that burden. And what's that saying about burdens being lifted off shoulders? That day will truly be a day for celebration. Not just for me. But for every Exiler and Second Chancer.

Night is the blotting paper for many sorrows.

Author Unknown

CHAPTER ELEVEN

Kira

Whatever uncharacteristic sweetness Blake had offered in the canyon quickly disappears the moment we enter the gym in our workout clothes and find Tristan and Bailey waiting for us.

"Welcome back," Tristan says. "Hey Blake, want to lift with me? Think you can bench more?"

"Uh, no thanks, I'm going to run," Blake responds. Thinking this must give him license to address me, Tristan wedges his way between us, pushing Blake aside with his right arm, and putting his left arm around me.

Tristan licks his lips and says, "I missed you while you were off canoodling with what's his name in the canyon. We haven't really had a chance to get to know each other," looking me up and down like I'm a slab of beef at the local steak house. I check him out in return like he's some sort of dead guy brought back to life. Oh wait...

Bailey wastes no time, grabs Blake's arm, and says, "You run. I'll follow. I love a good chase." Looks like it'll be a long night for both of us.

"Look," I say staring into the big brown eyes I once loved so much, but don't have the same glisten for me they'd used to have. "Tristan is it? I got a chance to know your girlfriend and she seems pretty cool. And, I've got a mandatory workout to get to, so…"

"I've got a killer circuit I can show you," he says, ignoring my hints. "I've whipped every girl here into shape." He starts to point at several girls and I note that he seems to only point out the exceptionally pretty ones, certainly not *every* girl. My eyes turn to plead for Blake to interfere, but he's already up to full speed on one treadmill, while Bailey's slowly walking on the next one.

"I love Tristan's circuit. Give it a try," Bri says, appearing out of nowhere. Of course you do, I think. When I was forced to take cheer, gymnastics and dance as my mom's clone-in-training, Briella played soccer and softball. In sixth grade, she grew from five foot two to five foot eight and took up basketball and volleyball, and her skills in both only improved as she grew another couple inches by eighth grade. She has the height and looks to be a model, though she could easily crush one. In contrast, I was all toothpick until ninth grade when I finally sprouted and curved. This secured me a coveted spot on the Carmel Valley High varsity cheer squad my sophomore year—or maybe my tumbling skills secured me the spot, I'll never know. But I never topped five foot six.

"Yeah, OK, fine. Circuits it is," I say, as Tristan leads me over to an area by the free weights and weight equipment. I follow along as he takes me through a routine of squats, chest presses and flies, tricep and bicep curls, lunges, leg extensions, crunches and more. He's shocked that I pick it up so quickly, and use the right form. Of course, I can't mention that I watched him do the same circuit dozens of times and suffered through it with him just as many. Every expression and grunt he makes ring familiar, not to mention his obsession with form and resting no more than thirty seconds between sets, and the way he slides his hands over his stomach ripples after doing crunches as if there'd be an immediate improvement. The only thing missing to complete the déjà vu is the kisses between sets and the thing added to create maximum awkwardness is periodic glares from Bri and Blake.

"What do you think?" Tristan asks, interrupting my thoughts.

"About what?" I mumble. I'm not sure I'm ready to make small talk with him.

"About all of it. Your new digs, the school, the people, the workout, me," he says. That all?

"Oh," I say. "It's a bit early to make judgments on anything a few hours in."

"You are an amazingly beautiful girl," he says. "There's something about you that is really… familiar and appealing. I can't decide what it is, but I'm going to figure it out." Could it be possible that some part of him remembers me, too? That he still feels a connection? Spud said that the Second Chancers often feel connected to the person they were last with… Well, Tristan in his stupidly drunken state that night kissed both Bri and me. I'm not sure how to respond to the flirting, though. A shower comes to mind, as the thought of kissing a dead guy still oozes creeper vibes from head to toe, just as I'd told Bailey and her vamp-seeking friends the night of her party.

"Thanks, I guess, for the inappropriate compliment and the workout," I say. "I'm going to go do some stretching so I don't feel like a pretzel tomorrow." And so I can shake off the willies.

"What's inappropriate about calling you beautiful?" he says, getting his sweaty, shirtless body a little too close for comfort, and reminding me how much taller he is than me. If I'd been expecting scars from where he'd been stitched back together, there are none, just the same swathe of chest hair he's always had.

"Well, uh, you have a girlfriend and I'm with Blake," I say. His eyes narrow and he shakes his blonde curls.

"Until I Cleave, I'm not tied down to anyone," he says. "I still have a month before I'm eighteen, and until then I have time to convince any girl, including Bri and you, to Cleave me before someone else decides for me." I shake at the thought. I'm speechless and just motion that I'm going over to stretch, leaving before he has the chance to say anything else, and quickly getting into a yoga pose, eyes closed.

"It's okay, you know," I hear, Bri's voice. "I don't blame him for being interested."

I stare at her incredulously. "No, it's not okay. At least I'm not okay with it. I think if you're with someone, you're with them and *only* them. From experience, I can assure you that anything else just leads to disaster and heartache." I may sound a little bitter, still burned by their stunt the eve of Winter Formal, which is hardly fair since she has no memory of that night. For me, I only have one positive memory of that night and I'd like him to be the one to reappear. Every other person I remember being at that party and blown to smithereens is here, but not Ethan. In some ways, it's worse to think that he *lived* and never contacted me, than died and resurrected here on Thera. He probably left the party, went straight to his girlfriend, and never looked back.

Bri cocks her head and gives me a look of pity. "Soon enough we're going to be Cleaved for life, so I guess I want to make sure it's right. And it wouldn't be right for Tristan and me if he's into someone else. He'd just be miserable. I knew the moment I first saw him that he was the guy for me, but it doesn't happen that way for everyone. Last day I thought we would Cleave, but Tristan was pretty teebed so I let him sleep it off," she says. This conversation sucks. How did I get to a place where I'm defending her relationship with Tristan and mine with Blake? And what exactly is "teebed" that Tristan had to sleep off? I went through all our cupboards and didn't see a drop of alcohol anywhere.

"Any guy would be crazy to not be into you. You're gorgeous," I say with all honesty. "And given Blake and I have only been here a few hours, it's pure craziness to even be talking about Cleaving or anything of the sort. I'm just trying to get through the first night, you know?"

"Yeah, sorry," she says, though I can tell she's still concerned about it. I dare to look around and can see both Tristan and Blake's eyes focused my way, though Bailey's over there trying hard to distract Blake. My feelings are a jumbled mess. How can I ever make sense of dead people made alive, impending lifetime Cleavings and the implications thereof, my fake relationship with Blake, and back-to-life Tristan hitting on me? I rub my temples and fight off a migraine.

I continue my stretching and my situation analysis until Blake shrugs off Bailey and comes to offer me a towel. He stayed shirted tonight as if he's embarrassed to be seen shirtless in the same vicinity as Tristan's bodybuilder physique.

"Thanks," I say. "How was your workout?" If I expected an answer, he disappoints, shrugging his shoulders as he winces. "Nothing's changed," I add, trying to reassure him. Why's he so worried about our stupid, fake relationship anyway? He leans in to give me a light kiss on the cheek and whispers.

"Sure it has," he says, and then louder adds, "I'll walk you back after showers." I open my mouth to object, but he puts two fingers against my lips. His defeatist attitude irks me big time.

Can he really think I'll give up my entire life back on earth, as pathetic as it's been recently, to live with my dead high school boyfriend here on rule-heavy Thera? Sure, I still have feelings for Tristan. How could I not? My life revolved around him before he died, but not always in a positive way. If I wasn't sure Tristan was *the one* after more than a year, how could I hope to decide that before his eighteenth birthnight? Those last few weeks before Tristan died had been a lot more negative than positive. If Blake has anyone to be concerned about for competition with our fake relationship, it's Ethan, not Tristan. A perfect fantasy boy's way more dangerous than a very imperfect, two-timing ex. Just thinking about Ethan makes my heart ache in a way that neither Blake nor Tristan can. With some effort, I re-bury the memory.

After Blake vanishes from sight, I scurry to the girls' locker area. Tristan heads my way. I pretend not to hear him call my name and close the door behind me. A shower soothes my sore muscles before I change back into my school uniform. I find Blake waiting for me outside the complex and for the first time I wish I knew how to skateboard, as our travel time 'home' would be cut dramatically. We walk silently past the spot I'd passed out earlier and I curse Spud under my breath.

"So, you're not talking to me?" I ask him finally. "It kind of seems like we should have more than ever to talk about."

"Not now, Kira," he says. I jump ahead and turn to face him all in one step, so that he has to stop. "What?" he demands.

"What has you so upset? So I worked out with Tristan. I felt stuck because Bri told me to, and as you said, it's not like they know the history, so I was trying to do my job and be nice."

"You looked like you were having a real nice time," he says. I guess this is Blake jealous and I really don't want to fight with him about it given I hate fighting under any circumstance. His emerald eyes and body language are fiery. It breaks my heart that he's mad and my heart can't stand any more destruction tonight. I motion him towards me as if I want to whisper something to him and I kiss him lightly on the cheek. He smells like Theranberry soap and shampoo.

"What was that for?" he whispers. The whoosh of skateboards behind us interrupts my thoughts, as I turn to see them screech to a sharp stop. My silent wish for instant teleportation goes unfulfilled and we are left face-to-face with Bri and Tristan yet again. Tristan looks ridiculous on a skateboard. He just doesn't have the body type for it.

"Wow, you're only getting cheek? You've got to go for the tongue action," Tristan says to Blake. I chuckle since I never had the guts to tell Tristan how much I hated his throat-seeking "tongue action."

"Uh, gee, thanks for the advice," Blake mumbles.

"Want to join us for dinner?" Tristan asks.

"Thanks, but not this morning," I say quickly. "Can we get a rain check? We're still getting settled and have someone stopping by later to make sure everything is well stocked and in order."

"Sure," he says with a smile that tells me he'll keep asking until we say yes. "We'll see you guys tomorrow."

"Uh huh," I say, thinking of how many tomorrows of this I'm going to have to endure before I get to go home. I wave to Bri as the two of them push off their boards and distance themselves within seconds.

"Promise me something," Blake says, mesmerizing me with his eyes.

"What?" I ask, not being willing to make a promise I can't keep.

"We need to talk. There's stuff about me you don't know… that might make you hate me," he says, avoiding eye contact.

"Why would I hate you?" I ask. I knew it. I knew there was stuff he wasn't telling me and that I couldn't completely trust him. It must be bad if he thinks I'll hate him.

He leans his forehead into mine and stares at me. His eyes look a little watery.

"Spill," I say.

"Not now. But soon. We've got to get back. It's time for your mental breakdown." I know that our sunlight quota is nearly up. Blake jogs up the hill. But as I contemplate our "date" with Spud and my pending meltdown, my feet feel heavy and I struggle to finish the climb to the top of the hill, falling well behind Blake. He patiently waits for me.

"Hey neighbors," I hear and look up to see Tristan and Bri, which quickly snaps me back to reality. You've got to be kidding me. They put us next door to them? Blake looks as thrilled as I do to see them watching us from their balcony, separated only by a half wall to ours. "How awesome is it that you guys are right next door?"

"So awesome. Bastards are going to pay," Blake mutters. He then says more pleasantly to our neighbors, "We'll see you guys tomorrow. I think I'm going to go cook this beautiful lady some dinner." He grabs my hand and pulls me up the ramp to our house.

"What, doesn't she know how to cook?" I hear Tristan saying. Neither of us responds and I'm relieved when the door shuts securely behind me. I stumble into the living room. Blake pulls me down onto the couch and into his arms. The tears start streaming and I release the emotions I've been holding in all night.

How the heck can this not be a dream? Is it possible I was actually injured in the blast at the Goodington's, am in a coma, and my brain has fabricated all of this? Didn't I see a TV show like that once? Isn't that more possible than traveling to Earth's sister world through a portal in the ocean to a place where dead people live again and some sick and twisted, faceless rulers force their loved ones to attend to them?

Do I still love Tristan? Or is that chapter of my life closed? Could I allow myself to develop feelings for Blake? Can he ever live up to the memory of Ethan, who I felt sure could be the one? Or will I turn on Blake when I learn his secrets? What has he done anyway? Did he spend time in juvie or something? Was he abused? Raised by meth dealers? What could explain those scars on his hands? Although I need to know his deep dark secret, I first need to deal with the existence of the Second Chancers.

The thing that I get stuck on over and over again is the "how"? How can my friends be alive? They were dead. Vaporized. Well, not quite given the number of body parts I saw in the post-disaster news coverage. But, mangled beyond repair, certainly. So, how did they get here? They weren't reborn since they showed up at the same age they were when they died on Earth. Someone needs to explain the science behind it, because nothing I've learned in school or training here can account for it.

Amidst the grief and anger, I also feel something for Blake that I can't quite define. He infuriates me most of the time, but occasionally shows me a tender side that tugs at my heart. By the time the doorbell rings, I realize we've completely missed our window for dinner. That mystery will have to be left for another day as we're due to be debriefed by the man whom I consider to be my captor. The doorbell rings again and I close my eyes to collect myself and let Blake pull away, though he whispers, "It'll be okay, Kira," before jumping up to get the door.

"Good morning, Mr. Sundry," I hear Spud say.

"Mr. Rosenberg," Blake responds. "Come on in. And please call us Blake and Kira. The whole formal thing's annoying. Sorry I was slow. We've just been, uh, working through the massiveness of the night."

"Yes, I'm sure," Spud says in an all-knowing tone as he enters the room and sees me in shambles on the couch. I don't bother to say hello, trying to wipe the evidence of my meltdown from my face. He helps himself to a seat and I watch Blake retreat to the kitchen.

"Ms. Donovan, or Kira, rough night?" he says.

"I got to hang out with all my dead friends. It was great," I say with the deadpan delivery I reserve for the man.

"As shocking as it must have been for you to see them, can you appreciate the miracle of the situation? You do understand that they are not dead *here*, right?"

"I'm not really a 'believe in miracles' kind of person," I say. "But true to your advertising, the Second Chance Institute has managed to find a way to give people a second lease on life," and then adding under my breath, "however disturbing it is."

"Well, I think it's a miracle," Spud says.

I look at him incredulously. How long did the SCI have to brainwash him? Deep down, does he understand that all of this isn't okay? I ask him, "How does it work? How do they get here? How do they get through the portals? I need to understand it."

"Sorry, even with my promotion I'm not privy to the details," Spud says.

"I don't believe you," I respond, full of indignation.

"Does it really matter? They are real. They are here. You are here. Deal with it," he says. I hate this man; truly despise him—his ridiculous looks, his condescending attitude, his inappropriate questions, and his pathetically insufficient answers.

"It matters to me," I say, pounding my fists on the couch, frustrated and upset.

"I assume you were careful not to discuss the past?" he says, ignoring my temper tantrum. I take some deep breaths to calm myself as I don't do angry well, being rather unversed at it.

"I assume you already know the answer to that?" I say, putting him back on the defensive. He glares at me with his signature, "be careful, you are pushing it" look. "But yes, to answer your question, I made no mention of the past. So all is safe, unless dead kids became psychic upon resurrection." This gets me a smirk and a nervous wiggling of his chin fat.

"Excellent. How did Tristan and Briella react to you?" he asks.

"How do you mean? I chatted with them. Bri and I hit it off, and Tristan hit on me," I say.

"Did that make you feel uncomfortable given his current relationship with Briella?" he asks. Why is it so important for him to know this? I try to read him and my best guess would be concern that I may be a spoiler in some evil being's Cleaving plans.

"Yes, it was uncomfortable and awkward for everyone," I say.

"Because of your feelings for Tristan or your feelings for Blake?" he probes. It takes a moment for me to realize that the powers that be think my relationship with Blake to be fully real and progressing much faster than in reality.

"Both, I guess," I say. I wonder what's taking Blake so long in the kitchen, but realize he's probably scrounging for food since we missed dinner. Blake doesn't have quite the appetite Tristan had when we dated, but pretty close. My eating habits more closely mirror my stress than hunger level. And since my stress level is at an all time high, I could use some munchies.

Spud continues his interrogation. "Did you get a sense that either Briella or Tristan had any memories from before?" Odd given he said that isn't possible.

"Hmmm. No not really memories per se, but more like feelings if that makes any sense. Tristan said he was drawn to me and he was going to figure out why, and Bri immediately felt like we'd be friends," I say. He jots down some notes on his tablet.

"Do you have any intention of pursuing a relationship with Tristan?" he asks bluntly. My eyes go wide. I let out a puff of imaginary steam and dig my fingernails into the couch.

"Mr. Rosenberg," I say, trying to keep my voice as calm and steady as possible, "I'm a little overwhelmed by the fact my dead friends are here and reanimated, and even more overwhelmed by the fact that you knew this and did not tell me ahead of time. So no, I'm not really planning some dream wedding with Tristan. Or I guess that doesn't even happen here since people either have premarital sex and get Cleaved for life, or get matched up by some random computer or whatever. Neither of which I'll allow to happen to me."

"But you have been pursuing a relationship with Blake?" he asks, his blubbery cheeks wobbling as he laughs over his intrusions. Well, not a real one. Or maybe? I don't know. But, for Spud, it's got to seem real.

"Yeah. As far as I know he's not dead," I say, biting my lip as Blake enters to hand me a plate of food. "Thanks," I say to Blake and then shove a bite of food into my mouth so I can avoid further discussion.

"Okay," Spud says. "You can eat while I talk with Blake and then I highly recommend you get a good day's sleep. Your doctor decided to move your surgery up to tomorrow evening after reviewing your test results, so I'm afraid you won't be able to eat or drink after dinner, and won't be able to have breakfast in the evening. And here's a medication you're to take right away," he says, handing me a couple of pills, which he waits for me to swallow. The mention of the surgery makes me feel ill. Blake grabs my hand to comfort me. I run my fingers across his scars, eagerly anticipating the moment he tells me what happened to cause such injury.

"Can Blake be there?" I ask. "I just can't deal with those needles on my own."

"I'm afraid not," Spud says. "Given your test results they're concerned about Blake as well, so they'll be running additional tests on him at the same time. I'll mention your concern about the needles to the doctor." The way he says it and the reaction on Blake's face makes me think that it's entirely intentional to keep Blake out.

"Can't they wait to run tests on me until after Kira's surgery is done?" Blake asks.

"No, I'm afraid not. You have classes to start. Kira will start her classes a night or two later, as I suspect she'll need some recovery time."

"I thought the surgery was no big deal. Should I be worried?" I ask, even more wary about it than before, and suddenly not so hungry. In fact, I'm very woozy and incredibly sleepy.

"It's not a big deal and no, you shouldn't be worried. Some people experience a little discomfort afterwards, but the doctor will give you some pain medication and with a little rest you'll be just fine," he says.

"What were those pills? I'm not feeling so hot," I say, putting my head down on the nearest surface, which happens to be Blake's lap. I'm sure to keep the ruse going, he runs his fingers through my hair and away from my face. The garden images on the walls relax me and before long I close my eyes, comforted by his touch and the silky feel of the couch.

"Yeah, what'd you give her?" Blake says.

"I believe it's just something to relax her and help her sleep. After the stress of the night it's important she be well rested for her procedure," Spud says. I'm too tired to speak, but those pills did not resemble those they gave us to sleep when we first arrived.

"I'd like to understand her surgery better," Blake says.

"She asleep?" Spud asks.

"I think so," he responds.

"As the doctors explained to her there are some side effects Recruits face by going through Thera's portals. Often small lesions form on the female's reproductive organs that if left unchecked can cause long-term infertility."

"And so that's what the doctor is fixing tomorrow?" Blake asks.

"Yes, of course," Spud replies.

"So then why are they messing with me?" Blake asks.

"Oh, well for males there can be issues will sperm motility, which can make it difficult to fertilize a female's egg."

"Seriously, stop right there. Don't ever talk to me about sperm again, okay? Besides, I'm not sure children will be in my future," Blake says. Why would he say such a thing? And why'd he stop stroking my hair? He's obviously upset by the exchange.

"Of course they will be," Spud says. "Which is why these tests and procedures are so important."

"What exact tests are they running on me?" he asks.

"I'm sure they're just going to take some samples and make sure all is well," he says. I can feel Blake shaking beneath me. Perhaps he hates needles as much as I do.

"Is that so?" Blake says.

"Yes," Spud says in such a tone I know that conversation is over. "So, tell me how the night went. Was it hard to see your sister? Or harder to see your girlfriend meet up with her old boyfriend?"

"Well, it's not like I got to chat with Leila since she's a freshman. And the whole Tristan thing sucked. What did you expect? That Kira would thank you? That I'd thank you?" Blake says.

"No, I imagined it would go as it did," Spud replies. "She needs to get past it."

"I don't know," Blake says. "Can she?" He's back to playing with my hair which feels amazingly soothing.

"I thought you'd like her," Spud says. "You've got a thing for her, haven't you?" He pauses, which makes me think Blake gave a non-verbal answer to his question. "She'd make an excellent Cleave for you, you know. Just remember that you came here to do a job, not just find the love of your life."

"I know. I got it. I won't let you down," Blake says. And then almost as an afterthought he adds, "As creepy as it is working with the Second Chancers, we'll do as instructed."

"Excellent. Well, I'll be going. I'll let myself out. I assume you'll see to it that Kira gets to bed?" Spud asks.

"I've got it covered, Ted," Blake says. Ted? Since when are they on a first name basis? I hear footsteps and then the door shut. Blake silently sits there for several minutes before sliding out from under my head so that he can scoop me off the couch and carry me to my room. He pulls the covers up over me and kisses me on the forehead before I drift off to sleep.

I'm barely showered and dressed before the doorbell rings and an all-too chipper Spud Rosenberg is at the door and ready to usher me to the clinic. Blake insists on accompanying me, but Spud says no, "His appointment isn't for a half hour." There's no chance to interrogate Blake about his debriefing with Spud. That will have to wait for later, when we can take a walk in the canyon, assuming I'll even be up to it. Actually, I don't care how I feel. My need for information will have to trump any pain or discomfort.

We traverse the path to the clinic through the glowing lights in the canyon, and I congratulate myself for my improved skills at avoiding the spiky brush lining the path. I try to start up a conversation with Spud, but he's clearly not an early evening person. He happily hands me off to the doctor who informs me that due to my "fear of needles" they've decided to put me under for the procedure, although it will be a "twilight" anesthetic so I'll wake up immediately following, just like when I got my wisdom teeth out a year ago. I remember Blake's clear instructions to not let them do this so I know exactly what's being done to me, but the doctor refuses to relent and I'm out like a light within moments.

My watch reads 20:10 when I come around, so I was under less than forty minutes. My abdomen feels sore and bloated, and there's a little bleeding, but other than that I appear to be functional. The doctor confirms that I'll likely have some discomfort and pain for a couple nights, but should be back to a hundred percent thereafter. He gives me a bottle of pain medication to help me deal before forcing me into a wheelchair and handing me to a nurse.

As we're wheeling out to the clinic lobby I hear a heated exchange coming from an examination room. One of the voices is my doctor and the other rings so familiar it hits me like a wrecking ball to the gut as he says, "What did you do to her? If you hurt her, I'll make sure you suffer." Ethan. But that's impossible right? Or not. I saw him at the scale model at Headquarters. At the time I was certain. But Brad Darcton scared me off. Why wouldn't Ethan come see me if he was here? Unless he's a Second Chancer and doesn't remember me. Which would suck. Although, wouldn't that mean he couldn't remember his girlfriend, either? What is wrong with me? I'm horrible and need to get a grip. Ethan's not mine to pursue, even if he is on Thera. Regardless, I want to know his fate.

"Who's in there?" I ask the nurse as I get out of the chair and attempt to open the door, which is locked. Thankfully she catches me when I collapse from standing up too fast. "I know that voice. I need to talk to him. I really, really need to. I've been looking for him. Please open up," I say through the door. "If it's you, please stop avoiding me." The voices in the room go silent.

"I'm afraid that information is privileged, Ms. Donovan," she says. "We take patient confidentiality seriously here. Should I get a member of the Ten or Council to address your concerns?" That's all the reminder I need to stand down. In my loopy state I'd ignored Brad Darcton's admonition to not go looking for people I'd previously known.

"No, no, never mind. I'm sorry. I think I'm just hallucinating or something," I say. She shakes her head and delivers me to Blake, who is apparently supposed to push me all the way home. I'm surprised he's waiting, but don't address him as I'm still muttering about the voice I heard. I want to stay and see the mystery patient come out of the room, but Blake's eager to get me out of there. The anesthetic they used has me in a bit of a fog, which I blame for my delusions. Finally, Blake breaks the silence once we're in the open canyon.

"You okay?" he asks.

"Yeah, I think so. Doesn't look like they removed anything life sustaining," I respond with a weak smile.

"I wouldn't be so sure," he mumbles.

"Huh?" I say.

"What did they do? What did you see? Tell me exactly?" he asks, his tone fearful.

"Sorry, I didn't see anything. They decided to put me out because of my needle issues. Why, what do you think you know? I heard you and 'Ted' last night, Blake. You seemed to be on quite the paranoia trip. You going to share?"

"Oh. I thought you were asleep," is all he says.

"Come on, isn't it time you tell me what your story is?" I say, turning in my chair to look at him, which wrenches my abdomen enough to cause extreme agony. "Ugh. My stomach hurts."

"I've got to get back to start my classes on time and you have to get some rest. Later, during free time I'll tell you anything you want to know," he says. "I promise."

As much as it pains me I stop our forward progress with my legs and stand up out of the wheelchair to face him. Since he's still pushing, he whacks me in the knees with the chair and I almost fall over.

"You'll tell me now or I'm not going anywhere," I say, although if my shakiness doesn't make me tank the heat may. It feels unusually hot and I can barely breathe. The relative darkness of the spot we stopped unnerves me, but I press on with my interrogation. "I have to know what happened to you that was so crappy that you think I'm going to hate you for it. I just can't hang out all night imagining up crazy scenarios while I watch you do a bunch of boring online classes. I won't do it. So, please tell me. Now." The discomfort I'm causing Blake is apparent in his eyes and body language, but I refuse to back down. Although, I may not be able to stay upright for long. The combination of anesthesia and pain medications has me swaying.

"Fine, but please sit so you don't keel over," he says, gently helping me back into the chair. He kneels in front of me, trembling, putting his hands on top of mine.

"I'm sitting. Go ahead," I say.

His eyes don't leave mine as he speaks. "I'm just going to spew it out. Kira, the deal is that I was born here on Thera. My parents were Exiled for stealing government secrets. My dad was a Daynighter—just like that guy from Foreign Affairs we met—so he traveled back and forth between Earth and Thera doing business between the governments. He discovered some things he shouldn't have—and shared them with my mom—not realizing everything they discussed was monitored. So they were both Exiled, despite the fact my mom was pregnant with me. My parents hooked up with a colony of Exilers in some caves outside the city. That's where I was born. I lived there until I was eight and it was no picnic—the kind of stuff that still gives me nightmares—like watching my Mom slowly die after giving birth to Leila. But, eventually the Exilers took control of an entry portal and found a new exit portal, and so my dad made good on a promise he'd made to my mom to get us out of here, and placed me with 'Jennifer,' his trophy wife on Earth."

My eyes grow wide and I'm shaking a little myself at the implications. He was born here? In Exile? I don't know him at all, I realize. "Keep going," I say. One swirling canyon light keeps illuminating and then darkening Blake's face—a creepy effect to accompany his equally disturbing tale.

"The thing is that I've been trained since I was eight to do what we're doing right now—to come back here as a Recruit and get information my dad and the other Exilers need to take control from the dictators who run this place. They're not good guys, Kira. They're seriously evil and the cities here are really just some large-scale experiments. Worse, the Second Chancers are just a bunch of pawns. They'd kill me in a second if they knew who I was or what I was doing." He stops, letting me absorb the information, though he can no longer look me in the eye. His whole life has been one big training exercise.

"Ted Rosenberg hatched the plan with my dad and helped me prepare for the Test, even though I was pretty much a shoo-in with my DNA. He's my dad's mole within the SCI organization, but until now he was stationed on Earth, not Thera. Ted knew that I couldn't get in and pull off the scam alone. Since Recruits are always partnered so that the SCI can try to Cleave them off and keep them on Thera, he had to find me a suitable match that we could trust not to blow my cover," he says, pausing. The pained look on his face tells me I'm not going to like what I hear next.

"So that's where I come into play? This has all been about getting me on board?" I ask, seething as the pieces start falling into place: the "pact" we made, the trust building, and the fake relationship. Blake pretending the fake could become real. He's the plant and I'm the pawn.

"I swear I didn't know about the partner thing until the day of the Test and I wasn't happy. I mean, they'd trained me to trust no one and then tell me that I can't do it alone, and that I'm going to be responsible for another life. A girl's life. Your life. Ted told me it was going to be you that afternoon after you insulted him in the interview. But he was worried you weren't going to be cooperative. So after the whole disaster unfolded at the Goodington's I knew they were behind it."

"What do you mean 'they' were behind it? So who are the 'they'? What are you saying?" I ask, though deep down I already know the answer and can feel my bones frost over before he even responds.

"The SCI killed your friends and my sister to make sure we'd commit—you'd commit. They caused the blast that night and engineered every single thing that followed," he says. He pauses to allow me to process and respond. It takes me a full minute to do so. I saw him at school every day for two months following the accident and he never said a word. He knew we'd end up here together and my life would be in danger.

"And you knew and you let me come," I say as the last puzzle piece ratchets into place and I understand why he thinks I'm going to hate him.

"I didn't know if I could trust you, didn't think you'd believe me, and was selfish because I needed you. Without you reacting to Thera the way you did it would've been obvious I knew too much. So yeah, I knew and I let you come, to preserve both our lives," he says.

There's nothing more he can say, or at least that I want to hear until I can process what he's already told me. He removes his hands from mine and proceeds to roll me up the path towards our home in dreary silence.

CHAPTER TWELVE

Blake

Kudos to Ted Rosenberg for scoring the job as our Handler and shedding new light on my deal here. I learned as much in our fifteen-minute debrief last night as I did the entire week of training, with exception of the visit to mini-Garden City which was the equivalent of the pot of gold at the end of the rainbow for me.

First, our house is bugged, but there are no cameras—at least not in the living area, because Ted's words didn't match his non-verbal signals. For one, after he described the so-called surgery for reproductive lesions I asked if that's what they were doing to Kira. His words said "yes" but he was shaking his head "no." When I said children weren't in my future—because I'm not sure I have a long life expectancy ahead of me—he says they will be, his body language screaming "count on it, whether you want it or not." And he made sure I knew that my tests have squat to do with making sure my sperm'll make the swim team cut.

Second, he was all in my face about my deal with Kira—even if it's a good cover I've got to keep trained on my real mission. Like I don't know that. Though I have to admit, holding her in my arms to comfort her last night had my body going haywire. Nothing a cold shower couldn't remedy.

Third, the powers that be are totally buying the whole relationship thing.

Four, there are moments where *I* forget the relationship isn't real. And that means I'm screwed. The moment I tell her the truth she's going to turn on me and that's going to open her up to Tristan's full court press for a quickie Cleave. I doubt she'd turn me in at this point, but the living situation could get unmanageable fast. And I need her to stay on my side so she can cover for me when I'm off doing daddy's bidding.

108

Five, Bailey's going to be a real obstacle for my fake relationship, no question. Almost makes me wish she had her memory back. She spent our entire workout educating me on ways to have "fun" without crossing the Cleaving line. If I'd thought she was pretty creative during our short relationship before… the stuff she whispered to me had me blushing (and otherwise reacting) and I don't embarrass easily. That conversation required an extra long cold shower post-workout.

Six, I'm pretty sure that my fake relationship with Kira and potential Cleaving has everything to do with Kira and me being the "future of Thera." I've got whacked thoughts like they want us to breed a bunch of super DNT babies, which would explain why they're all about our reproductive systems functioning. I just can't tell how far they're taking it.

All I know is the clinic just made me give them a sperm sample. And they're in there doing who knows what to Kira. With any luck she'll be able to detail it out for me, but I'm betting they'll make sure she can't. Ted told me the pregnancies were all done in-vitro, which screams "lab creations" to me. For all I know they're manufacturing a bunch of mini-me's right now and there's nothing I can do about it. Or maybe they're shoving my goods up her to try to get her pregnant, but that doesn't really jive either since we're not Cleaved, so that means any pregnancy, "assisted" or not and we'd be Exiled. However, it's equally likely my upbringing has made me overly paranoid and they're just trying to grow some DNT in a lab and the repro deal is a huge red herring.

My dad trained me for just about every scenario, but we never covered reproduction in a whole lot of detail. In fact, I don't think he ever factored female influence into the equation, which was a major oversight on his part. He shut down my relationship with Bailey the moment he found out. Beat the crap out of me for getting involved with her, so between his reaction and Bailey's reaction I equate girls with pain. Sure, I have a teenage sister. But it's a heck of a lot different having a girlfriend, fake or not. I could foist my sister on my step-mom when she got touchy and emotional, but I'm expected to shoulder that responsibility with Kira and I am way out of my element. I'd give anything for a laptop and an hour of Internet access because a little research is in order. Google'd be my best friend about now. I wonder if somewhere deep within the SCI administration buildings if they don't have some internet cable that runs through a portal.

I realize Kira hasn't been in for long, but I want to see her and find myself pacing the small lobby of the clinic. The receptionist keeps glancing up like I'm an annoying distraction, but I don't give a crap because I need to know what they're doing to her and whether they're hurting her. My sleep suffered as I spent the hours reliving how my body felt holding her. Though, if I'm being honest, I might have been thinking about some of Bailey's suggestions, too. Bad-news Bailey's the kind of distraction that could blow the mission completely.

The door to the clinic opens and I'm surprised to see Ethan the Intern stroll in.

"Hey, Ethan," I say. He looks as shocked to see me as I am to see him.

"Hi. Blake was it? What are you doing here?" he asks.

"Waiting for my partner, Kira, to get out of surgery. They're removing a lesion or something," I say, trying not to put too much emphasis on the "or something," but failing.

"Is she okay?" he says, looking concerned. His fists are balled and clenched enough that I almost think he might deck me, so I back up a step. What's got him strung so tight?

"She better be," I say. "She's supposed to be out any moment." He shoves his hands in his pockets and rocks back and forth on his feet, as if he's trying to figure out what to say. Sounds like he mumbles "Crap, not now" under his breath.

"I better check in for my appointment. I'm late," he finally says in a nervous tone and then walks over to the desk. After whispering something to the receptionist, he's immediately motioned to follow her back to a room. I had to wait twenty-five minutes for my appointment. "It was good to see you again, Blake," he adds before disappearing down the hall.

"You, too," I mumble. I hear some loud voices coming from the hallway, but can't make out the conversation. One of the voices sounds like Ethan's, but I can't be sure.

After Ethan disappears, I hear the fight continue behind closed doors. Then I make out fragments of a conversation between Kira and a nurse in the hall, which doesn't sound pleasant. About a minute later, the nurse wheels Kira out in a wheelchair. As much as I'd like to question the doctor about what they did to her, I decide to take her home. She's resisting a bit and mumbling something about hearing the voice of someone she knows and needing to wait to see if it's really him, but I assume she's just loopy on the drugs, so I get her out of there. Ethan's here and I'd still like to avoid the two of them meeting.

She tells me everything's okay, but doesn't know the details of what they did. But then the chair comes to a halt and Kira's looking for answers, and refusing to move until I tell her. So I do. I unload the stuff I know, leaving out the nastiness about what I think the SCI has planned, and it doesn't take her long to cut to the heart of the matter. She was headed for hell and I didn't warn her, and that is freaking betrayal with a capital B. Sugar coating it isn't going to help. I did what I did for good reason and it's too late to change it now.

I release my grip on her hands and push her on up the rest of the way to our house, cursing the screwed up situation. Letting them assign me a partner was a mistake, but allowing myself to care about her and what she thinks was an even bigger one. My chances with her were nil from the get-go between my sins of omission, she being way out of my league, her lover boy being brought back from the dead, and my focus needing to be on my mission and not some volatile chick who can't possibly understand how important my success is.

The truth is that I'm not sorry and I'd do it again. Had I told her at any point before seeing the Second Chancers, we'd have both been exposed as frauds and be dead—and it's not like we'd have been given another go at life on another planet. I'm done apologizing. It's time to stop fretting over my fake relationship and for me to get to work. She's going to have to get over it and help me. Because neither of us will have a decent future, if we don't deliver. Nor will my dad, the Exilers, or the Second Chancers.

Yes, whatever lust-filled or otherwise feelings I've got going for Kira (or my evil-ex) need to be extinguished for the duration. My father taught me to turn off my emotions. He's an expert, having done it to all his colleagues post-Exile. He'd practically worshipped the Grand Council and Presiding Ten until he'd discovered their rap sheet. After that, he axed the relationship cords. It was much easier to plot against them without consideration of the human factor— all the dinners, parties, and stories they'd shared. He figured "screw them all, they deserve what they have coming," comparing them to the Third Reich during the Holocaust. They were playing Gad and mucking with the natural order of things.

I knew precious little about Garden City or its inhabitants until my father allowed me to join his band of humanitarians on a stakeout of the Eco barrier as a "teaching exercise," wanting me to learn survival skills. The group hoped to figure out a way through, over or under the toxic strip so they could steal supplies from an outlying warehouse. Doc Daryn came along to attend to the injuries he was sure the group would suffer, leaving his Cleave as nurse to the rest of the Exiled.

Our humble cave dwellings sat just two canyons away from Garden City, less than a night's walk. So we'd left at sundown, traveled the night, and arrived by sunrise to a deep cave west of the city where we setup camp for the day. I was well accustomed to sleeping in sauna-like conditions, so curled in the back of the cave against a cool rock and slept until woken.

The first night we traversed a three-mile stretch along the barrier, throwing rocks from a distance to see if there were dead spots between the triggers of the deadly gasses. Despite it being mid-night the lights of Garden City glowed

—a vast difference from the canyons back home where we had to use lanterns or flashlights.

Our group was able to determine that there were indeed dead spots in the barrier. However, the men weren't able to throw far enough to map more than the first twenty feet of the pattern, and unfortunately the spaces appeared too small for a human foot to safely step between. While the men fought to uncover the barrier's secrets, my father taught me the plants of the canyons, showing me which varieties were edible, those that were poisonous, and others that stored water. He instructed me how to craft a makeshift rope from canyon brush, tie knots, and chisel foot holds into canyon rock.

I already knew to find shelter from the sun for the day, but he taught me tricks of how to tell which cave ran deepest. And upon our return that first night, he schooled me on ways to build a safe fire pit within the cave to ward off creatures, and to cook any available food or sterilize water. He had Doc continue on into the morning, teaching me first aid skills—from burn treatment, to bandaging a sprained ankle, to proper care for cuts, bruises, bites, or gashes. I look back and blame my eagerness to be taught for his later decision to make me a permanent student in his school of Theran life and coup d'état.

Night two had been spent trying to dig under the barrier, with zero success. I was forced to watch the debacle from a distance. The sandy, rocky nature of the canyons caused immediate collapse and the gas bombs to ignite, the men barely running to safety before causing permanent damage to their lungs and skin, even while wearing Doc Daryn's safety masks. This frustrated my father since Garden City had an elaborate tunnel system, but even the engineer in the group couldn't figure out a safe way to proceed given their limited tools.

The men, lungs too weak to try anything else, returned early to the cave to rethink their strategy. As they did so, and by request, my father told me stories of the evil men who controlled Garden City and the other cities on Thera, every story justifying why my dad found it okay to steal from them. For me it was enough to know that we'd die without the food and supplies, but my father chattered for hours without break, describing the government, the Second Chancers, and a bleak life of endless rules and lack of choices.

The men left me behind the last night as they walked the distance of the barrier all the way to the ocean, trying to determine if there was a way in by sea. I'd spent the early part of the night at the mouth of my cave, gazing at the city and canyon lights, pondering the words of my father, and wondering if I'd ever live in a city such as the one before me, or the fantastical one my father had promised my mother he'd take me to somenight. Things like running water, bathrooms with toilets and showers, kitchens with refrigerators and stoves, not to mention technological gadgets were absolutely foreign to me, no matter how accurately described.

Bad, evil men were also alien to me. The Exiled men could be characterized as rough, but who wouldn't be that way given our living conditions? From my father's tales, those Exiled from Garden City were done so for unjust causes. That night, however, I met face-to-face two very bad men who'd been Exiled for excellent reason.

I saw two figures scrambling up the canyon face towards me, and thinking they were part of my father's group I'd called out to them. But as they got closer I realized they weren't familiar. I immediately recognized their Exile attire, so knew they'd been in the city recently, as every Exiler ditches the orange suit first chance they get. One man stood at least six and a half feet tall, was at least twice as wide as my father, and curly black hair covered his head, neck and arms. His companion had a small build, but a bald head and scruffy gray beard. At first they were friendly and I'd always been taught to be polite, so I invited them into the cave.

"You Exiled like us, Boy?" they'd said.

"My dad was Exiled before I was born, and all our friends are Exiled," I'd responded.

"You live here?" the tall man asked.

"Nope, we live a night's walk from here," I said, wishing my father would return so he could answer their questions.

"Then why are you here all alone?" the small man asked.

"My dad and his friends are out, but should be back soon," I said, even though I had no idea when they would return.

"We'll hang with you and keep you safe, then," they'd said. And stay they did, making small talk and asking questions about Exiled life until my father and friends showed up a couple hours later.

As the group entered the cave and my father called out to me, the big guy grabbed me into a chokehold, my legs flailing beneath me. He threatened to snap my neck if my father didn't do exactly as prescribed. I remember gasping for air, but not being able to suck in enough. It felt like a three hundred pound weight was crushing my chest. Despite all the death I'd seen at a young age, it never occurred to me that kids could die. Or that Exilers could or would even want to kill other Exilers.

Exilers always arrived desperate, greedy, and willing to do anything to survive, so my father had been well versed in proper etiquette for diffusing panic. He greeted them warmly and assured them they were amongst friends and not harsh government dictate. Upon the promise of food, supplies, and lodging to the men, the man released his grip and dropped me to the cave floor.

I scrambled to my father's feet shaking, but my father's eyes stayed trained on the men as his sales pitch continued.

My dad peddled our community as a luxury desert spa, plus promised the men they'd have first dibs on the next ship to bring supplies to Garden City that the Interceptors planned to pirate. The men lapped up the vision of freedom and long-term survival, and then hiked the distance to our caves with us that night. The large man forced me to ride on his shoulders to ensure my dad kept his end of the bargain, but upon getting there and being offered a meal by Doc's Cleave, he'd let me join my sister as he and his cohort ate and surveyed the area. It's not like I could run and escape either of the guys, plus we'd led them to a place with hundreds of potential hostages.

During the meal, the men admitted to being Exiled for murdering an innocent family to steal their things. I could see my father digest the information. His band of misfits meant everything to him and having murderers in the group's midst meant unacceptable risk. He signaled his colleagues behind his back and one left quietly. When asked where the guy had gone, my father lied and said he'd gone to get the Captain of the Interceptors so the men could discuss the upcoming ship raid. The men continued to eat while keeping an eye on easy prey if things went sour.

When my father's friend came back alone, the men got angry and started shouting out threats. My father stepped in front of my sister and me. Leila buried her eyes in my stomach, but I watched the scene unfold. The tall man grabbed my father and dragged him away from us. He began to squeeze my father's throat.

I looked to my father's friend to help. The friend nodded to me and pulled a shiny black object from the back of his pants and pointed it at the tall man. I recognized the black object to be a gun. A split second later, my dad's friend pulled the trigger and a bullet spliced through the bad man's face, splattering blood and brains everywhere. The unsilenced boom echoed through the cave. The sudden sound scared Leila so much that she peed her pants and dug her fingernails into my skin. I kept my arms wrapped tightly around her to keep her from seeing the mess.

It took several seconds for the small man to realize that his partner was dead and that he was on his own. He'd likely never seen a gun before. Once his shock faded and he realized the same fate could befall him, the small man tried to run. Several Exilers blocked his exit from the cave. Trapped, he raised his arms to surrender. My father's friend gave him no mercy, however. He raised his gun again and fired at the small man, hitting him in the chest. Dead on impact, the small man fell into a pool of his own blood.

That was the first time I'd seen a gun used to kill men, but certainly not my last. The gun had been taken during a ship raid from an armed guard. The SCI had added security measures to all boats to discourage Interceptor raids. Although an Interceptor had been killed during the mission, the Exilers relished the score, previously having had to rely on dull knives, poorly fashioned ropes and clubs.

Thankfully, my father had whisked Leila out of the cave before she'd seen the bodies. I wasn't so lucky, as I'd been tasked with cleanup. It took me hours to scoop body fragments and blood-soaked dirt into a bucket by hand. Then, my father forced me to carry the heavy bucket a canyon over to bury alongside the dead bodies. I helped push dirt over the dead men's bodies in a shallow grave before being allowed to return to our cave and sleep in my dirty, bloody state. It wasn't until ten days later that I'd been given the opportunity to bathe.

I'd held Leila tightly each day for months after, recurring daymares haunting me. I woke frequently in pools of sweat as I relived the pressure of the man's arm against my throat and inability to breathe, the same man trying to squeeze the life out of my father, and then the executions of the two men by a close family friend. My dad rationalized the killings as self defense, and even had self-defense not been required, he said the executions were necessary for our community's safety. Judge, juror, and executor. How were my father's band of Exilers any different from those who'd Exiled them?

As I ponder my father's commitment to the Exiler's plight, the more I question his tactics. The adage says, "All is fair in love and war," but should you bank the success of your mission on your seventeen-year-old son? At what point do the rationalizations strip you of your humanity? My hypocrisy slams me in the face. Didn't I just rationalize my own crazy behavior to Kira? Convince myself it was okay to put her in harm's way because the cause came first? Although, doesn't the cause come first? I can't put one girl over the welfare of so many. And it's not like I knew her at the time I made the decision anyway.

The more I try to figure out a win-win solution, the more confused and unsettled I get. It's completely messed up that my fake relationship with Kira is as close to normal as I've ever come. Do I crave the pull of normality or the girl? Regardless of which drives me to question everything I've been raised to believe, I need to reject both and focus. Maybe if I'm still alive when the SCI has been defeated and Exilers and Second Chancers freed I can try to do normal and build a life with someone. Who am I kidding? The thought of being saddled to a Cleave and kids makes my body involuntarily convulse.

For I have sworn thee fair, and thought thee bright, who art black as hell, and dark as night.

William Shakespeare

CHAPTER THIRTEEN

Kira

I close the door to my bedroom and bury myself underneath the covers, not convinced I can ever face Blake again. My thoughts return to the night of Bailey Goodington's party. I'd left without forgiving Tristan and Bri. And look how that turned out. So, I know I need to forgive Blake. But he has a lot to answer for. Blake and Ted Rosenberg used me to get Blake unquestioned access to this hellhole. Worse, Blake manipulated me to trust and like him, all to further his cover.

The Second Chance Institute also needs to answer for their sins. They're behind both the explosion and Blake's terrible childhood. Can you give an entire government the death penalty? And, if I'm for that does it mean I should actively support Blake's cause? I'd certainly never turn him in, but I'm not ready to be a willing soldier either. Blake was trained for years. How could I possibly help him?

Avoidance is my best strategy for now and I have reasonable excuse to do so. My abdomen is swollen to five times its normal size and pain is shooting through my pelvic region as if an untrained acupuncturist assumed it proper to stick the needles in their full length. A gush of blood sends me running into the bathroom and the sight of it causes me to empty my stomach of bile and stomach acid into the sink. Better for the pain meds to take effect quickly, I think, as I reach for the bottle and down one. And, in case that won't knock me out, I swallow a sleeping pill to signal that I'm done with this night.

As my eyes close, my thoughts turn to Ethan and how flawless he seemed. Why do I get attached to the flawed guys and the one perfect one disappears the moment I meet him? I'd swear that was his voice I heard in the clinic. I'm starting to think he may actually be here. I allow myself to focus in on what I remember of his smile and the cute way he rocked back and forth on his feet, and drift off to sleep imagining meeting him again.

I manage to delay my start of classes for 48 hours to allow myself time to fully heal. The doctor pays house calls and assures me that my side effects, although worse than average, are still within normal ranges and that it is all worth it since the procedure was a success. The only time I leave my room is to nibble on the occasional meal when I know Blake is out of the house, not having a huge appetite anyway. I'm such a wimp where confrontation's concerned.

The rest of the time I hide away, trying to make sense of the nightmare I'm living. The holes in the information, the inconsistencies, and the deceptions have torn the fabric of my sanity. The hows and the whys may never be answered. I must move forward, fulfill my contract, and then take my scholarship, leave, and never look back. That's my goal anyway, although I have a growing suspicion that all will not go as smoothly as planned.

I've come to accept that Blake did what he did for a reason. His hand was forced as much as mine, his by his father and childhood, mine when the SCI decided to blow up my friends and remove my reason for staying my senior year. That doesn't make it any easier for me to sit down and work through my issues with Blake. Or for me to accept the situation I'm in. Thinking that the explosion had been an accident had certainly been traumatic and terrible. But learning that the SCI caused the accident just to get me here? The guilt's killing me. All that blood on my hands.

My evening's online classes are dreadfully boring, and I'm antsy to get out into the canyon again, as our sunroom isn't sufficient to walk off the bundle of nerves I've accumulated. Sitting next to Blake all evening has been torture, but I managed to put on my headphones and turn away. When free time starts I'm the first one out the door. To my disappointment, in a moment of sheer insanity where I forget that I'm on Thera, I expect to see sun and am greeted by a sea of darkness, swimming bits of artificial light, and Tristan and Bri. I resign myself to my misery and walk forward to greet them.

Bri gives me a hug, being careful to avoid my mid-section.

"So the princess is finally allowed to leave her castle," Tristan says. "We've missed you. Your BFF Blake isn't as fun to be around as you are, probably because I beat him at everything. And I mean everything! Come on, we'll walk you down, since I'm assuming you didn't master boarding on bed rest?" Blake's behind me and hears every word Tristan says, which I'm sure was intentional on

Tristan's part.

"Ha ha. No, I didn't," I say. I look over towards Blake, who speeds away on his skateboard without word to any of us.

"Trouble in paradise?" Tristan asks as we start walking.

"Paradise is lost," I say. Mumbling, I add, "Or misplaced at least."

"What happened?" Bri says, looking shocked and worried.

"Seriously," Tristan says. "You wanted to Cleave and he couldn't deliver?"

I ignore Tristan's crude remark and address Bri. "I guess I suck as a patient and he wasn't being very empathetic," I say, as close to honesty as I can muster, since I am a crappy patient and he showed zero empathy for me when he decided my life was worth less than his. No, that's not fair. We'd both be dead had he told me the truth up front and I probably wouldn't have believed him anyway. Given the rumors about Blake at the time, I'd have just thought he'd been partaking too liberally of some hallucinogens.

"Well then, next time you need a better caretaker," Tristan says, smiling and putting his hand on my shoulder. But he quickly realizes his mistake of doing so in front of Bri and adds, "I'll send Bri over. Guys are no good at dealing with girl stuff."

"Girls aren't good at dealing with girl stuff either," Bri says. "I'm sorry—I tried to stop by a couple times, but was rejected by Blake and that odd man with the huge head that seems to be at your house a lot."

"Thanks for trying. I was pretty much wailing and whining in my room, so you didn't miss much," I say.

"Sounds like you need a distraction," Tristan says. "Good thing we're hosting a dinner party at our house this morn and as our guest of honor your presence is mandatory." Huh, I wonder if Tristan found a stash of standard-issue alcohol on Thera after all, or if my friends have taken up Pictionary or some other wholesome form of entertainment. I'd bet on a stash. My friends suck at wholesome.

"You're right. A distraction sounds perfect. I'll be there. What time?" I ask.

"Right after we work out," Bri says. "Can we invite Blake? Or would that be too weird for you?"

"Yeah. Of course you should. I'll be fine," I say. I can't avoid him forever, nor do I think I really want to. He's my best source of information here and I plan to suck every last drop from him.

The rest of our walk goes quickly, but unpleasantly due to the discomfort of keeping my abs engaged as we climb downhill. I kick a couple lights on the way in disgust at their constant reminder of my sunless prison.

We arrive at the common area in time for Tristan to get talked into an impromptu game of basketball. Bri and I take a seat at the edge of the flat area, overlooking the lights of the canyon and shortly thereafter, Bailey joins us. She looks like she spent extra time primping today, and that she may have modified her uniform to show more cleavage. Not in the mood for her antics, I watch Blake's shadowy figure use one of the hilly paths as a makeshift half-pipe, doing various tucks, grabs and turns that I've only ever seen on television. If the powers that be are watching, I wonder how long it'll take him to get busted for boarding rather than spying on the lab rats.

"So what really happened between you two?" Bri asks me. To Bailey, Bri says, "They had a fight." Super. Bailey will be all over him. As if she hasn't been already.

"Blake's a great guy, but we see things differently and I'm having a hard time accepting his point of view," I say, since sharing the truth will never be an option.

"So you had a big blowout about it?" Bri asks.

"No. I don't handle the whole confrontation thing very well. We just stopped talking. I've been avoiding him. Which, I know is ridiculous," I say.

Bailey pipes in, "I'm not surprised you're clueless about how to handle this kind of thing, Kira. You got it part way right with the no talking. But where you failed—you forgot about the more touching. And rubbing. And kissing. Less clothes. I'm thinking shower and soap and some of that Theranberry oil…"

"Stop," I say. "That's disgusting."

"And that would be why you are incapable of keeping a boyfriend," Bailey responds.

"How would you know? And who says I'm not keeping him. We're just having a small disagreement," I snap.

"Oh, I know you, Kira," Bailey sneers. "Or at least girls like you. Miss Goody-Freaking-Ugly-Shoes. You're good at snagging the guys, because they all want to taint the whole innocent act you've got going on. But when you don't put out, they go looking elsewhere." If I didn't know any better, I'd swear she was talking about Tristan. Since, I'm pretty sure Blake hasn't been getting anything on the side of our fake deal. He's too freaked about accidentally Cleaving, just like me.

"Get. Your. Own. Boyfriend, why don't you?" I say. "Mine is taken."

"He's always been my boyfriend, Kira. He just doesn't realize it yet," Bailey says. "He will, though, I assure you."

"Gads, Bailey. You're seriously PMSing today," Bri says. To me, "You sure you can't talk it through with him and work it out? I still think you guys'd make great Cleaves and have wicked cute babies." I know the reason she's asking. The thought of me being on the market must have her panicked. Little does she have to fear. Tristan's toast and not so dear. Ha. I crack myself up.

"We'll eventually work it out, but I wouldn't start planning any baby showers," I say. Bailey smirks, but Bri looks at me oddly, and I realize she may no longer know what a baby shower is, so she's probably picturing babies falling from the sky.

We watch as Blake abruptly screeches to a stop in the canyon, his board flying up and nearly scalloping Spud Rosenberg's head. They're too far for me to hear the conversation, but with Spud's animated arm waving and Blake's defensive body language I can imagine the tone. Blake wasn't sent here to improve his boarding skills, but to befriend and spy on the Second Chancers, and his anti-social stance is contrary to the Plan. I see him glance at us before pushing off and heading our way.

"Ladies," he says with a nod to Bri and Bailey, before taking a left towards a group of guys.

"Hold on, Blake," Bailey says. "Not so fast. Come here, I have to ask you something." Blake looks a little fearful, but stops and waits for her to approach him.

Bailey puts her hands on his chest and rubs him up and down suggestively. "We're having a dinner party at Bri and Tristan's house this morn. You have to come," she says and then she whispers something in his ear that makes him turn beet red. Blake's eyes shift first to Bailey's lips, then to me, and then to Spud Rosenberg who is making his way up the hill before he looks back at Bailey and answers. She probably mentioned the oil in the shower thing and he kind of looks like he's considering her proposition.

"Sure. Sounds, uh, exciting," he says. "I'll see you there," looking Bailey directly in the eyes, which causes a visible swoon to occur. Even Briella looks affected. This isn't lost on Tristan who caught sight of the exchange from the nearby basketball court and exits to come protect his interests. Not wanting to watch Bailey and Bri ogle Blake any longer, I depart for the gym early, hoping to get changed and on a treadmill before the masses. There's no way my sore body can handle Tristan's circuit or the subsequent hate that'd be directed towards me if I agreed to a repeat of the other night.

Seeing the density of kids packed into Tristan and Bri's small home makes me shudder with discomfort, not because I'm unhappy to have plenty of distractions from Blake and Tristan, but because the last party I went to with these same people didn't end so well. The dining table is heaped with goodies and the kitchen filled with bottled waters and soft drinks. Seemingly tame, but something's off, because it's only a half hour in and kids are already pairing up and slurring words. What did I miss? I wasn't that late, only stopping home to take some pain meds, and psych myself up for the event by watching the sunrise from our sunroom.

I must have missed the memo about wearing party attire, probably because I didn't realize the skimpy stuff in my dresser was earmarked for that purpose and not some sleazy swimsuit photo shoot. The girls' outfits make our workout attire look modest, consisting of a sparkly gold tube top and an itty-bitty green tube skirt. The boys' attire is somewhat better, though still right out of some seventies' disco movie, with a shirtless gold vest and tight shimmery green pants.

Art skills are being put to use painting bodies, with what I hope to be temporary greenish-blue tattoos. Bri shows me the technique. Then has me practice on her. I'm able to apply a quick Garden Valley High logo to her exposed shoulder blade.

If the Grand Council were to stop by I'd envision a whole new host of rules would be born, unless they know and look the other way to encourage as many Cleavings to happen as possible.

I head towards the kitchen to find a drink, but when I see Blake practically drooling at Bailey's cleavage while she whispers more not-so-sweet nothings into his ear, I promptly turn around.

"Darn," I hear behind me. "I was looking forward to seeing you in… less." I turn to see Tristan, who appears to be imagining me in less than less. "Want a drink?" he says, offering me a glass.

"What is it?" I ask about the drink, studying his face. His eyes betray the fact that he's partaken of some mind-altering substance, which I want no part of. My pain meds have already kicked in enough to make me a little loopy.

"Relax," he says, as he hands me the cup. "It's just Theranberry juice." I smell it and it certainly doesn't smell like alcohol, but sip it warily regardless. Its flavor is strong, but pleasant like its scent, closest to Hawaiian passionfruit with a hint of berry and citrus. Despite my thirst there's no way I'm going to down it quickly until I know how Tristan and the others got their "high." Lucas and a pack of inebriated friends come over to bro-hug Tristan and nod their approval at our conversation, before making a kitchen run.

"Thanks for the drink," I say, raising my glass and looking around. "This is quite the rager. Are all your parties like this?"

"Everyone's got to eat, right?" he says. "We might as well have fun doing it. Let me show you around," he adds, motioning me forward, as if his house layout isn't identical to my own.

"Looks familiar," I say.

"Not the artwork," he says, taking my hand and leading me back towards the bedrooms. Crap, I do not want to be alone with my dead ex-boyfriend, particularly when his restraints are loosened. He ushers some kids out and closes the door behind us. "The painting's incredible, isn't it?" Not really, I think. Looks like a kindergartner tackled this mural, although I'm sure someone would label it modern art.

"It is different," I say, immediately turning around and towards the door. "I should get back out there and get to know more people." And make sure Bailey hasn't convinced Blake to Cleave her yet.

"What's your hurry? You have yet to get to know me and I promise you that I'm the most interested person here in getting to know you. Particularly now that you've dumped your loser boyfriend," he says, pinning me with my back to the door. I squirm and grimace at his proximity, but he leans in to try to entrance me. Doesn't work. Whatever he's on has sucked the luster right out of his eyes. And his breath's fruity, but too strong, reminding me of his drinking days.

"Blake's not a loser and this is not the way to get to know me," I say, feeling woozier than I should.

"You must be popping something stronger than TB to think that Blake has any redeeming value. He's a loner with zero social skills," he says, eyes lasered on me.

"Ugh. Please back up," I say, pushing him far enough to wedge my way around him. "You don't know the first thing about him, or me. And the only thing I've 'popped' is pain meds for my abdominal pain. What's TB?"

"Fine, defend the boy with the itsy-bitsy cleaver. You'll come around to my way of thinking when you see what he's not packing," he chuckles as he traps me again and pushes my hair away from my eyes. "And TB is chill. Don't worry about it."

I ignore the insult to Blake's manhood, since I doubt Tristan has firsthand knowledge. There's no love lost there. "Did you drug me?" I say. "What's in here?" I ask, sloshing my drink around my cup, before setting it down atop his dresser and vowing to never accept another drink from him that isn't in a closed container. From his expression, he confirms my worst fears.

"I didn't drug you—just gave you some of what we're all having. You just need to loosen up a little and have some fun," he says. He leans towards me, trying to work the smoldering eyes. "You are so beautiful. Can I kiss you?" I guess he must take my silence as agreement as he closes the distance. The move, altogether too familiar, fails as I turn my head in time for him to suck cheek. Just then the door opens to a very angry looking Briella and Blake. Bailey's behind them and looks thrilled to see my tenuous situation.

"In our house? Right under my nose? Really?" Briella says to both of us.

Tristan shifts nervously. "Uh. Well. Uh. She's been all over me." It comes across as a question instead of a statement. I roll my eyes, push him away again, and shuffle towards the door. My legs move robotically, the drugs hampering with my motor function. As I respond my words slur together.

"He's wasted. He gave me some juice that does not mix well with pain medicine. Nothing happened, nor would it have, despite the roofie. But you guys can believe whatever you want. I'm going home. Thanks for the party, Bri. Sorry about this whole deal."

"You drugged her?" Blake says, pushing Tristan against the wall. Tristan reacts by swinging his right arm towards Blake's jaw, which Blake avoids Matrix-style, before landing a hook of his own in Tristan's gut. This has little effect on Tristan who charges Blake full throttle, albeit impaired by whatever he imbibed. Blake sidesteps just enough to get the advantage and flip Tristan onto his back, knocking the wind out of him. Blake stands over Tristan and says, "You try it again and I'll have no issue facing Exile to make you pay. Understand?"

Tristan doesn't bother getting up. Still flat on his back and with belabored breath he says, "What's your problem? Both of you? It was just a little TB juice —not powder—and she barely had any. Besides, everyone gets teebed here and I had no freaking idea she'd downed pain meds before showing. The juice should have been harmless. I was just trying to get to know her a little better. It's not like I was going to Cleave her! I just wanted to kiss her and see if we had chemistry." Yeah, we *had* chemistry. Past tense. He simultaneously signs and says, "Forgive me, Bri. I was an idiot. I'm so sorry."

Blake gets in Tristan's face. "I couldn't give a crap what everyone else does. We don't do TB or anything like it, understand? And it's not harmless when you don't ask first." Blake then turns to Bri. "TB, teebed—what is it?"

"It's not real kosher to talk outside our group, understand?" she says to him.

"Spill," Blake says, putting a hand on her shoulder. "I won't mention it to anyone."

"The Theranberry bushes in the canyon… The boys figured out the berries and roots give a good buzz. When they're on it they're 'teebed.' So we always have the juice and root powder on hand for parties. It livens things up, but I've never seen someone react the way Kira has—it must be because of her meds. Typically the juice just relaxes people. The powder's a whole lot stronger," she says, likely referring to the fact I've become as flexible and useful as a wet noodle. Unable to walk, I slump into a pile on the floor. Blake looks even more furious now that the ruse has been explained. He starts towards Tristan, leg up as if he's going to stomp on him, but upon giving me a gander he thinks the better of it.

"I'm going to take her home. She'll never get there by herself," Blake says as he scoops me into his arms.

"Sorry," Bri says. I attempt to wave to her as we leave.

Blake carries me home and promptly dumps me onto my bed. In my uninhibited state he's looking pretty darn attractive and appealing.

"Don't leave," I say.

"What?" he says in an angry tone, though he leans over me to make sure I'm not having a medical issue.

"I want you... to stay..." I say, still slurring my words.

"No," he says, getting up to leave. Not content to let him go, I try to get out of bed to stop him, and instead lurch head first towards the floor, forcing him to catch me. We both end up on the floor and I'm in his arms as intended. I reach my hands up under his shirt to feel his chest, and attempt to deliver a passionate kiss, but he turns his head and all I get is a mouthful of ear.

"Stop it, Kira," he says. "This isn't cool. You don't get to go from hating me to mauling me, nor would you had Tristan not given you that juice."

"You saved me," I say, words still slurred. "You're my hero. Let me give you a proper thank you." I try to kiss him again, but he pulls away, and then hefts me back up onto the bed. I land with a thump.

"Sleep it off. If you still remember when you're sober we can discuss things. But my bet's on you still hating me in the evening."

"I won't, I swear. You're the guy for me, Ethan. I've known it from the moment I met you," I say. "We could Cleave," I add, wanting him more than ever, though that may be the drugs, I'm not sure. Is it Blake or Ethan that's here? And did I just call Blake, Ethan? It sure looked like Ethan.

"Good day, Kira," he says, slamming the door behind him as he leaves. Wow, Tristan wouldn't have blown me off like that. He'd have Cleaved me. But no, ugh, Tristan was repulsive tonight. Come back, Blake or Ethan or whoever you are. Please come back.

"Holy freaking crap. A suicide bomber just detonated a bomb in my brain," I say to myself as I rummage through the fridge for some juice, my throat so dry it could disintegrate at any moment. The orange juice I find doesn't make a dent in my thirst or headache.

"She speaks," Blake says, looking me in the eye for the first time in nights, although he looks a little angry.

"Yeah, but you shouldn't. At least not so loudly. What happened last morn? I remember being at that freak show party and then Tristan giving me a drink and a tour," I say, pausing to try to remember, but the concentration just sets off another blast in my head. "Nope, nothing but pain," I say to myself.

"Well, I've got good news and bad news," he says, gritting his teeth. "The good news is you won't have to play house with me anymore."

"Say what? Why?" I say, confused as to whether that truly constitutes good news. Despite his betrayal, he's the only thing here that gives me hope of returning to Earth. And before he betrayed me, I had some semi-positive feelings developing for him.

"Well, that's where I deliver the bad news—or maybe you won't see it that way. In your intoxicated state last night you Cleaved to Tristan, so you're now a full citizen of Thera and can live happily ever after with him and your to-be-assigned kids. You can teach 'em how to be self-righteous and Tristan can whip them into shape with that 'killer' circuit of his."

I got drunk? Cleaved to Tristan? Am stuck here forever? The horror slams me like a pro boxing knockout punch, and I slump to the floor and curl into a ball, rocking myself back and forth, attempting to sob but too dehydrated to get any tears to flow. How many times did Tristan try to convince me to give in to him back on Earth, to which my reply was always "no"? And now, I chose to do it drunk and don't even remember?

How did I let it happen? And why didn't Bri or Blake stop me? Or maybe they knew and looked the other way. Since Blake assumes I hate him over his betrayal, he probably figured it would happen sooner or later, so might as well get it over with and get rid of me so that he won't have to watch out for me while carrying out his plans.

"Anyway," he says. "Congratulations, I guess. I'm going to get started on my classes. I made waffles if you're hungry. And, here's something for your headache," he says, handing me a couple pills and a glass of water.

"Thanks for the pills. It's a great substitute for the pre-Cleaving intervention you should've done last morn. I guess you were too busy trying to sail down the Cleaving path with Bailey to notice," I mumble, but he just chuckles and leaves the room. The situation's so not funny, I think, but he must think I deserve it.

I stay on the floor for twenty minutes, allowing my headache to dull, and then grab a waffle and join Blake in the living room to start my classes. But first, I swivel his chair towards me and yank his earphones off.

"How did it happen, Blake? I wouldn't do something like that and I don't even drink. Why can't I remember anything? What's going to happen now? How will I explain to my parents that I can never come home? Did Tristan… did he, take advantage?" I ask, staring into his eyes and wondering how I could have possibly fallen subject to Tristan's charms when Blake was at that house.

"How would I know, Kira? You haven't exactly been buddy-buddy with me since you uh, dumped me." Huh? It's not like we were really dating, but yeah, I guess those listening don't know that. "I had to find out from Bri what you and Tristan were up to," he says, looking some combination of angry, sad, and smug.

"Oh no," I say, covering my head with my arms. "Bri must hate me. And who could blame her? I certainly hate me right now." *How will I ever face her again? Or Tristan? He'll be able to tell immediately how disappointed I am and that won't exactly start things off on the right foot.*

"Well, as much as I'd love to chitchat all night about this, I'm going to get back to my work, and I suggest you do the same thing if you don't want to re-consummate your Cleaving on Exiled ground," he says, pulling his earphones back over his ears and turning his chair away from me.

Time crawls the next few hours as I attempt to pay attention to my schoolwork, while trying to think of any loophole out of my current predicament. Blake doesn't glance my way once and retreats to his room at lunch to avoid further conversation. By the time we're cleared to leave for break I dread opening the door. Thankfully neither Tristan nor Bri await me. Blake exits on his board with a terse "see ya there," and I make my way down the path towards the common area as slowly as possible, not wanting to face anyone. Of course, that's impossible. Students—some I know from Earth, some I've met here, others I still haven't gotten to know—are everywhere. I dodge engaging in more than some basic pleasantries. As I approach the outdoor hangout spot, Tristan walks down the path to meet me.

"Hey," he says, eyes staring at his feet as if he's embarrassed. "I'm really sorry about last morn. It was a jerk move. I was wasted and just wanted to get to know you a little better, but let it go too far. I hope you'll be able to forgive me somenight. I'm really not that bad of a guy, but I know I've come across like it. I just got so caught up in the 'figuring out the right Cleave before it was done for me thing' that I screwed up." He honestly seems as distraught as I am over it.

"I… I just don't even know what to say Tristan. Can we talk about it later? I am just trying to get a handle on it, you know, and need some time," I respond. *In fact, I'll need a lot of time—like a decade or two.*

"Sure, fine, I totally get it. Thanks for hearing me out. I don't blame you for not wanting to talk about it," he says, continuing to look downward at his shuffling feet. I've never seen Tristan so humble and penitent about anything. I guess facing a lifetime with someone who doesn't want to be with you would do that to a guy.

"I know we eventually need to talk it through, but as I said, I just need some time," I say. He looks so hurt and I feel terrible that I'm causing him pain, but can't help it. *I can't accept what I've done and what it means. Cleaved to the former dead guy. How do I explain to our future kids why I look at him like he's a ghost, zombie, or some other creature from a horror flick?*

"Yeah, well okay, bye then," he says, walking towards the canyon and not back to the common area. Bri has been viewing our exchange from above and I can tell she's not going to let me walk by without a conversation. I approach cautiously; worried that she might just deck me for Cleaving her boyfriend in her own house. She motions me over to her table and I take a seat.

"Well, have you recovered from your big morning?" Bri says, eyes stabbing my heart.

"No, I don't think I'll ever recover," I say, unable to meet her glare.

"I trusted you," she says. "And yet you followed my boyfriend into his bedroom." This I vaguely remember. He wanted to show me his wall art, but all I recall is my desire to leave, not stay, and certainly not hook up.

"I'm so sorry. He was giving me a tour. I just never expected... Oh gosh, I'm just horrified Bri," I say, shaking my head in shame. "You must hate me. Absolutely hate me."

"I don't hate you. I already told you that I understood why he'd go after you. But what he did still sucks and I'm not ready to forgive him for it," she says. Is she honestly letting me off the hook? It takes two to Cleave. Surely I must have allowed it to happen and should be held equally responsible. When she and Tristan kissed at the Goodington's party I was furious. And that was over a kiss! She always was the better friend in our pairing.

"I hate me," I say. "The whole thing sucks. Just really freaking sucks."

"How'd Blake take it? He was pretty pissed last morn," she says. "I thought he was going to kill Tristan in that fight. He didn't, but sure humiliated him." Fight? What fight? Blake didn't tell me they'd fought. He acted like he didn't care that I'd Cleaved Tristan this evening, but he must have if Blake attacked Tristan. Too bad he didn't do that *before* the Cleaving.

"He seemed pretty indifferent to it all," I say, disappointed that it's the truth and still pissed that he didn't intervene.

"You are insane if you think for one second that Blake's indifferent to you. If you search for 'smitten' on your tablet, you're going to find his picture," she says.

"I doubt that's still the case under the circumstances," I respond, looking around for Blake, tears coming to my eyes at the thought of losing him forever, despite what he's done. "He was all over Bailey last night."

"Hardly! Bailey was the one mauling him. Blake bursts into Tristan's room to save you after Tristan gives you some Theranberry juice, fights for your honor, and then carries you home like a freaking princess, and you think he's into Bailey and not you? Geez girl, what's it going to take for you to Cleave to that boy?" Hold on. Did I hear her correctly? I can't Cleave to Blake if I already Cleaved to Tristan. My mouth's gaped open and I might as well have been struck by lightning given the shock I'm feeling.

"Uh wait. Say again. Last morn's still a little fuzzy for me," I say.

"I bet, given the state we found you in. Your painkillers didn't mix with Tristan's cocktail. Tristan was trying to kiss you when we came in. Blake decked him and then downed him before telling him if he ever tried it again he'd gladly risk Exile to get revenge. And then he carried you home and put you to bed. Your boyfriend is the ultimate gentleman, unlike mine."

Oh my freaking fake boyfriend. He was messing with me. I scan for the offender and see him talking to some boys and watching our conversation intently. How should I handle this?

CHAPTER FOURTEEN

Blake

Well, she doesn't look pissed, so she must not have figured it out yet, though I'm not sure how that's possible after talking to both Tristan and Bri. I don't know what possessed me to lie to her and tell her she'd Cleaved to Tristan, but after what she pulled last morn I feel justified. She shunned me for three nights after I confessed my sins without a single chance for me to explain or discuss it. And then she begs me to sleep next to her? Cleave to her? And calls me Ethan? When did she meet him? And fall for him enough to know he was "the one" from the moment they met? Granted she was on the TB plus pain killer express, but it still messed with me. Kept me up all day. Well, that and I can't seem to get some of Bailey's "offers" out of my mind. But, I'm too smart to cave, since I know what happens after things go sour and I'm not in the mood to have Bailey's "punishments" derail my plans for the SCI.

When Kira told me that last night was one big black hole, I filled in the blanks with a little misinformation. A harmless joke, or okay, maybe it wasn't so harmless since she looks like hell just froze over and she's stuck in the ice. She'll figure it out soon enough and that should get her blood flowing enough to reignite hell's fiery furnaces. If she were as evil as Bailey, I'd have to be worried about what Kira would dish back, but she's too nice to play dirty. Shame, really.

Perhaps if I could go skate the canyons rather than entertain the dead kids I'd be in better spirits, but Ted banned me from it. Yesternight I'd been getting some air that would turn a skate pro's head when Ted interrupted. He told me that my wings were clipped until I learned to be a proper social butterfly. That really fouled my mood and then to have to go to that whacked party, and find Tristan all over Kira, well, I flipped. That jerk has been testing my patience all week. Basketball, baseball, football, lacrosse, weights… it all has to be a freaking contest. When I suggested we go board or do some long distance running he laughed in my face, saying that it figured I'd pick stuff meant for loners with no friends.

Justified or not, I'm feeling guilty for my prank on Kira. Some part of me thought she'd be relieved at the notion of being reunited with her lost true love and being able to ditch me and my mess. Instead, she appears heartbroken and disgusted at the thought of a life with Tristan. Go figure.

Crap, she just looked my way. I'm toast. She's coming over. Best to just fess up and take the heat. Strangely though, she's still wearing the downtrodden body language, head bowed and shaking in disbelief. I clench my teeth as she approaches. I'm going to have to tell her. And there may very well be violence involved when I do.

"Could we walk?" she says. "I need to talk to you."

"Uh, yeah, sure, I guess," I mumble, following her down a steep trail, through the strobing lights, and to the bottom of the canyon.

"Sit with me," she says. "I'm still shaky." I do and she sits facing me Indian-style, her knees touching mine.

"I saw you talked to Tristan and Bri. How'd that go?" I say, not sure I want to hear the answer, but glance up to peek at her.

"Awkward on both fronts," she says. "Tristan apologized. I told him I needed time to get my head around the magnitude of it. And Bri, well she forgave me, which was hard for me to hear. She says you got me out of there afterwards, so thank you for that. It sounds like I was in no state to handle things myself." To this I can't respond or lift my eyes to meet hers, my guilt ulcering my gut like Swiss cheese. I definitely took my joke too far.

"Before they make me move in with Tristan, I needed to talk to you, to apologize to you for how I reacted the other night. Given the situation it's a lot to ask, but will you hear me out?" She pulls up my chin and looks into my eyes and I want to crawl under the cement floor of this canyon and rot. But instead I nod because I want to hear what she has to say. Need to know how she plans to handle what I told her. If she turns me in I'm Exiled at best, executed at worst.

"I am so freaked out, Blake," she says. "The thought of spending the rest of my life with Tristan here is, well, unbearable. I don't want to get into all the complications of my relationship with him, but I just don't know if I can do it. How can I spend a lifetime with someone I can't even be honest with? And who cheated on me back on Earth? I don't even know what I ever saw in him at this point. He's such a tool now that it's hard to remember the good stuff." She's shaking her head and staring at a line of ants a stone's throw away.

"But, my real problem and the real reason I can't do it is you," she says, looking back towards me. "My brain's been going full throttle since you told me everything and I admit I am angry and betrayed and hurt, but I need you to know that I do understand why you did it. You were stuck. Once they chose me, if you'd given me warning, we'd both be dead. I get that. It would've been impossible for me to fake my reaction when I saw Tristan and Bri had I known ahead of time. Besides, I chose to come here." She pauses. Maybe I haven't given her enough credit. She understands why I did it and even takes responsibility for her part in it? And I've gone and screwed it up worse by telling her yet another lie.

"So, Blake, I forgive you. I'm sorry it took me so long to tell you, that I shut you out, but it always takes me a while to work through stuff in my head." I never thought she'd forgive me; expected she'd hate me forever.

"But here's the most important part, because despite everything you've done, I'm going to ask for more. I have no right to ask this, but I need to anyway. Your mission here is now my mission. If you can't succeed—if you can't save the Exilers, and everyone here—well then I'm doomed to an eternity in hell. I need you to get me out of here, and preferably sooner, rather than later. If I need to, I'll get myself Exiled and hope to meet up with the others, but I can't play Tristan's life partner under any circumstances." She pauses and looks me directly in the eye with a look so predatory, I shift uncomfortably. Has Bailey been giving her lessons or what? "I can't pretend to love him when I'm pretty sure that you're the only one I have feelings for."

Her words penetrate me with the force of a cannon ball. Kira Donovan, the girl I once believed to be a vapid cheerleader, the girl who tried to seduce me under the influence last night, just told me that she has real feelings for me. What do I say to that? Crap. I don't do feelings. Not anymore. Especially mushy ones. She senses I'm not going to respond, sighs, and continues.

"Once I figured out I could forgive you the rest came easy to me. I'd always planned to wait for someone I could see spending my life with, someone I could give every part of myself to without hesitation or regret. I never felt that way with Tristan, which is why I never gave in to him back on Earth. In fact, I stayed sober so that I'd never even be tempted. With you, I'm tempted. Really tempted. So when you told me I'd Cleaved Tristan, everything snapped into place. I realized I'd destroyed the only future that could ever make me happy. I vowed to only ever be with one man, but I'm going to have to break that vow because I only want to ever be with you."

Okay, now I'm really tripping. She looks like she wants to eat me whole. The feelings thing freaked me out, but now she's decided I'm the only future that will ever make her happy? No expectations there, buddy. I am so freaking screwed. The pressure cooker is going to explode because I can't take any more.

I inch back a bit and open my mouth to speak, but she closes the gap and puts two fingers to my lips to silence me so she can continue.

"I'm really, really sorry to dump all this on you. I know it's so unfair given what I did with Tristan last morn, even if I don't remember it. But I don't want him. I want you, really, really want you. So badly that I'm not sure I can hold back from kissing you and feeling you in my arms, even if that means they Exile me for Adultery." She leans forward, pushing me back against the cement, stretches her body atop me and stares at me with those freaking gorgeous eyes before pressing her lips to mine. Stopping her action isn't possible because my body takes control from my brain. I roll her underneath me and return her kisses with fervor, thankful for the relative darkness of our location. It's not nuclear bomb action, but man it feels good.

After mere moments she pulls away from me, a fearful look in her eyes. She rolls out from under me and sits up to canvass the scene.

"Why haven't they come to get me?" she says, panicked. "What I did was cause for immediate Exile. I don't get it." She looks to me for answers.

Not quite in control of my faculties, I stand and face her. "Uh, uh, uh," I say. My heart pounds harder than it would with a fast run up a steep canyon. Suddenly, a huge grin washes across her face.

"Actually, that's a lie," she says. "As was the majority of the tale I just told you. But, I think I should let you try to sort out what's fact and what's fiction. Kind of like you let me do. But, then again, your story this evening was all fiction."

"Oh, gads. You figured it out." I finally say, a sheepish gape plastering my face. "Of course you did. You always do." I pause to let it sink in. "But, you retaliated. With kissing?"

"All part of the revenge plan," she says. With a laugh she adds, "And, well, you seemed to rather enjoy that part."

I can feel the blood rush to my face. "That kiss sure felt real, whether it was part of your wicked plan or not. In fact, it was pretty hot." I can't believe I just admitted that to her.

She bites her lip and looks at me through her long eyelashes in a fairly coy fashion that has me wanting to grab her and repeat the act in question. "I'm a *very* good actress. But anyway, it's time to go work out," she says, pointing to her watch and hopping up. "Don't ever lie to me again, Blake, or we'll have some real issues. I'm sure you meant it as a joke, but you let it go too far by letting me leave our house thinking I was Cleaved to Tristan."

"It wasn't a joke. If you want me to be honest, I'll be honest. I was trying to hurt you, because you hurt me. You promised you'd have my back no matter what, but completely cut me off and acted like you hate me. And then after nights of nothing, you freaking tried to seduce me into Cleaving you last morn after I pried that jerk off you. And," she cuts me off before I can tell her that she called me Ethan. Ethan! How and where did she meet him? We are always together. And yet, somehow she met the guy and he made enough of an impression that she's begs me to Cleave to her thinking I'm him. Her eyes go wide and she perches her hands on her hips like chicken wings.

"In my drug-induced state I try to get you to Cleave to me and somehow that warrants you telling me I'm Cleaved to Tristan? That's seriously deluded thinking. I never said I hated you or didn't have your back," she says.

"You just went all psycho clingy chick on me! You seriously freaked me out," I mumble. "You told me I was completely freaking responsible for your future happiness."

"You did tell me I was Cleaved for life to my dead ex-boyfriend and doomed to stay here on Thera. I think a little payback was in order and I didn't let you suffer near as long as you let me suffer," she says, pausing as if to think again. Her lips part slightly and all I can think about is how I'd like to part them with my tongue. Get it together, dude. You need her back on your side. And not by using your rusty seduction skills.

"I just need to know if you can get past everything I omitted before we came to Thera," I say.

She paces back and forth for a minute before answering. "I'm not happy, but I do get why you did what you did and I can probably even get past it. And I am super grateful to you and Bri for getting me away from Tristan before things did get out of hand, because if what you lied about had come true, I would have done something extreme to get Exiled, whether it meant my death or not. And despite your many, many, many faults, I do have feelings for you, but what are they? Like? Hate? Distrust? Fear? A bit of attraction? All those?" she says, counting off each one on her fingers, pausing between words. "Heck, I don't know." Thank goodness she left "love" off the table.

"Now *that* is something where I can say right back at you." No need to tell her that I might order the list a bit differently, but I'd replace the attraction with plain old lust and put it at the top of my list. In fact, something Bailey mentioned about whipped cream, cherries and hot fudge could sweeten things up at home with Kira.

"Okay then," she says. "Let's go exercise." Not what I had in mind, but I guess we can revisit this particular action-packed conversation later.

"Okay then," I respond, and we slowly march up the hill towards the gym. "One question though. Why'd you call me Ethan? How do you even know him?"

"Ethan?" she says, stopping cold and turning towards me. Even in the darkness I can see her face go pale. "What are you talking about?"

"Never mind," I mumble.

"Do *you* know an Ethan?" she asks.

"Well yeah. The Intern dude. I've run into him a couple times," I say.

"There's an Intern here named Ethan? What does he look like?" she asks.

"A little taller than me and a couple years older. Dark hair. Blue eyes. Looks like he could shave multiple times a day and still have stubble. Really into some chick he met at a party," I say. She looks like she might faint. "So you know him?"

"Huh. I haven't run into an Intern named Ethan on Thera," she says, but she won't look me in the eye. Her head is twitching ever so slightly. Can't tell if she's shaking it or having some sort of seizure. So she doesn't know him? I'm so confused.

"So why'd you call me Ethan?" I say, repeating my question.

"Sorry," she says, completely turning away, feet moving. She doesn't explain any further.

A muted explosion in the distance catches my attention, the light from it appearing no brighter than a bottle rocket set off on the Fourth of July. Had I not been trained to expect it, I probably wouldn't have noticed, given the canyon light show. Kira didn't seem to. I try to gauge the exact direction, and my best estimate without a compass would be that it had been launched approximately three to four miles northeast of our current location. Without question, this means my Dad has returned to Thera and is stationed at a resistance camp he'd established in anticipation of my deployment here.

Because of the changing tides and steep cliffs descending to the beach his team determined the Eco barrier to be weakest at the Northeast corner. The location had added benefits of harboring no Garden City population, only the desalinization plant to the immediate south, and main port farther south of that. If I memorized the city model correctly, the canyon we live in meanders that direction before exiting through a narrow passage into the ocean just north of the desalinization plant. So, technically, I could skate the distance, jog the beach and get within shouting distance of my father. I'm sure he is expecting this.

The last time I'd discussed the plan with my father was after we'd met with Ted to sign the SCI paperwork. Ted had explained the nuts and bolts of what to expect: a week of training, followed by meeting the Second Chancers, and settling into our role as fellow students and amateur psychologists. Given the SCI's strong interest in Kira and me due to our DNT levels, Ted thought they'd go all out on selling the Garden City experience. The hope was that we'd be given access to the scale model of the city, which they'd use to sell career options, but is actually used to track residents and plan the Eco barrier pattern.

My father once toured the Garden City model. The night he'd visited, a munitions' specialist happened to be testing a section of the detonators used in the model. They'd been having some issues with small animals on the Eco barrier and wanted to make some tweaks to improve the system to only detonate at certain weight levels. My father saw a pattern in the triggers, but at the time had no reason to commit it to memory, having been early in his career when he was still gung ho on the SCI vision.

Several vantage points from the scaled city were predicted to give me a reasonable "aerial" view of the model Eco barrier, and its chemical detonators. The triggers had been painted to mirror the soil color, but had a different sheen. So, in the right lighting, the pattern could be discerned. Their prediction held true. While Kira had been occupied checking out her DNT under the microscope, I picked folks to chat with who had the views I needed to figure out the pattern, confirm it repeated, and note some landmarks where the pattern stopped and started. So, I'd already completed one task.

Neither my father nor Ted mentioned the existence of the other city models, so either they are newer or a well kept secret within SCI ranks. My father assumed I'd have to get the other patterns out of the data center at headquarters, but what if I could get into the models instead? I haven't figured out how to defeat the SCI tracking system yet, though, and if I can't the SCI would know if I was anywhere near a sensitive area. I believe they inserted the tracker the moment we'd entered Thera with the shot they gave us, but it's also possible the tracker's in our watch. Ted thinks they may have redundant systems in place to ensure they don't lose anyone.

I, and by extension Ted now that he's on Thera, have also been tasked with assessing current security levels and weak spots citywide, determining whether a weapons stash exists and where, and ideally figuring out how to turn off the Eco barrier altogether. Permanently disabling the gas triggers would be ideal, but even if we could disarm them temporarily it would give time for the Exilers to infiltrate the city.

It's close to final exam time. And, if the actual final exam trumps the simulated one my dad gave me, I could be in trouble. I need to find a way to stack things in my favor fast.

I learned the layout of SCI headquarters during my training. My father worked within those walls for years before happening upon a whole lot of information he wasn't supposed to and getting booted. We spent the summer after my sophomore year of high school in a full-scale mockup of the building. The building sat atop a series of old mine tunnels, which my father used to approximate the secret canyon tunnels that lead to the headquarters. Mind you, he's never been in those tunnels, but promises they exist and will provide my only entry short of becoming a member of the Grand Council and inheriting a passkey, or getting Cleaved on my eighteenth.

My "final test" of that summer was to get from my "school residence" to the protected server bank in the Grand Council building, through pitch-black tunnels, locked doors and a half dozen security guards. He hired some ex-military buffs to play the tunnel security goons. They reminded me of my dad's Militant buddies—single minded and lethal. No question my dad wanted to show me my inadequacy for the task, so I stacked the odds in my favor with a little creativity—or as some might call it—downright cheating.

The night before the test I told my dad I was going for a run to calm my nerves, knowing he'd never deprive me the opportunity for more exercise. My eight-mile loop took me through an occupied horse farm we'd driven by upon arrival two months earlier. I circled the farm to confirm its occupants were away, and then broke into a locked bin in the stables where, even better than hoped, I found injectable horse tranquilizers, a tranq gun, and what appeared to be an anesthetic. The key would be to use my stash in moderation as to not kill anyone, although a prison life sentence might be preferable to my dad's plans for me. I kissed my treasure before stuffing it into the lining of my running shorts and jogging back. The four miles back home proved to be a little uncomfortable, as my loot chafed some rather sensitive areas.

First up on test day was locating the entrance from my digs to the tunnels. Officials use the tunnels to check up on kids during sleeping hours, scan for illegal paraphernalia and other rule violations, restock cupboards, and the like. Invisible to most, they present a huge security hole to the enlightened. I'd pretended to sleep, listened for the monitor to enter and from where, and after they'd left it took me less than twenty minutes to find and open the hidden door behind the bathroom cabinet.

Once in the tunnel, I allowed my eyes to adjust to the darkness before proceeding. Light on my feet, I jogged through the hot, musty passages, keeping an ear out for guards. The first was stationed at an intersection of pathways. I watched as he shifted his focus to each path every twenty seconds, giving me only twenty seconds with his back to me, and forty with his attention directed elsewhere. Dressed in black, with a dark hood obscuring my face, I inched towards him. As he turned to the passage to the right, I quickened, and by the time his back was turned to me, I'd pressed the horse tranq in a third of the way, before removing, capping and shoving it back in my pocket. I couldn't use the gun for the first couple doses or I'd likely kill the guys, so close encounters were my only option.

The dude didn't drop lightly, or quickly. He fought me for a good thirty seconds before tanking, nearly crushing my windpipe when he clipped my throat. I knew how to take hits and was able to absorb the blow by buckling backwards and rolling to the side. After catching my breath, I launched up, slamming my head into his with massive force. Full credit had to be given to the drugs because he was moving pretty slowly by this point. His reaction time withered and within a minute he dropped. Adrenaline pumped through my veins as I disrobed the guy, donned his uniform, stuffed my tools into my new pockets, and took the path to the left, running full speed.

I passed three guards without incident, they having ignored me after seeing my uniform. The fifth guard required some horse tranquilizer and a good kick in the ribs. I felt bad for sharing needles between the two guys but didn't want to waste any, not knowing for sure what lay ahead. Number six weighed at least two eighty, so I got out the new needle for him and gave him a half dose, and even with that he broke three of my fingers, a rib, and dislocated my left shoulder before he got woozy. I gave myself four minutes to recover and assess my wounds before proceeding. I searched my victim's pockets. He had a passkey on him, which I used to enter the building.

My dad had purposefully kept me out of the basement area, so that I'd have to improvise and find my way up six stories to the data center. I wasted many precious moments sorting through all the crap before finding a doorway blocked by a bookcase stacked with file boxes. I unloaded the bookcase before inching open the door and climbing the staircase.

I didn't expect much activity upstairs given the off-hour, but my dad was roaming the halls of floor five in an attempt to block my success. The anesthetic worked magic on him and his passkey worked magic on the lock to the data center. Not knowing how long he'd be out, I quickly located what I needed—which was a trophy my father had hidden—and reversed my path out of the building and through the tunnels. Carrying a large shiny metal object past the other guards gave my disguise away, so I'd had to deal with the three remaining guards by giving a third dose to one, and quarter doses to the other two. Using the trophy as a weapon compensated for my injuries, and I was able to get back to my "house" with only a few extra cuts and bruises.

Exhausted and in extreme pain, I waited out my dad who finally arrived an hour later to give his usual verbal thrashing, but at least he popped my shoulder back into place and let me get a few hours sleep. Despite the extended lecture to the contrary, I could tell he was impressed I'd found, stolen and used the drugs to my advantage.

The day after, I returned to school to start my junior year, still injured. I hid the cuts, bruises and breaks beneath a baggy hooded flannel, not wanting to have to spew lies to cover for them. After that, I left the hood on and let myself go until now, my hair growing long and shaggy, my interactions with others less frequent, my disgust for my dad at an all time high.

My dad wants to have a conversation, so my immediate task is to figure out a legitimate reason for visiting that beach. Perhaps if I could get Kira to ride with me, we could find an excuse to have a pretend romantic picnic there one sunset or sunrise? Any plan will require her help and even though she's forgiven me for my failure to disclose, and admitted she has feelings for me, I have no freaking clue where our relationship stands or if she still has my back now that she knows my mission.

I guess I better ask.

Deep into that darkness peering, long I stood there, wondering, fearing,
doubting, dreaming dreams no mortal ever dared to dream before.

Edgar Allen Poe

CHAPTER FIFTEEN

Kira

Even though our conversation warrants completing, I march towards the gym as an obedient Recruit should do. The look on Blake's face when I told him I imagined my whole future revolving around him… priceless. Guys don't react well to going zero to sixty on the emotional front in a relationship. They'll go from "hello to sex" in 5.5 seconds flat, but "you suck to I want to marry you and have your babies" and that'll cause them to sprout wings and fly away at supersonic speed. Blake clearly is inexperienced in the relationship front, because instead of running he got the whole deer in the headlights expression and for a moment I think I might have caused an aneurysm.

Speaking of aneurysm close calls—when I believed I had Cleaved to Tristan I truly did panic. Blake really did a number on me. Then I out-gamed the gamer with my spectacular performance. And it was going perfectly until I decided to seal the deal with a kiss. And he kissed me back. Really kissed me. In a completely turned on kind of way that made me think he wants to drop the "fake." Not that I let him know I agreed the kiss was hot. After his "joke" he gets no ego stroking.

Then things got blurry really fast the moment Blake mentioned a tall, dark-haired, blue-eyed Intern named Ethan who's here on Thera. It can't be a coincidence given my sightings and hearing his voice. If he's here, why has Blake run into him "a couple times" and he's managed to avoid me entirely? Blake said the Ethan he met was "really into a girl he met at a party." The same longing I've felt for months returns in force at the thought it was my Ethan and he might have meant me. If he liked me enough to consider marriage, kids and old age by my side, why would he avoid me? And guys accuse girls of playing games.

"Hold on," I hear from behind, as Blake grabs my hand, caressing it until I meet his gaze.

"We're late," I protest.

"I know. I just have to ask you a couple things. First, is my mission really your mission now? Are we still partners and do you still have my back?" Committing to this will put my life in danger. But, my life and future are already at risk, as is Blake's, and I've already decided our futures are tied, like it or not. His eyes intensify in purpose as he awaits my answer.

"Yes. I'll cover for you while you do your whole try to take down the bad guy thing," I respond. "I really do want off this rock." He closes his eyes, lifts his head upward, and clasps his hands together for a moment, before staring at me again.

"Thank you," he says. "Because I don't know if you noticed that flare a minute ago, but that means my father has arrived and will be eagerly awaiting an update on how my mission is progressing."

"That firecracker thing?" I ask, remembering vaguely a small blast and light in the sky, higher than the canyon lights, yet not a star. He nods. So, his dad's here to put on the pressure, which means whatever he's got planned is a "sooner rather than later" kind of thing. Great if successful, potentially disastrous if not. "So, when will you fill me in on the plan?"

"From now on, every bit of canyon time will be devoted to it," he says. "I have so much to tell you."

"Yes you do have a lot of explaining left to do," I answer. He twitches at my jab.

"My last question is… where do we stand? Are we resuming our quote-unquote 'relationship,' or what?" he asks. I know to complete Blake's mission we will need the canyon time, but I'm hesitant to define our relationship given the complicated nature of my feelings towards him and the news about Ethan. It takes a couple deep breaths to be able to answer.

"For public appearances, sure, we can resume our, as you put it 'quote-unquote relationship,' but it's going to remain fake." He looks disappointed.

"What about that kiss?" he asks.

"What about it? You're on a mission to take down the SCI, not on the freaking Bachelor. We keep up the ruse so we get our canyon time, but the PDAs going to be kept to a minimum," I respond.

"Surely after they observed that kiss, the powers that watch are going to expect more of the same. An escalation even," he says, leaning into my ear. My breath hitches a smidgen and I hope he didn't notice my body's betrayal.

"You guys have about two minutes to get into the gym," Bri yells. Saved by the yell. Thank you, Bri.

I look Blake right in the eyes with my best sultry look that used to get Tristan all hot and bothered. "In. Your. Dreams." And then I turn and run.

"You look absolutely freaking Cleavable," Blake says as I enter the living room in full party attire. We've been summoned to an all night to early morning dance-a-thon on the football field, mandatory for all students freshman and up, and so I've squeezed into my tiny tube top and skirt to appease the powers that be. I even dusted myself with Industrial City Party Sparkles and look like a human disco ball. Thankfully I've had a week off from clinic visits so my abdomen is flat and firm, the swelling from my surgery gone.

"You look like a 70s movie extra," I respond. He looks ridiculous in his party vest and pants. The SCI has no issue killing off a whole party full of teenagers, but can't give a single decent fashion designer a second chance? "Ready to get your groove on?"

"Absolutely," he says. "Happy to show you my moves." He pulls me close and grinds against me. The last couple weeks have been absolute torture as Blake seems hell bent on getting a repeat of that kiss. Sure, we've spent a lot of time discussing his mission in the canyon, but I'll be darned if he hasn't figured out how to discuss the SCI and their evil minions with bedroom eyes. But I've also seen him use the same look on Bailey and vice versa. So, I haven't given him more than a couple chaste pecks to keep our cover.

"You," I say poking him on the exposed part of his chest, "have become Testosterone's poster boy." He twirls me around and laughs.

"Ready to go?" he asks with a smirk. "I know how much you love parties."

"Why? You going to drug me?" I ask.

"Despite how hard you're trying to resist me, I know you want me, even without the drugs," he jokes.

"Yep, I'm right behind Bailey in line," I say and pull him out the door. I need some fresh air. I'm quite conflicted. Sure, I haven't been able to forget that kiss. But after hearing from Blake that an Intern named Ethan was in the city, I can't take things further. Blake thinks I'm playing hard to get, and Bailey thinks Blake's playing hard to get. Though the more Bailey plays "easy," the more he seems to be softening to her advances. Despite the fact he's been all over me.

I need to find Ethan and figure out what his deal is. I cornered Spud to ask whether he could get me in touch with him, but he told me that he'd do no such thing and that I should just focus on my own assignment. He didn't, however, refute Ethan's existence, so I'm as curious as ever about where he's hiding and why. And how he's here on Thera. If he has high enough DNT to cross over could that mean his being at that party wasn't a coincidence? The thought sends shivers down my spine.

Spud scored Blake a scooter that'll fit us both, so I've learned to close my eyes and hang onto Blake for dear life while he maneuvers us through the canyon paths at high speed. The pleasant breeze created outweighs the threat of injury, since walking the dark canyon in one hundred ten degree plus temperatures only results in sweat. The ride takes less than two minutes by scooter, so we're at the dance quickly.

Teens litter the football field, dancing to some new age crap that sounds like it belongs as the soundtrack to the canyon light show. At least it's music, I think. When I see Tristan eyeing me in my skimpy attire and licking his lips, I pull Blake in to dance with me.

"I like you in your skimpy party swag," Blake jokes. "You really move well in it." I push away and do a back handspring and flip to a split that gets everyone's attention. "That's what I'm talking about," he says, pulling me up and into a tight embrace.

We dance in a large group for an hour, rotating between slow and sweet, fast and crazy, and sheer athleticism. While Bailey pulls Blake off for a private dance that looks more like a strip-tease, I teach a line of girls several dance routines I know from cheer to tamp down my jealousy. My subjects eventually burn out and collapse into the arms of TB-enhanced boys.

"You're losing him, frigid minute by minute," a teebed out Bailey whispers into my ear. I turn to face her.

"He's been all over me lately, Bailey. Not all guys are into the 'I'm so teebed that I'll gladly spread my legs for you' thing," I snap.

"Little kitten Kira tries to have some bite, eh?" she says. "Well, my dear little promo for purity… what do you think has had Blake so hot and bothered these days? Surely, you don't think that one kiss you shared in the canyons did it, do you? Blake and I have had a… lot… to debate lately and he's been so… receptive to my arguments. It's only a matter of time."

"Whatever, Bailey," I say. "If he wants your brand of skank, he and I aren't meant to be anyways." I push through the crowd to escape her. Unbelievable. But then again, her case makes sense. Every time Blake returns to me from a conversation with Bailey, he's more aggressive about "giving the SCI a good show" than usual. If he's so into her, why's he still pursuing things with me?

I continue my brisk walk across the football field until I run straight into Blake.

"Where have you been?" he asks.

"Discussing your imminent Cleaving with Bailey," I say.

"Like that's going to happen," he says, though he refuses to meet my eye.

I glare at him and hope he can feel the heat, even if he can't see it. "According to Bailey, the only reason you've been so amorous with me as of late is because she's done such a good job of getting you worked up… and you guys just haven't had a chance to seal the deal yet."

Blake grabs me around my waist and presses his body to mine and whispers in my ear, "I have some rather bad memories of Bailey from my time back on Earth. You have nothing to worry about." The crowd considers Blake's move to be foreplay and shouts, "Cleave, Cleave, Cleave." Find some friends for the singular thought in your brain, people. I know their eighteenth birthdays are all staring at them in the face and the prospect of a lifetime with one person is huge, but honestly, I'm done with the Cleaving talk. Even if they are referring to the "lifetime commitment" instead of the "consummation" it still makes them sound like a bunch of freaking sex-starved robots.

"Raise my bet to thirty berries that they'll Cleave off after the dance," Bri says to Tristan. When she says "they" she means Blake and me. Bri and Tristan have been dancing next to us, as have Lucas and his new squeeze, Brooke. Bri adds, "They've been downright gooey since they got back together. Have you ever seen two kids more in love?"

"We heard that," I yell back. "It's a good thing you don't value your berries." Bri started a Theranberry pool to predict our Cleave date, and I believe everyone over sixteen (with the exception of Bailey) has entered since berry season ends soon. It'll be a long summer for those without good stock. Bri bounces over to Blake and me, dragging Tristan along.

"Come on guys. Help me out," Bri says, eyes twinkling. Her usually heavy makeup is doubled and particularly sparkly tonight, the effect being pretty sultry and I wonder if she's going to make a play for a Cleaving of her own with Tristan by morn. She pleads with Blake, "My summer party schedule depends on you. Blake, how can you possibly resist her dressed like that?" Tristan scans me, thinking he's safe holding Bri from behind, but Bri's sixth sense kicks in and she grinds her heel into his foot and Tristan whimpers like a dog.

"I think it safest to not answer that," Blake responds. "But I do agree that Kira's pretty hot in her party attire. Especially when she does all those flips and stuff."

"Seriously, you two," Bri says, her voice a bit pushy and urgent. "Get with the program. Cleave. Have wicked cute babies." Blake tenses at the mention of babies, having shared his concern of mini "Bliras" being grown in the Garden City labs. I think the concerns are unfounded. The doctors showed me ultrasound pictures of the lesion before and after my surgery. How would Ted know the specifics anyway? He's just guessing and spreading his unhealthy psychosis.

I dismiss her marketing campaign. "Sorry. I'm programmed differently." She purses her lips in disgust at my values. I always suspected she didn't share my views on waiting until marriage, but she wasn't one to kiss and tell either. She'd dig into my affairs—particularly where Tristan was concerned—but glossed over her own relationships. She'd dated Lucas for four months before her death. I have no clue what they did behind closed doors. Never asked. Didn't want to know.

Bailey says, "Yeah, you've got the 50s housewife programming." My head whips around to face her and I'm not the only one. What did she just say? She shouldn't know squat about 50s housewives. Blake clearly heard as well. Bailey's eyes jet around nervously, but then she lets out a squeal before I can ask her about it. Good thing. I could have exposed Blake and myself to the Second Chancers had I confronted her in front of everyone.

"Oooh. Lara and Johnnie came. She looks so cute pregnant!" Bailey says, waving her arms to get the couple's attention. She successfully lures them our way. I'll have to get Bailey alone later and subtly figure out what she knows.

Lara Stewart and Johnnie Sanders had been crowned royalty at Carmel Valley High… Homecoming Royalty, that is. Both seniors, they'd dated since freshman year and applied to the same colleges. I believe they'd been accepted and agreed to go to University of California Riverside. Before attending the Goodington Winter Formal after party. Now here on Thera, they're Cleaved and have Assisted Pregnancy Baby Number One on the way. Lara's working towards a degree in teaching administration and Johnnie's got a security gig of some sort.

While Blake plucks Johnnie's brain about Garden City security protocol, I politely listen to Lara dish about completely unnatural methods to get pregnant on Thera. The more she describes, the whiter I get, fainter I feel. Shots. Abdominal ultrasounds. Minor surgical procedure to remove the eggs. She might as well have been dictating my medical file. Our experiences vary on two fronts. First, she agreed to her egg removal. And second, a few nights after they removed her eggs they implanted an embryo, which took, making her pregnant.

Whereas Briella laps up every detail of Lara's story, my brain attempts to reject the similarities. Disprove Ted and Blake's theories of Petri dish-generated posterity. If they really did take my eggs and Blake's sperm, what happened to the embryos? Are they hoping Blake and I will Cleave soon so they can impregnate me? Or do they have some other plan?

I need air. The throngs of teens on the field seem to be closing in and cutting off my air supply. Without explanation to Bri, Lara or Blake, I sprint out into the open air and down a path deep into the canyon. The air feels heavy and sticky, different from usual, but I don't know how to attribute the change. I look to the dark sky for clues, but the canyon lights mask my view.

While I love my canyon time with Blake, I don't find the same appeal being out here alone. We usually walk the canyon as dawn approaches, but it is solidly middle of the night and the swirling lights can't cut through the blackness. Every sound rattles me. The bugs. Animals and reptiles camouflaged in the brush. And a rumble I can't place. It starts softly like fingers tapping on a keyboard, but then grows to a stampede of horses. So much for being able to think. Blake yells for me and then I hear a loud siren. It's familiar. Oh crap. That's the same siren they used in the flash flood drill. I scramble to climb the hill before the water assails me.

I'm fifty feet up, a third of the way, when it hits. Knowing I'll lose all progress if caught in a mudslide, I grab for the thickest bush, a thorny Theranberry. The briers slice through my exposed flesh, but keep me from being washed into the growing river below. Mud blankets me as it washes down the hill and the rain assaults from above. Our emergency drill hadn't properly prepared me. I'd relied on Blake's quick thinking and strength. He'd used rope ladders to scale the canyon, but how can I find a ladder if I can't see? The canyon lights are useless covered with mud. And the zip lines are way too high to reach.

Smaller brush, cacti, and unknown objects join the landslide and pummel me as they make their way towards the river of death below. I can feel the roots of my Theranberry bush loosen and tell that they won't hold me much longer. Where's a city worker on a zip line when you need them? I scream for Blake and for help until my voice fails me.

Twenty or thirty minutes later the rain abates from barrels to merely buckets and visibility increases. Enough to barely make out a human life form headed my way. The voice reveals that Blake has come to rescue me. He's on a rope ladder a half dozen feet to my left.

"Kira, listen to me. You're going to need to dive for it. Wait until I get farther down and I'll catch hold of you," he shouts, his voice shaking.

I attempt to dislodge myself from my destabilized Theranberry bush enough to slide sideways towards the rope. I get washed down ten or fifteen feet before I feel Blake's hand grab me and swing me towards him. Once I feel the rope ladder solidly beneath my feet, I let out a cry of relief and embrace Blake.

"What were you thinking? Why'd you run off by yourself like that?" he asks. I can only see the outline of his face, but can tell he's upset.

"Lara. She explained how she got pregnant. They took her eggs. Just like they took my eggs. You and Spud were right," I say, barely whispering, my throat raw.

"Oh crap," he says.

"Yeah," I respond.

"Maybe the procedures are similar?" he says. "Maybe we're jumping to conclusions we shouldn't without proof."

"It's possible. I mean they never did a second procedure to implant an embryo back in me like they did with Lara," I say. Perhaps Blake is right. The procedures could be similar.

"They couldn't do that anyway until you're Cleaved. If you got pregnant you'd have to be Exiled."

"Uh huh. More reasons to avoid Cleaving like the plague," I say. He looks upward at the huge climb ahead of us.

"Well, perhaps instead of freaking over something we can't prove or control, we should try to get out of here so we can live to see our labies," he says.

"Labies?" I ask, confused.

"Lab babies—labies," he says, his futile attempt to make a joke of it.

"Funny," I say. "They *stole* my eggs. You *gave* them your sperm."

"That's not fair, Kira. They made me. They said they were running fertility tests on me, just like they told you," he says, clearly upset by my accusation that he was somehow in on their plans, which obviously he wasn't.

Any further dissection of the state of our potentially existent labies will have to wait. The dumping of the heavens upon us has resumed with vigor and we can barely keep hold of the rope with the continuous lash of water and mud. I try to latch onto Blake so he can ascend the rope, but progress is impossible. Gale force winds pelt the rain at our faces with the force of a fire hose. As I reach up to try to clear my eyes of mud and water I lose my grip on Blake and free fall towards the river.

Panic overtakes me and it takes several seconds to regain enough faculties to grasp for something, anything to slow my descent. The rope should still be in reach, I think. I shove my hands into the mud and catch hold, nearly pulling out my elbow sockets as I abruptly halt, legs dangling in the raging river below. My upper body strength may not rival Blake or Tristan's, but between cheer, my nightly workouts here on Thera, and some major adrenaline, I ratchet myself up a few rungs and get my legs out of the water.

Taking some deep breaths to try to get my heart rate down, I survey my situation. Blake didn't fall with me, so he must still be above. How far, I have no idea, as I'm still blinded by the rain. How much longer can this storm last? Fatigue plagues my muscles, and the rain and mud sting the flesh wounds sustained by the brush and debris. I've swallowed enough mud to craft a childhood mud pie. My stomach protests the non-nutritive meal and I dry heave between belabored breaths.

I work out a rhythm. Inhale ten times facing down to keep the mud out of my mouth. Climb two rungs. Rest. Repeat. Several minutes go by. Eight rungs.

Ten rungs. Twelve rungs. It's progress.

And then Blake and a mass of sludge slam me into the river below.

With no time to react and no way to hold on, I hit the cement floor with enough force to hurt, but not kill. The rapids churn us like laundry, sweeping us towards the ocean. Thirty or forty seconds later, I pop my head out of the water and gasp for air. Where's Blake? He'd been right next to me. A tug at my legs pulls me under for a moment and then we both rise to the surface. My lungs burn but I refuse to die this way so I look for options. I motion towards the "shore."

Swimming against the current, we target anything along the shoreline that can be used to pull ourselves out. The river carries us at least a mile before we can get across ten feet of rapids and grab hold of a dense patch of brush. Blake shoves me up with one arm, his other wrapped around a monstrous cactus. The rain has slowed again enough to see his face every few seconds as a strobe flashes around the canyon.

"Stay above the brush and search for a ladder with your hands," he says. "Try to yell out every couple minutes so they can get a handle on your location."

"Take my hand, Blake. I can pull you up," I say.

"They have a well trained rescue team. It shouldn't be long before they find you. They'll be using the zip lines," he says.

"You're scaring the crap out of me, Blake. Get up here," I say. As the light shines on his face I can tell he won't be joining me and that it is by choice. "No, no, no, no, no. You are not leaving me here. You don't get to leave me and our babies while we suffer an eternity on this cursed planet!"

"Chill. I'll be back. I promise. Trust me. If I don't come back, at least you have some great other options here—Tristan and Ethan, the chick-magnet Intern," he says in a joking tone, although I don't think it's funny. "By the way, it's not fake to me anymore. I'm falling for you, Kira." Then he lets go and the river swiftly carries him away.

"What the hell?" I yell, though he may be too far to hear me. How dare he tell me he's falling for me right before launching into that suicidal stream of sludge? I know him. He has some hare-brained idea that he can get out to the beach and within range of his father. But the far more likely scenario is that he drowns or gets pulled out into the ocean by a riptide and I never see him again.

The agony of his departure paralyzes any action on my part for what seems like hours. I numb myself to the rain and mud as the intensity cycles between brutal and barely noticeable. As dawn approaches the skies shut off and the drains built into the canyon floor suck the remaining liquid, leaving behind a graveyard of debris and silt. The clouds dissipate and the sun sears the mud to my skin. The minuscule remaining rational portion of my brain urges me to scale the canyon, but my angst of not knowing Blake's fate squashes any upward momentum.

Eventually, rescuers find me. I get hauled to the clinic by way of mule. The mule's stench and the jarring ride barely register. An unnerved Spud Rosenberg meets my rescue party at the top of the canyon.

"Where's Blake?" he asks me. No need to look up to know his chin fat is swaying and thin brows furrowed.

"The river. He pushed me up and out of it, but got swept away." Intentionally, the jerk.

"How long ago?" he says.

"Hours," I respond, although I have no idea of the exact timing.

"We'll find him," he says. "The rescue team will scour the canyons until they do." Only if he wants to be found. Or if his dead body is amongst the riverbed debris.

Two nights and no news. They've kept me drugged most of the time as my wailing "distracts the doctors and nurses." My wounds are healing. Appetite, not so much. I've been stuck in the clinic, hooked to tubes that force nutrition into my body. Bri and Tristan have been swapping shifts to keep me company. I'm surprised Bri trusts Tristan to sit with me, but I guess she figures I'm too distraught over Blake to put up with any crap from Tristan. She'd hate the truth, which is that I prefer Tristan's bedside manner to hers. Bri's overly sunny "everything will be fine so that you and Blake can finally Cleave" talk drives me insane when the outcome may be much less than okay. The rescue teams have failed to find Blake, dead or alive. Tristan has avoided the topic of Blake altogether, catching me up on every bit of Garden City High gossip.

"You mind if I read you a children's story?" he asks.

"Is it because I've been acting like a child?" I respond.

"Ha ha. No, because the girl in the story reminds me of you," he says. He shows me pictures from the book on his tablet and I gasp at the resemblance of the girl in the story. The girl wears her long strawberry blonde hair in ringlets and has pale green eyes ringed in gold. Even her facial structure resembles my heart-shaped face. The boy looks like a cross between Blake and Ethan, if I even correctly remember what Ethan looks like at this point. I must be doomed to a life of loss.

"Yeah sure, a children's story is about all I can handle right now," I say, pretending to not be that interested. Far from the truth, because Blake and I are supposedly Originals I am very intrigued about my legendary ancestors. I burrow into my pillow, pull my blanket up and listen to Tristan bring life to the magical tale.

Centuries ago, a beautiful princess named Helina of Light stood at the precipice of a volcanic crater at dawn. As firstborn daughter, her family had to sacrifice her to the Gads in exchange for seven years of plenty in the lands surrounding the volatile and fiery volcano. As the sun peeked over the Eastern horizon, she boldly dove towards the fiery pits.

Instead of being consumed by flame, Helina found herself engulfed in warm water. She flopped and flailed in the water to keep herself afloat. A strong breeze whisked her to a shell-covered beach. Too weak to move, she awaited death.

Death did not come. Hadrian of Dark found her while fishing. He abandoned his haul, carrying her to his garden home miles away. The garden was lush, fertile and beautiful beyond measure. Helina thought she was in Heaven with the Gads. She fell in love with Hadrian and, in time, agreed to cleave to him.

A year hence, Helina bore twins to the delight of her husband. Csilla favored her mother. Cole, his father. The children thrived in the gardens, though Csilla yearned for adventure. She'd grown hearing stories of the 'mortal' land of her mother's birth. After Cole took his uncle's daughter to cleave, Csilla set out to find Light. She wove a raft of reeds of the garden and pushed out to sea, never to be seen by Helina and Hadrian again.

Years after her parents' death, Csilla returned to her parent's garden home with her children and grandchildren. Cole greeted her and marveled at tales of travel between Light and Dark. After nights of feast and celebration Csilla invited Cole to journey to his mother's birthplace and see Light with his own eyes. He acquiesced to his sister's pleadings, bringing his own children and grandchildren. They visited the very volcano where Helina was sacrificed before Cole returned to Dark. Despite the lure of Light, he missed his cleave and his father's gardens.

Generation after generation passed between Dark and Light. Only those of the blood of the Originals could make the journey. Until, that is, Helina's great-great-great-great granddaughter, Ilana, who lived on Light, struck a deal with the Gads when her husband died before his time. The Gads agreed to bring her husband back to life in the Dark land of her distant grandfather. Eventually, others were granted a second chance at life on Dark.

"Cool story, huh?" Tristan says upon finishing. "I love a good romance." I envy his naivety. He thought some author imagined the story. Although I imagine much of it to be fiction, the folklore justifies Original domination over Second Chancers. Tristan doesn't even realize he once lived in Light and his benefactors in Dark Exiled him here by execution.

Choosing my words carefully I respond, "Kind of grim. I can't believe someone wrote a story for kids about a girl jumping into a volcano."

"You wouldn't jump into a volcano if it meant finding your one true love?" he asks. I might actually jump if I knew I could find Blake. Or see Ethan again. But to jump thinking I'd die? Crazy.

"She didn't know she'd find love," I say. "And since when are you such a romantic?" A slip. Not one he'd recognize, but a slip nonetheless.

"I'm a regular Prince Hadrian," he says, brown eyes sparkling and impish grin shining. And with that, I smile for the first time since Blake disappeared. We talk for hours until Bri arrives, covering every kosher topic on Thera, from Cleaving, love and romance, to friendship, sports, exercise and food. It is the Tristan of our early relationship. Fun. Talkative. Charming. Sweet. I fell in love with *that* Tristan, not the soulless, drunken oaf who cheated on me with my best friend.

"Have you found him?" I ask as Spud Rosenberg enters my living room unannounced, a second man behind him. Although I'm thankful to be out of the clinic, being in the house I share with Blake without him has been excruciatingly painful.

"I'm afraid I can't say," Spud says. "Our search and rescue operations are confidential. But you should prepare yourself for the worst."

"Are you kidding me?" I say. "He's my partner. I need him back and to know that he's alive. Why won't you tell me?"

"We're not here to discuss Blake. My colleague, Ethan Darcton, requires a word with you—and I do believe you've been wanting a word with him, as well," Spud says.

"Ethan *Darcton*—as in related to Brad Darcton of the Ten? " I ask, straining my neck to get a look at the guy who's still obscured by Spud's large head. My stomach lurches toward my throat as if I've just taken a plunge down a roller coaster. I instantly recognize the face. Striking. Magazine cover material. Young twenties. Dark hair. Twinkling sapphire eyes. Stubble from a couple-night start to a beard. And definitely not a ghost. Ethan. How could he show up now after all this time? He just now comes to see me? He walks towards me so I can get a better look and I can finally confirm he's as incredible as I remember. He's a Darcton? The Ten was responsible for that explosion and Mr. Senior Ten's son was there that night striking up a conversation with me? That can't be a coincidence. Could hot college dude be a terrorist?

"Yes, I'm his son and we've met previously," he says as if he might have slipped my mind, taking my hand in his and sitting down next to me on my couch, close enough that his knee touches mine. My heart races at his contact, but my brain is doing somersaults at the thought that Ethan may have been involved in the Goodington disaster.

"I'll leave the two of you to talk," Spud says. I shoot Spud an icy glare, but he waves me off and exits through the front door. My attention returns to the Darcton heir and I find his eyes transfixed on me. I sigh deeply and try to find my voice amidst my astonishment.

"So, after all this time, you show up. At first I thought I'd lost my mind," I said. "I kept seeing you on Earth, or so I thought. And again at the scale version of the Headquarters meeting with... your father. I heard your voice at the clinic, but you wouldn't open the door. And then Blake said he'd run into an Intern named Ethan with your description. Why wouldn't you say something to me and let me know you were alive? Or perhaps you were purposefully avoiding me." He closes his eyes and takes a deep breath, as if to compose himself before addressing me.

"I'm so sorry that Blake's gone missing," Ethan says, ignoring my questions. "He seems like a really nice guy and from what I understand, you two are close."

"How did you survive the explosion at the Goodington party? How are you here on Thera? You're really Brad Darcton's son?" I ask. To think that I obsessed over every word he spoke to me that night... wondering if he felt even a fraction of the connection I felt... wondering who his girlfriend was... and ridiculously wondering if he could forget her and want a forever with me.

And then the fantasy fizzles. He's a Darcton. "Why were you even there that night?" Heck, they can Exile me for all I care. "Did you cause the..." Ethan cuts me off as he firmly plants his hand over my lips, but shakes his head "no" at my intended question.

"I know you have a lot of questions. But, let me address one thing at a time. I was at the Goodington party, because as part of the interview process the SCI does a 'spot check' on the most promising Recruits to confirm they're of the right kind of character to represent the Second Chance Institute. The Ten asked me to observe you and your friends. It was during my observation I happened upon an unfortunate incident," he says, as if reciting a script. "It's easier to show you," he says. "I brought a video that should... shed some light on the events of that night."

"Video?" I ask. He briskly leaves the couch, takes a memory card from his pocket and plugs it into the side of my tablet. I follow him. A few moments later images appear on the monitor and I take a seat in my desk chair. Ethan's not acting at all like the flirty, sweet guy I remember. In fact, he's awkward and seems nervous. His hands are shaking. The all business demeanor doesn't suit him.

"I apologize in advance for the content," he says. "I was directed to show you."

"By?" I ask.

"The Ten," he says. "They have... concern about the time you've been spending with your former boyfriend, Tristan. Given your importance... as a

Recruit… they want you to be fully informed as to his behavior leading up to the accident." I clench my teeth to keep from correcting him. Accident? Don't insult me.

Mr. Darcton the Younger skips forward to the segment I'm to watch. Briella and Tristan fill the screen. They're sprawled out on a bed, presumably within the former Goodington estate since they're dressed in Winter Formal attire.

"We need to tell her," Bri says.

"Why now? If you haven't told her about us after a year, what's changed to make you want to come clean?" Tristan asks.

"I love you," she says. "I always have. Since our first time up at Mammoth, and that was before I stupidly introduced you to Kira and you blew me off for her."

"I didn't blow you off at Mammoth. You were playing head games and then you blew up at me after I spent the afternoon keeping Kira company in the lodge. I didn't want to deal with your crap. No matter how good of a time we'd had at that party," he says. "Besides, you said you were okay about it. That you wanted her to be happy and I made her happy."

"I don't think either of us have been making her happy lately. She has to know something's up and I don't think she could handle finding out about it from someone else," Bri says.

"I thought we'd talked this through at iHop this morning and decided *not* to tell her. She'll probably be leaving soon anyway to go do that stupid internship and then I can use that as an excuse to break up. When she gets back we can tell her we hooked up while she was gone," he says.

"No, it's not enough. You can't date my best friend while having me on the side. We need to tell her. Tonight," she says.

"That's crazy. You're drunk," he says, and then shoves some tongue down her throat.

"*You're* drunk. I'm just enough drunk to give you what you've been wanting all night," she says before slipping off her dress and unbuttoning his tux shirt.

"Please turn it off," I say to the monster I assume filmed it. How could I have been so wrong about Ethan? I'd built a freaking pedestal so high to put him on, so I guess I shouldn't be shocked to see how far he can fall. At least I've kept a perfect record in falling for only schmucks who disappoint.

"Of course," he says. He closes out the file and slips the card back in his pocket. He turns to me, putting his hands on my shoulders and whispering in my ear, "I'm so sorry. Know that I had no choice and disagree with the Ten's methods." His touch sends shivers up and down my spine, attraction and repulsion converging.

I pull back, step away from him, and practically spit out my words. "You followed me? Taped my friends? How did you survive the explosion? Why won't you answer my questions? Why have you been avoiding me?" I ask, furious at his involvement with the Ten. Furious at the Ten for sending someone to spy on me and for killing my friends.

"I followed you when you left the party and planned to offer you a ride home. But then the explosion happened and Blake carted you off in his truck," he says. "After that, well, I wasn't purposefully trying to avoid you, I swear." I look into his eyes for hints of sincerity. He appears to be telling me the truth, but I can't possibly trust the son of a member of the Ten, no matter how attractive and how big of a fantasy I've built up in my head about him. His father and the other nine exterminated more than a hundred people to get me here. No good can come from that bloodline.

I retreat back to the couch, tuck my legs into my chest, and rock back and forth. My entire relationship with Tristan was a lie. And Bri? She loved Tristan the entire time we dated. Slept with him. Even before we'd met and started dating. We'd gone on a big group thing to Mammoth. I got carsick on the way up so she went to the party that night without me and must have hooked up with him. Then the next day, he'd come over to our table—probably to see her —and since I thought he was cute I nervously monopolized the conversation. And told Bri afterwards I was interested in him. At that point, she decided not to tell me what had happened between them. And then he'd asked me out and I was dumb enough to accept.

At some point, though, they'd hooked up again. Or maybe they never stopped. But things shifted. I recognize that now. They both started pulling away. Right around when I told them I planned to take the Test. Tristan distanced himself after that. Started drinking more. When I'd left iHop the day of the Test, I'd seen them deep in conversation. Why couldn't I see it? She thought I was onto them. Stupid, stupid, stupid. I should get an award for my abject stupidity. And then I come here and get partnered with Blake. And our fake relationship starts to progress to something real and he tells me he's falling for me. I still can't quite forgive him for letting go of that cactus and leaving me to fend for myself in a flash flood. Not to mention risking his own life just to chat with his father. And now he may be dead. Or joined up with the Exilers with no plans to return.

Blake and I may be the unwilling parents of who knows how many offspring. There's still that possibility weighing on me. My eggs. His sperm. Future of Thera. Blood of the Originals. Dark and Light reunited. Fantasy or fiction, I do not know. What I do know is that I'm not ready to parent a brood of crossovers. Or Daynighters as they're called. Why do they care so much about having people that can go back and forth? It's not for Recruits, that's for sure.

And if all of that isn't enough, the incredibly hot, sweet guy who I dreamed about spending my life with turns out to be the son of my worst nightmare. He's not dead. He's not with his girlfriend, if she was even real. Instead, he's Brad Darcton's son and errand boy for the Ten. His flirting was just another assignment and my fantasy was just that. A fantasy. That stings most of all.

My silence and mental breakdown lasts at least twenty minutes. Ethan stays put, silently watching and waiting for me to snap out of it. Finally, I speak.

"I can't… I can't deal with this. Blake's missing and may be dead. The whole Bri and Tristan thing. You… being here and not at all who I thought you were. I want to go home. Mr. Darcton," I say, purposefully emphasizing his family name.

"Please call me Ethan. And, that's just what we're going to do. I'm going to take you home for a visit," he says.

CHAPTER SIXTEEN

Ethan

"Still moping over the pretty redhead?" The voice startles me from my daydream. I may or may not have been slacking on my job.

"You scared the crap out of me, Jax. Can't you ever ring the doorbell or something?" I jump out of my desk chair and turn to him. He's in a white tank and athletic shorts. Hair's rumpled and in its usual "needed a haircut a few weeks ago" state. Golden eyes are full of mischief.

"And ruin the surprise? Never. Let's go discuss your woes over some basketball," he says. "I take it the moratorium's still on."

"Yes on the moratorium. No on the basketball. Some of us have to work... harder than others."

"Ha. As if, Mr. 'I'm too in love to have picked up my tablet in the last hour.' Never fear, love-deprived boy. Doubt you'll be stonewalled much longer now that Blake's gone missing," he says.

"What? Missing?"

"Didn't your *daddy* tell you," he mocks. "Happened during the flash flood. He floated right on out of Garden City, or so it would seem."

"I take it you know different?" I ask. With anyone else, I'd worry about having this conversation listened to. But Jax has the ability to block any surveillance within a 50 foot radius. One of his many talents. I keep trying to get him to hook me up, but he tells me that although he can work miracles, he can't (or won't) work that one. Selfish bastard.

"When will you get it through your thick skull that I know all," he says with a jovial shove. "Blake's not good enough for her. He's got a thing for that blonde named Bailey. And, he left Kira to die in the middle of the flood. All to meet up with... drumroll please... the Exilers." He shows me what's happening in a manner only Jax can. I can't believe my eyes. "Blake's daddy is head hauncho of the Militants. And they are plotting against Garden City's own and quite dear Grand Council. Blake was sent here to play hero." His tone's mocking. My parents love Jax and would never guess he isn't a willing pawn in their Grand Cause. In the same way they don't realize I'm not quite on their side. Dr. Christo made sure of that.

I let Jax's words and the images sink in. Blake's a traitor? A plant from the Exilers? I knew something seemed off with him. Could Kira be in on it?

"No, Kira's not an Exiler plant," he says. I hate it when Jax reads my mind. "Only the boy. Though he told her and she hasn't turned him in. Nor will you. It's all meant to be played out," Jax says.

"I don't want her involved," I say. "She could get hurt."

"Relax. I'll watch out for her," he says, eyes aglow. "I may even enjoy it."

"No. I don't want you around her either," I huff. The last thing I need is more competition. Between Blake and Tristan, the dead boyfriend, the situation's already barely manageable. I doubt Kira would be enough for Jax anyway. He's even pickier than I am about the female race.

"Alas, you'll be with her soon. Don't blow it. If you do, a real man may have to step in and take charge," he says as he straightens his shoulders and puffs out his chest. Did I just see him flex his bicep?

"And who might that real man be, Jax? Surely not you," I jest.

"Indeed, indeed. I'm what they model the real men after," he says with a smirk. "She's quite unique, you know. More so than the Ten realizes. My dad's been overseeing her medical treatment and I've been tracking her progress."

"Why would your dad be involved in her medical care? Does she have a heart issue?" I ask.

"You're asking the wrong questions, Ethan. As usual," he says. "You'd be best to ask why my father was involved in *your* treatment. It's not like there weren't others *brought* to Thera to see to your care." Jax understands that my parents like to take an occasional dip in the Sea of Depravity. But he's never been one to spout the family secrets.

I'm used to Jax's lures and refuse to bite. Doesn't mean I can't throw out my own barb. "I know plenty about your family's business, too. Did you so quickly forget we did all our schooling together?" My family may rule the Second Chancers, but his family's responsible for the Second Chancers being here. On the grand hierarchal pyramid, neither Dr. Christo or Jax ever let me forget that they've got the "better view," a carefully guarded secret that no member of the Ten or Grand Council knows. Which is why I always wondered why Dr. Christo gifted me a "partial view" to his lifestyle. According to Dr. Christo I'm well situated to help with his family business and so, like everyone else around me, he's appointed me to assist.

"Some things can't be learned. They must be," he says, brushing off my dig with ease. "And I think you know better than to threaten me or my father. We've always been there for you and you can't say that about the others in your life."

"Jax, I wasn't threatening you. I made a vow I plan to keep. Forgive me for being frustrated. My parents. My Uncle. You and your father. I'm always at someone's beck and call. I just wanted this one thing—one girl—for myself."

He slaps me on the back. "And so you will. The lovely Miss Kira Donovan fell prey to your spell that night and hasn't forgotten. So relax and enjoy the ride. I've got to be off. Duty calls. Keep me posted."

He departs in a flash and I return to my desk and work, pondering the gift of hope Jax left me.

The doorbell rings. Well, at least I know it isn't Jax.

I open the door to a giant and rare smile on my father's face. "Hello, Son. I come bearing excellent news."

"And what would that be?" I say. I assume he's finally here to tell me about Blake's disappearance, nights after Jax filled me in.

"How'd you like a little vacation to San Diego?" he says. Not the news I was looking for. The last thing I want is to be a world away from Kira.

"Uncle Henry needs me to escort some brainless bimbo to a fundraiser?" I thought Uncle Henry planned to be on the road all summer, but that doesn't mean he wouldn't slip back into town for a weekend to make a few bucks.

"No fundraisers. I need you to escort one pretty Light Original back home for a visit. The girl's distraught. Her boy toy disappeared and she's not taking it well. And Tristan, the girl's ex, is trying to dig his claws into her. I want her far away from here for a spell," he says. I get to take Kira home for an extended vacation? Now that sounds too good to be true.

"Jax filled me in on Blake's disappearance. His dad's her doctor?" I say, trying to get a reaction or a rise out of my father. "Since Blake's out of the picture, does that mean I have the Ten's approval to move forward? I get a chance with her?"

"Jax should spend less time meddling. And yes, our plan can move forward. Though, not without conditions," he says. Of course. I'd expect nothing less, even if it is *his* plan, not mine.

"Which are?"

"Well, for one, we need Tristan out of the picture permanently. We need you to show her the video you took at the party."

"No. No way. That's seriously perverted stuff. She'll hate me," I say while vigorously shaking my head. "She'll know the real reason I was there that night."

"It's required. But, here's the incentive. You'll need a reasonable excuse to stay with the girl at her home. So, you get to be her boyfriend for the duration of the trip."

"You think she'd say yes to that after I've just shown her a video of her long-time boyfriend cheating on her?" My father is nothing if not delusional.

"She has no choice in the matter."

"Ugh. I don't want a *fake* relationship with her. I want a real one. What happens after the trip?" I ask, although I'm not sure I want to know the answer.

"Well, that depends on how the trip goes, whether Blake magically returns, and how she feels about you," he says with a chuckle. "Keep her in line. No deviations will be tolerated. Her life and your life depend on it. The Ten expects her silence while there and her immediate presence back when required."

"Yes, sir," I say. It should floor me that he threatened to kill his own son, but that's standard issue parenting for him. Who am I kidding? Dr. Christo has been more of a father to me than my dad will ever be.

Most pre-teens get "the talk" on the birds and the bees. Instead, Jax and I got the "Dark and the Lights" lecture from Dr. Christo. Over and over again. Dr. Christo drilled the concepts and then tested. Perhaps had Jax let me get a word in, the good doctor would have realized I knew the material. But, Jax felt the need to show his superiority and I let him.

"What is DNT?" Dr. Christo would ask.

Jax immediately would answer, "Markers that determine whether we can pass between worlds."

Dr. Christo: "People can be DNT(l) or DNT(d) or DNT(ld). What do the sub-markers represent?"

Jax: "Well, duh, that represents the root source of their DNT. Light, Dark, or Both. Light originated on Earth and Dark on Thera."

Dr. Christo: "Jax, please let Ethan answer. Particularly since you didn't answer in full."

Jax: "Only because you interrupted me. Pure Lights or Darks are extremely rare. Almost non-existent. So, the (l) or (d) sub-marker only indicates what the 'majority' is in the mix. The (ld) marker is the theoretical sub-marker for the perfect union between a pure Light and pure Dark, which of course only happened at the beginning. No pure Lights have been known to exist since."

Dr. Christo: "True. But it can and will happen again. In your lifetime in fact. What happens when someone has the (ld) marker?"

Jax: "Magic. Among other things, the ability to freely travel between the worlds without issue."

Dr. Christo: "Is DNT the only marker of interest?"

Jax: "No. ARB is also of interest, but highly uncommon. Like those with DNT(ld), those with ARB may also freely pass between worlds. Their talents are many and thus, much is required of them. You and I have ARB, Daddy."

Dr. Christo: "Indeed we do, Son. Can DNT and ARB co-exist?"

Jax: "Yes, in rare circumstances."

Dr. Christo: "Jax, *please* let Ethan speak. Ethan's special, too. Ethan, you're a pure Dark with a 'little something extra.' This is why so much is expected of you, even much more than your parents realize."

I finally get a word in. "I know. Though I'm hardly special. I'm broken."

Dr. Christo sighed. "No, not broken. Fixed. Whole." I'd just recently had my last surgery. "Now, why was Light lured to Dark? Why was it crucial in the beginning to have those who could cross over?"

Jax: "To make all things equitable. Things were architected so those who were not afforded ample opportunity to achieve their purpose—through no fault of their own—would be given that opportunity. A Second Chance."

Dr. Christo: "Isn't that what the Second Chance Institute does?"

Jax: "No. That's what we do. We bring them here. The SCI manages them once here. Or mis-manages, I should say. To bring about their own purposes."

Dr. Christo: "And what purposes would that be?"

Jax: "Research. They test ruling methods here to use back on Earth."

Dr. Christo: "Is this acceptable?"

Both Jax and I answer this one in unison: "No."

I hadn't thought about Dr. Christo and Jax's differences in a long time. I'd spent so much time with them that their oddities seemed to be the norm. Not until I'd moved in with my Uncle Henry did I realize Jax and Dr. Christo were anything but the norm. Dr. Christo told me that my pure Dark DNT had a "little something extra." Even when pressed, he'd never told me what that meant. Other than the fact I have "an even Grander Destiny to fill."

After my "vacation" with Kira, I do believe I owe the good doctor a visit. My parents placed me on Earth with my Uncle Henry for a reason. They want me to have political aspirations and use Theran knowledge to "better" a "declining" society on Earth. But, I need to understand how that meshes with Dr. Christo's plans for me. Since Dr. Christo has the big picture, it's time he shares it.

CHAPTER SEVENTEEN

Blake

I'm a real jerk. I can't believe I told Kira I was falling for her and then ditched her in the middle of a flash flood. Who knows how long I'll be gone and I wouldn't want Kira hooking up with anyone while I was gone and ruining our cover. Better to have her pining away while I'm away. Am I really falling for her? After Bailey, I thought I'd never want a relationship again. And now… living with Kira and Bailey tempting me at every turn, it's making it near impossible. My hormones are raging. From a strategic standpoint, hooking up with Bailey would only hurt my cause. The SCI wants me with Kira. And, that kiss with Kira was hot. I'd like to try it a few more times to see if I can get the kind of volcanic reaction I had in the past with Bailey.

All moot if I don't return. Or if Kira doesn't get rescued—she could die if another mudslide puts her back in the river. What was I thinking? I saw an opportunity to get word to my dad and took it. Even if the SCI tries to track me they'll just assume I got swept out to sea by the current. I have a foolproof excuse to be where I shouldn't and I took it without thinking it through. No turning back now. To prevent being tracked, I rip off my watch so the SCI will think it came off in transit down the river.

I've completed four triathlons. That's child's play compared to swimming river rapids full of debris. I have zero visibility. No way to gauge how far I am from my target. I'm saddled by my less than swim-friendly party attire. And the canyon lights are covered in mud, so it's pitch black. I use a breaststroke to push the debris from my path while I think strategy. Worst case I end up in the ocean, swim far enough north to clear the Eco barrier, and then ride the waves into shore. I'd prefer not to go that route since I'm bleeding from at least a dozen spots, which means I'm some pretty attractive shark bait. My standard issue party vest has been ripped to shreds.

Without warning I slam into a rock wall. I churn alongside large chunks of debris in a small pool for quite some time, periodically being pushed back into the same surface. The clouds break for a moment and I can see that I'm at the mouth of the canyon. This means the beach, Eco barrier, and the ocean are around the corner. I can't feel the canyon floor with my feet, so the water must be pretty deep between the ocean waves coming in and storm water flowing out. I'm able to see a small rock shelf jettisoning out of the canyon wall a couple feet above water level. It appears to continue around the canyon's mouth. That's my opportunity to get a safe view of my situation since I don't know how close the Eco barrier is.

I dive low and then push upward with all my might, popping out of the water. After a few tries I'm able to grab hold of the shelf. I fall off and have to repeat the maneuver. On the fourth try, I pull myself onto it. Thank goodness I added pull-ups to my workout routine. The shelf's about three feet wide and slick from the rain. I gouge my hand pretty bad getting up, so hope it's worth it, because I really don't want to get back in that water. The shelf is too slick to walk on, so I inch forward on my stomach, using my forearms to propel myself.

The shelf angles upwards and narrows as it rounds the bend of the canyon mouth. But I press forward in darkness. The clouds have closed and the only way I can tell the shelf continues is by reaching out with my arms. It seems like hours pass before I have a decent view of the landscape again. I've managed to go from the inland side of the canyon wall, around the corner, and to the beach side. Waves are furiously breaking against the canyon wall below me.

Gads almighty. I had no idea I'd climbed so high. I'm at least thirty feet above the ground on a shelf just more than a foot wide. The Eco barrier may be directly beneath me, but I can't tell. There's less than ten feet of progress to be made before the shelf disappears entirely. The only thing I can do is wait for daylight. If the storm clears and sun appears I'll burn. My arms and head are exposed. The mud layer I'd once had on me washed off in the river. Perhaps the ocean route would have been wiser. Exhausted, I scoot my back against the cliff and close my eyes.

Scalding sun wakens me. My skin has turned a bright pink. The stone ledge burns to the touch. I allow my eyes to adjust. Despite the debris left on the beach, I can see the edge of the Eco barrier at least twenty feet to the south of me. Keeping all but my head atop the ledge, I peer over the side to see if the canyon face is uneven and might provide enough footholds to allow me to climb down. I see a few, but not enough to descend thirty plus feet without injury. That leaves me two options. Signal my dad and hope his team can help, or return to the other side of the Eco barrier and swim the ocean.

Signal first. I put two fingers in my mouth and whistle loudly in a pre-planned pattern of long short long short for about a minute. And then I wait. Given the Exilers will likely be sleeping, I try again. And again. Finally, I notice a figure jogging down the beach, hugging the cliffs to keep from being too noticeable. About fifty yards from me he stops and whistles a short long to respond. Only after I echo his tune does he catch sight of me and wave. He closes the distance and shouts up at me.

"Blake? Is that you?" says Doc Daryn. He hasn't seen me for nearly a decade, but perhaps my father showed him a recent picture. I figure he's pretty old by now and may not have stellar eyesight, particularly in the bright sun. His hair's long, white, and pulled back in a braid.

"Yep. Hey Doc. I'm getting fried up here. Any chance you have a thirty foot ladder handy?" I say.

"Sorry, buddy," he says. "I will, however, go get your father and his team and we'll try to figure something out."

"Hey, no hurry. I'm just in Garden City party attire and my sunscreen washed off. Take your time," I say. He waves his hands in dismissal of my snarky comments and jogs back up the beach. It's a full half hour before the rescue brigade arrives. They're wearing large sun hats and other protective gear, and have a shovel and large fishing net. Looks like they want me to play aerial circus clown. Super. My dad confirms my worst fears when he tells me that he expects me to jump.

"You know, Dad. We could just chat right here and then I can reverse my course. That might be a little safer than diving into your shoddily built fishnet," I say.

"We're going to dig a hole under in case you break through," he says. Sure, that would delay the pain, but who's he kidding? He's asking for me to jump to my death. "A ship will be arriving within the hour, so we're going to have to get this done and move our conversation to the caves. Otherwise, we're sitting ducks." True, given the heavy raiding activity of Interceptors, the ships have taken to firing upon any suspicious activity upon beaches or in the water.

They don't get much of a ditch built in twenty-five minutes, so they better hold that freaking net tight. I may bounce, but that's better than a thirty-foot free fall. I try to mentally calculate how far I'll need to jump outward to land directly above the ditch and center of the net. They roll it out and the men take their positions.

When my father gives the signal, I stand and pretend I'm jumping off the high dive at the local pool, rather into a twenty foot diameter fishnet held up by two dozen Exilers. I aim for center but am off by several feet when I land.

They've held the net too tightly and the cords slice into my skin before giving way and thunking me to the ground on my legs and back. I avoid hitting my head, but twist my ankle. Thankfully, though, I don't think I have any broken bones and I'm off the cursed ledge. Who knows how I'll ever get back to Garden City, but I might as well take this one step at a time.

Two men carry me back to the caves so that Doc can give me a once over. The lacerations and bruises will heal, as will my ankle. Of bigger concern are my burns. My party clothes are removed and I'm lathered with a thick gooey substance, and told to stay put for a few hours while it works its magic.

"So Doc, how's your Cleave?" I ask, trying to make conversation. Doc's Cleave will always hold a special place in my heart. She was practically my mom after my own mother died. Doc looks away for a moment, before turning to answer me.

"She passed a couple years back," he says. "It's been rough without her." I can tell it still hurts him. They were as tight as any couple I've seen.

"Oh no. I'm so sorry. How'd it happen?" I ask.

"In an unfortunate skirmish," he says. There's obviously a story behind it, one that likely involves the SCI.

"With SCI security?" He gets a very serious look on his face and clears his throat.

"Things have changed since you lived here. Not all the Exilers have the same goals. Linda went to bat for our beliefs and the opposition took issue," he says.

"Exilers did it?" I say, wondering if they were like the evil men who'd hurt me when I was young.

He shrugs his shoulders and says, "What's done is done and she's got no second chance at it. I can't dwell. It does no good. All I can do is try to do right by my people and avoid violence in the future." I nod, tears in my eyes, it hitting me hard that Doc's Cleave is gone.

Doc forces me to eat some nasty cooked grain, which makes me wonder how I'd survived my childhood. How spoiled and picky I've become. I used to be grateful to get any food at all. Though, I do remember a time when I'd gotten a taste of the good life and it soured my opinion of Exiled food for the rest my time spent living on Thera.

At age six, the Interceptors scored "the big haul." They'd sieged a freighter that was hauling supplies from Food City and Farm City to Garden City. Without any fancy-shmancy deep dock to pull into, and desiring to hurt the SCI's transportation system, they'd run the ship aground north of the Interceptor caves in a lagoon between canyons. The Interceptors set traps to dissuade any SCI men from entering the lagoon to retrieve the spoils.

Knowing the food couldn't survive the trip to our hot caves, they'd decided to move the people to the food. Our family and countless others trekked the relatively short distance and spent a month aboard ship. The accommodations were grim and cramped, but not enough worse than the caves to complain about it. Plus, after months of famine we welcomed the plenty. But even more than the food, I embraced the change of scenery. What little boy wouldn't want his run of a ship? One night I was an Interceptor. Next, a Spy. Then, a Militant. The younger kids on board, including Leila, served as my minions, the enemy, or my forces, depending on which game we played. Every adult had been assigned a full time job, so we had little to no supervision.

On one particular night, the adults dispersed to fend off an anticipated attack. Garden City's next shipment was due, which meant a new ship and fresh crop of security detail aboard. They'd be on the lookout for us and would eagerly await the opportunity to recapture their ship and supplies, although the ship had been so badly damaged when maneuvered into the lagoons it had a questionable future back on the open seas. The SCI had no way to know that, though. So, the adults camped near the feed from the lagoon to the ocean and waited, leaving their misfit kids aboard the ship. An adult or two may have been left on deck, but the bowels of the freighter were fair game for deep exploration.

That night I became "Blake the Great," a fearless explorer of unknown territories. We ventured into every nook and cranny of the ship, seeking great fortune and adventure. The metal ladders aboard presented no obstacle, as I found them infinitely more stable than the rope ladders of the canyons. Collecting items of great worth in a small plastic bag, we amassed a sizable treasure by midnight. By then we'd worked up a huge appetite and I decided to transform from "Blake the Great Explorer" to "Blake the Great Hunter." The supply hold was strictly off limits, but the usual guards were absent. I'd figured we'd be in and out long before the parents returned, so no harm done. We unlatched the door and entered.

The vault had been so vast that the light of our headlamps couldn't extend the length of it. Rows and rows of supplies. Boxes piled to the ceiling. Labels I didn't recognize. I'd been taught to read off a tablet the Interceptors stole in a raid, but had been limited to the text contained on that particular tablet, so most of the supplies were unfamiliar. We finally found boxes labeled "Food City" and figured that whatever was inside had to be edible. We opened the only box we could reach without toppling an entire stack.

Jackpot. The box had been filled with raw sugar and chocolate chips. We divided the spoils and kept eating until we'd devoured every last bit. I'd never tasted anything like it, the sweetness overloading my taste buds in a good way.

If the Interceptors had ever happened upon this stuff before, they'd kept it for themselves.

Despite being stuffed, we were desperate to find more of the same for later. We sent an entire stack of boxes flying, which had a domino effect on the entire row. If we'd hoped our intrusion wouldn't be noticed, we were out of luck. Thankfully no one had been hurt, as any of us could've been crushed had the boxes fallen a different way. Food had been strewn everywhere. We sampled everything that opened upon impact. Bananas. Cereals. Vegetables. Cookies. Many of the things needed cooking, but we didn't know that. So we moved on quickly from things like dry beans and pasta, and hoarded the good stuff in a pile. I don't remember a happier time in all my early years on Thera. We'd fallen fast asleep by morn with our mountain of goodies, for once without a care in the world.

Our parents had not enjoyed a peaceful, bountiful night as we had. They'd engaged in a bloody battle with an armed SCI security detail. Ultimately the Exilers overpowered the security forces, but not without a couple dozen losses on our side—men and women. Many of the dead were parents of the kids who'd joined my feast. The good times never lasted long as an Exiler on Thera.

Upon returning to the ship to bind wounds and prepare the dead for burial, the remaining parents found their children missing. A small search party scoured the ship before finding us sleeping, circled around our heap of favorite foods.

There's a couple ways it could've gone. The parents might have laughed about their kids getting their hands caught in the cookie and chocolate boxes. Admired us for being self-sufficient. For finding food and feeding ourselves. Or, they could whip the little thieves with leather lashes and confine them to assigned quarters for the duration.

I don't remember a whole lot of laughing on Thera, but I do vividly recall my father giving me twenty stripes for being the food raid ringleader. He and the Militant faction had taken out their anger and frustrations with the SCI on their children while the practical faction looked on with horror. With our wounds still fresh we'd been carted outside to help dig graves for the deceased in the marshy ground surrounding the lagoon. That included the kids whose parents died. I don't think I'd even dug a full grave in a couple hours' time, but that wasn't the point. The Militants wanted us to feel so much pain for the loss of these Exilers that it would erase any and all pleasure we experienced during our feast. Living Exiled is about survival. Not sugar with whipped cream and cherries on top.

Many tears had been shed as the remaining Exiled men lowered their friends' dead bodies into their shallow graves. I'd seen dead bodies before. It had been earlier that year that Leila and I were caught in a flash flood and the two men who'd gone looking for us drowned in the impromptu canyon river. But it wasn't until that moment I'd realized how hopeless life as an Exiler was. The odds weren't with us. Starvation. The elements. Unknown forces of evil. There'd even been deaths in our community from spoiled food, snakebites and severe sunburns.

The service was simple. Family and friends spoke kind words about the deceased having been committed to our cause until the end, the valiant way they'd fought our enemies, and that their sacrifice would be remembered by the living. The few Daynighters of the group who'd become acquainted with religion on Earth shared their beliefs that the dead would live eternally in heaven, a completely foreign concept to Therans who'd have been Exiled at the mere mention of a deity.

Following the burials, our leaders chose to have all of us return to the caves. They didn't want to risk another altercation with SCI security details. Our location was known so we weren't safe. Our group carried as many essential non-perishables as possible, but the bulk of supplies were left behind. The plan had been for a small group to return to get more boxes, but a large team of SCI security members had promptly reclaimed the ship. So, our men returned empty handed.

I never tasted sugar or chocolate again until I left Thera for Earth. Just the memory of my sweet encounter causes me to reject the pasty slop Doc gave me. I spit it back into my bowl and await my father. The sooner I get my message to him and updated orders, the sooner I get back to Garden City, real food, and to Kira.

After waking up from a quick nap, I seek out my father. I find him in the adjacent cave entrenched in a war of words with Doc Daryn. No one seems to notice me so I play fly on the wall while they finish out their "discussion." The cave's enormous—long and wide, with jagged ceilings low enough that I can almost reach out and touch the bats who are hanging. There's a few hundred men gathered in the cave. More than half are positioned behind Doc, the others behind my dad. The contrast between the two sides strikes me. My dad's men are lined up military style in an attention stance, waiting for orders. Doc's men are lounging about in an unorganized fashion, watching the exchange, many nibbling on some hard biscuits.

"Just go home, Doc and take your men with you. We've got this," my father says.

"You and your militant maniacs are on a suicide mission," Doc says. "You are completely underestimating the capabilities of the SCI."

"The security in Garden City is weak. I worked in Headquarters for years, remember? There were never more than a dozen security guards in the building and they don't even carry weapons. And throughout the city? There were none," my father says. He's pacing and waving his arms to emphasize his points. "The Ten and Grand Council? Completely unprotected. We have weapons and military training. They have no chance."

"That's what they *want* you to think. That they're weak. It's a trap. They want nothing more than for you to march in there expecting to take them out so that they can annihilate you," Doc says.

"And how will they do that, pray tell? They'll be lucky to get a ship from Military City to Garden City in a week with support. By then the leadership in Garden City will be replaced and we'll use their own Eco barrier to keep the security forces out. We'll easily get the community's support once the Second Chancers find out how far they've been misled," my father says.

"Hank, have these imbeciles you surrounded yourself with polluted your brain so much that you actually believe that? You really think you can march in there and take over?" Doc says. He's whirling his finger around his ear, indicating that he thinks my father has gone insane.

"And what glorious, brilliant plan does your band of pacifist losers have? Keep scrounging for morsels of food and water until the Exilers become extinct?"

"We *Survivalists* are strong in number and growing every day. Ten thousand plus, including our two sister communities. With the recent additions of several prominent Daynighter defectors we have the political clout to negotiate with the SCI. We're structuring our own government and will ask the SCI to recognize us as a valid entity on Thera. We control several entry and exit portals and could easily expose the SCI on Earth, so the SCI government leaders will have to listen. If you go in there and attack, you'll ruin any chance of negotiation." My father laughs wildly at the Doc's plans and signals his men to join the mocking.

I had no idea that the factions within the Exilers had become so fractured. What was once mere annoyance now borders on full-blown civil war. My father never told me that there was more than one way to handle the situation and provide relief for the Exilers. I look around the room. Of the men I recognize —the ones I trust are with Doc Daryn. The ones I don't are with my father. My mind reverts to what Doc said about the skirmish that killed his Cleave. Were the Militants responsible?

My father, once done with his laughing fit, addresses Doc again. "You think you can *negotiate* with the SCI? You're way more deluded than I am. If you threaten to interfere with their plans to create a master race of Originals and

167

inflict their political theology on Earth, they will unleash all of Military City on you."

"We wholeheartedly disagree," Doc responds. "But, the conversation's moot anyway since you'll never get into the city. Your idiotic plan to send your men across the Eco barrier on stilts will never work. You'll just alert the SCI to your presence and/or blow yourselves to bits."

"Actually, thanks to my son we now have a way into the city that doesn't involve stilts at all. We plan to build a ladder and enter in on the canyon ledge Blake found." Great. I seem to give my dad all his bad ideas. Unintentionally, of course.

"With all your guns and equipment? That ledge is fourteen inches wide at most from what Blake told me," Doc says, holding up his hands to show how small fourteen inches is.

"It will take time, but it can be done," my father says.

I've heard enough. I step out to address the group.

"That's crazy," I say to my father. "It took me hours to inch up that ledge."

"You did it in a rainstorm," my father says. "Stay out of this, Blake." He motions for me to exit.

"No. You put me front and center of your plan without informing me that there was any alternative. I have to agree with Doc. The SCI has greater capabilities than they're letting on. They killed a whole party full of kids to get my partner, Kira, to Thera. That kind of extreme action doesn't come from a government with lax security," I say. "Their technology seems sophisticated."

"Advanced technology won't help them when they don't have weapons or forces," my father says. "Back off. You gave us what we needed and I won't have a seventeen year-old kid who doesn't know squat telling us what to do."

"Well, if you don't need me, then I think I'll be going at first dark," I say.

"There's still work you need to do to prepare for our coup. I expect you to do what you are asked," my father says in a threatening tone.

My father wants me to find a way to permanently or temporarily disable the barrier, in case they need to retreat quickly. If Garden City authorities are pursuing them the Militants won't want to take the time to exit by the canyon shelf. He directs me to put the screws to Ted and get his help in accessing headquarters.

I stand by as the Militant leaders finalize their plans for entering the city, while individual units practice maneuvers. The Survivalists are forced out of the cave at first dark by gunpoint, although Doc Daryn is allowed to stay. Despite the harsh feelings between the two groups, Doc is still one of my father's oldest friends and the best doctor in the region.

Doc addresses me when my father is twenty hours into his strategy meeting and well occupied with his "generals." Whereas I'm ready to crash, he looks well rested. His wet hair smells like saltwater and looks like a limp jellyfish. "You don't need to do your father's bidding any more, you know." He pauses to reflect before continuing, "His approach is all wrong and I would hate to see you caught in the crossfire of his harebrained plan."

"Right now I just want to get back in the city," I say. "If I don't I'll have a lot worse problems than dealing with my dad and his crazies. The SCI will kill me if I can't explain my whereabouts."

The doctor turns to me with a hopeful gaze. His grip on my arm is so tight that it's cutting off my circulation. "You could be invaluable to our efforts in negotiating with the SCI," he says. "If we could guarantee the Exilers a better future without using force... if they could see that we aren't a threat, but as a neighboring country...." His voice trails off. He looks away and drops his hand as he sees me shake my head.

"I get it," I say. "But it wouldn't even help. Recruits are pretty low down on the hierarchy. How'd it get like this? The Militants and Survivalists? Is it as bad as it looks?"

"Worse," Doc says. "The split happened a couple years after you left. Your dad and his crew moved here and we stayed back in the canyon. I assure you, though, that the majority of the Exilers want a peaceful existence, without violence. I wasn't lying when I said I had more than ten thousand with me. Your dad has about three hundred. Unfortunately, they've stolen all but a small stash of our weaponry, so we've been powerless, despite our numbers."

"I'm all for peace, but what about the Second Chancers? How does your plan help them? If you simply coexist with the SCI, you help the Exilers at the expense of everyone else the SCI is oppressing," I say. He purses his lips. No one likes to be asked the hard questions.

"One step at a time, Blake," he says. "If we're recognized as an alternate entity on Thera we can grow in power and prosper. Then we'll have the strength to consider other options." That's all fine and good, but in the meantime a lot of people, including Kira, will suffer. From the expression on his face I can tell he knows his plan is deficient, but that he doesn't see a viable solution to help the Second Chancers right now.

We talk for a long while about the split of the Exilers and how it came to pass. And more about Doc's ideas to keep the peace. Although I think both sides are a little extreme in their stances, Doc seems to have thought things through better than my father. He refuses to confirm that the Militants were responsible for the death of his Cleave, though he didn't have to. The expression on his face when I asked spoke louder than any words he could offer.

I grow weary of the planning exercise and retreat to the cave next door and collapse on an old tarp in a dark corner that reeks like dead fish. It's critical that I get a few hours sleep before I attempt to return to Garden City, and to Kira. I have some begging of forgiveness to do.

To prepare for reentry, Doc scrapes the silvery burn ointment from my skin. As it pops blistery welts across my back, I scream in agony. It's not that he or I want to shun good medical treatment, but that I can't explain it. And if I can't explain it, it has to go. Hopefully I'll be found before sunrise. I'm not sure I can handle the pain of one hundred fifty degree sun on my burns.

On night two of my visit to my father, I get ready to depart. If I wait any longer, it's less likely the SCI rescuers will still be searching for me. My plan counts on being found. I want the SCI to assume I'd been too disabled to return home myself. That way I won't have to explain my disappearance.

I put back on my party attire—what's left of it—wishing the flash flood had happened during school hours. My regular school uniform would provide much better sun protection. Oh well, got to work with what I have. I drink a full flask of water and gnaw on a hard biscuit before bidding farewell to the Exiled Militants, and to Doc. My father tells me to ignore anything Doc Daryn said. He also emphasizes that his life and the lives of his people are in my hands and that failure isn't an option. Really, Dad? I'm glad you mentioned it, because I really haven't felt the pressure until now. I hope Kira's wrong and I don't have a whole host of children being grown in some Garden City lab. The only thing parents can possibly offer their child is disappointment, unrealistic expectations, and heartache.

The sand feels hot on my feet. I'd ditched my uncomfortable party shoes back in the river. I jog down the beach towards the Eco barrier. Depending on whether I can see a partial pattern, I'll decide whether to swim around or try to cross it. The sun's lingering above the horizon and sizable waves are crashing onto the beach fifteen feet away. Too bad I don't have my surfboard here. Given it is high tide most of the barrier is covered by the waves. I wonder if I could body surf it? If I swam out and across, I could potentially clear the barrier if I rode a big one in.

Despite piles of debris, I can make out sections of the pattern. The storm must have eroded the soil covering it. Either I've remembered incorrectly, or the layout has shifted. It's almost as if each detonator has moved ninety degrees on an axis from where I'd expect them to be, creating a completely new pattern. I stare, trying to figure out an explanation, when the detonators shift again. Some shift ninety degrees clockwise, others counterclockwise. I openly curse my father's naive assumption that I could ever cross the barrier on stilts. All that insane training in the desert was for nothing.

Even though it delays any futile attempt to cross, I wait out the next adjustment. I don't have my watch, but my best guess would be five minutes between rotations. My father definitely underestimated the intelligence of the SCI. Had I not found that canyon ledge, they'd have all died trying to cross the barrier. Best case, it would take me twenty minutes to cross with stationary detonators. It's impossible with randomly rotating ones, as the movements can't be anticipated. The barrier is foolproof.

That leaves my original idea of body surfing over the barrier. The barrier remains intact, even under water, per the folks I spoke to at the scale model of the city. In low tide the barrier is completely exposed on the beach. In high tide, it's at least partially covered with water. My hope is that if I catch a big enough wave that I can clear the barrier when I come crashing in. I'd swim farther to the South where the ships come in, as there is no barrier there, but in place of the barrier is a solid, sliding wall that only opens to let ships in and out of the docks.

Because I waste the remnants of sunlight studying the shifting patterns, I have to enter the water at twilight, which will make it more difficult to see what's coming.

No time like the present to die. I have zero desire to return to my father's cave to tell him I gave up without trying. The exit portal to Earth is a three-night journey. Even if I could remember the exact route, I have no supplies. And I couldn't leave Kira on Thera without attempting to rescue her. So, my decision's made before I can second-guess it.

I wade out into the ocean and the salt assaults every open wound. Clenching my teeth to keep from screaming, I dive under an incoming wave, and swim out twenty yards to keep the surf from prematurely pushing me to shore. Then I swim south fifty yards to clear the North border of the Eco barrier. I tread water for a few minutes waiting for the right swell.

"Here goes nothing," I say to the unseen ocean life.

The wave's a good pick. I swim with all my might to catch the crest, silently pleading with the Gads to deliver me safely on the other side of the barrier.

No such luck. The Gads must side with the SCI. I crash ashore right atop several detonators. They ignite immediately. The water absorbs a chunk of the lethal fumes. Not enough to protect my exposed areas, however. I can feel the skin melting from my arms and back, unprotected by my threadbare party vest. I'm not there for more than a second, however, as the combination of the blast and the next wave catapults me like I'm one of those dudes who flies out of cannons. When I land again, I realize I've cleared the remaining detonators, but the damage has already been done. If I'm not found quickly, there's no question I'll die. With my last bit of energy, I roll through the sand towards the canyon mouth. I hope the sand can mitigate the effects of the poison. Plus, I don't want to risk a larger wave sucking me back towards the barrier.

Help arrives quickly. Detonating the barrier must have set off alarms. The rescue team attempts to ask me what happened, but I'm too weak to speak. I can barely breathe, my lungs filled with burning gas. Head's pounding. Vision's blurry. Whispers of my bleak situation abound. Unstable heart rate. Severe chemical and sunburns. Scant breath tones and pulse. Unresponsive.

I'm transported on a board and by mule through the canyon. Brad Darcton and Ted Rosenberg await me at the burn unit. They chat while doctors clean and douse me with chemicals to diffuse the poison.

"Will he make it?" they ask the doctors.

"It's too early to say. We'll do everything we can. But it may not be enough," one of the doctors replies. Nice that the doctor is so optimistic.

"It's time to have Ethan show her the video and then distract her with a trip back home," Brad Darcton says to Ted. Ethan? She said she didn't know him. Was she lying? She certainly knows *some* Ethan by the way she looked at me when I asked her about him.

"You sure? Shouldn't we wait to play that card until we know if Blake lives or dies?" Ted responds.

"No. We play the card now so that we have her under control if he dies. Ethan's my pick for her anyway. He's equally qualified," Brad says.

"But he's not all of the Ten's pick," Ted says. "Some think you're biasing the panel because he's your son."

"At this point he's got the vote. Besides, I hardly think you're in a position to counsel me about Ethan or the girl. If Blake lives, then we'll see where the girl's at and adjust our strategy as necessary," Brad says.

Did I hear that right? Is Ethan the Intern really Brad Darcton's son and pick for Kira's Cleaving? It's too much to take in and I drift off to sleep, ready for the night when I can muck with all of Brad Darcton's plans.

Have the courage to live. Anyone can die.

Robert Cody

CHAPTER EIGHTEEN

Kira

Three zips. Two trains. A long mule ride. A short hike. All blindfolded and attached to College Boy. Obviously the powers that be do not want me to know the route to the exit portal. I spend the time in silent meditation hashing through the pathetic details of my life. And stressing over Blake's fate. I'm beating myself up for begging to leave Thera instead of waiting to hear whether they find him. Call me a wimp but I can't. Can't hide out waiting for a knock on the door bringing bad news or risk a confrontation with Tristan or Briella. What do I even say to them? They have zero memory of the crap they pulled, so I'll never get an apology. Guys can be real idiots, but what's Bri's excuse? Something lame like "I saw him first," I'm sure. Whatever. I just have to put it out of my mind for a while and enjoy time off this God forsaken planet. Ironic that I left Earth to escape my memories of them and now I'm fleeing Thera to do the same.

Ethan removes my blindfold once we're well into a dimly lit tunnel.

"Sorry about that," he says. "Security protocol."

"Yeah, you wouldn't want the Recruits leaving Thera. You'd have people sneaking off to go out to dinner. Or shop. They might even try to smuggle back in contraband like music or games or something," I joke.

"Funny, yes, we can't have that," he says. "Here's some clothes to change into. You can't wear your Theran clothes home." He hands me a bag.

"You expect me to change here? In front of you?" I say, my cheeks flush with color. "I don't think so."

"Please, if you want to go home, you'll do as I ask. I'll turn away to give you some privacy," he says. How thoughtful.

I partway undress and then peek at Ethan to see if he's peeking at me, and catch a glimpse of him with his shirt off. He's changing, too. Wow. I hesitate to take in the vision and allow myself to remember the way I'd felt about him when we first met, and how he took my breath away. A silvery scar on his chest —likely from some sort of surgery—serves as the only blemish on his otherwise perfect body.

He finally notices me watching him and we lock eyes for a moment, but then he sees I'm half dressed, swallows hard, bites his lip, and turns away. I quickly finish stripping down and replace my Garden City High uniform with a t-shirt, sweater, pair of jeans, and some flats. All my size, but not my original clothing.

"All set," I say as I hand him the bag filled with my discarded attire. He's now in low rider jeans, a tight fitting long-sleeved blue t-shirt and knit cap. The look works on him. A garbage bag would work on him. He's a Darcton, I remind myself. The Ten gave him this assignment. He may or may not be responsible for my friends' deaths. I can't allow myself to be attracted to him; need to bury my feelings for his alter ego.

"Excellent," he responds, throwing my bag to the side while keeping his eyes locked on mine. "Let's go."

"Thera's no place like home. Thera's no place like home. Thera's no place like home," I say while clicking my heels together. "Didn't work. I don't have the right shoes. Can I get some red sparkly ones?" I frown and cross my arms defensively.

He tries to hide his smile, but his shimmery sapphire eyes defy him. "Sorry, all out, Dorothy. Just walk the corridor and wait for me in the room with the light at the other side." Even though he's dressed now, I can't get the image of half-naked Ethan out of my brain. How can someone so beautiful be spawned by someone so evil?

As excited as I am to go home, I can't believe I have to be chaperoned. By Brad Darcton's son. The Ten must really not trust me to behave while home. I could cause all manner of trouble for the SCI if I went to the press with my story. The headlines would be killer: "Second Chance Institute Front for Zombie Slavery Enclaves on Earth's Sister Planet"; "Aliens Exist—But They're Really Your Dead Friends."

To rebel against my orders ever so slightly, I launch into a light jog before doing a couple perfectly executed back hand springs, an aerial, and then a back flip into a large, circular room. The room's round and paneled in cherry-colored wood. The electric sensation of the tunnel and parched feeling I'd gotten on the way in bothers me less on the way out. I look around and find the place odd. There's a metal circular staircase that goes down to another level and a lot of seams in the panelling that seem unnatural, although there's only a single opening where I came out and one doorway which is marked "EXIT" in large red letters.

Ethan's out of breath when he gets through, so I figure I might as well use that exit and see exactly where I am. Another warehouse in the middle of the ocean? I skip through the doorway and up a windy staircase that leads to a trap door. I push it open, climb a rope ladder, and find myself at the end of a concrete jetty.

"I know this place," I say out loud, looking to my left to see the ocean and my right to see Children's Beach in La Jolla from the jetty I'm standing on. A wave hits the sea wall and douses me with water. I feel cold for the first time in weeks. The sky is just turning light blue as the dawn breaks and dozens of seals are littered across the beach, less than twenty minutes from my parent's house. I love to come here to watch the seals, even if it's a huge controversy for the city. The space had been designated to be a children's swimming beach before the seals took over. What an odd place for an exit portal. Of course, the portal existed long before La Jolla and the jetty may have been built to help Daynighters get to shore with ease.

"Not cool," I hear behind me. Ethan's shaking and looks ten shades paler than he did on Thera.

"I'm sorry that I circumvented your precious Theran security protocol. If you need to, you can take me down a notch on the Circle of Compliance. But, seriously though, I can't enter through it. And I don't know where the entrance to it is back on Thera, nor would I rush to get back there if I did know. So, what does it hurt? Besides, you removed my blindfold and I didn't hear anything about putting it back on," I say.

"Can I expect this much trouble our entire trip?" he asks as he puts his hands on my shoulders. Despite his mild annoyance with my disobedience, the right side of his mouth is turned upward in a smirk.

"Trip? I thought I was coming home for good," I say, raising my eyebrows. I know it'd never be allowed, but he deserves to be tweaked.

"I wish you could stay, but you have yet to fulfill the terms of your contract. So, you will be returning to Thera," he says. He almost looks sad for me. The guy really doesn't show a lot of enthusiasm for his job.

"I was just joking," I say. "You were so much more fun the first time we met. Oh yeah. I forgot. That was just an act." He grimaces at my reminder of his betrayal.

"I wish it was a joking matter," he says. "Come on, let's get some breakfast before we head to your house. We need to get our stories straight."

Ethan obviously knows La Jolla well as he leads me off the jetty and up the hill towards a swanky hotel buffet breakfast. The walk dries me off and returns some color to Ethan's cheeks, but he's still looking a little off. Oddly I feel fine, though to me it feels like dinnertime, not breakfast. But it won't be the first time I've had breakfast for dinner. Yummy. I pile my plate full of eggs, waffles, pancakes, and fruit. And wolf down every bit. It's not that the food's bad on Thera—it's that the selection's limited and often far too healthy for my liking. He manages to get down some dry toast and a banana, but abstains from the rest.

"The return trip's always easier, but wow, you're amazing," he says. The slight twinkle in his eyes as he labels me amazing makes my stomach flutter. I almost buy that he means it about more than my world-traversing skills. Darcton. Darcton. Darcton. Evil. Evil. Evil. I repeat over and over in my head.

"What can I say? For some people, inter-worldly travel's just in their blood," I respond. As I stare at him, I'm reminded of his age and something strikes me. "What does your wife or Cleave or whatever you call the girl you told me about think about you playing babysitter to an unCleaved girl? Wouldn't she be kind of ticked to find out you flirted with me at that party, even if it was part of your *job*?" That brings a huge smile to his face.

"What makes you think I'm Cleaved?" he says, his amusement making the topaz twinkles in his eyes appear to jump out in three-dimensional fashion.

"You're old. Or older. Obviously over eighteen. You're Brad Darcton's son. I'd assume you'd have no choice but to follow the Canon strictly," I say, as if it's completely normal to be talking about while I push my remaining food around the plate.

"I'm twenty but am not Cleaved," he says. I cock my head and scrunch my face as I try to figure it out. "I live here—not on Thera. My dad brought me over when I was fifteen to live with my Uncle Henry. I started college at UCLA at sixteen and got my international relations degree by eighteen. And I just finished my second year of law school at University of San Diego. I spend summers interning for the SCI on Thera. The current plan is for me to go into politics—here." I note that he's careful not to say that it's *his* plan, just *the* plan for him to enter politics. Wow. Bizarre. Brad Darcton created a loophole for his own son.

"Oh, I guess I should have asked you a few more questions that night," I say. Under my breath I mutter, "About a lot of things."

"You have nothing to apologize for," he says. "I didn't want to bore you."

Although the details of his life are far from boring, what I really want to ask is about the girl and I can't let myself do that. Can't let him see how much he got to me that night. "So, what politically correct story have you concocted for my parents? Cause I'm betting we're not going with the truth." I study his face as he takes a couple deep breaths before answering.

"I'm a fellow Recruit in Unit 27. We fell for each other the moment we met and you just couldn't wait a full year to have your parents meet me. The program has helped put things in perspective for you. Helped you move on," he says, sharply inhaling and holding his breath as he waits for my reaction.

"And your alternative story is?" I say. "Because I'm not sure I can go along with that one. First, you're a Darcton. Second, you filmed my ex having sex with my best friend which is disgusting. Third, you may have been responsible for that explosion. Fourth, other than you being incredibly attractive and being able to fake a good conversation, I don't know you well enough to pull off a pretend relationship. Fifth, I'm in a relationship with Blake. Sixth, I'm going through a lot right now with Blake maybe being dead and the whole ex-best friend debacle. So, please come up with something else." I don't mention that my relationship with Blake has mostly been fake with some real undertones as of late, including the surprising declaration that Blake is supposedly falling for me.

He doesn't smile at this. His face is devoid of emotion as he speaks in a soft tone. "Listen to me very carefully, Kira. This is the only story that will explain the fact I'll be at your side every moment. And I *will* be at your side every moment. Many lives, including your own and your family members depend on your cooperation."

"You're threatening my family now? It wasn't enough to off all my friends?" I whisper. He leans across the table within inches of my face and stares into my eyes. I get a little dizzy at his proximity. His breath still smells like cinnamon.

"I had nothing to do with that, nor did I know it would happen. I almost died. My job that night was solely to keep track of you and your friends. But you are just going to have to trust me when I tell you that the Ten is serious. So please stop putting both our lives in danger and do as you're told," he says. He looks pained, as if he's seen the Ten in action a few too many times. No, worse than that. It's personal to him.

"What'd they do to you?" I ask.

"Nothing, and if they did it'd be none of your business. The less you know, the safer you'll be," he says, pulling back and looking away.

"Fine. Whatever. But, if you expect anything beyond some hand holding to pull off this scam, I'll warn you that my parents do not like public displays of affection. It's uncivilized," I say in the snottiest tone I can muster. He chuckles.

"As long as you can convince them I'm the love of your life without the PDA, then OK," he says. "You are attracted to me, so how hard can it be?" He's relaxing and showing off the flirty side I remember. Or starting up his act again.

"I said that you're attractive, not that I'm attracted to you. Besides, you don't want me in love with you," I say. I'm trying to focus on the negative things about him to keep my attraction at bay, but I know I'm failing. If there were a formula for perfection in appearance, Ethan would be the natural output of it. "Bad things happen to the people I care about."

"Well, then you must be head over heels for me already," he says with a wink. "Because I've been kind of down on my luck lately."

"What? Did the love of your life reject you or something?" I say, obviously striking a nerve as a sad look sweeps across his face. Is his girlfriend no longer in the picture? "Because, since you're not dead or presumed to be dead like I thought you were and Blake likely is, I wouldn't be complaining," I say.

"Understood. There's degrees of bleak," he says. "But, if you're in hell, you're still in hell whether directly in the fire or standing right next to it."

"Whenever you're ready to tell me about it, I'll listen," I say. I may or may not believe what you say, but I'll listen, I think.

He looks away for a moment and then nods before saying, "The check's paid. Time to meet the parents."

My parents adore Ethan. In fact, if they knew about Cleaving I bet they'd lobby to institute it here. Who wouldn't want a twenty-year-old son-in-law who's already completed his second year of law school? And who has political aspirations with the face to pull it off? He's charming, polite, and listens to every boring story they tell like it's the best tale he's ever heard. They're not privy to the small little details of his life to round out their impressions—like the fact he was born on another planet to a dictator father.

Jared, on the other hand, refuses to buy that I left a few weeks ago a complete mess, miraculously healed, and fell in love all over again. Well, I did fall for Fantasy Ethan. Just not Reality Ethan. And I have feelings for Blake, but am not ready to declare my love for him.

We've been at my parents' house for thirty hours. Ethan slept on the living room couch next to my downstairs bedroom. And even that level of proximity took Ethan selling my parents that he'd only enter my room in case of a non-romantic emergency. The "time change" has decimated my internal clock so I was out cold. I'd barely made it to seven o'clock last night before passing out. I have no idea how I got into pajamas and into my bed and I'm not sure I want to know. And right now I'd love to take a seven or eight hour nap, but that's not in the cards.

Jared pulls me aside while Ethan's busy tasting my mom's dinner concoction.

"Spill, sis," he says. "You and Mr. Model? I'm not seeing the sparks. You look like you're pissed at him all the time." He narrows his light blue eyes at me. Typically I'm brilliant at masking my feelings with a smile, but I just can't get over the fact that Ethan's a Theran, a Darcton, and that he was at that party on the Ten's business. I wonder if I'd have been better off if he'd kept avoiding me. No, perhaps I needed to know the truth. Fantasy Ethan was seriously interfering with my ability to consider a relationship with Blake. Reality Ethan is flawed like all other guys. He isn't some character from a fairy tale.

"You know how Mom and Dad are," I say. "If I showed sparks, they'd get out the fire extinguisher."

"Hardly. They like Ethan so much that I'm sure they've already driven down to get your marriage license. But the way you used to look at Tristan... totally different from how you look at Ethan. And where's the brushing hands against each other and sneaking kisses in the pantry?" he asks.

"Ethan's not just some high school fling. He's a little beyond that," I say, trying to cover my tracks. It's true that I've done little to perpetuate the fantasy of a real relationship. I'm terrified to trust myself around Ethan, because I could so easily forget his lineage and give into him if I was just to go on the attraction factor. Ethan sees that Jared has me cornered, which must worry him, because he's over in an instant.

"Hey, beautiful. I missed you," Ethan says, staring into my eyes. He leans down to kiss me and I'm so taken aback by the surprise, and quite illegal, sweet tasting move that it takes me a couple seconds to pull away. My heart's going haywire, but my brain resents his gesture. I involuntarily lick my lips to savor the touch of cinnamon he left behind. He gives me his patented smile, spreading from right to left. Lawyers and actors share a lot of attributes, and I'm ready to give him an Academy Award for his "save" performance. I want to hurt him, but instead I plaster on my fake smile and hold my tongue.

"How's the dinner tasting?" I ask. "Would you rather eat out? I know a great place." I'm trying to decide between ten-star spicy Thai food and a five-diamond restaurant that would put him back a few hundred bucks as punishment.

"It's dreadful," Ethan whispers, his lips touching my ear, which makes me shiver. "But, I wouldn't want to disappoint your parents."

"This is my vacation and I really feel like I've had enough family time for tonight... or today," I say, correcting my mistake. "I insist you take me out and put a dent in your daddy's trust fund for you."

Ethan leaves to smooth over our decision to eat out with my parents, while Jared continues to grill me.

"He's infinitely more believable than you are," Jared says. I roll my eyes at him.

"Did you ever think I might just be tired from the time change?" I say.

"What's the time change again?" he asks, trying to narrow down the possibilities for where I might be stationed. Or to catch me in a lie. If Jared was half as curious in school, he'd be top of his class.

"You know I can't talk about it," I say. "I'd be kicked out of the program. I'm not willing to risk my future over it." Or your future. Or mom and dad's futures. I can't handle more deaths on my conscience. Especially not my family's.

"All I know is that the secrets can't be a good thing," he says.

"You're just irked I left you behind to deal with Mom and Dad all by your lonesome," I say. "A few weeks ago you were begging to come with me."

"Does Ethan have a cute sister?" he says, changing the subject. Yikes, I have no idea. I hope my face doesn't betray my ignorance.

"Sorry, buddy. No sisters," Ethan says, coming up behind Jared. To me he adds, "Your dad gave me his keys to the Mercedes. Let's go. I'm taking you for the most romantic date you've ever had." Ethan pecks me on the lips again and then grabs my hand to drag me towards the garage. Jared's down on one knee and pretending to open a ring box. Funny, Jared. Ethan sees it and winks at Jared. I'm not amused. Once in the garage I pull my hand from Ethan's and bring my fingers to my lips to pretend to wipe off his cinnamon taste.

Ethan takes me through the McDonalds drive-through. I hate to say it, but I'll take the McRib sandwich, a chocolate shake and french fries over my mom's cooking any day. We drive to the beach and Ethan lays out a blanket he must have found in our garage. I'm a little irked my fries are cold by the time we get there. Eating in my dad's car though... never going to happen. He'd contact the SCI to make sure they grounded me on Thera and may still do that if we can't air the car out by the time we get back.

"Romantic enough for you?" Ethan says. "Restaurant food. Beautiful view. Fabulous company." He's kicked back on the blanket shirtless, enjoying the relatively hot day for San Diego. He's like the perfect combination of Tristan and Blake, physically at least. Six foot one, toned, oozes sex appeal. Even the six-inch scar he has on his hair-free chest somehow makes him look more appealing. His abs... holy smokes. But as nice as he's been to me, I can't get over his pedigree chart.

"You must not have dated much in college. McDonalds on the beach really doesn't scream romantic date. Too busy racking up the degrees to figure out the dating protocol, eh?" I say.

"Not at all. I dated. And none of those dates warranted a trip through the McDonalds drive-through. You, on the other hand, are lucky to have gotten fed given your lackluster performance the last couple days," he says. "A steel post could have mustered up more excitement about that kiss. I expected so much more from you."

"We'd agreed *not* to kiss," I say. "You caught me off guard."

"I agreed to no such thing. You were supposed to sell everyone on our incredible whirlwind love story. I managed to get your parents to like me, but your brother's not buying any of it," he says. He narrows his eyes and adds, "And I knew you wouldn't dare react to the kiss. You know what's on the line."

"Keep up that line of talking. That'll warm me up to you," I say with a sneer. "I'm so sick of this crap. Do you honestly think I've forgotten the threats? Please don't treat me like an imbecile."

"I don't think you're an imbecile at all. Just a terrible kisser, so I was disappointed. I could give you lessons," he says, laughing.

"You think I don't know how to kiss?" I say. "I assure you that I do. I just don't want to kiss *you*. I don't like you and I don't trust you," I say. He scoots closer to me so that I have to look him straight in his gorgeous sapphire eyes.

"Really? Can you tell me with all honesty that you didn't feel anything for me at that party?" he asks. "I kind of thought you were into me, but maybe I was just deluding myself." He doesn't say it in an "I think all girls love me" way, but in almost an embarrassed to even be asking way.

"Why do you think I did?" I ask, answering his question with a question.

"Well, other than all the flirting and blushing, you just seemed really concerned about whether I was alive when I showed up on Thera and so annoyed that I didn't come see you sooner. You were keeping track of my whereabouts," he says in a tentative tone.

I gaze out towards the ocean, not wanting to look at him any longer. I'm embarrassed my feelings were so apparent. "That was before I knew who you were. Your sweet act at that party was just a ruse."

"Come here," he says, motioning me towards him. I lean forward slightly. "Closer." I don't want him to kiss me to make his point so I make sure the only thing near his face is my ear, although even his breathing in my ear makes me reconsider. When his lips brush my ear by accident I have to take a deep breath to keep from suggesting we head back to Thera and Cleave. A move I'd regret, as I don't ever want Darcton in-laws.

He strokes the side of my face and then says, "You're going to have to trust me at some point that I have as much on the line as you do. Do not for one moment think that because Brad Darcton is my father that I get preferential treatment. I do what I'm told or the consequences are as severe for me as they'd be for you. Stop punishing me for who my father is. I'm nothing like him and you know it. I never misrepresented myself at that party."

I turn my face towards him and realize his lips are a mere inch from mine. Swallowing heavily, I whisper, "Really? Are the Ten threatening to kill your family? I don't think so. Your dad is one of the Ten and your family is safely on Thera."

"No, but the Ten will have the girl I love killed," he says. If he's being honest, which it looks like he is, his perfect girl is still in the picture and her life is on the line. Which means he's as terrified as I am. I should be relieved to know he's not evil like his father. But instead I'm jealous of his girlfriend and angry that Ethan wasn't born into another family.

Once Ethan confessed his precarious situation to me and I could see he was a fellow "blackmailee" in this whole mess, I relaxed and decided to enjoy my vacation. We did all the things I'd missed while living on Thera, from shopping, to eating out at my favorite haunts, to seeing a movie at a drive-in theater, to afternoons at SeaWorld and the zoo. And we hung out by the pool to soak in sun that wouldn't fry us. We played games and had fun. Ethan acted like a little kid everywhere we went. For the level of enthusiasm he showed you'd think he was doing it all for the first time.

It hasn't been hard to pretend that Ethan's my boyfriend. In fact, sometimes I have to remind myself that it's all an act and that I'm not just living out the fantasy I dreamed about in the months I thought he was dead. Dates, cuddling, holding hands, laughing, joking around. After all, even though Ethan treats me like a queen and an outsider would never know he's not completely devoted to me, he's in love with someone else. In the moments that makes me jealous, which has happened a bit too often, I remind myself that Blake cares about me, assuming Blake's alive and returns to Garden City. Somehow, though, I've come to doubt that Blake is alive or, if he is, that he will return. Wouldn't they have summoned us back from vacation if they'd found him?

Jared's now completely sold that Ethan and I are head over heels in love. Or he has been since he taunted us for not being affectionate enough and we kissed again.

"Do you think you can sell it this time?" Ethan had whispered, although he said it in a joking, flirty fashion.

I sold it. I didn't feel it, but I did sell it. No, that's a complete lie. I felt it. It was impossible not to because of my convoluted feelings, the fact Ethan's a really exceptional kisser, and that he sold it like I was the love of his life. We were in the pool. I was in my bikini, Ethan in his swimsuit. The whole thing played pretty steamy, but I figure actors and actresses have to do it all the time. Doesn't matter, I only did it to support our bogus story. Ethan hasn't teased me since about needing kissing lessons and he's encouraged as much repeat behavior when Jared's around "to further the cover" as possible. Why do I get saddled with the bogus relationships? By deceit or design, they all suck.

The way Ethan looks at me sometimes has me wondering "if that's the way he looks at me, how does he look at his real girlfriend? And does he melt her heart, too?" Tristan told me he loved me. I know the look. I just don't know how Ethan pulls it off with me when his heart lies elsewhere. The guy's a brilliant actor, because he acts smitten even better than Tristan or Blake. How easy it would be to fall for him if he didn't love someone else and I wasn't so stressed about Blake. He's just so nice to look at—and fun.

During our time off, I also spent some time researching "assisted pregnancies" and believe, more than ever, that the doctors harvested my eggs. If they used Blake's sperm to create embryos, those embryos could have been implanted as soon as five days later. Or they can be frozen and stored for later. Ethan caught me researching it and insisted I explain. He thought I was being paranoid, but I could tell that he saw there were too many similarities to be dismissed as coincidence.

If I never appreciated my circumstances before, this vacation has helped me count all the blessings I'd enjoyed before becoming a Recruit for the SCI. Daytime living. Choices. Open schedules. Capitalism. Even the loving concern of my parents beats being used by dictators. The more I contemplate going back to Thera, the more claustrophobic I feel about my freedoms being quashed. Somewhere in the back of my head I hear a voice screaming to remember what happens when I outwardly rebel, but I ignore it.

It's during this moment of reflection, at the height of my appreciation for earthly life, that Ethan informs me our vacation is over. We're out by the pool, I'm happily getting my vitamin D fix, drinking a diet soda, and reading a trashy novel. His timing sucks.

"I won't go back," I say, openly tempting Karma and not caring as I do. "My parents aren't perfect, but they don't threaten me with death and Exile if I don't follow all the rules." I slurp down the rest of my drink and return to my book.

"Kira," he says softly. "If it was up to me, you know that I'd let you stay. But, it's not. Bad things will happen if we don't go back."

"Did they tell you that my *real* boyfriend, Blake, is alive and well yet?" I ask. "Because that would be motivation for me to go back. Short of that though…" It's one of those thoughts that I should have left in my head, because Ethan looks offended and hurt by my jab.

"Well, no," he says, looking at his hands and nervously running his fingernails across his thumb. "They didn't. I wish I had good news for you, but they haven't said anything about him. I'm so sorry. That doesn't mean he's not fine. You can't assume the worst."

"Sure I can. Truth is, I can't handle the bad news. If and when they have good news, then they can come get me," I say, not even bothering to look up from my reading, even though I haven't progressed more than ten pages in the last hour.

"We have to go. Our boat will be here this evening and they'll make sure we are on it one way or another," he says. He looks terrified. What's he expecting? That they'll come drag me out of my parents' house? Let them. My parents can issue an Amber alert and perhaps the goons from the SCI will get arrested.

I finally put down my book and turn to him, speaking in a bitter tone. "Look. I know you're probably worried about your girlfriend. But it's not like they are going to punish you for failing to compel me to return. So, feel free to leave any time. Go Cleave Ms. Perfect and enjoy the rest of your summer internship with your daddy." I shouldn't bring up the girlfriend, but I think to myself, the girl should dump him anyway. Assignment or not, Ethan's been playing my boyfriend a little too well. There's nothing I dislike more than cheaters. I mean, sure, he's doing it because he's being blackmailed, but I think he could have toned down the PDA and still made his ruse about our relationship work.

"I'm not leaving without you, Kira," he says. He's sits up straight and grabs my hand. "They will punish me, but that's not my concern right now. I'm concerned about how they'll punish you."

"What? They'll blow up my friends? Been there. Done that," I say. "I'm not discussing it any further. I think I've had enough sun. I'm going to go in to watch some bad TV or listen to some music while I eat some junk food." He closes his eyes and takes several deep breaths.

He droops his head and shakes it vigorously. "Oh, Kira. You don't know what you've done. You have no idea."

Ethan's super clingy all afternoon, almost as if he's shielding me from the storm that he thinks is coming. He hasn't let me do anything short of use the bathroom by myself. I had fun most of the trip with him, but this afternoon— it's gotten to the point of being stifling. He completely ruins my recorded season finales marathon with his whiny pleadings.

When the doorbell rings at dinnertime, I assume it's the pizza guy and answer the door with enthusiasm for some grease-covered bread. Imagine that. You go on your computer, place an order, and someone brings food to you that you don't have to prepare. Bonus.

But it's not the pizza guy. I curse at Karma in my head when I see our visitors. It's two men toting guns with silencers. And they have four girls in tow. The men are hooded and are wearing dark sunglasses. They herd us all towards the kitchen, where the rest of the family has gathered for the expected pizza. The color drains from every face in the room. It's clear this won't end well. The mystery girl guests' hoods are removed and they all seem shocked to see Ethan.

"I thought you were gone for the summer," one of them says. She's your typical Southern California blue-eyed blonde, with enough unnatural curve to make me wonder whether her plastic surgeon daddy helped her fill a D cup.

"How? Why? And who is she? Wait, that's the girl who you had a picture of on your phone that you refused to delete," the girl adds, pointing at me. He kept that? Is this his girlfriend? Seriously? Yuck. I'll add that to "being a Darcton," "can get clingy," and "cheats on love of life" on his list of negatives. Bad taste in women. Really bad taste.

"That's Ethan's girlfriend—my daughter, Kira. He plans to marry her," my father says. Idiot. My dad's obviously deluded. Did Ethan give him that impression? That we'd get married? No way. He'd have no reason to set that expectation. Ethan shyly avoids my gaze when I look at him.

"You're what? You are going to *marry* her?" the girl screams. The other girls look equally as disgusted. "Don't believe him—Kirie, or whatever your name is —Ethan is seriously anti-commitment."

"Shut up. All of you," one of the gunmen says. "You will speak only when directed to do so." I'm down with that. It has been quite a while since I've been in a room with such a low average IQ level, Tristan and Bri's party being the last time.

"Ethan, if you feel the need, please explain your behavior to your host of girlfriends from the past year. And, of course, say your goodbyes." Everyone looks confused. I believe the girls think the men plan to execute Ethan. But both Ethan and I know better.

"I'm really sorry, Sarah. And, Beth and Courtney and Aliya. When I... dated... each of you I had no idea that I was putting you in danger. I should have, but I was naive. If it helps, I can assure you there's life after death in this kind of situation," he says, fumbling over his words, shaking with anger and fear. He appears to be collecting his thoughts to say something more.

Too late. The impatient gunmen execute them—two at a time. Courtney and Aliya first, and then Beth and Sarah. Less than ten-seconds passed and four lives extinguished. They'll likely show up on Thera somewhere and will gratefully not know Ethan or me from Adam and Eve. Ethan steps in front of me to shield my body, rigidly holding my arms, as if he's worried that I'm next. We're all covered with bits of brain, although it's somehow not as messy as I had imagined. It occurs to me I may be in shock.

My parents don't react well to seeing four college-age girls executed and oozing blood all over their kitchen floor. They weep. Beg. Scream. And try to run. They don't get far, stopped in their tracks when they see guns pointed at Jared's head.

"Ms. Donovan, I assume you have some final words for your family?" the speaking assassin says. I wriggle out of Ethan's hold and step to the side to address the man.

"I do, but first I have a thought for you. Jared's as much of an Original as I am. Do you really want to make the same mistake you made with Blake's sister, Leila? Does the DNT stay active when you cross over that way?" I ask. I can tell I struck a nerve. I'm playing a hunch, guessing that someone with DNT who crossed as a Second Chancer has less appeal than those who cross over alive. Otherwise, they'd have just killed Blake and me, and spared Blake's sister and my friends. My parents likely have DNT, but since they're past reproducing ages, I know they have no chance of being saved. The two men whisper amongst themselves while I address my parents. While I speak, I try to think of a way out of this. A way my parents and brother can survive.

"I'm super sorry, Mom and Dad. I love you so much and appreciate everything you've done for me. I'm so sorry to have been so difficult after the explosion and put you through so much agony. It's not like you'll remember this or believe me, but I promise these gentleman will arrange for you to live the remainder of your lives on a planet named Thera. You won't recognize Jared or me, but everything will be provided for you. It'll be a clean slate and a chance to be happy again." No words can soften the blow, convey my pain, or my guilt.

My parents look like they want to respond. Perhaps even tell me they love me, too. But before words can leave their mouths the bullets enter their brains. Six bodies now. I collapse to the floor, unable to breathe. Because I know I did this. I defied a direct order to return. My own parents are dead because of me. I deserve to return to that hellacious rock. I deserve death. But I won't be granted death or the peace of a second chance with erased memories. The assassins grow weary of my display. I swallow my sobs, kiss each of my parent's foreheads and then close their eyes. They've been so unhappy—with me and with each other. Perhaps a fresh start will be good for them. To hold it together I have to embrace one good thought. I'm yanked back to my feet.

What will they do about Jared? He is frozen. Paralyzed. Likely thinking if he moves an eyelash the men will put a bullet through his brain. Ethan steps back in front of me, holding both my hands tightly to keep me from moving. The assassins confer quietly while keeping one gun pointed at Jared, another at Ethan and me. I mouth "I'm sorry" to Jared, but he doesn't respond. One gunman circles Jared, gun pressing into Jared's head. Jared lets out a low groan as he awaits the bullet. The other gunman heads towards Ethan and me. Ethan turns to embrace me, pressing his body hard against me, his lips to mine, with a level of desperation that I've never experienced. As he does so, the gunman pries our lips apart with his gun and shoves it into my mouth. His partner has dragged Jared over and has both Ethan and Jared covered to keep Ethan in check, knowing that Ethan would make a move to protect me.

The seconds feel like hours. Ethan's screaming "No, no, please don't. It's my fault. Kill me." Jared's still moaning. I stay perfectly still and look directly into the assassin's sunglasses. Please kill me, I will him with my eyes. I can be another SCI Second Chancer puppet or waste away into nothingness. Although I can feel the beads of sweat drip down my face, that bothers me less than the waiting. I taste metal and am keenly aware that the gunman's finger is pulsing against the trigger. Do it.

The creep shoves the gun a little farther into my mouth, hitting the back of my throat and making me gag. He whispers into my ear, "You best not disobey orders again" before yanking the gun back out of my mouth. He then drags me by the hair over to Ethan and Jared. Looks like I'll live to see another night. I don't deserve the easy way out anyway.

The gunman kneels before me and says, "So, if you can only take one of them with you, who would you choose? Your brother or the boy toy?" He alternates pointing the gun at each of them chanting, "Eeny, meeny, miny, moe, shoot a traitor in the toe. If he hollers, let him go? I don't think so, no, no, no." I look neither to my right to Ethan or left to Jared, not trusting the gunman to honor my choice, even if I could make one. "Now don't make me kill them both… or do you have another deal you'd like to strike with me?"

"How about we go try to make that boat? All of us," I say. "Haven't you hit your quota for today on 'accidental deaths' to provide new labor for Thera? Doesn't the SCI only get to pull across 50,000 a year?" I'm angry. Devastated. Determined to be the one to die. To keep Ethan and Jared alive.

My quip earns me a pistol whipping with such force that I end up in Ethan's lap and his soothing voice pleads, "Don't leave me, Kira. Please don't leave me."

CHAPTER NINETEEN

Blake

I awaken having no idea how long I've been out or why. I'm flat on my stomach, with my head cradled in a large donut attached to my bed. As I attempt to get up and feel pain at the attempt, my memories of crossing the Eco barrier return. I'm attached to dozens of tubes and machines and am bandaged like a mummy.

"Excellent," a voice says. I turn to see a potbellied man with a bad combover in a white coat. My doctor? I think so, but the circumstances of my rescue are still pretty fuzzy. "You're awake. I'm going to remove your bandages and see how things are healing." I'd respond but as I try to vocalize I feel the tube running down my throat and start to gag.

"Don't try to take it out. Let me examine you and if I think you're ready, then I'll remove the tube," he says. I nod and wait as he painstakingly removes bandages and inspects every inch of my body. After what seems like hours, he slowly slides the tube from my throat. I choke, cough and sputter before I speak.

"Kira? Is she okay?" I say, barely recognizing my voice.

"I'm sorry," the doctor responds. "I'm not familiar with anyone named Kira." I vaguely remember a conversation between Ted Rosenberg and Brad Darcton about her, a video, and Ethan. Was that real or did I dream it? I have no idea.

"When can I go home?" I say.

"You're doing remarkably well for someone who came in contact with the Eco barrier. We were able to get an antidote for the poison in you quickly, but it will take quite a while for you to build your lung capacity back up. You sustained some pretty severe burns on your shoulders, back and arms that required skin grafts, and then some more modest burns on your hands, feet and face that are healing nicely. We induced a coma to allow your body time to focus on regenerating," the doctor says.

"Can I see a mirror?" I ask. I've never been vain, but the way he describes my injuries, I fear I look like Frankenstein. He complies, getting a couple small hand mirrors. A two-inch gash extends along the hairline of my forehead. It had been closed with stitches, which are already removed. I can live with that. My skin looks patchy from the healing burns. I find similar stitched abrasions on my hands and feet. My clothing had covered part of my chest and legs, but the chemicals in the blast had dissolved the clothes and skin from my back and arms—thus, the more severe injuries.

He has to hold one of the mirrors to help me see my back and backs of my arms. There are four patches of graft. Each appears raised and pink, with vein-like swirls and dots of red.

"Your body is accepting the grafts well. There should only be minor scars. You won't be able to do any exercising for at least three more weeks," he says, before describing in disgusting detail the process used to graft the skin to my body and risks of over-stretching it. A knock at the door interrupts and my buddy, Brad Darcton, joins us.

"Well, well, well," he says. "Wonder boy pulled through after all."

"I'd like to see Kira," I say, adding, "if possible."

"I'm afraid she's not here," he says. "I'm here to discuss the events that led to your injuries, Blake. What happened?" Thankfully, this is a conversation I'm prepared for.

"Kira and I went to the dance… the night of the flash flood, however long ago that was," I say. I have no idea how long I'd been in a coma. "She left to get some air and must have been quite a ways down the canyon when the alarms went off. I heard her calling for me."

"Fast forward to the part where you end up by the Eco barrier nights later," he says. I stare at him for a moment and notice that he has a small, circular pin with the number ten on it fastened to his city headquarters attire. For how much respect these folks expect, I'm surprised they don't wear a flashier nod to their authority.

"Sorry. I'm still a little fuzzy, so I'm trying to remember as I go. We ended up in the river at the bottom of the canyon. We were able to swim to the edge and I pushed Kira up into some brush, but the current carried me away. I couldn't see because it was so dark. I was carried a long ways with a lot of debris. At some point I grabbed onto a plank and managed to get myself on top of it. By daylight, I was in the ocean. I could see the shoreline, but was quite a ways out."

"You were in the *ocean*? How'd you get over the Eco barrier to get into the ocean?" he asks in an accusing tone, obviously not believing my story.

"I don't know. As I said, I couldn't really see. But the water in the river was deep. I assume I just floated over it," I say. Had I continued and not climbed up on the canyon shelf, this is exactly what would have happened.

"So then, how'd you get back in?" he asks.

"Well, I paddled towards my best guess of where I'd come out of the canyons. I remembered from the city model we visited that the desalinization plant was south of the canyon that the school was in. I was pretty weak, but finally I decided I might have a chance at high tide of clearing the barrier if I body surfed in," I say. This is true.

I can see veins pop in his forehead and neck. Perhaps in his anger he'll have a small stroke. "You thought *what?*" he asks.

"I just figured that the water would be higher at high tide and that I might be able to float over like I did on the way out. Obviously it didn't work very well. When I tried, I crashed into the barrier and the explosion sent me flying," I say. I describe in detail exactly how I hit, the effect of the water on the blasts, and how I'd finally cleared the other pressure points. Honesty will serve me well here. There's no way I could describe the event so vividly without having experienced it. Not to mention I have the injuries to back my story. He seems satisfied with my explanation. At least for now.

"Well, I'm happy I won't have to deliver bad news to your parents," he says. "The Second Chance Institute prides itself on taking good care of our Recruits. We have our very best doctors on your case." I'm sure you do. I'm the future of Thera, after all, aren't I? Or am I? The memory of his conversation with Ted Rosenberg still haunts me. He said Ethan was his choice for Kira. I can't believe I'd joked with Kira that she should go for him if I didn't return. Of course, at the time I had no idea that Ethan the Intern was Ethan Darcton, son of a member of the Ten.

"Yes, thank you for the excellent medical care," I say. "And for the rescue." He nods.

"I'll talk to the doctor and will expect you back on duty as a Recruit as quickly as possible," he says. "There have been some unfortunate activities happening with your Second Chancers that we need someone on top of."

"Like?" I say. What have they done while Kira and I have been away? Did Brad and the rest of the Ten find out about their parties and TB pimping? I'm interested to know.

"Just get better and your Handler can apprise you of the situation when you return," he says, before upping himself and promptly leaving the room.

With strict instructions to abstain from any physical exercise, including boarding, running, and anything else I might do in the gym, I'm released a few nights later and taken home. They dress me in a loose fitting Garden High shirt to protect, but not irritate, my grafts.

Bri and Tristan happen to be out on their patio when I'm wheeled up the ramp to my house in a wheelchair.

"Hey, man," Tristan says, jumping over the barrier to my patio. He's got his Garden City High shirt off and draped over his shoulder. "Can I help?" he asks the nurse.

"Yes, thank you," she responds to Tristan. He takes control of my wheel chair. To me she says, "Remember your release instructions. A nurse will be by twice a night to check you out. Get plenty of rest and drink lots of water."

"Yeah, I got it," I say. The nurse departs and I get up out of the wheel chair and go inside. Tristan and Bri follow and make themselves at home in my living room. I ditch the wheelchair and hobble in to join them.

"So, what happened to you? I thought… Kira thought you were dead," he says. "She was pretty freaked."

"Was?" I say.

"Haven't seen her in forever. She just vanished out of thin air. We've both asked around. No one's seen her," he says. I look at Briella, but she just shrugs her shoulders.

"How could she just disappear? Was she OK after the flash flood? Tell me exactly what happened," I say. Tristan and Bri each take turns telling me Kira's story. It sounds like she disappeared shortly after being released home from the hospital.

I need to talk to Ted Rosenberg. He'll know. Wait. Brad Darcton directed Ted to "have Ethan show her the video and then distract her with a trip back home." Perhaps she really did get to go home?

"Could she be with a guy named Ethan?" I ask.

"The only Ethan I know is Brad Darcton's son," Briella says. "I met him on one of our field trips. He's helping his dad with some stuff for the summer, but lives somewhere else the rest the year. You better hope Kira isn't with him as she might forget all about you, Blake." Thanks. I hadn't been worried about that already.

"You mean that guy you were crushing on?" Tristan accuses Bri.

"I wasn't crushing on him. He was hot. So what? He has to be at least twenty so I'm sure he's Cleaved. Gads. I can't believe you'd accuse *me* of crushing on another guy after you mauled Kira," she says.

I ignore the rest of their quibbling. All I know is that Ethan is Brad's pick for Kira—so he can't be Cleaved—and that Brad arranged for Ethan to take my girlfriend on vacation. He said Ethan was "equally qualified" to be Cleaved to me. I wonder if they've collected sperm samples from him, too. He showed up at the clinic the same night Kira and I were there. Are there little Kethans being created in those labs? Perhaps. Or perhaps not, as Brad Darcton only played the "son" card when he thought I might die.

"So hey," Tristan says. "We're having a killer party at dawn. The flash flood killed off the rest of our uh, party enhancements, so we're going to use our reserves and do it up right. Of course, you don't have to partake if you don't want to." This sounds like the kind of thing I could get bonus points with Brad Darcton for attending and "keeping an eye on things."

"Sure. I'll come. But I'll bring my own water bottle," I say with a wink.

"Good to have you back. Hopefully Kira will come back soon, too. It's not the same without you guys being all judgy judgy on us," he says with a laugh. "Plus the three of us—me and Bri and Kira—had gotten to be pretty good friends when she disappeared."

"Yeah, she better show up soon," I say.

They leave after a bit more small talk, having to return from break to their online classes. I make myself a peanut butter and jelly sandwich and then reward myself with some sugar and chocolate. Being fed through a tube—and before that eating Exiled food—has me craving some real food. I'd kill for some McDonalds and hope Kira really has been able to get off this rock and enjoy some earthly treats.

I jump when I turn to see Ted Rosenberg. He must've let himself in and I didn't even hear him. Perhaps my hearing was affected in the blast? I shove my fingers in my ears to see if there's some excess wax buildup.

"Where's Kira?" I say after Ted sinks back into the couch and smoothes his newly grown salt-black moustache.

"Hello to you, too," he says with a glare. "Nice to see you're still alive."

"Yep, I'm alive. Where's Kira?" I repeat.

"She was having a hard time with you missing, so we sent her back to Earth for a respite from her worries," he says. "So let her enjoy her break while you recuperate."

I study his face. "When will she be back?"

"Despite my promotion, I'm still the last person to know anything," he says. Sure you are, I think. Brad Darcton's been giving you personal orders. How can he lie to my face?

"So tell me about Ethan Darcton," I say. His chin fat wiggles, a clear indication he's uncomfortable.

"How do you know Ethan?" he says.

"I've met him a couple times. And then, Briella mentioned him tonight. I was wondering what his story is," I say.

"He's Brad Darcton's son. I believe he attends law school during the year back on Earth and interns here in the summer," he says, avoiding eye contact.

"Is he Cleaved?" I ask. Ethan told me he wasn't, but I want confirmation.

"I don't believe so," he says. "Why the curiosity?"

"Oh. I had to listen to a stupid argument between Bri and Tristan about him," I say. Whoever's listening would have heard the same thing and back my story. Hopefully Ethan's still obsessed with that girl he met at the party, and won't find Kira interesting or vice versa, assuming either of them has a choice in the matter. I don't like the idea of that guy being her escort home. He's too nice, too good looking, and too ready to settle down. And Kira still never explained why she called me Ethan. What if they really do know each other and she has a crush on him?

"I see. Well, I know you aren't supposed to exercise, but the nurse did mention that I should get you to stretch your legs once a night. Shall we take a short stroll in the canyon?" he says.

"Sure," I say.

We don't walk far. I update him on how I'd really spent my flash flood time and about the timing of the Exilers' attack, and my father's directive to shut down the Eco barrier, which will be particularly important to him given my new data about the shifting detonators. Ted slips me a card key that will give me access to headquarters. Even if he can't see the benefits of his promotion, I can. He also issues me a new watch with the instruction to perform any "extracurricular" activities without it; having confirmed it is indeed a tracking device and supposedly the *only* tracking device used.

The chunk of our walk is spent brainstorming the potential ways to disarm the Eco barrier. He feeds me bits and pieces of conversations he's heard about it and we narrow the possibilities of a switch to three rooms within headquarters. Even better, he provides an access password to the HQ central computer system that he claims to be two levels above his security clearance.

"Did that strain your grafts too much?" he says as we walk back into my house.

"Nope. I'm good," I say, a bit of a lie. I'm pretty exhausted.

"You should get some rest," he says.

"Yeah. I'm going to head over to Tristan and Bri's for a big party they're having at dawn and then I'll get some sleep," I say.

"Really? They're having a party?" he says.

"Yep. Sounds like they're going all out," I say. "I figure it's a good way to get to know some more people and catch up on Second Chancer scoop."

"Excellent. I'm glad to see you are jumping right back into your role as a Recruit," he says. "Just remember to keep well hydrated—with water."

"You think?" I say. I'm not stupid. I saw how TB interacted with Kira's pain meds. Sobriety won't be an issue for me.

How much freaking TB did these kids have stored? This party's insane. Not that I'm a party expert, but I thought Tristan's last party lacked inhibition. This one has no restraint whatsoever. I do my best to chat it up with folks, but they're slurring sentences so badly I can't understand one freaking word they say.

The spread looks tame, but every morsel of food and drink contains Theranberry. And for those who want the quickest hits, raw berries and powder have been provided. I sip my water and listen to Briella justify the portrait of Tristan she had Bailey paint on her stomach with Theranberry juice. Bailey has no future as a Theran artist, but she still offers to paint me in some rather private and sensitive areas that I want her nowhere near. When in her teebed state she lifts up her tube top to show the "work" she did on her breasts, I try to leave. Not that they aren't attractive, but I've seen them before and the girl could be renamed Pandora. I don't want in her box.

"Not so fast, Cowboy," Bailey says, grabbing me and yanking me into the bathroom. "I need to talk to you." She pushes me hard and fast against the cupboard and presses herself against me. She's got on 5 inch stilettos, so we're eye to eye. I'll give her two minutes, I think. I don't trust her and haven't since our relationship ended.

"It's not going to happen, Bailey. Sober up," I say.

"No matter what you say, Blake, I know you find me attractive," she whispers in my ear. "You've been quite responsive to me for weeks now."

"You know I'm with Kira," I say. Unfortunately, I can't tell her the whole host of reasons her devoid-of-warmth personality trumps her gorgeous body or I'd be Exiled.

"I don't see Kira here. Haven't seen her for a long while. I heard she's otherwise occupied with a *very* attractive guy," she responds without so much as a glance away.

I glare at Bailey. "I trust *Kira*. You, not so much," I say.

"Why do you act like you hate me, Blake? I can't think of a single thing I've done *here* to piss you off so much. I've been nothing but friendly." Yeah, like the freaking neighborhood welcome wagon.

"I'm not getting your game, Bailey," I lie. I'm totally getting her game. The sultry look, licking those plump lips, a wardrobe "malfunction" that has her breasts spilling out of her tube top, and the grinding against my hips in a way that I'm having trouble ignoring. Brain understands "vindictive tramp"; body not so much.

"Sure you do, Blake," she says as she stares at my lips, which gets me staring at hers. Before I know it, her lips are pressed against mine and she's parted my lips with her tongue. Like riding a bike, the muscle memory comes back and I'm helpless to resist. She's surely talented at this, but there's a reason I don't want this, if I could only remember what it is. It occurs to me. I hate her. Really hate her. And then there's Kira. My "girlfriend" who's off with Ethan the freaking Abercrombie-model intern. I told Kira I'm falling in love with her and she can't stand guys that cheat. Not that I am cheating. Bailey kissed me. Crap. I'm kissing back and wanting more. Wherewithal regained, I push Bailey back.

The only thing I can bring myself to say is "No."

She smirks as she licks her lips, roughly gropes my pelvic area, and whispers, "You're saying no, but I can tell you're not really feeling it."

"I'm out of here. Don't touch me again," I say a bit more half-heartedly than I should have.

"We're not through, Blake. Not even close. We've got more in common than you think and I'll be seeing you sooner rather than later," she says.

I practically run towards the other end of the house and figure that Bailey won't be able to catch me while teebed up.

What I see happening in the rest of the party makes my encounter with Bailey look tame. Guys are slurping TB from girls' bellybuttons. Licking TB powder from lips. Chewing up berries and sharing the slop like a mother bird does with her babies. The "sizzler," where they allow the TB juice to boil on their skin out in the courtyard and whiff in the fumes disturbs me greatly. And then there's the random making out with multiple people to see who's most teebed and will put out more.

I'm contemplating how disgusting they all are when Tristan slaps me on the back atop one of my grafts.

"Holy crap, Tristan. Don't slap me on my skin graft—or anywhere," I say.

"Sorry, dude," he says. "Didn't know they'd put cow skin on you."

"Huh?" I say.

"You said skin calf right?" he says.

"No. Graft," I say. No lights on upstairs this morn. "Never mind. Don't worry about it."

Time for me to leave, I think. I'm getting nothing out of this party other than new images to add to all the other disturbing ones in my nightmares. I make my way to the front door, when a host of men in official looking uniforms burst in, led by Brad Darcton.

"Blake," he says, narrowing his eyes at me. In an accusing tone he adds, "I'm surprised to see you here."

"Mr. Darcton," I respond. "Just doing my job as a Recruit and attempting to mix with these folks. I can assure you I have done nothing of concern." I wave my water bottle at him.

"Go home, then. We're moving their party to headquarters," he says. Holy crap. What's he going to do to them? Mass execution? Appearing to read my thoughts he explains, "They'll be fine. We've figured out a… creative… way to deal with their complete disregard of the Canon."

"I do believe I will head home, then. I could use the rest," I say, being truthful. I am so tired that I can barely keep my eyes open. "The only circumstance I'd like changed is for Kira to come back."

"Patience, Blake. And thanks for giving your Handler the heads-up on the party," he says with a wink, before shooing me out the door. Great, whatever life-changing circumstances he has in store for them will be on my conscience. I just hope it isn't Exile. These kids would be zero help to my father's cause.

I watch from my balcony as the gaggle of drunk teens are escorted off—at least a hundred of them—in the blaring hot sun. They can barely walk, much less adhere to the strict instructions being yelled by the security detail. Once the kids have been ushered through the door that leads to the train, I see another half dozen men carrying evidence in carefully labeled bags. SCI Security is well trained to carry out raids. I've seen it happen before. But this raid has been far more civilized than the one I remember.

My fifth birthnight was rapidly approaching and the summer heat was deadly. I remember begging my father for more water. Leila cried around the clock. Collectively, our band of Exilers became pretty sluggish, lacking the energy to do even the most basic tasks. However, desperation had driven the men to help the Interceptors forage for food. Only women and children remained in the camps and no one had thought to stand watch as we slept during the day. That must be why we didn't see them coming.

A large team of security detail from Garden City showed up toting shotguns and whips. Threatening to kill, the men went cave to cave and poured out water supplies, trashed food, and stole supplies. They ripped apart the soft brush we used for bedding. Destroyed fire pits. And burned excess clothing. It was chaos and everyone started to scatter. We feared for our lives.

A few gunshots brought us into line. The men corralled our group together at the bottom of the canyon, by pushing and shoving us down the hill, guns pointed at our backs. I carried Leila and my feet struggled to keep up with the fast pace of the unfamiliar men. Several times I'd fallen and been kicked by heavy black boots. Leila wailed and wailed. They insisted I shut her up or they'd do it for me. Thankfully, Doc's Cleave made her way to us and took Leila from me and calmed her down.

What the men did next still gives me chilling nightmares. A half dozen kept their barrels trained on us, while the rest troweled a ditch around us, a couple inches deep. The process took less than twenty minutes with their tools. Then they poured some sort of powder into the ditch and lit it on fire. Ringed with hot flames, exposed to the searing hot sun, we were powerless to escape. Laughing, they'd gone on their merry way, toting large bags of our life-sustaining supplies back towards Garden City.

One of the more resourceful women figured out that we could extinguish the flames by scraping the hard soil with our fingernails and pushing it into the ditch. Once we'd cleared a path out of the ring, Doc's Cleave led the children back up the canyon to the caves, while the other women stayed to put out the rest of the fire. A single spark could have set the entire canyon ablaze. Any remaining supplies would have been destroyed and we'd have all died from burns or smoke inhalation. They weren't willing to risk it.

Hours later, the ladies trudged up the canyon, blistered from the sun, hands bleeding from their toil. They discovered what we had already. The supplies kept in our caves were gone or burned. But, our meager reserve, camouflaged by boulders in a nearby cave, remained undiscovered. So, resources were rationed and we'd subsisted on sips of water and crumbs of food for a full week until the men returned with more.

I find it interesting that the security detail didn't kill us. Perhaps they rationalized that they weren't responsible for our deaths if they left us to dehydrate, starve, or burn rather than put bullets in our heads. And, after all, they'd just been "retrieving goods stolen from the good citizens of Garden City," or at least that's what they said.

Yes, whatever Brad Darcton has in store for the delinquent Garden City high schoolers, it will pale in comparison to the Ten's treatment of the Exilers.

"What the—?" I say out loud as I approach the common area at school on foot. Did I miss my invite to some sort of date function? Most nights the girls group together and gossip while the guys play basketball, football or board the canyons. But tonight… it's a whole different scene.

All I see are couples splattered about. Holding hands. Kissing. Laughing. Talking. Staring dreamily into each other's eyes.

I walk over to Briella and Tristan, who are sprawled out atop a picnic table looking at the obscured stars.

"What happened after the party? Why has everyone paired off?" I ask in a loud voice.

"Oh hey, dude," Tristan says. "Keep your voice down. My head's pounding." Really? Shocker. Don't do TB. Just say no.

"Last I saw, you guys were being carted off by security. Where'd they take you?" I say, this time quieter.

"Oh yeah. We went to the SCI headquarters. It's all a little fuzzy. But that Darcton dude from the Ten. He Cleaved us," Tristan says.

"You and Bri?" I ask, looking at each of them. Briella smiles at Tristan. Tristan opens his mouth first to respond.

"Yeah, first he Cleaved us. And then, he Cleaved all of them," Tristan says, sitting up enough to wave his arms towards the rest of the couples.

"Seriously? The Ten Cleaved all of you?" I ask. "No. Freaking. Way."

"Way," he says. "Well, except for Bailey who apparently managed to get herself Exiled. She wandered into a high security clearance area at HQ. So I guess you won't have to worry about her pawing you any more."

I know the powers that be are listening in, so I've got to be careful what I ask. "I'm so confused about how this all went down," I say. Bailey Exiled? What was she doing in a classified area of headquarters? I always thought there was something off with her after her 50s housewife comment. And all the Second Chancers were Cleaved? I'm teeb-free and I'm still tripping.

Tristan's all too happy to share his warped memories. "Mr. Darcton seemed a little tweaked about our party. Apparently TB's illegal or something. But instead of Exiling us the Ten decided to give us the 'opportunity' to become all responsible by Cleaving us. Which is pretty much the most awesome punishment ever." Kira may be the only one who can appreciate the brilliance of Brad Darcton's punishment for the partying Second Chancers. And she's not even here to gloat.

"Wow," I say.

"Wow is right. Wait, how come you didn't come with us to HQ?" he says. Let's see. How *do* I explain that? I look at my shoes and then back at Tristan.

"I was just leaving when the security guys arrived. When they saw I was sober, they told me to go home," I say. "I guess I missed out. How'd they do the Cleaving?" I doubt Tristan, Bri and the others got the full Cleaving treatment, given their inebriated state. Typically, physical tests and questionnaires proceed the pairings, to insure good Cleaving matches. Following the official pairing, the SCI provides a ceremony and grand dinner celebration.

"They just called off names by pairs and then had us sign some paperwork to make it all legit," Tristan says. "Then they sent us home to consummate the Cleaving. Which we did several times." Given how hopped up on TB he was, I'm surprised he could perform or remember.

As if narrating a documentary, Tristan starts to detail the consummation for me. My eyes go wide and I scan for an excuse to escape. Briella pretend slices her throat to try to get him to stop. Too much information. I see Ted Rosenberg and pretend like I have something urgent to discuss with him.

Ted confirms Tristan's story. The Ten had the Garden City High sixteen-and-ups mass-Cleaved at SCI headquarters overday. Every single bone-headed kid who attended that party, with the exception of Bailey and me, has been Cleaved to their "perfect" mate. Given there wasn't an exactly equal number of girls and boys at the shindig, a few others got whisked off to HQ from their homes to join the party by afternoon.

"What does this mean for Kira and me?" I ask. "Are we going to keep working with them now that they're Cleaved? Cause I'm not so sure I want to listen to all that Cleaving talk."

"For now, yes, it's business as usual. I realize as the only unCleaveds of your age range that it will be awkward, but it was awkward anyway, right?" he chuckles. I nod. "The Ten will be reviewing the program, and will adjust it as necessary. I'll let you know if your duties change."

I think what he meant to say is he'll let me know *when* things change. The Ten's likely still hoping Kira and I will Cleave—assuming they ever bring her back. Or, they'll move us elsewhere—to another city. I shudder at the thought. Having two singles amongst dozens of Cleaveds just isn't going to fly for long. The dynamic would be too awkward. They'll be saddling the couples with kids before long and then what would we have to talk about? Our mythical babies?

"Kira's going to freak when she finds out about all this," I say.

"If you're referring to Tristan and Briella, I really don't think she'll be bothered that they Cleaved," Ted says to me.

"Well, no, I just meant the whole thing, although I guess that might still bug her," I say. I don't know. Tristan and Bri had said they'd all been getting along well before Kira disappeared. I'm not sure how she'll react.

"I don't think so. The two—meaning Tristan and Bri—apparently had a long-term sexual relationship back on Earth behind Kira's back," Ted says.

"Serious?" I say. "How would you even know that?"

"They were caught in the act on video. Kira viewed the video prior to her vacation," he says.

That's the video he and Brad discussed? And the same one mentioned when he was talking to that other guy in the steam room? That makes sense. When they decided to place her in spitting distance of her ex-boyfriend, they'd made sure to have a smoking gun to keep her from ever being tempted to reunite with him. When they feared I might die, they decided to show it to her so that she wouldn't turn to Tristan. But with me out of the picture, they wanted her to have someone to confide in. Insert Ethan Darcton—the alternative heir to Thera.

"Wow, that's extreme," I say, mostly to myself. "She must've flipped."

"I wasn't there to see her reaction, but I'd imagine she was upset by the news," he says.

Upset? With that news and me missing, I'd be surprised if she didn't go insane.

Anything less than abject submission has to have some attack in it.

Frank Herbert

CHAPTER TWENTY

Kira

I awaken groggy, nauseated, hooded, and with extreme facial pain from where I was whacked with a gun. From the intensity of the pain I'd guess I have a huge welt and am in for some very attractive bruising. My captor drops me in a heap onto a hard surface. It's then that I hear a familiar voice indicating that I've returned to Thera. Brad Darcton. My hands are tied behind my back with something thin and cutting. A tight gag keeps me from speaking. Oddly, I feel better than I did the last time through. Physically, that is. Mentally, I'm just waiting to be shoved into a padded room as the memories of the deaths at my childhood home flood my brain. Have to keep it together, I think. I wriggle to indicate I'm awake and await to have my hood, gag, and cuffs removed—and to see if Ethan and Jared made it through with me. The thought of either of them dying at my hands is unbearable. I've already killed my parents; their blood soaks my hands.

"Ah, it appears our little rebel has awoken," I hear Brad Darcton say. "Keep her hands in the restraints until I know that she plans to behave." A pair of ice-cold hands removes my hood and then my gag. I wrench my head around and am devastated to see neither Ethan or Jared in view.

"Where are they?" I ask, struggling to speak.

"Who?" Brad asks in a menacing tone.

"My brother, Jared. Your son, Ethan," I say, emphasizing the "son."

Brad strolls over to me and with a nasty glare says, "I'm so sorry to hear about the untimely deaths of your parents. It's so tragic when those we love die —especially when the deaths could have so easily been avoided." I drop my head and try to contain the sob growing in my throat. Is that his way of telling me that Ethan and Jared are dead, too? Everyone I care about. Gone. Do I dare confirm my worst fears? Could there still be one person left?

I ask yet another question I'm afraid to hear the answer to. "Blake? Is he alive?"

Brad paces back and forth for what seems like an eternity before answering. "We found him, though his situation is dicey. Honestly I don't know which way it's going to go. Your cooperation the next couple weeks would go a long way to lifting his spirits and giving him the fight he needs, don't you think?" Brad says. He's alive. I've never been more relieved or scared at the same time. This time I'll take Brad's threat seriously. If I don't cooperate, Brad will make sure Blake dies. If I cooperate, he's got a fighting chance. With Jared and Ethan presumably gone, I can't lose my one last thread tying me to life and hope of a future.

"Whatever you need me to do," I say, bowing my head in submission, even if it's mock submission in my head.

"You three will be placed in a… quiet area… where you can contemplate the bigger picture of things," he says, a sickeningly amused look on his face. Wait. Three?

I'm afraid to take his bait. "Three?" I whisper. Brad motions to a colleague and two hooded figures are dragged in and dumped beside me from an adjacent holding area. I let out a gasp of relief as I recognize the clothes to be Jared and Ethan's. Their hoods are removed and they get the luck of having their cuffs removed, which I see to be simple zip ties. Jared looks bewildered. Ethan bursts into tears when he sees me, but Brad's colleague keeps him from running to me to have a happy reunion.

Brad steps forward to address Ethan. "Son, welcome back. I assume you've learned some vital lessons while away. One, to always follow orders. Two, I warned you to avoid the women on Earth. You've got to stop fighting me on the Cleaving thing."

How can he be so cavalier about killing my parents and Ethan's harem? What a monster.

Brad turns to Jared. "And, here we have an unexpected guest."

I walk over beside Jared and plaster on a smile. "This is my brother, Jared. And I'm afraid in my passed out state that I didn't have a chance to educate him on where we were headed. Perhaps you'd like to do the honors?"

"Absolutely," Brad Darcton beams. "Jared, welcome to Garden City, Thera."

"And where's Garden City, Thera?" Jared asks.

"It's the location of Unit 27 of the Second Chance Institute. You left Earth by traveling through a portal to Earth's sister planet, Thera. It'll take some getting used to and we'll be sure to get you properly trained as Kira and Blake were, but first I think all three of you need a little 'me' time. You'll all be able to talk things through and gain some needed perspective," Brad says.

"No, Dad. You can't do that. Can't lock us up. Me up," Ethan says. He's got his hands on his father's shoulders and looks desperate.

"I can and I will," Brad says, pulling away from Ethan.

"I have no idea what you guys are talking about," Jared says, his mouth gaped open. "Can someone tell me what the hell is going on here?"

"First, recuperation. Then, education. That's what I tell every Recruit. I'll see you all real soon," Brad says. He pauses to scan us and our disheveled, bloody state, "Oh, and get yourselves cleaned up. What a mess."

To the casual observer, one would think Ethan, Jared and I were sharing a typical Garden City two bedroom home. Ethan and Jared took the twin beds in one bedroom, and I got the queen, just like in the house I share with Blake. This house, however, connects to the center city clinic and has been completely locked down. A team of physicians and psychiatrists manage our "care."

It takes a couple nights for us to lose the drug-induced haze shot into us after our entry. And much longer to get over the shock of the events that happened. Brad Darcton knows he crossed a line executing my family and Ethan's friends in front of us. There's no going back to presenting the Second Chance Institute as a benevolent cause. So, his only choice is to terrorize us into compliance, brainwash us into acceptance, or eliminate us.

In case he needs to go for plan C, he plans to extract another round of eggs from me. Despite being drugged, I recognize the shots for what they are. When I try to protest, I'm kindly reminded of Blake's fragile physical state and my brother's tenuous mental state.

Yes, Jared. He's like a raving lunatic. Take note for future recruiting, SCI— don't execute a Recruit's parents in front of said Recruit if you want them to like you. While, I'm currently terrorized into compliance, Jared's far from willing to feign even a little obedience.

"I'm going to kill them. Every last one of them," he says. He's pacing the living room and kicking the furniture.

"That will be difficult without weapons and I think you're a little outnumbered," I say, tucking my feet up onto our couch so that he doesn't whack me in the shins.

"They freaking killed Mom and Dad. For no reason," he says, spitting out the words and his fists slamming into an imaginary punching bag.

"Not true. They had a reason. They wanted me back on Thera and I wasn't cooperating. I called their bluff and they called mine. It's my fault, Jared," I say. After all, it's the truth.

"It's not your fault, Kira," says Ethan. He's barely said a word since we returned. I'm shocked he doesn't blame me. "They were looking for a reason—any reason—to do it. I don't think it was avoidable." I'm worried about Ethan. He doesn't look well. Not that I do either with a giant gun-shaped, multi-colored bruise on my face. In contrast, Ethan's face is deathly white. I've seen him muttering to himself and hyperventilating. He checks the door lock every few minutes. If the average claustrophobic hates being in small, enclosed spaces—well then, Ethan goes nuts by simply being locked in any space.

"Thanks for trying to make me feel better, but I need to take responsibility," I say. "Six people lost their lives because of me." I'm not taking my current situation well, but need to stay strong for Jared. Ethan. And Blake. I save my tears for my pillow at day, in the privacy of my own room.

"Well, technically they're no longer dead. They're here somewhere," Ethan says. He's on an adjacent chair and looks ready to call for help if Jared gets any more violent.

"Sure, the zombie or shell versions of them are here, but it's not really *them* if they can't remember their lives. For instance, how can you learn from mistakes you've made if you don't remember making them?" I say.

"What zombies?" my brother asks. He still doesn't get it. I explain it all to him again. The Second Chancers. Daynighters. Recruits' roles on Thera. Inverted days and nights. Cleaving. The Circle of Compliance, Grand Council, and the Presiding Ten. When do they plan to start his training? Or are we his training? I hope not, though I'd be a whole lot more interesting than Video Dude. I'm careful to try not to color the facts with my personal interpretations. We're being monitored. Any admission to things I shouldn't know or "misrepresentation" of Theran doctrine could cause things to end badly. I'd already played the "Originals" card and admitted I'd known they'd killed Leila. At some point, I'll be called to explain my "wealth of knowledge" to Brad Darcton and prefer not to add things to have to rationalize.

"The people who run this place are total quack-jobs," my brother says. "Certifiable. And they lock us up? I'll tell you who needs some 'me' time. The Ten Assassins for their Circle of Compulsion or whatever it's called."

I shake my head. The anti-psychotics didn't help. Information's not making a dent. I've got to figure out some way to get Jared to keep his opinions to himself or we're all dead.

"I'm not insane," I say. "Nor is my brother, or Ethan. We're just… upset… over the deaths of our loved ones… and the roles we played in those deaths." We're in our nightly group brainwashing-centric therapy session and I've decided we'll never get released unless we redirect blame to ourselves, rather than the leaders of the SCI. It's like a play-acting exercise from drama class, except I actually do blame myself. Each mind warp session lasts four hours and we cover the same things over and over and over and over again. Presumably, we'll continue to cover them until we get the answers "right" in the eyes of the Ten. And believe it.

"So, you understand that you are responsible for the incident which is causing you so much pain?" the silver-haired therapist named Lily says.

"Absolutely. I defied a direct order and there are consequences when we don't abide by the law," I say. All true. It is my fault.

"She is full of CRAP," Jared says. He stands, kicking his chair back behind him. "You are all full of crap!"

"Jared, it isn't your turn to share," Lily says, as if Jared is a misbehaving toddler. "Please pick up your chair and return to the circle."

"Lily, would you mind if I have one minute to speak with my brother in the kitchen? I think it might help, but I'll leave the decision to you," I say, trying to be as pleasant, yet submissive as possible.

"One minute," she says to me. "We want to keep our discussion on track."

I pull my brother from the dining area into the kitchen. To reach his ear, I have to get up on my tiptoes. When did he get so tall and why hadn't I noticed while I was at home? He's easily past six feet now. His tan and freckles are fading from the lack of sun.

"You need to get your temper under control, Jared," I say, reaching up to steady myself by putting my hands on his shoulders. "They will keep us locked up forever—or worse, Exile or kill us if you can't. If you want any hope of a relatively normal future, then you'll get a grip."

"Sorry. You may be used to the whole move to a different planet full of psychoapathetic killers thing, but I'm not," he says in an angry, hushed tone. Did Jared stop his SAT prep classes when I left? Or did coming through the portal tweak his long-term memory? He just shouldn't use big words. Unless he's doing it on purpose as he always did back home, to get on my nerves.

"It's not a planet full of *psychopaths*, I promise you. Just a bunch of normal people going about their lives. But the Garden City leaders do strictly enforce the rules. That, they're quite up front about," I say. For the most part, I speak the truth. Other than forgetting their past on Earth, the Second Chancers live their lives as best as possible given their circumstances. It's only those in charge who have redrawn the line between right and wrong.

"They killed our parents. And those girls," he says, backing away from me and putting his hands on the back of his head. "How do I forget that?"

"Our parents and those girls are alive. Here on Thera," I say. "I'm sure they're fine. Happy even."

"Will I ever get to see them again?" he says.

"I don't know. But if we don't get out of here, then I can assure you we'll never have the chance," I say. I'm not as eager to see my parents as Jared is. It could be unwise to destroy my fantasy of a perfect "hereafter" for them.

"I'll try to do better," he says, walking back to the living room calmly.

I catch up and whisper in his ear, "Try harder. Because I can't stand confinement another night."

After Jared shows restraint for a couple sessions, he's allowed to start his official training. He still attends group therapy, but spends the remainder of his non-sleeping hours learning Theran doctrine. Meanwhile, Ethan and I are going out of our minds. There's only so much we can do within the confinement of our locked down home. I teach Ethan games like charades and hide and seek from my childhood to distract him. We garden. Have cook-offs. Do a lame aerobics routine since we're gymless. Read to each other. Sleep a lot. And I do my fair share of crying behind closed doors for my failure to consider how my actions would affect my family.

After stuffing ourselves with veal schnitzel that I cook and chocolate soufflé that Ethan makes, I excuse myself to my room to hide a pending mental breakdown. Within a few minutes, a knock at my door forces me to dry my tears on my pillowcase and answer.

"I'm sorry to bother you," Ethan says. "But, I could tell you were upset and thought you might need a hug. And I know I could use one."

"I could," I say. I let him join me on my bed, although I face away from him and let him hold me from behind. We both silently contemplate our situation for a while. Finally, I speak, turning to face him. "I'm so sorry. I should have listened to you and not fought coming back. I've made such a mess of everything. Even though I didn't hold the guns, I pulled the triggers."

He takes my face in his hands. "It's not your fault and I don't blame you. I'm just happy that you're okay—that Jared's okay,"

"It is my fault and now I've ruined your life. I assume the blonde girl they killed was the girl you spoke of at the party? The one you wanted to grow old with?" I say. He shakes his head.

"No, Kira, she wasn't. Not even close. You haven't ruined my life," he says. "Don't ever think that." He presses his forehead against mine and touches his nose to mine for a moment before pulling back.

"Why were you dating her then?" I ask.

"My girl's been a little tied up, so I'm in a bit of a holding pattern. To be honest, I only took Sarah to a couple events my uncle was hosting. She's the daughter of a colleague of his and Sarah wanted those dates to turn into a relationship. I didn't feel the same," he says. So Sarah was a bit of a stalker and forever girl's been giving Ethan the brush-off. I feel terrible for him. What girl would keep a guy like Ethan waiting? Even if he is a Darcton.

"Do you think we're ever going to get out of here?" I ask.

"We'll definitely get out of here. You're handling this... them... Jared... well," he says.

"They took more eggs from me," I whisper.

"Are you absolutely sure?" he says, his blue eyes narrowing.

"Positive. Same process as before," I say.

"They took a sperm sample from *me* during my 'check-up'—they said they needed to test my reproductive system. It was the second time they've done it, in fact. That night you heard me at the clinic... that's why I was there—for my routine reproductive system check," he says.

"Great, looks like we're going to have lab-produced babies together, too," I say. "Don't they have any other high-DNT, Original-blooded girls to spread the joy of motherhood with?" I ask. I'd be more disturbed, but the fact is that I'm well beyond being surprised at the absurdity of the Ten's actions. I bury my head in his chest and he holds me tight. Despite our situation, I feel safe with Ethan. That hasn't always been the case. It's taken a while for me to trust him and I still have doubts. It's hard to believe that he didn't have anything to do with the Goodington explosion and that he's not an evil pawn, but an unwilling pawn in the Ten's terror games.

"Somehow, everything's going to work out. We have to believe that," he says.

I look up at him and wonder if he really thinks that, or if he's just trying to make me feel better. An absurd line of thought trickles through my brain as I wonder if my babies with Blake or Ethan will be cuter. I laugh out loud.

"What? Are you mocking my optimism?" he says.

"No, no. Not at all," I say. "I'm just truly going bonkers. Don't worry about me. Can I ask you something that I've been meaning to ask you for a while?"

"Sure," he says.

"How'd you get the scar on your chest?" I ask, rolling his shirt up gently and running my fingers across it and down the contours of his muscles, despite the fact I know how intimate and inappropriate my action is.

"I was born with a heart defect," he says. "The doctors weren't sure I'd live, but they were able to correct it with a bunch of surgeries."

"Oh, wow, I didn't know," I say. "I'm so sorry."

"It's long done with and fixed, although my parents continually remind me of my shortcoming," he says. "I think they... and others... are worried that it's genetic and I may pass it on to my children. It makes me a less-than-appealing Cleaving candidate. So I guess it's a good thing I don't live here full time."

"There's absolutely nothing that could make you unappealing," I say and I mean it. He's downright beautiful. We lock eyes and I can see him melt at my compliment. I can't believe that his parents have killed his self-esteem so much. His eyes drift to my lips and I can't help but drift my eyes to his.

"Likewise," he says. He leans in to kiss me, the first time since we've returned to Thera. His cinnamon-tinged lips hit mine and then he parts and teases my lips with his tongue. He alternates between gentle exploration of my mouth and nibbling on my bottom lip. For a sizable moment, I allow, respond, and even enjoy this sweet, passionate gesture, my heart pounding and desire for him building. Until I remember Ethan loves someone else. And, Blake's alive and fighting for his life. The guilt pummels me. I have feelings for Ethan. No question. He's gorgeous, fun, a great listener, an even better smooth talker, a fabulous cook, my best friend at the moment, and I feel comfortable with him. He's the only reason I'm getting through this. But, we're no longer faking this to support our cover. This is all too real and feels wrong. I can't and won't be "the other woman."

I pull away. "I'm so sorry. We need to stop. This isn't right. Not now. You're in love with someone else. And, there's Blake. I forget all that sometimes… being here with you and not having them around. But, I'm just not one of those kinds of girls. Just look at what Briella and Tristan did to me. I don't want to ever be like that… ever." My loyal tendencies are a good trait, right?

He closes his eyes, unable to look me in mine. "I understand and I shouldn't have done it. Forgive me? I just caught up in the moment… beautiful girl I care for in my arms… but I'd never want to disrespect what you have with Blake. I'm not that guy either. I promise. We just seem to have bad timing," He rolls off the side of the bed and then comes around and sits on the edge, facing away from me, head in his hands.

"It's okay and of course. There's nothing to apologize for," I say, rubbing his back. It's hardly his fault. I put my hand up his shirt and told him how incredibly appealing he is. What guy wouldn't act on that?

"I hope we can be friends," he says, though I'm not entirely sure he means it. He looks sad, but I don't see why he would be, since he's still got his dream girl in the wings. I couldn't stand to be his "fill-in" girl anyway.

"You are already my friend, Ethan. The best friend I could ask for," I say, pausing for a moment to wonder if it's really possible for a girl and a guy to be just friends. Sure we can, I think. How could we not after what we've been through together? "How about I go trash your butt in charades? Because you really, really suck at having to keep your mouth shut."

"I'm a lawyer-in-training," he says with a chuckle, although I can tell he's still upset. "What'd you expect?"

I'm so excited to see the familiar sights of my canyon I loosely hug a giant cactus and kiss the dirt. Never mind the fact I almost died in it. And discovered the truth about the Second Chancers here. Blake and I spent so much time here amongst the Theranberry bushes and cacti, and for that reason alone I'll always appreciate the place.

Ethan and I were released on a "probationary" basis. If we continue to toe the party line, we stay free. If we start spewing unflattering words about the Ten or SCI we'll be re-confined or Exiled. Jared had to stay behind to complete his training. I expect he'll also be receiving a little extra therapy time, too.

"Come on," I say to Ethan who seems less enthused to deliver me back home than I am to get there. "Let's go." I grab his hand and drag him along the canyon path and up towards my house. He stops me at the ramp to my front door.

"Things are going to change now that we're out. You and Blake will be together. I have my internship. And soon I'll return to Earth for my last year of law school. I just wanted to tell you that I, uh, am glad to have gotten to know you better. That first night I met you I thought you were amazing and I was right. You are, well, incredible. I'm really going to miss you," he says. He's got his hands in his pockets and is rocking back and forth on his feet. Just like he did that night.

"You can come see me anytime you like," I say. "And, if I'm allowed, I'll come visit you. We're going to stay friends, Ethan Darcton, despite the fact you were spawned from Satan. You don't get to use law school or Blake or anything as a cop out. I'll miss you just as much." He smiles at the reference to his father.

"Promise?" he says.

"I promise," I say. "Now can I go see if Blake's home?"

"Sure, I'll be going," he says, motioning towards the doors to the train. He looks so sad that it makes me want to cry.

"Uh, no you won't. You're coming with me. If Blake's not home, you'll handle my meltdown and help me track him down. If he is home, I still want you there. You guys should be friends, too," I say.

"I don't know about that. I don't think he's going to like me much now," he says. "After all, I did pretend to be your boyfriend."

"Right, you *pretended*. On orders," I say.

"What about all the kissing?" he says, biting the edge of his lip and looking at me through his long eyelashes. I feel a pang of longing at the memories, particularly of our last kiss. But I feel even more desire to see if Blake is home and well.

"What kissing?" I say with a wink. "I don't remember a thing and even if I did, I think you compared me to a post and suggested I need lessons."

"Kira," he says, cocking his head to the side. "You know…" I don't let him finish, shushing him by placing two fingers over his mouth. Then I put my hands on his shoulders and push him up the ramp backwards until his back is against my front door. I pause, my body pushed against his, our eyes locked, knowing it will be the last moment we have for a while, so I soak in the fabulous nature of his sapphire eyes, strong jaw, full lips and stubble. Finally, not wanting the moment to get any more awkward than I've let it, I knock with one hand while keeping him trapped with the other. Trapped being an overstatement, as he could easily overpower me, but he's going along and laughing while he does.

It seems like an eternity before the door opens. Ethan has to catch his footing as the door gives way. To keep him from escaping, I shove him inside, shut the door behind me, and then jump into Blake's arms. Blake feels a whole lot skinnier than he did the last time I saw him, if that's even possible.

"Whoa, whoa, Kira," Blake says, setting me down gently. "I guess no one told you about my skin grafts? Ow!"

"Skin grafts?" I say. "No one told me squat. Last I heard you were 'barely hanging on.' I didn't even know if you'd be here when I knocked on the door."

"Well," he says looking at Ethan. "It looks like we have a lot of catching up to do."

"Blake, I think you've met Ethan Darcton. After the flash flood I kind of flipped out. So, the Ten allowed Ethan to escort me back to Earth for a vacation of sorts. He's been a good friend."

"Friend?" Blake says, narrowing his eyes and looking Ethan up and down. Perhaps it does look a little sketchy for me to show up with an incredibly attractive male "friend" who I've just spent several weeks with.

"Yes, friend," Ethan says, offering his hand to Blake to shake. Blake hesitates for a moment, but finally accepts the gesture. "I'm glad you are back and feeling ok."

"That was quite a long vacation you took," Blake says to me.

"Well, it wasn't all vacation," I say. "But, no matter. Thank goodness you're okay. I have been sick with worry."

"You know, I'm going to get back into the city to see how my house held up while I was away," Ethan says. "It was good to see you again, Blake. Kira thinks the world of you. You're a very lucky guy."

"Thanks for bringing me back," I say. I'd like to hug him, but don't think Blake would react kindly. So I smile and tell him I'll see him soon. When the door closes, Blake wraps his arms around me.

"I thought he'd never leave," he says. "I've been waiting an awfully long time to do this." He backs me against the front door and kisses me. He's holding back, though, and I wonder why. Or maybe it's me holding back. For that I'd know why—but I push the comparisons with Ethan aside.

"What's wrong?" I ask.

"You must hate me for leaving you like that during the flash flood," he says.

"That sucked, but how could you even think it would be possible for me to hate you?" I say.

"I love you, Kira," he says.

I pause. It's funny how once one person says those three little words that it's expected to reciprocate and keep saying them. And at some point you stop questioning whether you meant it in the first place and the words continue to leave your mouth. That happened with Tristan. And now, here I am again. About to tell a guy I love him. He nearly died. What else can I do? I might love him. But am I sure? Why am I second-guessing myself?

"I love you, too," I finally say, though the crack in my voice may reveal my uncertainty about it.

"What about Ethan?" he asks.

"He's a friend. I thought I mentioned that," I say.

"As in friends with benefits? Or just friend-friend?" he asks.

"You are so jealous," I say. "It's too bad you didn't lose that attribute with your skin." I'm well aware that I don't answer his question, but we're not going to discuss it in this house with others listening. "You know, I feel like I've just been locked up inside forever. Can we go for a walk? On the upper trail of the canyon? I'm not quite up to hiking down it yet." I'll never let myself get trapped down low in canyons again.

"Sure," he says. "Bear with me, though. I'm a little slow."

We walk. And talk. Oh how I've missed our conversations in the canyons. I breathe in the putrid, warm air and run my hands along the prickly shrubbery, thrilled to be outside. Blake asks me for details about my "vacation." I gloss over my recovery from the flood, the video, and my trip home. And even though I'm talking to Blake, I take care when speaking of the traumatic "incident" with my parents and Jared. The brainwashing had the intended effect.

I explain that the SCI had Jared return with me after there was an "accident" with my parents. I'm honest about the faked relationship with Ethan, including the kissing, although I say the kisses meant nothing. *Liar*, I think to myself. I may be attracted to Ethan, but it doesn't matter since I made a choice to just be friends with him and let him pursue the love of his life. Blake's less than happy to know I shared saliva with Ethan.

"I think there's more to your trip that you aren't telling me. You really expect me to believe your parents died in an accident?" he says. I knew he wouldn't buy it.

"Blake, please don't push me on it," I say.

"You don't know me very well if you think I'll let it go," he says. His body language tells me he'll never forgive me if I don't tell him the truth.

"It's my fault they died. I didn't want to come back. In fact, I refused to come back. My parents and several girls Ethan dated died because I wanted to be able to eat out, watch movies and lay out by the pool," I say. "I'd been clearly told there'd be consequences if I wasn't cooperative, but thought I could get away with it. I should have known better. The last time I tempted fate all my friends died."

"Oh, Kira," he says, taking me in his arms. "It's not your fault."

"You can't breathe a word," I whisper. "Or they'll lock me back up or Exile me. Or kill Jared. They still have him."

"What do you mean lock you back up?" he asks.

"Ethan, Jared and I have been back on Thera for a while. But in lockdown. Brad Darcton felt we could all benefit from therapy," I say. "Jared hasn't been too cooperative, though, so he's stuck there for longer. I can't risk his life, Blake. I just can't."

"Perhaps there's hope," he says. "That we'll all be free soon. My dad and the other Exilers plan to attack. I found a way into the city that doesn't involve crossing the Eco barrier. I'm not sure it's the best idea, but they're going ahead with it whether I like it or not."

He proceeds to catch me up on his ridiculously dangerous mission and near-death inducing return. He tells me about the different Exiler factions with competing strategies. The Militants' plan is crazy. Suicidal. I don't want Blake to have any part in it. It doesn't sound like he wants any part of it either. He assures me that Ted's given him a foolproof, risk-free way to help his father, but avoids mentioning the details. Which means it's not foolproof or risk-free. What to do? I'm not willing to lose him again. We can't fight the SCI in the way his father is advocating. Our best hope's to avoid making waves and stay alive until we can find a way to get out.

"Gads," he says. "I forgot to tell you the biggest news. Right after I got back, Tristan and Bri invited me to one of their out of control parties. They got raided and hauled down to SCI headquarters. The Ten Cleaved them there."

"Ha ha," I say. "Serves them right. The two of them belong together."

"Not just Tristan and Bri. All of them."

I've been back for three nights and still haven't seen all the happily Cleaved couples. Spud Rosenberg brought us orders from the Ten to refrain from any interaction with them to "allow them time to acclimate to their new circumstances." Fine with me. I have no desire to rush the reunion with Tristan and Bri and wanted the alone time with Blake. Not that our private time's gone as well as I'd have liked.

Spud completely mucked with our schedule. To avoid the Second Chancers, Blake and I have had free time and exercise time in the evening, with classes after midnight. So, we spend all evening in the canyons disagreeing over his plans to help the Exilers, the late night hours quietly fuming while trying to concentrate on school work, and early morning "making up" by making out. And even that's been tame since Blake moans every time he's touched. The grafts are pretty nasty, I must say. They're healing, but his back and arms look like skin patchwork quilts. I just thank my lucky stars that he survived. Had the detonators not catapulted him farther up onto the beach, I'd be saying goodbye to yet another boyfriend.

Our area of contention is that Blake's still intent on delivering a knockout punch to the leadership of the SCI—although he'd like to devise a plan more proactive than his friend, Doc Daryn, and less extreme than his father. I'm determined to avoid any contention with the SCI until we have a foolproof plan. Enough people have died at my hands. He doesn't understand my point of view and although I sympathize with his, I think the outcome of his plan will be failure for the Exilers and pain and suffering for the rest of us.

Tonight, we've been invited to attend the first ever Garden City Cleaving Festival at Headquarters Plaza. The entire city's been summoned and special attire has been issued to wear for the event. Surprisingly, I like the outfits they picked to represent Garden City. I'm wearing a lightweight, wispy dress with floral pattern and hidden pockets. Blake has a light yellow short-sleeved shirt, green pants and tie to match my dress. He's been complaining about the short sleeves as one of the grafts on his arms shows, but I assure him they're healing so well that no one will notice. A small white lie.

We arrive shortly before midnight and the crowds have amassed. It reminds me of how Times Square looks on New Year's Eve, though it's at least a hundred degrees out and everyone's dressed in the same clothes. The heat generated by all those bodies is being offset, only slightly, by ventilation holes in the concrete surface that are blowing cool air up into the crowd. So, at least my feet and legs feel mildly comfortable. The air being piped in has a slight pleasant scent to it. Aromatherapy to combat all the body odor, perhaps, or a drug to pacify the masses?

A large stage has been constructed in the middle of the crowd, with booths surrounding the plaza. Giant screens sit atop the booths and have projected images of some of Garden City's most prized murals. The entire plaza has a warm glow. Not bright enough to wash out the screens, but enough to see well in the dark of night. Did they portal in a party planner from Earth? It's uncharacteristically festive for Thera. I scan the crowd to see if I know anyone. Or, should I say, to see if I can catch sight of Ethan, not having seen him since I reunited with Blake. I'm sure he's here, but with everyone dressed the same it's worse than playing Where's Waldo.

At midnight sharp, seven men and three women take the stage, Brad Darcton among them. Brad climbs onto a five-foot tall podium atop the stage and addresses the crowd. Then he introduces the Presiding Ten of the Grand Council. Was one of the women another Darcton? Blake whispers something about going to find a restroom and I'm left to watch the spectacle alone.

"We are thrilled to have the opportunity to address the Garden City residents tonight," Brad says. "And to celebrate our heritage and beautiful prospects for the future with each of you."

He tells the love story of Helina and Hadrian and how they tenderly cared for their garden. How their children were special and had the ability to overcome Day and Night, Dark and Light. How the blood of the Originals still runs through the veins of those on Thera. And how we honor the Originals by Cleaving and bringing new generations of Original-blooded Therans into the world.

"The Ten is thrilled to present Garden City's newest Cleaved couples," he says, motioning for them to come up on stage. I scan the stage. Notably missing is Bailey Goodington. There's no way she would have missed that party. I'll have to ask Blake why she isn't up there. "These forty young pairs put their faith in the Cleaving process. Furthermore, they agreed to parent the next generation of Theran youth without delay. It is with great joy I announce that each couple is confirmed pregnant thanks to our Assisted Pregnancy process."

Wild cheers and shouts of congratulations fill the air. The couples on stage look genuinely happy. However, I stay silent. The math's not working for me. I know how long it took to shoot me up with drugs before they took my eggs. There hasn't been enough time since they Cleaved to retrieve the eggs, create embryos, insert the embryos back in, and confirm the pregnancies took. Unless they'd already done the egg retrieval on all the girls previously? Perhaps they'd been planning this for a while?

I feel a tap on my shoulder and turn around. Guess who is better at playing Where's Waldo than I am? My heart starts thumping wildly.

"Ethan," I say and give him a huge hug and kiss on the cheek, noting he's not as scruffy as usual. We're both slow to let go and I know I spend a few seconds too long staring at his lips, which he most definitely notices. "I was hoping I'd see you tonight. You haven't come by even once. I've been going through major withdrawal."

"I thought you'd be sick of me after being around me twenty-four seven for weeks," he says. "And that you'd want the time with Blake. Where is he?"

"He went to find a bathroom or something, but I'm not sure he'll ever be able to find his way back in this crowd," I say, watching the hordes of people fill every gap in the makeshift arena.

"Things going okay with him?" he asks and I can tell he regrets it the moment the words leave his mouth. "Sorry, that's none of my business."

"We're friends. You can ask me anything," I say. As long as you don't ask me to betray Blake or your girlfriend, because you are too much of a temptation and I really don't want to be that girl. If my relationship with Blake was fake before, I can no longer say that. It's real, fights and all. What choice did I have, since Blake declared his love for me, I felt obligated to return the sentiment, particularly since Ethan's in love with someone else. I have to get over Ethan and fully commit to Blake. "It's going okay."

"You look beautiful in that dress," he says, changing the subject. "And it could even pass for something you'd find at the mall," he adds with a whisper.

"Thanks and yeah, shocking huh—patterns. You look pretty handsome yourself, College Boy," I say. I can feel the blood rush to my cheeks. It's one of those awkward deals that can't be avoided after two people have a "moment" and then try to retract it and just be friends. I'm really happy to see him. He's been on my mind a lot. I haven't been having much fun lately. Plus, it's hard to spend that much time with someone and then go cold turkey. I want to look away but I can't take my eyes off his. Under the festive lighting of the plaza the topaz sparkles in his eyes are more prominent than usual.

"My dad's on a roll," he says, changing the subject again.

"He's quite the dynamic speaker. When he was introducing the rest of the Ten did he mention another Darcton?" I say.

"Oh yeah, that's my mom—Vienna Darcton," he says.

"You never mentioned they *both* were members of the Ten," I say. "Yikes. Why didn't you tell me?"

"I'm not them—and you thought the worse of me already," he says. I've hurt his feelings and I run my hand along his face to show him I'm sorry. He softens when I stare into his eyes and then down to his lips and we're back to uncomfortable, so he lightens things up. "So, what's the deal with all the Cleaving? Did all those kids really turn eighteen at the same time?"

"Nope," I say. I tell him about the partying and consequences, and then add, "I didn't know about the pregnancies though. That's a bit of a surprise."

"When did you say they Cleaved?" he says. I can tell the math's not working for him, either. He saw the same in-vitro information I did while we were back on Earth.

"Not long enough ago for them to be pregnant already," I say.

"Huh, you should ask them about it," he says. "In the meantime though, since Blake's probably lost in this crowd somewhere, why don't we make a round of the booths and look for him? There's free food and fun to be had. Or at least that's what my dad announced." I missed the part of his speech about food.

"I am hungry," I say. Ethan takes my hand and leads me through the crowd.

We get half way around the booths and still haven't seen Blake. The booths are a mix of industry-sponsored informational stations and ladies who volunteered to bring their favorite meals in bulk to hand out samples. I managed to eat a full meal, though I haven't tasted anything to beat Ethan's chocolate soufflé. We skip over a full section of booths aimed at small children and end up in the "Cleaving propaganda" section where we run into Tristan and Bri. Ethan drops my hand, probably thinking I don't want to have to explain it, although Bri definitely noticed.

"Kira, you're back," says Bri, who gives me a huge hug. She's sporting her party look, her eyes a dark sea of eyeliner. "Where's Blake? And hi, I'm Briella. We've met before, but you probably don't remember," she says to Ethan, outstretching her hand to shake his. She looks to Ethan, then to me, and back as if she's trying to figure out how and why we are here together.

"I remember. Nice to see you again," Ethan says. "I'm Ethan Darcton," Ethan says to Tristan.

"I'm Tristan. Bri and I are Cleaved," Tristan says. As if we didn't know, although the comment seems to be directed to Ethan. Tristan is marking Bri as his personal territory.

"So where'd you say Blake was?" Bri says, glancing at Ethan again, implied text being "Did you dump him for this hunk?" I can tell she wants me to explain why I was holding Ethan's hand when I'm supposedly committed to Blake. How can I explain it? I shouldn't have been, but I love the way Ethan strokes my hand while holding it and have missed it since we got back to Thera.

"Blake disappeared to find a bathroom and seems to have gotten lost, so Ethan's been helping me try to find him," I say, though I'm starting to wonder if that's where he really is. I thrust my hands in my pockets to wipe off some of the sweat and I find an object in my left pocket. A watch. Blake's watch. What's he doing? Something where he doesn't want to be tracked. You're an idiot, Blake.

"Huh, we haven't seen him either," Bri says.

I don't want them raising any alarms so I change the subject. "I guess congratulations are in order. Wow. Cleaved and Pregnant. That's, uh, just, uh, huge." I try to imagine her nine months pregnant. She'll barely turn eighteen by the time the baby's born, being young for our class.

"I know," she says. "It all happened so fast." Yeah. Too fast to be believable. Ethan nudges me to tell me that's my cue.

"Fast is an understatement. Tell me about the whole Assisted Pregnancy thing. How'd that work?" I ask.

"Well, a couple nights after our Cleaving we went in to the doctor and they put the baby in," she says.

"Huh?" I say. "I'm confused. How often had you been seeing the doctor before that?"

"Well, almost every night for the month before. They'd put me on a few extra medications, but that was just because my thyroid was out of whack or something," she says.

"When did they retrieve your eggs? I think I remember your friend that you introduced me to—Lara Stewart—she mentioned having a surgical procedure to get her eggs out," I say. "Did you have the same thing done?"

"What? Just the one procedure, but they assured me that was all I needed. And obviously it worked because I'm pregnant. I've been having plenty of evening sickness to prove it," she says as she rubs her stomach.

I turn to Tristan and ask, "When did you give, uh, your contribution to your child's DNA?"

"Oh yeah, that happened the same night they put the baby in," Tristan says. I shake my head. Obviously they're clueless and will be no help to me. For all I know the only assistance they did was to take a syringe full of Tristan's goods and insert it into Bri. It seems like a pretty huge coincidence that the timing would be right and that they got *all* the girls' cycles aligned. Although, they've had them all on birth control so it could be possible.

"I haven't seen Bailey around. What's she up to?" I ask.

"Blake didn't tell you? She got *Exiled*. The night we were at Headquarters for our Cleaving, she apparently snuck off and got caught in some secret area. She totally missed out, though I'm pretty sure the only one she'd want to be Cleaved to is your boyfriend," she says. "She was super teebed and all over him the night of the party."

"Huh, interesting," I grimace. "No, Blake never mentioned it." Why wouldn't he tell me Bailey got Exiled? And that she'd been throwing herself at him at the party?

"So, when did you get back exactly?" Bri asks.

"A few nights ago," I say. "I would have stopped by but heard you guys were having 'private time' or something."

"Yeah, we've had a *lot* of private time," Tristan says. I cringe. Whatever.

217

That's nothing new, apparently. Not that he remembers. Ethan rubs my back to calm my nerves. He knows better than anyone what these two did to me.

"Where were you?" Bri pushes. "You just disappeared without saying goodbye to us. Blake was pretty freaked when he got back and you were gone."

"I'm really sorry about that," I say. I look to Ethan to help me out. He can spin some sort of story that'll fly.

"It's my fault," Ethan says. "I'd been working on this project for my dad that had this huge deadline. My dad told me I could pull Kira out of school to help me out. She didn't want to leave but it's not like anyone can say no to my dad, right?"

Both Tristan and Bri nod. They're quite aware of who Brad Darcton is and had they been asked, they'd have jumped without asking to say goodbye to friends, too. "Oh yeah. I think Blake said something about you maybe being with Ethan." Huh? Blake knew? How?

Speaking of the literal devil. "Hello, Son. Kira," says Brad Darcton. He appeared out of nowhere. I wonder how much he heard? His eyes are fiery and trained on me.

"Hey, Dad. I was just explaining to Kira's friends why she disappeared for so long and how much I appreciate you having her help me out on my project," Ethan says.

"Yes, Kira has been a huge help to the Second Chance Institute," Brad says. "In fact, I wanted to discuss your work with you, Kira, if you don't mind."

"Sure," I say. Oh crap. He must have heard me interrogating them about their Assisted Pregnancies. I keep my face emotionless and avoid looking at Ethan who might invoke a reaction. My mother taught me well to control my emotions and bury them when necessary. Which on Thera—is all the time.

"Can I join the two of you?" Ethan says, a stern glare affixed to his father.

"Sorry, Son. I need to talk to Kira alone. I believe Councilman Hunt would like a word with you," Brad says to Ethan and then gestures to a man a few feet away. To the others he says, "Please excuse us and enjoy the festivities. And my personal congratulations on your pregnancy, Tristan and Briella."

"Thanks, Mr. Darcton," they say in unison.

"I think we're past the pretenses now," Brad says to me as he pushes his glasses higher onto ,the crown of his nose. It took a few minutes to weave through the crowd, out the back of a booth, and to an empty bench overlooking the city canyon where we could talk. He removes a gun from a leg-holster and sets it on the bench, loosely pointed toward me. I guess he'd like me to take our conversation seriously.

"Yes," I say, as I study the face of Ethan's father. He's handsome for an older man. I don't entirely see the resemblance to Ethan other than the dark hair. Ethan must have his mother's general demeanor and physique. Brad has dark hazel eyes and is pencil thin, compared to Ethan's evenly toned body.

"I'm pleased by the reports of your progress during therapy and am counting on you to maintain an objective view of your circumstances," he says. I simply nod. If he wants my opinions he'll ask—and I'll give him the version of the "truth" that he wants to hear.

"Your brother isn't adapting as well as you and Ethan," he says. "So he'll be remaining with us a while longer." I nod again. "You were very smart to play the Originals card to get Jared here," he says. "How'd you know about it? And how'd you guess his DNT would diminish if he came over as your parents did?"

"You say we're past the pretenses?" I ask. He nods. "Blake overheard a conversation that we were descendants of the true Originals and important to the future of Thera. And then Tristan read me the story of the Originals when I was recovering from the flash flood. I made an educated guess from there that our DNT was important—and perhaps not as potent if we came over as a Second Chancer. Otherwise, why not just kill us?"

"Why do you think you're important to the future of Thera?" he asks, avoiding my comment about offing us.

"Well, I assume you want more pure-descendant blood in your midst. I don't know why, but given you've harvested my eggs twice now, my progeny must be important," I say. If my bluntness surprises him, he doesn't show it.

"I believe the doctors told you they were removing lesions on your reproductive system," he says, sitting a little more upright.

"Let's just say that's one of the first things I checked when I went home. It's amazing what you can learn with internet access. So, what have become of my eggs?" I say.

"They've been put to excellent use," he says. "In fact, the fruits of your labors were on stage tonight. Your friends are carrying your children." Are you freaking kidding me? I knew something was off with the timing of their pregnancies, but this revelation shocks the crap out of me. But even though my insides are churning, I maintain an aloof appearance on the outside by digging my nails into my palms.

"All the Cleaved couples are pregnant with my children? Forty babies?" I ask. "From what I read, doctors are lucky to get fifteen eggs during a retrieval. And, don't doctors usually have to insert multiple embryos to get someone pregnant?"

"We've had a lot more experience with Assisted Pregnancies on Thera, and thus have much higher success rates with retrieval and implantation than our counterparts on Earth," he says, beaming with pride.

"I'm impressed," I say. "So, who's the father of my children? Blake? Ethan? Or both?"

"Ah. Excellent question," he says. After a long pause, he answers. "Both. Whereas you will uniquely be the Mother of New Thera, we have yet to decide who will win the role of Father. That may largely depend on you."

"How so?" I ask. Best to keep him talking. How will I ever explain to Blake that he's fathered half my children and Ethan's fathered the other half? Worse, how will he feel about our friends being used as permanent surrogates? Briella will birth and raise my child with Tristan. I have no words to describe how I feel about that. At least nothing I'd say out loud.

"There's two ways this can play out. One, you get your boyfriend, Blake, under control, Cleave him and stay on Thera with your new extended family," he says. I see zero chance of getting Blake to agree to Plan A.

"And the other option?" I ask.

"You Cleave to Ethan. You'd be trained here on Thera in the family business and to be a Daynighter and politician's wife, and would eventually return to Earth to help him move forward SCI interests," he says. I'm not sure Ethan would be happy about plan B, since that would keep him from the girl he truly loves.

"Interesting," I say, my heart being tugged in two directions. "Which plan does the Ten prefer for me?" Hmmm, which of those do I prefer for me?

"It's undecided," he says. "I'm preparing you for either eventuality. Either way, you'll have an important role in propagating SCI interests." Ah, the Ten still hasn't come to an agreement on my exact role, but they all agree I'm a permanent fixture in their plans.

"When you say I need to get Blake under control, what do you mean by that?" I ask. I know very well where Blake's allegiance lies, but I wonder how much if anything Brad Darcton knows. He shifts his head to the side and smiles.

"Don't insult me, Kira. I know Blake's father well, or did before his Exile. I've tracked his whereabouts and the company he keeps since. And I have some strong evidence that Blake met with the Exilers during the time he was quote-unquote "lost" during the flash flood," he says.

"I didn't see him after he disappeared down the river. What evidence?" I ask. People like Brad Darcton like to hear themselves talk and show how smart they are, so tend to give away more than they intend.

"He was treated for severe sunburn with a silver paste that is a trademark cure concocted by an Exiler named Doctor Daryn. Most of it had been removed by choice or by the saltwater, but enough was left to prove he didn't spend his entire time paddling ocean waters," he says.

"Assuming you are correct, how can I affect Blake?" I say.

"He says he loves you. Wouldn't he rather live out his life with his true love than die fighting a battle that can't be won? Surely, you could help him to see things more clearly," he says. As if. I have tried to persuade him to abandon his ideals for a chance at a life with me, but have been entirely unsuccessful.

"What happens should my clarity and his clarity fail to converge?" I ask.

"Nothing good, I'm afraid—for Blake or the Exilers," he says. "You see, I think people underestimate the strength of the Second Chance Institute, both here on Thera and on Earth. One might incorrectly assume we're weak since our cities are small and spread apart. Our security force appears to be limited and our only defense from outside attack seems to be the Eco barriers. I'm afraid those same people may delude themselves into thinking they could succeed in an attempt to overthrow or undermine our efforts. Unfortunately, we'll be forced to reveal the full extent of our capabilities if and when attacked." He could be bluffing. Or not. Probably not. They killed off an entire party full of kids to get me here. And executed my parents in front of me to get me back. Why would they be any less ruthless with the Exilers?

"I can see your point," I say.

"I'm afraid I need to get back to make an important announcement about a huge threat to our beloved city. We have intelligence that deranged Exilers have plans to harm our fair citizens. They need not fear, though, because their government will protect them," he says. So, this entire "celebration" has been a ruse to spread ill will about the Exilers—so that if and when they attack—sympathy will be with the SCI and not the Exilers. Smart on the Ten's part. "But, before we convene, I have one more piece of advice for you."

"Yes, what's that?" I ask.

"I strongly recommend you don't mention our conversation to anyone—especially Blake. I'm afraid I wouldn't be able to guarantee the safety of Jared, or of Blake, if you were to discuss these highly private matters," he says. "And I will know if you do, no matter where the conversation occurs. Understand?"

"I understand," I say. Jared and Blake die if I warn Blake. And Blake and my canyon time has never been just "ours."

CHAPTER TWENTY-ONE

Ethan

"You locked me up like a caged animal. No, I'm not going to forgive you," I tell my father. After spending my childhood as Heart Defect Poster Boy in a room-shaped bubble, I vowed never to allow myself to be confined again.

"Given the circumstances, it was quite necessary. And, I locked you up with the girl, so what's the problem?"

"She went back to him," I say, more to myself than to my father. "All because she thinks I love someone else. And I can't tell her otherwise, since I haven't been given the go ahead to freely pursue her." I've been going crazy the last few nights. I kissed Kira and she responded with enthusiasm. It felt different from the passionate, lust-filled embraces we'd shared back in San Diego. There was no "audience" (e.g. Jared) to impress or cover to support. No, this was so personal, so intimate, so full of love. Dropping her back with Blake and her reaction to seeing him... heartbreaking.

My father puts a hand on each shoulder and looks me squarely in the eye. "Forget about her. She and the boy are liabilities and as good as dead. We have what we need from them. Anything more is too risky." My heart beats erratically and vision blurs. "Dead" and "Liability" are not acceptable descriptors for the woman I have fallen so deeply for.

I pinch the bridge of my nose and take a deep breath. Contemplating making a deal with the devil brings on sharp sinus pains. "I'll do anything to keep her alive. I won't fight you any more on your plans for me. Just don't have her killed. Please. Blake either. She cares about him." I can't bring myself to say or admit she loves him, even though I can tell she does.

"You're more of a sap than I thought. Fine. I'll protect the girl. In return for your 'cooperation' in our plans for you. I cannot, however, guarantee she ends up with you. And you are not, under any circumstances, to share anything with her that would put me, your mother, the rest of the Ten or Grand Council at risk, including the events of your childhood. Understood?"

A small price to pay to keep her alive. And besides, I can feign my compliance and enthusiasm. At least I hope I can. "Understood. And Blake?"

"I'll do my best. He's not exactly a friend to the Ten," he says. This, I'm well aware of thanks to Jax, but I don't let my father know it. "He may be able to be… persuaded… to come around."

"How?" I ask.

"You leave that to me. In the meantime, I'm going to arrange for you to shadow some Council and Ten members for the remainder of your Internship. To further your education and preparation to take your rightful place in the affairs of the SCI. Henry's arranged for you to work on his campaign during the school year as well."

I groan. So much for free time to visit Kira. He sneers. "If it's a problem, we could annul our agreement."

I'm quick to respond. "It's fine. I'll do what's required to keep Kira safe." Why do I get the feeling I've been manipulated? I have to wonder if he threatened Kira's life solely to gain my cooperation.

"Excellent," my father says with a wicked grin. "I've got to leave for the Festival, as do you. It's going to be an exciting night for Thera."

"I'll never find her in this crowd. It's a regular clone-fest," I complain to Jax. Seeing Jax in Festival attire is jarring. He rarely wears color. Lots of heads turn our way as we push through the hordes of people here to celebrate the messed up institution of Cleaving.

"That's why you have *me* with you," Jax says. "I've got my Kiradar on since she's just entered the premises with one very suspicious looking Blake Sundry." Would it be too much to ask for Blake to make himself scarce for a bit?

"Well, then, by all means. Lead the way," I say, eager to find her. It feels like an eternity since I've seen her. Jax takes his time meandering, our progress slowed by Council members and other acquaintances who want to exchange small talk.

My father's on the podium driveling on about the Originals. I'm only marginally paying attention, but then he introduces "Garden City's newest Cleaved couples" and my head snaps up. Kira better not be up there.

"Kira remains as virginal and nearly as pure as when you last saw her," Jax says. I clench my fists, ready to mar Jax's pretty face when he adds, "Fascinating. Forty newly Cleaved couples. Pregnant. That's a lot of babies. Magical, don't you think?" Jax double-speak for "I've got information that you don't."

"What do you know?" I ask.

"I know the tide's a'changing and this is history in the making and the Ten's playing with fire," he says without answering my question. Typical.

"Why must you always speak in riddles?" I ask.

"To keep your brain from atrophying," he says with a chuckle. "Looks like your love interest's a little shocked by the news." He points to a crowd twenty feet away and I immediately see her. She's a vision. The most beautiful thing I've ever seen in my life. Her hair's in perfect ringlets and cascades down her back. The Festival dress clings to her curves. She looks to be deep in thought and has a slight scowl directed at my father.

"Wow," I say.

I glance at Jax and notice him salivating at Kira. When his eyes darken with lust and he licks his lips, I re-clench my fists and prepare for a fight. But then he slaps his hand on my back and says, "I'm not fighting you, Ethan. Despite the fact she's breathtaking. Positively glowing. And alone. Chop, chop. No time to waste. Get over there."

"Want to meet her?" I say without thinking and then mentally berate myself.

"In due time. But not tonight. I have business to attend to. Enjoy your evening. And the girl... while you can," he says with a smile. When I scowl at him, he adds, "Blake will be back for her eventually."

I waste no time, leaving Jax behind. Has she even thought about me? Will she be excited to see me? Has she missed me a fraction as much as I've missed her? I tap on her shoulder.

She turns around. "Ethan," she says as she embraces me and lands a huge kiss on my cheek. I flush red as she holds on, staring at my lips with such desire that I'm tempted to pack her over my shoulder and back to my house. "I was hoping I'd see you tonight. You haven't come by even once. I've been going through major withdrawal."

Oh, Kira. Me, too. Me, too.

CHAPTER TWENTY-TWO

Blake

The moment I see the Ten all on stage, I know I'll never have a better opportunity to explore SCI headquarters. I'd been hoping this would be the case. Although I don't want to support my father's plans, I figure I may be able to find something to help Doc Daryn. And, if my dad and his men do need to escape and I can figure out how to turn off the Eco barrier, I'm saving lives. Lives spared, even if they are Militant lives, is still a good thing. Avoiding the situation altogether would be even better. Doc promised me that he'd continue to work on my father and see if they can come to an agreement that will stall or avoid the invasion.

I tell Kira I need to use the restroom and slip my watch in her dress pocket so I can't be tracked. She'll assume I got lost in the crowd when I don't return quickly. Unless she notices the watch. Then I'll have a lot of explaining to do, because she wouldn't agree with my choice. All of the sudden she's pro-subservience and anti-rebellion. Seeing her parents executed really did a number on her. The Ten have convinced her that she's responsible. And that if she deviates from strict obedience to the Canon ever so slightly, they'll put a bullet in Jared's brain.

As I wind through the crowd I notice that although all the security personnel are wearing the standard issue Cleaving Festival attire, they are also wearing hats. I hunt for the right situation and then "accidentally" push a large woman into one of the security guys. They both topple over, sending the guard's hat flying. While the guard's busy helping the woman return to her feet, I snag his hat and tuck it into my shirt.

Because booths circle the plaza, with only one entry in from the train station, I have to exit through a booth to get to headquarters. I don my new hat and explain to a nice lady offering fried chicken samples that I've been dispatched to check the perimeter. She sends me with some chicken to go, I thank her for the service she's rendering by providing food for the festivities, and I'm on my way, discarding the chicken into a trash bin in front of headquarters.

I'm surprised I don't encounter anyone as I enter headquarters. Not a single soul. How could they possibly leave the entire building unattended? I don't waste time to analyze the situation, as the security guards could return at any moment, but I do take a second to look up in awe as I walk into the center court of the building. Made entirely of intricate glass mosaic and six stories high, the dome-topped atrium depicts the loveliest garden I've ever seen. A circular staircase rings the outside of it and shines lights through the glass to create a spectacular three-dimensional kaleidoscope feel. It's the most stunning thing I've ever seen in my life and I have a sudden desire to go get Kira and show her, but I suppress it. That will have to wait for another time.

Instead I locate the fully enclosed back staircase and start to climb. Ted's instructions prove accurate and I head to the first target room on the third floor. I keep my face shielded by the hat in case any cameras are recording my visit.

The first room has banks of servers, but no computer to access them from and no switches other than to control the lights. So, I head for the second room Ted suggested on the fourth floor. This one appears to be a boardroom of sorts and has lots of monitors and cords to connect to tablets, but nothing else of interest. I'm starting to worry Ted sent me on a wild goose chase.

Room three's smack dab center of the sixth floor and I find both a computer and host of control panels. Jackpot. This appears to be the main control center for the city. There are panels to adjust the solar panels, monitor the city's water reserve, and track incoming cargo ships. Pretty cool. The Exilers—from either faction—would love access to this room.

One control panel is labeled "EB" and appears to be a good bet. An LCD screen sits atop the screen and shows a ring the shape of the Eco barrier and dotted lights, likely representing the current pattern of the detonators. Perfect. Unfortunately, I have no idea if switching it off will trigger alarms or switch it off permanently. So I turn to the computer and enter the password GCM47CoCL10 that Ted gave me hoping to find more information.

With a bit of hunting I find a manual for the Eco barrier. Apparently, the switch only disables the barrier for ten minutes. To disable for longer—in whole or in part for maintenance work, an additional switch must be enabled from one of the Ten's tablets. Worse, to prevent someone being able to steal the password and deactivate the barrier from their tablets, the Ten must memorize a twenty-digit code to enter into the Eco barrier program on their tablet. Man, I thought the password Ted gave me was bad. I hope ten minutes will be enough time for my dad and the other Exilers to cross. Because I have little hope of getting one of those tablets, or the code.

The other thing I run across while hunting for the manual is a master calendar of upcoming activities at headquarters. One particular event catches my eye: Theran City Heads Meeting. It's scheduled over a two-night period— three nights prior to my dad's planned attack on the city. I have to get my dad that information. The Exilers could deliver a definitive blow to not only Garden City's government structure, but also every city's structure if they were to capture and imprison the heads of every city. A list of attendees who've accepted an invitation to the meeting may also be useful to my father so I commit the names to memory, noting whether they are from Garden City or elsewhere.

I logoff the computer, glance around the room to make sure I've returned everything to the state I found it in, and depart. As I approach the stairs, however, I hear the familiar whir of the elevator shaft. Crap, I took too long and folks are returning. I duck into the back staircase and jog down the stairs, being careful to stay light on my feet and check for anyone entering or exiting the staircase. But the coast is clear and I'm able to get down to the basement. My dad had the layout all wrong. I don't have to hunt for trap doors or climb up storage room shelves. There's a simple exit to the tunnels.

Of course, I have no clue where to go once in the tunnels. My hope is that the majority of Garden City inhabitants are still partying at the Festival and that if I go farther than a hundred yards in any direction I'll be in the clear. So I pick a path and run quickly, but carefully, just as I had in the coal mine tunnels. At my current pace, I should hit a quarter mile in two minutes. I count it out and once past my mental quarter mile mark, I look for an exit. About ninety seconds later I see a small ladder. I scale it and find a trap door at the top, which opens using the passkey Ted gave me.

Here goes nothing, I think as I push up and peer out. All I see is hanging Garden City attire, and not just any attire. Grand Council attire. If caught, I'm dead. They won't even bother Exiling me. On the other hand, it's likely the resident is still at the Festival. I listen for any sounds in the home, but hear nothing and so I decide to go for it.

A minute later I'm out the front door and down the home's ramp. I recognize the street from the Garden City model, as this street is the only street with residences built atop the canyon and close to the city center. If I follow the road towards town I should hit the plaza. I jog down, staying clear of the street lamps, until the backs of the booths and large screens come into view.

And that's when I hear an announcement that makes my hair stand on end. I recognize the speaker as Brad Darcton and he's spinning a tale about barbarian Exilers planning to mount attacks on the city. He claims that hordes of blood hungry savages stand waiting to kill women and children to get Garden City's resources. They've already attempted to infiltrate the Eco barrier on numerous occasions and have attacked incoming ships, executed the sailors, and stolen supplies meant for the city's residents.

Well, despite hating the message and the Ten's manipulation of the general public, Brad's given me the perfect opportunity to enter the Festival again unnoticed. Because I guarantee everyone's focused on that stage, awaiting his next riveting words. So I duck into the bathrooms to wipe the sweat from my face and ditch the security cap. When I come out I add my shock and dismay at the gall of the evil Exilers to the crowd's.

Someone demands to know how the Ten and Grand Council will keep them safe. Have no fear Garden City citizens. The Ten and the Grand Council have a Grand Plan. They will protect the residents of Garden City, even if it means the annihilation of the extremist Exilers. The crowd cheers "Thanks to the Ten" over and over again. If security in Garden City has ever been lax, it isn't now. Brad wouldn't create widespread panic if he didn't have a plan to defeat any intruders. Doc Daryn was right when he warned my father not to underestimate the SCI.

While joining in the chanting I circle the crowd looking for beautiful strawberry blonde ringlets. I finally spot Kira and am dismayed to see Ethan by her side looking at her like a puppy in a pet shop window who wants to be taken home. Friend, my booty. Guys don't do girls as friends. At least not hot girls like Kira. Why's he not Cleaved to his dream girl again? Right, he doesn't have to Cleave, as he's not under Garden City jurisdiction. His daddy made an exception until he could find Ethan the right girl. One with the right blood type. For a guy who told me he'd never be able to look at another girl again, he surely seems to be in love with my girlfriend. I'm sure that was daddy's plan by sending them away and then locking them up together. With that much time alone some feelings were bound to crop up.

I sneak up behind Kira and hug her from the back, slipping my watch back out of her pocket and onto my wrist.

"I've been looking everywhere for you," I say as I unwrap my arms and slip between her and Ethan. I give her a juicy kiss for good measure.

"Likewise," she says. "We finally gave up and decided to stay in one place so you could find us."

"Thank goodness for that or we'd have probably kept missing each other," I say. I can't tell if she's buying it. In fact, since she got back I don't have a clue how she feels because no matter what she *says*, her face shows nothing except a smile.

"Ethan's in love with you," I say to her as we walk back from the Festival.

"You are way out of line. You have no idea what you are talking about," she says. "He's in love with someone else. Not me."

"I see the way he looks at you. Don't pretend like you can't see it, too," I say. I hate that she affects me the way she does. Even my father can't hurt me or make me angry like Kira can. "I think you understated your relationship with him."

"Are you accusing me of lying to you?" she says. Her eyes and body language scream defensive.

"No. Omitting," I say. I know I'm being a hypocritical jerk. It's not like I told her Bailey kissed me. Since Bailey got Exiled, I didn't see any real reason to bring it up. And I'm the one who escalated my relationship with Kira. The moment I saw her come back home with Ethan in tow, I knew I had to raise the bar and tell her I love her. Or else I'd lose her. Bailey had been Exiled by that point, so I could give Kira my undivided attention.

"Wow. I mean, wow. That's so choice," she says. "You ditch me for the entire Festival and suddenly I'm a lying, cheating whore when I spend a little time with a friend?" Now she's pissed.

"That's my problem. I don't think he sees you as just a friend," I say.

"How would you even know? You don't know him like I do. I like him. He's important to me. We went through some crazy stuff together. But, we're just friends and that's the last time I'm going to say it. Believe me or not, I don't care," she says with her poker face. I do have a bad attitude about Ethan. His daddy wants him to Cleave my girlfriend. And, the thing I keep coming back to —he's nice and devoted and ready to settle down. More so than me. What bugs me about Ethan is that he has that same look as his father and the other SCI higher-ups. Pretty on the outside. Talks a good game. But probably masking a whole lot of ugly under that beautiful façade.

"I'm sorry I mentioned it," I say. "I don't want to fight with you." I know she's hiding something from me and it involves Ethan. But the conversation's going nowhere, and who am I to talk? I haven't exactly been forthright about my own plans and activities. Though none of my activities involve a "friend" that's a girl (only a hot girl enemy who's no longer in the picture).

"I don't want to fight either. I wish we could just be on the same page about things. I feel like we're heading down divergent paths and that really scares me," she says, finally showing some emotion, as I can see the fear in her eyes.

"How can you be so complacent after everything the SCI has done to you? It seems like you've just given up and decided to live with it. I can't do that. I'll fight to the end to get my freedom and the freedom of the Second Chancers and Exilers, even if I decide to go about it differently than my dad. Why can't you do the same?" I ask.

"Because I decided I *can* live with the status quo, for now, if it means that we can be together and live in safety. Or at least try to affect the status quo from the inside," she says. "I have nothing to go back to on Earth. Everything I care about is here. I'm not willing to risk a life with the people I love over an effort that I think is hopeless. "

"So let me get this straight," I say. "You want to Cleave me, have two kids, and live unhappily ever after on this hellhole?" She stares directly into my eyes and pauses only momentarily before responding.

"That's better than the alternative," she says. "Think it over. Since we're so important to the future of Thera, perhaps we can have a positive effect on the way things are run. Regardless though, what's more important to you? A futile cause or the potential of a life together?"

"Is that an ultimatum?" I ask.

"No, of course not. I just have spent a lot of time thinking about it myself and well, it's obvious what conclusion I came to. It'd just be nice if you did the same—I mean the thinking, not to necessarily come to the same conclusion," she says, shrugging her shoulders.

"That's not fair. It's not black and white. One or the other," I say, crossing my arms.

"Life's not freaking fair," she says. "I think we both know that."

We walk the rest the way in silence.

I had completely forgotten until just now, but Ted Rosenberg once told me "life wasn't fair but that it's my life, so I need to get over it and make the most of what I have." My father dumped me on him for a week when I went through a period of rebellion at the age of ten. The first thing Ted did was to take me to the graveyard where his daughters were buried to give me a little object lesson.

"Well, life isn't fair," I'd told him.

"What's not fair exactly?" he said.

"My mom died. I had to grow up on that dark craphole Thera and then my dad makes me learn all this stuff I don't care about just so he can send me back there," I said.

"Let me tell you something, Blake," Ted said. He takes a picture out of his wallet and hands it to me. It's of two darling girls that remind me a bit of Leila when she was little. "My beautiful, beautiful daughters were born here on Earth. But they died way before they should have—when they were just little girls. They got a second chance to live—on that 'craphole' Thera as you call it. They love it there. They're happy. Really, really, happy. So I hold a really special place in my heart for Thera. It's a place of miracles for my daughters and for me."

"Well, it wasn't for me," I said, kicking a clump of grass out of the turf and sending it flying.

"Did you know that if it wasn't for your family—and they go way, way back —that my daughters would have never gotten a second chance and people like you and me couldn't travel back and forth between Earth and Thera?" he said.

"Nope," I said.

"You are going to have the opportunity one day to help make sure the people on Thera—like my daughters and the rest of the people living there—get treated right, including the Exilers. It's your birthright," he said.

"What's a birthright?" I asked.

"It's something that gets passed down from father to son to father to son and so on. If Thera had Kings you'd be one. You've got royal blood in you, Blake. You and your brother will one day get to rule Thera as goodly Kings," he said.

"You mean sister, right? I don't have a brother. Only Leila," I said.

"Yeah, sorry. When you get old you say stupid things," he said with a laugh. "Leila can be like a Queen. And you both can have children that will get your birthright, too. That way more people can travel back and forth and help the people on both Thera and on Earth."

"I don't see how going there helps anyone," I said.

"You'll understand someday," he said.

"Why do you care so much what I do?" I said.

"I would do absolutely anything to protect my daughters and the people I love. Your dad feels the same way about the Exilers. But one day all the people that your dad and I care about will depend on you to make good choices and do the right thing," he said. "Can you promise to do that?"

"I guess. I have no clue what you're talking about, but I'll try to be good," I said.

"I'm counting on that," he said.

I remember that I asked my dad about the whole birthright thing and he told me that Ted must've been making up a story to get me motivated. But now I know it wasn't a story at all. Which means that Ted knew who I was all along and about my importance to Thera and the SCI. And he didn't tell my father. Well, Teddy boy, time for you to step up and show where your allegiance lies. If you're really on the side of "good for all Therans" then you can play a bigger role in helping my dad's coup. Why should I risk my life to sneak into headquarters again—during regular business hours this time—when Ted Rosenberg works there?

And if Ted's loyalty has drifted over the years… well then, he's got a date with the Reaper a.k.a. my father.

"I'm going boarding," I tell Ted and Kira. Ted's here first thing in the evening for our nightly Handler meeting since it's a Sunnight and we don't have school.

"You're not supposed to exercise for another week," Kira says, her green eyes stabbing me with accusation of poor judgment.

"I feel fine and I need some air. Thinking time. No tricks, I promise," I say. It's ironic I'm using Kira's "suggestion" I spend some time thinking to do the things she'd prefer me to avoid like the plague.

The truth is that I'm not really ready to ride, but I need to get a message about the meeting of the city heads to my father. So I grab my board, walk out the front door, and roll down the ramp before Kira can stop me. The temperature is brutal. I note the sun is setting to the East, so it shouldn't be long before the heat backs off. It's a long ride to the beach, but I've left my watch at home, so unless I encounter someone who has the audacity to ask me what I'm doing, I should be fine.

Despite continual adjustments to my stance while boarding I feel like someone's trying to rip the grafts off my back with a giant claw. The new skin doesn't stretch well. I start to worry that my back will look like it's been through a shredder by the time I get back. The paths get bumpier the closer I get to the beach, having been ravaged by the storm. Apparently the Garden City maintenance crew hasn't bothered to fix this stretch. The pain from being jostled on my board slows me down. It takes a half hour to get to the mouth of the canyon and by the time I get there the sun has fully disappeared.

Without the lift of the flash flood water it takes a couple minutes to find some footholds in the canyon wall to help me climb to the shelf. I manage to get up, though I can feel blood seeping through the back of my shirt. Not good. My doctor will be most displeased with me. I turn my focus to maneuvering up the shelf. The slickness of rain slowed my forward progress before. Tonight, vertigo attacks me as a full moon and stars illuminate the increasing distance between the beach and me.

When I finally hit the end of the shelf I give the signal. Short long short long. I repeat it several times and get a response within minutes. My dad comes personally, lantern in hand, which sheds light on his mood. Angry.

"Why are you here?" he yells up at me.

"Nice to see you, too," I say. "I just missed you so much that I thought I'd come for a visit."

"I don't have time for your sarcasm, Blake. We're busy preparing for our mission," he says.

"Well, I have some intel that could and should influence your plans," I say. "After what I tell you, perhaps you'll listen to Doc Daryn. You've way underestimated the SCI." I detail my visit to headquarters and the information I obtained, including a warning about the ten minute time limit to cross the Eco barrier, the ever-changing barrier configurations, list of meeting attendees, and Brad Darcton's speech about the Exilers.

"Are you sure about the timing of the meeting?" he asks.

"That's what it said on their master schedule," I say. "So unless Ted set me up, it should be accurate. He gave me the passkey and code to get on the computer."

"Ted can be trusted," he says.

"Really? I'm not so sure," I say. I recount the memory of my trip to the graveyard with Ted and how it proves that he knew about me being an Original long before I arrived in Garden City.

"Just because he knew doesn't say anything about his loyalties," my father says.

"Doesn't it?" I say.

"If Ted has turned and you can prove it I'll personally put a bullet through his oversized head. But until then, we're going to act on this intel. The opportunity to remove all the city heads at once may not come again."

"The SCI is expecting you. They've warned the entire city. There's no way you can come waltzing in and expect no resistance."

"We haven't seen a single ship come through—so where is the Ten's supposed security force? Every security detail we've encountered from Garden City has been a dozen or less people. We can easily overpower whatever they have."

I shake my head, incredulous at how overconfident he is. "So, you're still coming? Same timing, just different night?"

"Yes, we'll be there on meeting night at 1930 hours—just prior to the start of the work night. Dressed in city attire. The Interceptors got lucky on their last run a couple months back. The clothes will help us blend," he says. Indeed, that will help. Once within city limits, officials won't know who to be on the lookout for. "You should get back. It was a huge risk to come."

"Infinitely less risky than what you're about to do," I say.

"Just give us three hours to get in and out and have that barrier down at 2230 hours sharp," he says.

"OK," I say. "But, I just want to be on the record that I think this is a bad idea from everything I've heard and seen. I'll do what I can to preserve lives, but I think you're making a huge mistake." I still plan to ask Ted to disarm the barrier. I'm not sure I want to be anywhere near headquarters when this all goes down.

"Get off your high horse, Blake. We see the atrocities being committed by the SCI and we're doing something about it. Unlike Doc's bunch, we refuse to be a bunch of pansies who are fine to let those evil men continue to torment us —and the Second Chancers. Have a little faith. We know what we're doing."

He turns to leave without a goodbye. I surely hope he's right. The largest security detail I've seen since I've been here came to cart off Tristan, Bri, and the other partiers. From our "aerial flight" and visit to the scale model of the city I didn't see any obvious place to stash large numbers of security men or an arsenal, but they could have just left something off the model or failed to fly over a secure area.

I retrace my path down the ledge and then jump off once I get inland, twisting my bad ankle again when I land on a rock that I didn't see in the poor lighting. Great. Now my return trip will take longer. I'd estimate about an hour and twenty minutes, with a lot more uphill riding and energy spent. I have an uneasy feeling about my father's plan. Everything rides on whether Ted is truly loyal and whether Brad Darcton and the Ten have more capability than my father thinks. I plan to distort the truth when I communicate my dad's plans to Ted. I'll tell him I need him to turn off the barrier to let my father and his team in and not tell him it's their exit strategy. That way, my dad and his team will have a three-hour start and can hopefully avoid an ambush. Any advantage is better than no advantage.

The other thing that makes me feel uncomfortable about the plan is the invariable fallout if the Militants fail. Every Exiler knows about my involvement. So, if caught and questioned, there's a high probability someone will give me up. How would the SCI handle my treason? Death? Exile? Or would they hurt Kira to get to me? What about our lab babies? Will they destroy them if their father is proven a traitor? I've always known the risk to me, but if Kira or the babies suffered for my actions… that I can't deal with.

When I arrive back at my house, ready to collapse, I'm surprised to see Ted still there. I've been gone for at least two and a half hours, if not longer, and they look pissed.

"You aren't supposed to exercise at all and you go ride for three and a half hours?" Kira says. Oops. My calculations on time gone were way off. "We were about to send out a search party." I need to think up an excuse fast. A variation of the truth usually works best.

"I haven't slept well lately… I've been reliving the explosion at the Eco barrier—having nightmares where all my skin melts off my body. I dunno… I just thought if I went back the spot that I might be able to get some sort of closure or whatever. Sorry, I know that probably sounds really lame, but… it's the only thing I could think of to help me sleep better," I say.

"I could have arranged to have you taken by mule," Ted says. "It was irresponsible for you to board all the way to the beach. The doctor should be here any minute to give you a once over and make sure you haven't done irreparable damage to your grafts."

"I'm fine," I say, a small deviation from the truth. "My back's a little sore, but I just need to rest. And drink some water. It's hot out there." It was pretty stupid to leave without bringing at least a bottle of water.

"A little sore? I see blood on your shirt. And, where's your watch?" Ted asks, pointing to my wrist.

"Oh, shoot. I must've forgotten to put it on," I say. "Let me go grab it." I slip away to my bedroom and put on the watch. Why would Ted say that out loud when he knows we're being listened to? It wasn't necessary and will just make the powers-that-be wonder what I'm up to. The fact he did it has my suspicion about Ted's defection from the Exilers' cause at an all time high.

I let the doctor check me out. I'm so severely parched that he has his nurse insert an IV and tells her to run three bags of fluids through me so that the grafts can rehydrate. Kira bails at the mention of the IV, knowing that it will involve needles. It takes six tries in four different veins to get the needle in. After the juice is flowing the doctor tends to the damage to my patches, stitching a few dissolvable sutures into a dislodged area. Then he wraps my ankle to stabilize it.

Once all needles and sharp objects are put away, Kira brings me some bland toast. I try to make some light conversation, but I can see she's clenching her teeth to keep from chewing me out in front of company. She knows better than to discuss our issues within the walls of our house. So, she stays silent.

Maybe it's better she's ticked. If the Ten thinks we're on the outs, there's a chance she won't be blamed or punished for my actions. It was far more irresponsible for me to start up a relationship with her than to board down to the beach. I knew better than to get involved, but did it anyway. I let myself be tricked into thinking I had hope of a normal future. People like me don't get normal futures.

Whenever two good people argue over principles, they are both right.

Marie Von Ebner-Eschenbach

CHAPTER TWENTY-THREE

Kira

"So, you had plenty of time to think on your long ride," I say to Blake.
His story about not sleeping and wanting to face the source of his nightmares is
not believable. He could sleep like a baby even if tornado sirens were blaring.
We are sitting on the upper path of the canyon looking out at the lights. Blake
still thinks it is safe to talk here. I know that nowhere is safe, but can't tell him.
All I can do is persuade him to abandon everything he believes in—or he dies.
"What's your verdict? Adjust to life here or fight your father's cause?"

"I want to support my father's cause and be with you. If his mission fails, I'm
all yours and we'll do things your way. But I can't abandon him or the other
Exilers now. They've sacrificed too much for me," he says.

"Is it worth your life?" I ask.

"I'm not really involved at this point. I got my dad his intel and now I just
have to wait and see what happens, so don't stress. I'll be fine," he says.

"Since you met with them on the beach you haven't done anything to help
him? No intelligence gathering? Nothing?" I whisper. Although I don't want
Brad Darcton to know the answer, I need to know whether Blake will lie to a
direct question. I stare directly into his eyes so that he has to do it to my face.
After finding out my entire relationship with Tristan was a sham, trust means
everything to me. If I can't trust Blake... if he can't be completely honest with
me, even when I completely disagree with his actions, then how can I possibly
fathom spending my life with him?

"No," he says, although he seems to be sweating more than usual. "What
good would that do? It's not like I could get any information back to my father

in time to make a difference. I've done my part."

"You're sure that you aren't keeping things from me? Because, whether it's to protect me or avoid disagreeing with me, I'm not okay with dishonesty and secrets. After the whole Tristan and Bri thing I realized that trust is paramount," I say. I'm giving him a second chance to fess up. He pauses for a few seconds before answering.

"Nope, there's nothing important to tell," he says, brushing some large beads of perspiration away from his eyes. "Other than the fact I love you." He leans in to kiss me, but I pull away.

"The watch at the Festival? Your board trip? I *know* you're lying," I say, again with a whisper. "Plus, Ted told me about the passkey and code he gave you." I stand up, brush off my pants and turn to leave. It's time for me to do some thinking. He just lied to my face. Twice. Unbelievable.

"Kira, wait," he says, popping up. "Let me explain."

"No," I say. "I gave you the opportunity to come clean."

"You set a trap for me," he says. "That's not fair."

"What's not fair is lying to the person you say you love," I say. "I thought we were partners—that we had each other's backs."

"So, that's it? You're done with me just because I don't give you a freaking log of my whereabouts?" he says. Typical guy reaction. They're the jerk and they try to make the girl look like a taskmaster.

"I think you know the difference between me being a control freak and you doing stuff behind my back that puts us in danger," I say.

"Well, at least I didn't go spend a few weeks with some girl behind your back," he says. Ah yes, when the taskmaster accusation doesn't work, he accuses me of cheating. "If you want to talk about omission, let's talk about you and Ethan and what's really going on between you two. Obviously you've had a thing for him for a while since you called me his name when you were all hopped up on TB."

Blake has been relentless in his accusations about Ethan. He is one-hundred-percent convinced that Ethan's in love with me and that I return his feelings. No matter how much I try to explain that Ethan's heart lies elsewhere, Blake responds that "feelings can change." Sure they can. I know that. But Ethan's been consistent about loving another girl since the first night I met him. So, Blake is just being jealous and paranoid.

"Let's not, because we've already discussed it and it's not at all relevant to you lying to me," I say.

"You lied to me," he says.

"I'm going now," I say, throwing up my hands in defeat. "You go do your thing. I'll be back later. After I've had a chance to cool down and think things through."

"I bet you go see Ethan. That's your plan, right?" he says. "You can whine about me to him, and he can comfort you and tell you how much better he is for you than I am." Wasn't my plan. Not until he put the idea into my head.

"Goodbye, Blake. I'll see you later," I say, done with the fight. How could Brad Darcton ever think I had a shot at getting Blake under control? I walk off, shaking my head, disillusioned about any hope of a happy ending to this bleak situation.

Not wanting to go home, I take the mini-rail into the city, a couple short zips across the canyon to get to a residential area, and then walk around. Part of me wants to go see Ethan and the other part doesn't want to validate Blake's theory. It can't hurt to at least figure out where Ethan lives, I think. I've been meaning to do it for a while and I have his address, so I start walking until I'm horribly lost. The heat is brutal, even in the middle of the night. My clothes are clinging to my body and my hair is matted against my head. A hubbub of activity under a portable spotlight catches my attention and I turn towards the crowd to find someone who can give me directions.

Bad move. As I approach I'm pummeled with dirty water along with the rest the onlookers. Dirty, *hot* water. Even the water in the main lines gets heated. On Thera, there's no need to heat your water, only cool it. I try to brush the gooey, sticky mess out of my face so I can see. A young female worker apologizes to us and explains that a water main had broken earlier in the night. While they thought they had it fixed, the patch didn't hold. Murphy's law in action. The good news is that she kindly gives me directions to Sunflower Lane, where Ethan lives.

It occurs to me as I ring his doorbell that Ethan's probably at work. And even if he is home, that he might prefer a visitor who isn't covered with mud. On the short walk from the water main break to Ethan's house, the mud dried to my body and itches like mad. Just as I turn around to leave, the door opens.

"Kira," Ethan says, chuckling at my ridiculous appearance. "What happened to you?" He must've worked tonight. He's in Garden City headquarters attire, which looks like it was designed just for him. The shimmery blue top matches his eyes perfectly, and the tan pants look as good as any pair of jeans would on the model-worthy boy. His appearance literally steals the breath from my lungs.

"Well," I say. "I was walking around trying to find your place and happened upon a broken water main."

"Come on in," he says, looking me up and down. "I was going to come by your house, but you saved me a trip. I have a surprise for you, but first... do you maybe want to get cleaned up?"

"Getting cleaned up would be good. Unless you want mud all over your house," I say as I come in and immediately remove my shoes. His house smells oddly like a fast food restaurant, which makes me really hungry. "What smells so good?"

"Stay here," he says with a mischievous grin. "I'll be right back." He returns a couple minutes later and has me follow him to the bathroom. A fresh towel, robe, and one of his shirts are on the counter.

"Just throw your stuff outside the door and I'll wash and oven-dry your clothes. It's as close to instant laundry service that I can offer here," he says, brushing my mud-covered hair out of my eyes. "My shirt's pretty big so I figure you can wear it as a dress in the meantime."

"Thanks," I say. He leaves and I take a look around his bathroom. Although it's identical to mine, the products are suited to men. I undress and open the door to put out my clothes and am thankful to be largely shielded by the door when I find Ethan waiting to take my clothes. He blushes, I bite my lip, and hand him my filthy attire before closing and locking the door. It's not that I don't trust him, but want to secure any possible temptations. On both our parts.

Despite it being awkward to bathe in his house, I take a quick shower, dry myself and put on Ethan's shirt over my wet, but still clean underwear. The shirt's barely passable as a dress, extending no more than six inches past my butt, but it'll have to do. I crimp my wet hair with my hands and use some lotion on my face as men aren't issued makeup. After, I join Ethan in the kitchen to see the source of the smell.

"Are those french fries?" I say as place my hands on his waist and peek around him. He turns and feeds me one, doing his best to keep his eyes off my rather exposed legs, but largely failing. I grab another fry. Yummy. Thin and salty, just as I like them.

"For you, my dear, I have tried my best to recreate McDonald's french fries, a McRib sandwich, and a chocolate shake. I planned to drop it off to you. But it will taste even better fresh," he says.

"Are you kidding me?" I say. "Did I do something to tick you off again? The first time you took me to McDonald's it was for punishment." I try to look upset, but my grumbling tummy gives me away.

"Oh, so you don't want it? It's fine," he says, winking at me and then covering up the plates with his arms. "More for me."

"I *do* want it. Come on... hand it over. I'm starved, cranky, and could use some major comfort food," I say, tickling him to get him to release his grip. He smiles, hands me the plate and we both sit down at opposite sides of his dining table. I savor every bite of the greasy, calorie-laden meal and slurp down the chocolate shake while Ethan watches me.

"So, are you going to tell me what brought you here?" he says after he knows my mouth is food free.

"Can't it just be that I missed my lockup buddy?" I say.

"Is that the truth?" he asks, biting the corner of his lip.

"Yes, I did miss you. Terribly," I say.

"But is that really why you're here?" he says.

"Yes. And no. But, I prefer not to talk about it. I just need a good distraction. Can we play a game or something?" I say. "You think of something while I do the dishes." I jump up from the table, stack the dishes, haul them to the kitchen and start scrubbing.

"Twister?" he says, although I can't tell if he meant for me to hear that or not. I glance back at him and catch him staring at my backside, and he blushes.

"Are my clothes dry yet? Because I think I'm being more of a distraction to *you* and you're supposed to be distracting me," I say. I open the oven door and check. Still wet, though making progress.

"Sorry," he says, walking over to me and sizing me up head to toe. "I promise to stop noticing how hot you look in my shirt and focus on entertaining you in a wholesome manner." I shoot him a disapproving glare for his compliment, but also can't completely conceal a smile, as I have zero immunity to Ethan's flirty side. He then lifts my chin up, stares into my eyes, and says, "Do you know that you are the only girl I know who can manage to be even more beautiful without makeup than with it?"

I blush and say, "You're a great liar."

"I'd never lie to you," he says. After taking a deep breath he adds, "So, how can I best distract you? Do you want some dessert? Charades? Pillow fight? Tell ghost stories? Play tag? Marco polo? Hide and seek? Cuddle? What strikes your fancy?" A smile spreads from the right side of his mouth to left at the inclusion of "cuddling" in his list.

"Let's see," I say. "Everything except the cuddling, because that could only lead to trouble." I want to blot out my disappointment with Blake and what will be the consequences of his actions. So I need distractions. But given how bad things are with Blake and how attracted I am to Ethan, it would take very little cuddle time to let things get out of control. And I'd like to maintain what little control I have over my life.

"I was just messing with you," Ethan says, looking away. "Sorry."

"Don't be sorry. You apologize altogether too often," I say, getting on my tiptoes to plant a kiss on his cheek. "You're it." I dash away and get to the other end of the house before I'm tackled. Ethan and I play hard for a few hours until well past dawn, and then take two spoons to some ice cream, polishing it off. Stuffed and exhausted, I sprawl out on the floor amongst piles of pillow fluff giggling. We had a couple purposeful casualties during our pillow fight.

"Distracting enough for you?" he says as he inches as close as possible without touching me. I find it very hard to be this close to him. He oozes Cleave appeal from every pore. Gorgeous, sweet, sensitive, fun, attentive. But not my boyfriend. Ethan and I have terrible timing. First time we met I was stupidly with Tristan. And now, despite all the fighting, I'm still with Blake; have told Blake that I love him. I have to keep reminding myself, though, that Ethan's not mine to desire.

"Do you still love her? The girl you told me about way back when?" I ask. He rolls onto his back, inhales, and then exhales slowly.

"Madly," he says, glancing at me. "I didn't think it was possible to love someone so much, but she is the smartest, most beautiful, most kind, most loyal, most caring, most fun, most incredible girl in the universe. When I'm with her I just want time to stop forever and when I'm not I can't even think straight. My heart pounds, I'm antsy, and I can't get her out of my mind. She's in my every thought, every moment, so much so that I have trouble getting my work done. I constantly wonder what she's thinking and if she feels a fraction for me the way I feel about her. I'd like to grow old together and be surrounded by our kids and grandkids and great grandkids."

He pauses and I feel sick. My stomach's in my throat and my own heart's pounding a billion times a second. I'm so jealous I can barely function. Both because he feels that way for someone else and that no one feels that way about me. Sure, Blake loves me, but it's not the kind of undying love that Ethan has for this girl. And doesn't every girl deserve that kind of love?

"So, why haven't you Cleaved her or married her or whatever?" I ask, my voice strained. Why do you keep tormenting me, flirting with me, and making me have second thoughts about being with Blake? That's what I want to ask, but can't. No wonder he didn't even think to come see me after I got to Thera. The other girl is the only thing on his mind all night long. He looks at me like I'm a bit crazy and shakes his head.

"Well, for several reasons. My parents, for one, aren't fully on board. And more important, I'm not sure she is either," he says. Great, so it's my fault they're not together. His dad has Ethan on hold as a potential Cleave for me and Father of Thera.

"I'm so sorry," I say, and then mumble, "Here I am taking up all your time when I'm sure I'm a terribly poor substitute." He rolls his eyes at my pity party.

"That's just silly talk," he says, grinning from the right side of his mouth again.

"Tell me about your childhood and your family," I say. "You know everything about me. Return me the favor. What was it like to be sick? How'd you react when you had to move to earth at fifteen and live with your uncle? Was it better or worse than here? What's your mom like? Your uncle? I want to hear every single detail." He ponders my request for a minute before answering.

"I, uh, don't think you'd be very interested. I grew up in one boring little bubble. My story would put you dead asleep. Which reminds me that it's very late. Do you want me to walk you home?" he says, looking away. Why won't he ever talk about himself?

"I am interested and I'm too tired to go anywhere," I say, closing my eyes. "Especially home. So put me to sleep telling me all about your boring life." Blake would want to fight it out and I can't deal with that right now. I'm all about delaying confrontation. And I'd feel too guilty being at home with Blake when I'm so busy coveting the guy I cannot have.

"But Kira…" he says. I open my eyes. He turns to face me again and I reach up and shush him with my fingers, which he starts to kiss but stops himself.

"I can't. Please let me stay. Please? I'm fine to sleep right here. I know that puts you in an awkward spot, but I wouldn't ask if I didn't need this," I say, staring into his eyes. The wheels appear to be spinning as he tries to figure out the right move.

"You can have my bed," he says. "I'll take the couch."

"I'm really fine here," I say, but he lifts me up in his arms and takes me back to his bedroom, kissing me on my forehead before tucking me into his bed.

He lingers on the edge of the bed and takes my hand in his. "I'm here. If you want to talk it through. But I won't push." He lets go and gets up to leave.

"Wait. Where's my bedtime story?" I ask. "I really want to hear about your life." I have a deep desire to know what makes him tick. And how he turned out the way he did given his parents and environment.

"You should sleep," he says, getting up to leave the room. "Good day, Kira." What is he hiding from me? Why is it such a big deal to tell me about his childhood?

"Thanks for being such a great…" I stop myself before I say, "friend," as it doesn't accurately describe my feelings despite it being an accurate representation of our relationship. In the back of my mind I'm fully aware that if Blake continues to screw up, I end up Cleaved to Ethan. I should be repelled by the notion of a Darcton Cleaving. I wonder to myself if I could live with it, but I realize that I would be depriving Ethan of happiness with his true love. I feel guilty and selfish for even contemplating it.

"I know. I'm your good friend," he says with what I detect to be a slight bit of resentment. I want to ask him to hold me in his arms while I sleep without it meaning or implying anything, but I can't and it would, so I let him leave and I hug his pillow, wafting in his scent until I fall asleep.

It takes me a few moments to realize I'm not in my own room. The murals differ from mine. My clothes aren't in the dresser. I'm still wearing Ethan's shirt. I stagger out of his bedroom and towards the kitchen to retrieve my clothes so I can change and go home, but I stop in my tracks when I see the scene at Ethan's dining table. Ethan. Daddy Darcton. Mommy Darcton. All eating breakfast as if it's a normal, everynight occurrence. Ethan's back is to me, but Brad Darcton catches my eye. I try to smooth out my messy hair and pull Ethan's shirt down to cover more of my body, but I'm afraid that won't really make this look any better.

"So Ethan," Brad says. "How are things going with Kira? You guys looked pretty cozy at the Festival. You like her as much as I think you do?" I keep my feet firmly planted and fold my arms, not wanting to ruin Brad Darcton's nightly amusement. If I did, he'd surely take it out on me somehow.

"Keep your voice down, Dad. I told you that she's here and sleeping. I don't want to wake her. She seemed like she could use a good day's rest," Ethan says.

"But how do you feel about her?" Brad pushes.

"You, of all people, know how much I care about her. She's fantastic. We're good friends. But if you're asking about anything more—well, she loves Blake Sundry, not me," he says, a hint of disappointment in his voice. Why does he always seem to want more from me when he loves someone else?

"I don't know. I think they've been fighting," Brad says. OK, that's enough. Time to silence this conversation.

"Yeah," I say as I approach. "Relationships suck when there's outside influences setting all the parameters." Ethan looks terrified that I heard him talking about me with his parents. "Good evening, Ethan. Mr. And Mrs. Darcton."

"I'm sorry. I didn't know you were up," Ethan says, standing up and offering me a chair. His hair's more disheveled than normal, stubble more pronounced than last morn, eyes dark. I like the fresh out of bed look on him. If only I could pull it off as well, I think, feeling frumpy. "My parents brought by some breakfast. I was hoping they'd be gone by the time you woke up." He glares at his father and I stay standing.

"On the contrary," Brad says. "Your mother's been wanting to meet Kira. And how often do parents get to catch their grown son having a sleepover with his female 'friend'? I just love those awkward situations, don't you?" he says, a huge smirk on his face. Yes, to Brad Darcton this must be like Christmas.

"Hi, I'm Vienna Darcton," Ethan's mother says, outstretching her hand towards me. I shake it. She's stunning up close. Dark hair. Bright green eyes. Milky skin. Ethan definitely favors her over his father, but he's more beautiful than both of them.

"Kira Donovan. It's really nice to meet you," I say. "I'm so sorry to barge in on your breakfast. I'm just going to change and get going."

"No, you'll stay for breakfast. Sit down," Brad says. "I always enjoy our conversations." I comply and sit in the chair Ethan pulled out for me. He squeezes my hand under the table.

"Kira, please tell me something about yourself," Vienna Darcton says.

"What would you like to know? About my life back on Earth? Or my dead parents and friends who are now on Thera? Or my boyfriend, Blake, who is making bad choices and will probably face death or Exile? Or, how about my brother, Jared? He's here on Thera, too—but in lockdown—because he's being a little too rebellious. Actually, I'm sure you know about all those things, being one of the Ten and all," I say. Ethan's mouth is gaping open and his parents look aghast at my tirade. I should know better than to tempt the universe again.

"Blake may face death?" she asks Brad, a look of sheer disappointment on her face. Brad doesn't respond. I assume that's a topic they're not going to discuss in front of me. She then turns to me and says, "How do you feel about your situation?"

"I'm resigned to it," I say. "Though I would be more comfortable if a) Jared were released and b) Blake's safety could be ensured." Might as well put it out there. Brad said no pretenses.

"You'll see Jared soon. Later tonight, I'd assume," Brad says. "And as for Blake… you were supposed to get him under control." I avoid looking at Ethan. I'm not sure how much he knows, but obviously Brad has no issue discussing in front of him.

"You know that's not possible," I say. "He fears his father as much as he fears you. And you know that I've tried. What I've offered to get him to abandon his plans." Given how Blake reacted to the idea of a future with me, I'm not even sure that's what I want anymore.

"Yes, I do know the lengths you've gone to get him on board," he says. "And that kind of loyalty won't go unnoticed or unrewarded. I'll do what I can. As long as you continue to do as asked. Now, why don't you enjoy this delicious meal my Cleave has prepared." I pile some food on my plate and get no more than a couple bites in before Ethan's mom interrupts.

"I know how you feel about Blake. But how do you feel about Ethan?" she asks. I look at Ethan, who has covered his face with his hands, he's so embarrassed, and then back at Vienna Darcton. "You came to him when you had problems with Blake. Spent the night here. Are you toying with his affections?" Why does it not surprise me that Brad Darcton got Cleaved to someone as blunt as he is? As invasive as the question is, it'd be a valid question from any parent—whether or not they are members of the Ten.

"I think it should be obvious to all of you, Ethan included, that Blake and Ethan share my affections. How could they not? Both have fathered my children—babies you've impregnated my friends with. Both are candidates to be my Cleave and 'Father' of Future Thera. I've spent considerable time under stressful circumstances with each of them," I say. "So it's only natural that I have feelings for each of them."

"What?" Ethan says, his head whipping around to me and then to his father. "How come I'm the last one to know about this? Babies? Surrogates? Cleaving? Father of Thera? Explain!" Oops. Did I let the babies out of the lab? Shame on me. At least I'll have someone to talk to about it now. If Brad doesn't Exile me on the spot.

"Son, why don't you and your mother discuss it in the garden while Kira and I finish our talk." His mother forcibly pushes Ethan from the room. I mouth "sorry" to him.

"Well played, Kira," Brad says. "I never give you enough credit."

"Sorry. I figured he knew about your Grand Plan, since you felt like you could openly discuss the rest of my life in front of him," I say.

"Is it true that you have feelings for both Blake and Ethan?" he asks.

"Yes," I say. The exact nature of those feelings may differ, but there's no need to mention that, particularly when the balance seems to be continually shifting.

"How do you plan to reconcile that?" he asks.

"I thought you planned to do that for me," I say. Didn't he make it clear that I have no choice in the matter?

"And you will abide by whatever the Ten decides?" he asks.

"Yes—with the caveat that if Jared or Blake are harmed my loyalties could fade," I say. "Let me be blunt. You know Blake is being forced to help his father. And he has every reason to do so given his precarious upbringing. Given his circumstances, I ask you to consider this when making a decision between Exile and death. One night his father could push him too far. Or if the Exilers fail as expected, he may see the error of his ways."

"We shall see if you can keep from slipping sensitive information to Blake like you did to Ethan," he says, appearing to be deep in thought. "Now run along home and try to explain to Love #1 why you didn't come home last day and I'm going to go help mop up the mess you created for me with your Love #2. Be at SCI headquarters promptly at 2200 hours Thursnight. I'd like to show you and Ethan something."

"What?" I ask.

"It's classified, but I promise you'll enjoy it," he says.

"The last time kids my age showed up at headquarters they got Cleaved," I say.

"True, but that's not my plan for *Thursnight*," he says with a smile. "Go home. Perhaps Jared will be there by now. You should be there to celebrate the terms of his release." That's all the motivation I have to leave. I'd like to say goodbye to Ethan, but Brad makes it clear that's not going to happen. So I change into my dry clothes and head home.

I can hear his drawl the moment I enter my house.

"Jared," I yell. I run into the living room and am a little confused when I see not only Jared, but also Blake and his sister, Leila. "Hey, you're out. Thank goodness. How was training? You okay?" Jared has a guilty look on his face. Leila's stroking his arm in a fashion that seems a little too intimate for my liking. She's pretty, I think, but she and Blake don't look much alike. She's got long, straight dark hair, but small hazel eyes in contrast to Blake's large emerald ones.

Jared responds with a half-cocked grin and, "I'm all trained. I never thought I'd get done, but then Brad Darcton came by yesternight with an interesting proposition for me. After weighing the alternative, I accepted."

"What proposition?" I ask, glancing over at Blake, but he won't even look at me.

"Kira, I'd like you to meet my Cleave, Leila. We did the whole Cleaving ceremony and feast at headquarters, and then they gave us a house a couple doors down from you," he says. "We came over as soon as we, uh, made everything official." Leila kisses him on the lips and both Blake and my eyes go wide. They apparently waited for me to arrive to drop the bomb. They Cleaved my little brother to Blake's little sister? Can the Ten be Exiled for disregarding their own Canon?

"The kitchen. Now," I scream. I don't wait for him to obey, yanking him along with me. "You agreed to what?"

"It sounded a whole lot better than a bullet through my brain, Kira," he says in a whisper. "I'm fine with it. Leila's cool and you're right that it's better to go with the flow than face the consequences."

"Uh huh," I say, pacing the kitchen. My brother—Cleaved. At sixteen. Insanity. Brad Darcton gave him the option of a bullet in the head or Cleave Leila. If I maintained any hope of a future that didn't involve Thera or the SCI, it just vanished. The only thing I don't know is who my future will be tied to. I have to try again with Blake, but can't with Jared and Leila here.

"Come on, Kira. Chill. Come get to know Leila. For me?" he says. "Hey, since you're not Cleaved yet I bet I'll make you an Aunt before you make me an Uncle." He's wrong about that. He'll be an uncle 40 times over soon enough. The thought of my baby brother having kids makes me a little ill. He can't even clean his room, do basic chores, or wake up for school on time. How can he possibly handle raising a child? Heck, how can any of my friends raise children? My children!

I return to the living room after making a pit stop to the bathroom to brush my teeth and freshen up, and I make nice with Leila for a half hour while Jared and Blake talk. Then Jared and Leila leave to have some more "alone time," which means I've got to smooth things over with Blake.

"Can we talk?" I say. He still won't look at me, his eyes focused on a patch of garden on our wall with yellow sunflowers.

"How's Ethan?" he says, still turned away. "Did you have a nice slumber party?"

"Ethan's fine. Nothing happened, if you are curious. We just ate and played games. Slept in separate rooms. Had breakfast with his parents," I say.

"Sounds like you'll make a happy Cleaved family," he says, his tone bitter, eyes narrow and brooding.

"I love you, Blake. If you recall, I offered to Cleave you and spend my life with you. I haven't offered that to anyone else and you know what a big deal it is to me," I say. I sit by him on the couch. "Please look at me." He turns his head to me, but his look is sour.

"You'd Cleave with me—right here, right now?" he says.

It takes some effort to shove thoughts of Ethan out of my brain and say, "If you agree to have your sole focus to be on us and nothing else from here on out. Then, yes, I'll Cleave you. Here and now." I can see him struggle with my offer. He rubs his temples and I reach up and stroke his face with the back of my hand.

Moments later, he kisses me and then pushes me back on the couch. Takes off his shirt. Lies atop me. More passionate kissing—the most intense it's ever been. I'm extremely nervous, not really ready, but knowing that I need to keep my word. To keep him alive. He starts to lift my shirt off and then abruptly stops. Did I hear a door slam?

"I've got to go," he says. "I can't do this." Huh? That's supposed to be the girl's line.

"What's wrong?" I say, but he's already up and has his shirt on. "Blake, don't leave. Why won't you talk to me?"

"I just can't commit to what you're asking. Had we gone through with it, I would have ended up disappointing you by going back on my word. I love you, Kira. As best as I can. But as amazing as you are, I'll never forgive myself if I'm not true to myself and what I believe in," he says. "As much as it kills me to say it—I think Ethan's the better Cleave for you."

"You can't mean that," I say, tears filling my eyes.

"I'm sorry. That's just where I'm at," he says.

Lovely. Where does that leave me?

I arrive at SCI headquarters at ten to 2200 hours Thursnight. I'm a little nervous to see Ethan given the bomb I dropped on him at breakfast the other night and hoping he is in good spirits and can cheer me up. Blake's barely been home since he rejected my offer to Cleave. When here, he's been silent. It's breaking my heart.

Ethan shows up precisely at 2200 hours.

"Hi," I say. I'd hug him but his body language says he won't be receptive. Hands in his pockets. Tense. Cold look on his face. Looks like he hasn't slept in nights.

"Yeah, hi," he says, distant and businesslike. I'm repelling all the men in my life. Before I can delve into which thing I did that pissed him off, Brad Darcton shows.

"Excellent. You're both right on time," he says, as if we'd dare be late. "Kira, I wasn't sure you'd be here with all that Cleaving you've been trying to do with Blake lately." Well, kudos on making things even more awkward, Brad. Of course, that's his intention.

"That's a bit of an overstatement," I say. "Blake hasn't spoken to me in nights."

"Well, looking at it from his perspective… you stay overday at Ethan's house and then come home and throw yourself at him. Those kind of mixed messages would be a huge blow to any guy's ego," he says. If he's attempting to solicit a reaction, he'll be sorely disappointed.

"I did what I thought was right to try to protect his life. And your interests, as requested," I say. "My sales pitch failed."

"Yes, didn't he suggest that Ethan would be a better Cleave for you?" he says. Ethan shoots his father a glare so cold that Brad must have brain freeze.

"Ethan's not happy with me either. Do you have a plan C for the Father of Thera?" I quip. "I should have some more viable eggs left."

"I'll make note of your willingness to provide more offspring. In the meantime, let's proceed with our tour," he says. Unwise to plant ideas in his head, but they'd do it whether I agreed or not.

Brad leads us into headquarters and facilitates an express route through security. He then leads us into a multistory atrium of sorts that takes my breath away. A short overweight man signals Brad by waving a folder.

"You two stay here for a moment while I consult with a colleague," Brad says. Fine with me. I want to take this place in. It's the most beautiful thing I've seen on Thera... maybe ever.

"You get to work here?" I say to Ethan. "This is incredible."

"You offered to Cleave Blake?" he says. I guess he doesn't want to discuss the stunning glass mosaic gardens that bring the atrium walls to life.

"Yes," I say. "To keep him from proceeding with activities that will lead to his death. He'd prefer sticking to his plans than a life with me, however."

"You said—that evening at breakfast—you have feelings for both of us. Is that true?" he asks. Why's he so worried about my feelings when he's declared that the only girl who will ever make him happy isn't me?

"Yes, I shouldn't, but I do. I'm sorry," I say, looking into his eyes. I watch as he swallows hard. I've been really jealous the last couple nights about his admission that he's still in love with the other girl. And beating myself up over it for stupidly caring.

"Yet you rejected my kiss and said you just wanted to be friends?" he says.

"Just because I have feelings for you doesn't mean I can act upon them, or that you should want me to given the fact you are in love with someone else. When you kissed me you were in love with someone else, and I can't condone cheating. Plus, I had a relationship of sorts going with Blake and needed to figure out if that was going anywhere. I felt guilty enough pretending to be your girlfriend back on Earth, knowing what it must be doing to the other girl. Had things been different... had you not had someone else...," I say. "But they aren't different and anyway, you're the one that suggested we stay friends. If you don't want that, then tell me."

"I came by to talk to you after my parents left—to talk about all the stuff you said at the breakfast table. Your front door was open. I knocked, but no one answered, so I came in. I saw you and Blake on the couch. Needless to say, I left right away," he says. That explains the door slam I heard. I shake my head. Ethan must think I'm such a jerk—talk about a huge blow to a guy's ego. No wonder he's giving me the cold shoulder. But wait, he shouldn't care. He loves someone else, I remind myself yet again.

"I don't know what to say. I'm sorry," I say. "Obviously I'm an immature idiot and an excellent argument for raising the Cleaving age to 21 or higher. I'm just not equipped to deal with this."

"I'm not sure any of us are equipped to deal," he says, turning away from me. I feel guilty at what he saw and how much it hurt him. Why is this bothering him so much?

"Ethan, who's the girl you are in love with?" I ask.

"What do you mean?" he asks. I can see the nerves kick in as he shoves his hands in his pockets and starts rocking.

"Because you're confusing me," I say. "You tell me that you love this other girl so much that you'd do anything for her, yet you are upset that I haven't acted upon my feelings for you. The way you look at me and flirt with me... how can you do that when you love someone else? You say you aren't that guy who'd ever cheat or convince someone else to cheat. But you are being that guy. Every moment we spend together you're that guy. So who is she?" He throws his hands up in air and rolls his eyes, before settling his hands on my shoulders.

"Do I really need to answer that? Isn't it obvious? Wasn't it obvious the first time we met? How can you not know? I never said it was anyone else," he says, staring into my eyes.

Oh. Holy crap. It's me. What an idiot I am. I can't help it but my mouth and eyes go wide.

"I wasn't even supposed to talk to you that night," he mumbles. He shakes his head and walks off a few feet. I'm having trouble processing this.

Before I can discuss it with Ethan, Brad returns and tells us the history of the glass mosaics. I attempt to listen to try to get my mind off Ethan and what I've done to him. I'm not sure I can ever fix the mess I've made. Ethan won't even look at me. How could I have been so stupid? It should have been obvious all along; it certainly is now. The SCI needs to revamp their tests. If they thought I was good at puzzles and problem solving they were dead wrong.

Brad tells us that it took two-dozen artisans more than ten years to complete and represents the garden of Hadrian and Helina—where the first Cleave occurred. Now, every Cleaved couple has their feast in this very spot and is sworn to secrecy to keep the experience fresh and new for every Cleaved couple. Well, except for me. And Ethan. And Blake, since I know he's been in the building with Ted's passkey.

From the atrium, Brad leads us through a series of turns until we arrive at a familiar hallway where Blake and I took our field trip to the Garden City model.

"Kira, I thought it was time I introduced you to the whole of Thera. You need to understand the importance of the Second Chance Institute, how far reaching our program is, and why you are so vital to it," Brad says. He's going to let us see all the cities? Cool! I watch as he signals four different people to use a combination of passkeys and codes on floor panels. The moment deserves to be celebrated with my best friend, but Ethan's still shunning me and my heart aches for him.

And then the walls on either side of us lift and give way to a sight more spectacular than the glass mosaics in the atrium. In every direction there are full-scale city models—every one completely different from the other. One city has spindly skyscrapers. Another appears to be completely underground. A third has been built entirely of white and blue marble and a fourth of jeweled glass. One city looks like it has thousands of "pods" made of shells and cement. A very mysterious city is surrounded by mirrored walls.

"It would take weeks to explore every city," Brad says. "Tonight we'll just take the moving sidewalk from one end to the other so you can get an idea of the diverse nature of the Theran landscape." He motions us to step onto the walkway, which we do.

"Why is every city so different?" I ask, watching the models while we converse. I don't want to miss anything, even though I'm having trouble absorbing it all with my mind on Ethan's revelation. I keep shifting my attention from the cities to Ethan, but Ethan still refuses to look at me.

"Excellent question. Each city has a unique personality—from landscape to people to government to architecture. We track best practices from each city," he says.

"How so?" I ask. "That sounds complicated."

"We have quarterly meetings with all the city heads here at headquarters. In fact, the next one is next Monnight and Tuesnight. The first night we will discuss and record good practices from each area, and the second night we will meet with top government officials from Earth to share our findings," he says.

"How do Earth's officials use the information?" I ask in a very professional manner as if I'm representing a non-existent Theran newspaper.

"We give them ideas for new legislation and effective methods to manage diverse groups of people, with obvious goals of reducing crime, increasing productivity, and personal accountability for citizens," he says.

"So the folks back on Earth can expect to be Cleaved or face Exile?" I ask.

"No, but perhaps there should be accountability for premarital relations to try to ratchet morality back up. And an adaptation of the Circle of Compliance could be useful so citizens know whether they're in good standing or not—especially if they know the better they act, the more influence they'll have on society's rules. But those are minor thoughts in the grand scheme of things. We get hundreds of ideas from other cities. We create systems that work for Theran citizens, but obviously change must happen in degrees back on Earth," he says.

"From my interviews with your Recruiters who match Recruits to cities I can tell that some of the city governments would be considered pretty extremist back on Earth. Are the Theran citizens in those cities happy and well cared for?" I ask. His theory only works if the quality of life is good for everyone.

"We take care to place Recruits and Second Chancers where they'll have the best experience. Some people need more structure than others. Others need nurturing environments. So yes, we like to think that our citizens overall are much happier than those on Earth," he says.

"Interesting," I say. I'm not sure I agree or condone the extreme actions the Ten take to protect their secrets, but at least I understand better how the Theran government works and why they want and need people to travel between the two worlds. I wonder why Brad Darcton trusted us with this information. Blake's dad and his Militant Exiler gang would kill to know that all the city heads would be here next week.

We continue down the walkway in silence. Ethan shifts closer to me and presses his arm against mine, but he still won't look at me. We watch the bizarre scenery while leaning against the handrail. A floating city built on giant pylons with marshy land underneath. Farm City with no visible residences above ground—only farmland. And in what seems to be the very center of all of it, there's a large, two-story circular platform with dozens of long, narrow tubes emanating from each level in every direction. It almost looks like two giant bicycle wheels laid atop one another, with the tubes being the spokes of the wheels.

"What's that?" I ask.

"That's the secret source of our power and reason we'll never be defeated," he says with a smirk. "But, I think I'll leave it undefined for now other than to say it helps us with resource allocation and management." It reminds me of something, but I can't quite place what.

Our moving walkway circles the spokes, but a close-up view gives no additional clues to its purpose. Beyond it, I see a triangular city with what looks like large manmade canals through it—like Venice on steroids.

"Let me guess—Import/Export City at the Bermuda Triangle?" I say.

"Yes," Brad says.

When our tour concludes I've counted at least thirty distinct cities, though I may have missed some.

"Are all the cities represented here?" I ask.

"Not all," he says. "We're always expanding and the models take a considerable amount of time... and real estate to build." He finishes out our tour and then we retrace our steps back through the headquarters building. Once back out, Brad reminds us to keep our mouths shut about what we've seen and leaves us.

"We need to talk," I say to Ethan. "Really need to talk." He cups my face in his hands, rests his forehead and nose against mine. It's impossible to be this close to him, knowing how he feels about me, without having my feelings bubble to the surface. No matter how hard I try to shove them to the back of my mind—for Blake's sake, not my own.

"Not now," he says. "I have plans. But we'll talk soon." He leans in to kiss me, but instead plants one on my cheek after grazing my lips with his. I stand there for a long time watching him walk away. He turns once and stares for a moment, but then vanishes around a corner and I feel completely and horribly alone.

Blake's sound asleep when I enter his room and slip into bed next to him given it's well into the morning. It takes a while to rouse him. When traditional methods don't work, I kiss his eyes, ears and nose and rub his chest.

"What are you doing here?" he asks. "I haven't…" I peck him on the mouth to shut him up. He doesn't need to tell me that he hasn't changed his mind. I know that, but feel strongly that I need to tell him about the city heads' meeting and this is the only way I can think to do it discreetly. After all, Brad thinks I'm spending all night, every night and day trying to Cleave with Blake…

"Play along," I whisper. "I need to tell you something important." He kisses me back, but I can tell there's little feeling to it.

"What? Be quick. I need my sleep," he says.

"Every city head is coming to Garden City for a meeting," I say, kissing him along the neck.

"I know that," he says. "Why do you think I'm trying to get sleep? My father and the Militants attack tomorrow night."

"Why tomorrow?" I say. "The meeting is next Monnight and Tuesnight. Monnight's meeting is for city heads only and then a bunch of Daynighters who work as government officials on Earth show up on Tuesnight."

"You're positive?" he says.

"Brad Darcton told me," I say, leaving the part out about the city models. It takes four guys with proper access to open the walls, so the Militants have zero hope of ever getting in there.

"Ted set us up," Blake says. "I had a bad feeling, but my dad wouldn't believe that Ted had turned."

"I'm sorry," I say. "I just thought it was important that you knew. If Brad finds out I told you, it won't be good for either of us." I want to tell him everything, but know Blake would end up dead if I did. He'll be at huge risk come tomorrow when the Militants show. I'll only be able to bargain with Brad Darcton if I've kept the bulk of the truth from Blake.

We kiss for a short while longer, but it feels more forced than my kisses with Ethan on Earth. Pure drudgery, because Blake's not responding at all. Now I know what Ethan meant when he compared me to a steel post. I find myself thinking about Ethan the whole time and wondering what plans he had to keep us from talking. Or if he lied to avoid spending more time with me given how much I've hurt him. The whole time we were home, he wasn't faking it. When he told my father he wanted to marry me, he probably meant it. He wants to have kids together and grow old with me. Thinking about another guy, even if I'm not imagining him in an inappropriate way, makes it difficult to keep kissing Blake.

It's not that I don't still care for Blake. My feelings for him are strong, but all the fighting with no compromise has left me feeling depleted. Completely void of emotion. I feel like I've been beating my head against a battery of knives and they've carved the life right out of me. I'm more of a zombie than my Second Chancer friends.

"You should go," Blake finally says. "Thanks for trying again, but I'm still not ready for that kind of commitment."

"Yeah, I know," I say. "You've made that really clear."

I turn and leave to go sulk in my room. That's what they'll expect. This morning, I'll have to fake it.

CHAPTER TWENTY-FOUR

Blake

I rise mid-afternoon, unable to sleep. Kira's revelation about the true date of the city heads' meeting deeply disturbs me. Although I warned my father that Ted might be setting them up, I still feel as if I've failed the Exilers. I wasn't able to persuade my father not to attack and gave him the wrong information about the date of the city heads' meeting. Ted's a traitor and has assuredly informed the Ten of the impending attack. They'll be ready and waiting. The only things going for the Militants will be their city uniforms and three-hour head start. They better use this small advantage well. I do think Ted will disable the Eco barrier at the appointed time believing he's luring the Militants into the Ten's trap. There's still a chance my father can get out safely.

After a quick shower I get dressed in a Headquarters uniform Ted brought to me. It would draw too much attention to wear my school uniform in the city during class hours. I eat a hearty breakfast before collecting food, sunscreen, extra clothes, flashlight, duct tape, and other necessities, the necessities being absolutely anything I could use to help capture SCI officials or protect myself if needed. Knives. Rope. Bag of flour—it can be used to create a lame and very temporary smokescreen. Sleeping pills and pain pills that I've ground into powder—easier to slip into a drink or food. Perfume that Kira doesn't use—it should blind someone if sprayed in the eyes. If not, it'll surely make them gag. I have to be prepared to leave with the Militants or fly under the radar for a while, in or out of the city, and defend myself if attacked. The loot blankets our dining table as I try to figure out how to efficiently pack it all in a small pack designed to cart my tablet computer.

"Going somewhere?" I hear from behind. Crap. Figures this would be the one time she'd wake up early. I've done my best to avoid Kira since I made my choice. But this morning when she crawled into bed with me and gave me a heads up about the real city heads' meeting date, it took every ounce of energy to treat her like an inanimate object. I thought about bad-tasting foods, negative experiences, and eons of SCI control to keep from mauling her.

It's best Kira think I'm a heartless prick who chose my father's cause over a life with her. Actually that's exactly what I am and I did make that choice. Not because I don't have feelings for her. I owe the Exilers too much to let them down—and although I'd have preferred that my dad and Doc Daryn agree on a strategy that would keep the peace and grant freedom to both the Exilers and Second Chancers, I realize that my father will never compromise. So, I'll do what I can to help overthrow the SCI today, even if it means sacrificing my deal with Kira or my own life.

I make the mistake of looking at her. She's got her arms crossed, a foul look on her face and distrust streaming from her eyes. It's kind of hot. "Good evening—or I guess it's still afternoon," I say. "I'm just getting ready for my night." She circles the table, perusing my stash, running her fingers across it all.

"Need any help?" she says, stopping in front of me and looking directly into my eyes.

"Nope. Thanks for offering, but I'm good," I say, avoiding her gaze. I start to stuff everything into my pack, trying to remember my preferred order despite the current distraction in a daygown.

"You sure?" she asks. I shake my head to indicate I am. "OK, well, let me know if you change your mind." I'm tempted to stay here, spend the night with Kira, and let whatever's going to happen happen. If I leave and join the fight— or even just observe—there's the possibility I'll never see her again. The taste of blood brings me out of my trance and I can feel sharp pain. In my attempt to block out my desire for Kira I bit the inside of my cheek so hard it'll be difficult to eat for a week. That'll stretch my meager supply further if I'm forced to switch to an Exiler's diet.

Should I say goodbye to Kira? She disappeared back into her bedroom, likely to take a shower and get ready for the night. If I walk in and find her in anything less than that daygown I won't be able to resist. It would be best to avoid a teary, dramatic farewell. I hope that it'll end up being unnecessary. The Militants need to prevail tonight so I can return home in the morning and celebrate with Kira. Assuming she will forgive me and take me back.

I leave my watch by my desk where I'm supposed to be starting lessons for the night. Then I quietly slip out the front door. It's still light out but the sun's quickly fading behind the canyon hills to the East. The air is hot and sticky and it smells like a campground, which concerns me a little. Fire of any kind is strictly forbidden within the city. I worry the citizens may panic. They're already on edge about a potential Exiler attack thanks to Brad Darcton.

I dart into the entrance to the train and am happy to see it empty, but running. Minutes later I'm at the city center. The sun disappeared while I was aboard the train. The booths and stage have been dismantled so I have a clear view of the vibrant lights of the Headquarters building. All looks quiet, so I take a seat on a bench next to a city worker and pretend to peruse my tablet for evening news as he is doing. The smell of fire's stronger here. Could it be a diversion of some sort?

I'm thankful that the lighting is better in the plaza than elsewhere in the city. The street lamps give a hundred feet of visibility or more. Out of the corner of my eye I see small groups of men in city uniforms on the offshoot street where city officials reside. That's where I came out of the tunnels the night I'd infiltrated headquarters to get Ted's bogus planted information. They're at a considerable distance, but a couple of them look familiar. Although I don't have my watch on, I know what time I left the house. The Exilers planned their arrival to shortly precede the normal worknight at HQ, so if I'm right and it's my father's men, they are early.

"Not again. This is Mandy's tablet," I say out loud. The man next to me gives me an odd look. "I grabbed my Cleave's tablet by accident. It's the third time this month I've done that! Here I thought I was so early and now I risk being late." He chuckles as I get up to leave, giving him the impression I'm off to rectify my stupid mistake. I head towards the residential area to get a closer look and confirm the men are Militants.

It doesn't take me long to find my father. As promised he and his henchmen are in city attire, although their equipment implies they are part of a fire safety crew.

"I need to talk to you. It's important," I say.

"Take this," my father says. He hands me a toolbox. "Don't say a word. I mean it. Now's not the time. Just follow." I nod and follow him to the front door of the next house. A woman answers.

"We are so sorry to alarm you, ma'am. Is your Cleave home? As you can tell from the odor in the air, there's something burning in the city and we've been dispatched to find the source," my father says. She calls to her Cleave who arrives promptly at the door. Medium build. Receding hairline. Cold brown eyes. He's wearing that telltale symbol that all members of the Ten wear—a silver pin carved with a circle representing the Circle of Compliance and a small number ten in the center of the circle.

"How can I help you gentlemen?" he asks.

My father and his colleague don't bother to answer. My father puts a bullet through both the man and his Cleave's brains. I gasp in horror at the sight of my father executing two human beings. The man may have been a member of the Ten, but what about his Cleave? My father pushes me back and closes their front door.

"Go home, Blake," my father says. "We've got this."

"Dad, the meeting isn't tonight. Ted set us up. It's next Monnight and Tuesnight," I say, words stumbling from my mouth.

"I see," my father says. "No matter. We've hit six of the Ten so far and numerous members of the Grand Council. Garden City's government will be crippled. Now go." I back away from the group who has already made their way to the next door, wanting no part of their mass executions. At no point during my father's planning sessions do I remember him discussing killing and not simply capturing city officials.

I slowly walk back towards the square as my father's men finish out the rest of the street. Masses have gathered to report for work at HQ and are making their way through security and into the building. Pretending to be one of them, I join the line and get out my HQ passkey to prepare to enter. My gut says my father and band are headed here next. As I approach the main doors I'm proven right. I see my father to my side. He glares and motions for me to leave but I ignore him. If there's a way to stop further executions, I'll figure it out. I'm ashamed to carry my father's DNA right now.

How could things go so wrong in ten minutes time?

Two hundred plus Militants stormed Headquarters with a vengeance, executing twenty security guards in seconds and surrounding the crowd. The workers screamed and frantically tried to escape. To protect myself, I grabbed an executed guard's gun and tucked it under my shirt and into my pants.

That's when I saw her. Kira. She must have followed and slipped in behind me. I froze as I tried to figure out how to keep her out of the clustered crowd and safe. Our eyes locked for a moment and that didn't go unnoticed by my father. He pounced on her faster than a cat on its prey.

"Well, well, well," my father said, pulling her beside him. "You must be Kira Donovan. Stick by me and I'll keep you safe."

"Let her go, Dad," I said. "As my partner, she followed me here. But she has nothing to do with any of this."

"On the contrary. If you reported correctly, Kira is a coveted Original. The SCI has big plans for her and likely wants to keep her alive. That's about as useful as anyone could be to us," he said.

"Dad, no. You are not using Kira as your security blanket," I said. He didn't reply, but pointed his gun at her head.

"It's okay, Blake," Kira said, her gold ringed green eyes showing infinitely more confidence than I have. "Everything will work out. I'm not worried." She mouthed 'I love you' to me. I paused too long, leaving her sentiments unanswered.

"Move. Everyone to the atrium now!" my father said, yanking Kira with him.

So, here I am, watching as the HQ employees are coerced into the atrium where Militants systematically look for Ten or Council pins and begin to terminate wearers accordingly. In the chaos and panic I ditch the crowd. Before I can climb the stairs to watch from above, I run into Brad Darcton. Behind him are hordes of heavily armed security forces.

"This is not my doing," I say to him. "My father has Kira with a gun to her head. You have to get her out safely. Please." Brad tilts his head to the side as he weighs his options, one of which I assume would be to eliminate me on the spot.

"How many men?" Brad asks.

"Two hundred or more trained Militants. I didn't get a good count. It all happened so fast," I say.

"Is Ethan or my Cleave in the crowd?" he asks.

"I don't know," I say. "They have everyone in the atrium."

"I'll do my best with Kira," he says. "And you will answer for this later. For now, it would be helpful if you could think of something to divert your father's attention."

"Yes, sir," I say as I start to creep up the stairs.

"Careful," he says. "You'll be a tempting target through all that glass," referring to the glass mosaics that won't hide my silhouette as I climb the stairs. Chills go down my spine. Despite the risk of being shot at, I creep up the circular staircase until I am safely behind a post and then get down on my stomach. I watch the scene through holes cut in the glass for spotlights to shine through.

Brad makes a grand entrance, parting the crowd as he greets my father by name.

"Hank, my friend. So good to see you," he says. Two hundred guns track his march to the center of the atrium.

"Brad. Long time no see. I can't say I missed you," my father replies.

"Wow. My feelings are so hurt," Brad replies. "What brings you and your friends to Garden City tonight?"

"I thought a little reorganization of your government was in order," my father says. "And hell, the revenge is good, too."

"Let the girl go, Hank, and let's talk this out like two grown men," Brad says. He starts to speak again, but a shot is fired by a Militant that hits him squarely in the chest. It sends him catapulting back a few feet, although I don't see any blood. Body armor.

"Hold off," my father says to keep more shots from firing. "There'll be plenty of time for that and I'd like to do the honors." It takes a minute for Brad to catch his breath and stand back up. In the meantime, while everyone's busy trying to catch a glimpse of one of the Ten's fate, Brad's soldiers have the opportunity to surround the Exilers and disengage their safeties in unison.

"Checkmate," Brad says in a more belabored tone. "I believe you are outnumbered, my friend. And I have endless reserves to take their places. It's time for your men to stand down." I don't know where they came from, but Doc Daryn was one hundred percent right. The SCI's illusion of weakness was the work of a master magician.

"You harm anyone and your precious Original dies, and then you won't be able to use her for your ridiculous purposes," my father threatens. Kira is ignoring my father. Her eyes are trained on someone in the crowd. Ethan. If Kira ever questioned his true feelings for her or if I ever doubted that she had feelings for him, both are crystal clear now. He looks ready to sacrifice his own life for her if needed. I watch him inch towards her. She appears to be waiting for his signal to make a move. Fabulous. She's going to get herself killed.

"Ridiculous purposes? Your son's alive thanks to those ridiculous purposes. As for Kira, if you want to kill an innocent girl over your futile plans, then go for it. She's already provided what we needed to preserve the future of Thera," Brad says, walking forward to meet my father face to face.

"Don't you dare bring up my son," my father says, scanning the crowd. Is he looking for me? He looks more scared than I've ever seen him.

"Why? You don't want him to know about his true lineage?" Brad says.

"I am his father," my father says.

"Perhaps, but your dear Cleave who died in Exile is most certainly not your son's mother," Brad says. "I bet you never mentioned that to him."

What? I stumble a little, but catch myself before going headfirst through the glass. My mom—who I watched die in agony—wasn't my real mother? He has to be lying. But then I think about the whole Assisted Pregnancy process and it occurs to me that they could be implanting any embryos in the mothers.

"Shut up or I'll kill the girl," my father says, pressing the gun harder against Kira's head.

"Really? Because if finding out that you lied about his mom won't kill your relationship, I really can't guarantee your son will ever support you or your cause if you execute his girlfriend." The look on my dad's face is priceless as he tries to absorb that nugget of information. I guess I'd failed to mention my relationship with Kira expanded beyond plain old partners.

"Is that true?" my father asks Kira. "Are you involved romantically with my son?"

"Sorry, I missed that. What are you accusing me of? I can't hear with the gun shoved in my ear," she says. He keeps hold of her, but shifts the gun ever so slightly away from her head and repeats his question. That's just the opportunity I need to create a more significant diversion without risking her life.

I remove the security guard's gun from my pants, release the safety, and aim for the glass mosaic directly behind my father. Then I pull the trigger and watch as thousands of shards of glass rain down on the crowd below.

The diversion works. My dad loses his grip on Kira as he spins around to see the source of the explosion and starts firing shots wildly. Ethan tackles Kira, pushing her to the ground so he can act as a human shield. I see blood oozing from Ethan's shirt. He may have been hit by a bullet. By the time my father realizes the rain of glass was meant to distract him and jolts back around, Brad Darcton shoots my father. The force of the bullet puts a grapefruit-sized hole through my father's heart. Dead on impact. His lifeless body falls to the floor.

The execution of my father causes a domino effect. A Militant shoots Brad Darcton in revenge. Then one of Brad's security personnel shoots the Militant. Brad's still down, but I can't tell where he was hit. Security forces rush and secure Brad's body and the area. While there, they grab Ethan and Kira and whisk them out to safety.

After that it's an all-out slaughter, with the Militants outnumbered at least five to one. I see some of the Militants drop their weapons and try to blend with the HQ employees, but most get outed by residents who saw them with guns. When both sides start shooting at the glass in my direction, I scramble up the stairs to the third level, use my passkey to enter the floor, and run for the back stairs and down to the safety of the tunnels.

The problem is that the tunnels are used to evacuate important SCI personnel to safety in case of emergency. I see a group of security goons escorting a group. I'm in the open with no place to hide. And this group includes Ethan and Kira. Ethan's shirt is off and he's using it to apply pressure to his wound. Showoff.

"There you are," Ethan says. "I worried you might have been amongst the injured." To his security escort he adds, "He works with me. We were together in the crowd, but I lost him when I went for Kira." Why would he help me? Guilt over his father killing mine?

"I barely escaped. Two of those beasts were after me," I say, playing along.

"Let me see your headquarters passkey," the security guard says. I show him and he nods to accept me into their brigade. Kira starts to drag as if she can't handle the hike and within minutes we're at the back of the group. The security detail's way more concerned about the Council members than us, so leave us alone as we march.

"You've got to get out of here," Kira whispers to me. "Once they figure out who you are... given the number of dead up there... they'll blame you."

"I know. I wasn't exactly planning to run into company," I say. "I'll ditch you at the next intersection. I know where we are."

"I'm sorry about your dad," she says. "About all of them."

"You were right about it being a futile cause," I say. "I just had to try to help. But when I saw the way my father carried out his plan—by executing innocent people—well, I couldn't support that. So, I got them all killed by bringing down that glass wall."

"That was you?" Ethan says. I nod. "Great timing. But, the deaths aren't your fault. That would have happened anyway with the security detail surrounding the Militants."

"Maybe you are right and that the outcome was inevitable. Doesn't make it any less hard," I say. I slump my shoulders, feeling the heaviness of the burden I'll have to carry for the rest of my life.

"Thank you. What you did... probably saved both our lives," Kira says as she brushes her hand against mine.

"I'm sorry," Ethan says to me. "About my father... what he did to your dad."

"Your dad paid the price of the conflict as much as my father did," I say.

"Perhaps," he says.

"Is your arm okay?" I say, motioning towards the wound.

"It's just a graze. I'll be fine," he says, though I can tell he's gritting his teeth.

"Time for me to take off," I say. "I'll see you soon," I add to Kira.

"Hope so," she says.

And with that I dash to the right and sprint to the next bend where I take a left and head towards the exit I'd found through the Council residence previously. I should have told her I still care about her, but until things settle down I'm poison to her. It sucks to have to leave her in Ethan's care, though. His perfect, nice-guy, risk-his-life-to-save-hers deal is pissing me off.

Once through the trap door and into the residence, I listen for sounds but there are none. I check by the front door and see two decimated dead bodies, likely executed by my father. Seeing the couple conjures up images of the hundreds massacred at Headquarters. I splash some water on my face, and grab the victims' tablets so I can look for information and track time. Thankfully the owners had left their tablets logged on. After, I settle back into the closet and allow myself to mourn my losses.

I find maps of the tunnels on Walter Hunt's tablet, Walter being the homeowner. The maps prove to be useful since staying at a murder scene doesn't seem too wise. It'll be a while before officials finish with the mayhem at Headquarters and fan out to search residences, but with the number of forces that magically appeared out of nowhere, I can't count on a long reprieve. After studying the maps I decide where to go.

My father had been right. The tunnels do extend all the way to student residences. I take the "long way" back to my school, hoping to run into as few people as possible in some of the outer tunnels. It's eerily silent the entire way, other than creaking and squeaking sounds. All security personnel must be at Headquarters, but there's plenty of rats and even some large bearded lizards to keep me company.

When I reach the narrow tunnels that lead to school residences I'm pleased to see small markings to indicate which trap door leads to which residence. It's a sketchy hour to make an entry—middle of the day—but I don't hesitate to intrude. The trap door leads to the back of the kitchen pantry and as I swing it inward, the shelves and food move with it. Leaving the door open so I can get back out, I remove duct tape from my backpack and tear off two mouth-sized pieces and then two larger pieces to secure hands.

I tiptoe into the sole bedroom in the residence and am pleased to see the occupants sound asleep. I'm able to get the duct tape on without much struggle, but it does wake them both up. Thank goodness they're clothed. After removing both their watches and turning on the light, I bring my finger to my mouth to encourage them to be quiet and motion them to follow me. They look a little angry, but comply. I lead them back into the tunnel where I'm fairly certain our conversation can be private and have them sit down.

"I apologize for the midday invasion," I say. "But everything we say in our own homes is monitored by the government and I wanted our conversation to be private. If I remove the duct tape from your mouths do you promise to be quiet and listen to what I have to say? I promise that I'm not here to physically hurt you, but to give you information that you need to know." They both nod and I remove the duct tape. From the shrieks they let out, it must've hurt to pull it off. Bummer.

"Ow. What the hell, Blake?" Tristan says. "You better start explaining yourself fast." He looks like he wants to kill me. Get in line.

"I will. It's a bit of a long story, so just calm down," I say.

"I'll freaking calm down when you explain what's so important that you need to kidnap us in the middle of the day and drag us into this nasty, smelly dark place," he says.

"Did you ever wonder why you guys are called Second Chancers?" I ask. Both shake their heads sideways to indicate they don't. "Well, it's time you both partook of the fruit of the Tree of Knowledge."

"Huh?" Bri says.

"You both have very interesting pasts that you can't remember. So I'm going to fill in the gaps for you. Starting with the fact that you lived and died elsewhere before being given a second chance here on Thera," I say. I tell them everything, start to finish, as best I know from what Kira's told me about them including the pertinent details about what they did to her on Earth. Bri soaks it all in, but Tristan looks skeptical throughout.

When I'm finished telling them the whole story, Tristan chimes in first. "It all sounds like a bunch of crap you made up."

"No, I think he's telling the truth," Bri says. "I got chills. The whole thing rings true."

"You got chills because it's freezing!" Tristan says. Funny. It's a humid eighty-five or ninety degrees in the tunnel, but to a Theran that feels cold.

"What if we really did all that stuff to Kira, Tristan?" Bri says. "We'd deserve to die for it."

"He's just trying to give us a guilt trip over Cleaving before they had a chance," Tristan says. I watch them banter back and forth for a while before inserting some well-needed advice.

"Well, don't take my word. By all means, spread the news, gather your friends, and go ask the powers that be at Headquarters about it," I say.

That should keep the remaining Ten and Council members occupied while I figure out my escape plan.

For everything you have missed, you have gained something else, and for everything you gain, you lose something else.

Ralph Waldo Emerson

CHAPTER TWENTY-FIVE

Kira

"You asked to see me?" I say, entering Vienna Darcton's executive office on the sixth floor of the Headquarters. An armed security guard delivered me here. He made sure to take me past the masses of dead bodies on the way up—an object lesson in the perils of rebellion. The blood, body matter, and stench struck me like an oncoming train.

It's been twenty-four hours since Ethan saved me and we were evacuated to an underground stronghold. Since then security forces have secured the city and city officials have returned to Headquarters to assess the damage.

The commander of the security forces briefed officials in the stronghold. Only three of the Ten remain. Sixty percent of the Grand Council members were executed—either within their homes or at Headquarters before security forces intervened. Fifty-seven additional innocents lost their lives. Husbands or Wives of the Ten or Grand Council. Headquarters employees. City residents who were caught in the crossfire, when the battle expanded beyond Headquarters. Two hundred seventy-seven Militant Exilers perished, with others wounded and captured.

Everyone within the city had been tracked down and afforded the opportunity by security forces to present proper credentials proving they were Garden City residents. If they couldn't do so and no other resident could vouch for them, interrogations, followed by executions happened on the spot. Those who were vouched for by Cleaveds, friends or family await confirmation in lockup. Whether Blake's alive or dead I have no idea. He disappeared in the tunnels with a promise to see me later. The security commander didn't mention specifically searching the tunnels, which are only accessible by official passkeys, so I'm holding out hope.

"Yes, Kira. Please have a seat," she says. I sit in a lush green velvet guest chair in front of her large mahogany desk and admire the view of the canyon lights. While I wait for her to explain why she summoned me, I chew on my finger. She looks at me in disgust for my nervous habit and says, "We've been unable to locate your partner, Blake, despite our city-wide manhunt. Do you have any idea where he might be?" Thank goodness. At least he's still alive.

"Honestly, I don't," I say. "I haven't seen him since yesternight."

"A security guard claims to have seen him with you and Ethan in the tunnels during the evacuation," she says.

"No," I say. "There was some colleague of Ethan's, but he went back to see if he could find his Cleave when he saw she wasn't with us." Ethan and I had discussed how we'd handle questions about Blake if asked. She narrows her eyes, clearly doubting my answer.

"I understand your desire to protect him, Kira, but given his father's role in the Exiler attack on the city, we need to speak with him," she says. I stare into her bright green eyes and feel the same contempt I've felt from Blake lately. A good time to change the subject.

"Mrs. Darcton, I am really sorry about your loss. It must be terrible for you. Can I ask you though—what did your Cleave mean about Blake's dad being his real dad, but that his mom wasn't?" I ask. The statement kept me up all day, as I'm sure it did Blake.

I watch Vienna's face closely for clues on two fronts. First, to see how she reacts to my statement about her loss. Although it has been widely reported that Brad Darcton died from the gunshot wound he received, I know he was wearing body armor and security ushered him out quickly. To this, she does genuinely look upset. Second, I'm curious about how much she knows about Blake. Her expression is contemplative, as if she's deciding how much she wants to share.

"His parents used the Assisted Pregnancy process to get pregnant, just as all Therans do. A donor egg was used to insure he had Original blood," she says.

"Can I ask who his mother is?" I say. She looks away and it's apparent she's not going to give me an answer, although I can tell she knows. After a moment, she turns to me again.

"It's likely Blake will come to you," she says. "If so, I need you to persuade him to turn himself in." I start to laugh, but then cover it up with a fake cough.

"I have a poor track record of convincing Blake of anything. If he comes to me I'm happy to try—if you promise me that you will spare his life, no matter what the circumstances. He's not like his father. He must take after his mother,"

I say, trying to strike a nerve. She turns her chair around to look outside for quite some time before turning around to face me again.

"I'll agree to spare Blake's life if you agree to stay on Thera and submit to the will of the Ten and Grand Council," she says. I think to myself that she means the "Three" and the "Less Grand Council," but don't voice my snarky thoughts. The decision requires little thought. Blake lives if I do what she wants. No brainer. Every time I've rebelled horrible things have happened. This time I'll happily comply to keep the people I care about alive.

"Yes," I say. "I'll agree to those terms."

"Even if that means that you and Blake won't have a 'happily ever after'?" she asks.

"Yes, I think I'm well past the fantasy of a happily ever after," I say.

"I'll count on you to keep your word. Besides Blake, you have a lot of family now on Thera—Jared, your parents, and all those babies—who will benefit if you do," she says. She does threats as well as her husband, although I do sense she has more heart than he did or she wouldn't have agreed to spare Blake.

I mask my disgust of her threats with a small smile. "Yes. My family is here now."

"How's Ethan?" she asks.

"Physically, he's okay. He was grazed by a bullet, but we managed to get the bleeding stopped quickly. Emotionally, I'd expect he's devastated. Seeing his father kill Blake's to spare my life and then be shot by an Exiler. It was terrible," I say.

As much as I despised Brad Darcton, he did do what he did to save me. Well, I'm sure to make a definitive statement to the Militant Exilers, too, but his actions did save my life. "Both your Cleave and your son saved my life. I'm grateful." My gratitude will only go so far. She and the rest the SCI still need to pay for their actions.

"Ethan cares for you deeply," she says. "He would have sacrificed his own life for yours yesternight."

"I know," I say, blushing a little. Both Blake and Ethan did their part to save me with little thought about themselves. It blows me away and I feel unworthy of either's affections. I spent the entire day tending to Ethan's wound, and then together we mourned the dead. It took three armed security guards to persuade me to leave and bring me here.

A knock on the door interrupts our conversation.

"We have a situation," the security forces commander says. He looks at me suspiciously, but Vienna encourages him to continue. "The plaza is filled with Second Chancers demanding answers about their 'previous lives.'" My eyes go wide. Somehow I don't think the Second Chancers having newfound knowledge is by chance. Someone broke the cardinal rule. And unfortunately, I think I know how Blake spent his day—and it wasn't sleeping. This will definitely test my deal with Vienna Darcton.

All the Mass Cleaved have filled the plaza and don't seem to be dissuaded by the security forces pointing guns at them. Those girls are carrying my babies so the situation's making me pretty nervous, given the massacre I saw yesternight. All the questions you'd expect are being shouted from the crowd:

"Why can't I remember anything before February?"

"How did I get here?"

"Is it true that I died?"

"Was my name the same?"

"Where's my family? Who are my parents?"

"What happened to my memories?"

"Where did I live before and what was it like?"

"If I got blown to bits how'd my body get put back together?"

Vienna Darcton turns to me and says, "You're lucky we made that deal about Blake before this." I nod. There's no use trying to convince her that this isn't Blake's handiwork.

"How can I help?" I ask.

"We have a strict protocol on how to deal with these situations," she says. "Watch and learn. And *never* contradict."

Vienna steps forward and signals the security commander to blow a loud whistle, which stifles the masses. Although her demeanor had been stiff and businesslike with me, she softens as she addresses the crowd. Smiles and disarms them with her warmth. I'm surprised to see that she's capable of showing emotion.

"Greetings, Garden City residents. Thank you for bringing us your concerns tonight, although I assure you they are unfounded. Regardless, we invite each couple to meet with Council members and staff to have your worries addressed personally," she says. As she says this a large group of what appears to be remaining Council members and doctor staff pair off and approach each couple, walking them off towards the psychiatric clinic where Ethan, Jared and I had been imprisoned. All the couples cooperate, except Bri and Tristan, who refuse to leave without talking to me.

Bri looks like she's been crying, her face a mess of mascara and eyeliner. She grabs my arm and says, "Kira, we need to talk to you. You need to tell us whether what Blake told us is true. Did we go to high school with you on a place called Earth? Did we die in an explosion?" I can sense the doubt in her voice as she says it out loud. The story, albeit true, sounds preposterous. It's obvious who Blake targeted to incite the crowd. I'm sure he'd been more than happy to dump a whole load of guilt on them.

Vienna pats Bri on the shoulder in an effort to comfort her and says, "Kira and I will personally answer your questions. Just follow us." Then, she whispers in my ear. "Lie. They'll have the hardest time letting go of the truth since they were given details."

Vienna leads us to a small room in the clinic with a table and chairs. She directs us to sit. A mirrored wall leads me to believe we're being watched. Despite a member of the Ten being there Tristan and Bri unload everything Blake told them. My friendship with Bri and relationship with Tristan. Tristan and Bri's affair The Goodington party. The explosion. A sordid tale of betrayal and just desserts.

"Wow," I say when they're done. "That's quite the story. But it's not true. I'm sorry. Blake was just messing with you. It's clearly revenge for you giving me that Theranberry juice, Tristan. He unleashed his rather overactive imagination on you." I've had plenty of practice masking my emotions, so it's unlikely my face will reveal it's a lie.

"Are you sure?" Bri asks. "I really felt like it was true and, as much as I try, I can't remember anything that happened before I came here. No one can."

"We've brought in a doctor who may be able to help," Vienna says. "She specializes in helping people with their memories. She uses a combination of medications and mental exercises. Would you like to give it a try? The process takes a couple nights, but it is well worth it."

"Will the medicine hurt the baby?" Bri asks, rubbing the not-yet-existent bump on her belly. Tristan squeezes her in tightly as if that will protect her from whatever Vienna Darcton has planned.

"Not at all," she says, taking Bri's hand in hers. "We'd never do anything to harm your baby. That life you are carrying inside you is precious." Bri and Tristan both relax.

"Well then, yes," Bri says. "We'd like to meet with the doctor."

"We will send her right in," Vienna says, getting up to leave.

"Could we have a moment with Kira?" Bri asks. Vienna nods and then leaves. She'll be watching. "I just wanted to ask you again without her in the room. Are you positive there's no truth to what Blake said? If so, what we did would be unforgivable."

"Positive," I say. "And, even if it were true, which it isn't, it would be forgivable. I'd forgive you." A little risky, but I needed to say it. I needed them to know in some small way that I'm over it and forgive them.

"I didn't sleep a wink thinking I'd betrayed you like that," Bri says. "Is everything okay with you and Blake?"

"I'm sorry you lost sleep over it and am really sorry Blake did that to you," I say, avoiding a discussion about my failed relationship with Blake.

"He took us into some creepy tunnel behind our house. Why would there be a hidden passageway into our pantry?" she asks.

"They are probably delivery tunnels. I wouldn't worry about it," I say.

"Do you trust that woman?" Tristan asks of Vienna Darcton. "Will the doctor really help with our memories?"

"Yes to both," I say. I put my hand on Bri's arm for effect. Vienna Darcton will absolutely send in a memories expert to help them. Erase their memories of Blake's indiscretion, that is. "I'm going to go and see if I can find Blake. He's got some answering to do for this." We say our farewells and a kind-faced lady in a white coat passes me as I leave.

A security guard opens an adjacent door for me to enter and join Vienna. I watch as she gives them some medication and then hypnotizes them. It only takes about an hour, but apparently she'll repeat the process every six hours for two nights. Vienna explained that most people only need two to three treatments, but given the specific details Blake unleashed on them, they'll need more extensive therapy.

"You should understand that the alternative isn't possible," Vienna says to me. "Second Chancers come here happy and stay happy. Introducing a troubled past creates guilt, worry, comparisons, and trauma that they can't handle. They can never go back to Earth. And in most cases they wouldn't want to. But they might think they do and that can only cause pain."

"Indeed," I say, agreeing with her. My recent memories of Earth are all about pain.

For some strange reason, Vienna Darcton invites Ethan and me to sit through the last hour of the city head's meeting to hear a portion of the overall recommendations they'll be giving to Earth's delegates tomorrow night.

A rotund man with a bad comb over proceeds to read the minutes from the meeting and within moments I'm nodding off.

"I know that voice," I say to Ethan. "That's the dude from the training videos. If they want anyone here to retain any information they should really let someone else read. He gives new meaning to the word monotone." Ethan nods his agreement.

"I guess I'll have to entertain you then," he says. "Or you can use me as a pillow. Up to you." I snuggle up next to him and put my head on his shoulder, taking care to avoid his bandaged arm.

"I'm exhausted. Your mom kept me up half the day watching the experts extract the unpleasant memories Blake provided to the Second Chancers," I say. "They were all pretty messed up over it."

"Have you heard from Blake?" he says.

"Nope. Who knows if he's even still in the city. He has to know he painted a giant target on his head by inciting the Second Chancers to riot," I say.

"He wouldn't leave without saying goodbye to you," Ethan says. "Or taking you with him." His voice trails off and I can tell he thinks it's a distinct possibility that I'll be heading off into the desert with Blake "any time now."

"I'm not going anywhere," I say, looking directly into his eyes to show how serious I am. "Leaving would be counterproductive to the health and happiness of my friends and family." Plus I doubt Blake really will try to come rescue me and whisk me off with him. I'd have to decline, for the safety of my family, and that would make the break from him harder.

"What about your happiness?" he says. What about it? I once thought I was happy with Tristan, but that was a joke. My best friend wasn't a true friend to me. Blake chose his father's fight over the hope of a happy life with me. And the fun I'd had vacationing with Ethan at home ended with my parents' deaths. Since back, I've been angry, confused and torn between Blake and Ethan... anything but happy.

"I'm good," I lie. I bargained away my happiness to save Blake's life and keep my family safe here on Thera. That's good, right? "How are you, though? With your dad and everything?"

"I could be better," he says. He takes my hand, squeezing it tight, and then intertwining his fingers with mine. We sit silently for a couple minutes, each of us needing the other's company but not knowing what it should or can mean under the circumstances.

"You know how much I care about you, right?" he finally says, shifting his body weight to look at me with an expression that could melt the hardest of hearts. We still haven't had "the discussion" about his feelings for me and whether I return them. It didn't seem appropriate after the scene at Headquarters and I don't think I'm ready for it.

"Yeah. I care about you, too," I say. Even though he loves me, I'm glad he didn't put me in the awkward position of having to return the sentiment, given my feelings for Blake and generally being unsure about the whole love thing after two strikeouts in a row.

We're both shocked to attention when we hear a recommendation from one of the remaining Ten to locate and execute Blake for his role in the Exiler's attack, and for creating unrest with the Second Chancers. Blake's father had executed the man's Cleave. She was a member of the Grand Council.

"That is not possible," Vienna Darcton says. "The boy will not be harmed."

"You are hardly unbiased in the matter," the man accuses. "Blake Sundry's father shot my Cleave."

"And his men shot mine," Vienna says. "But we're not going to punish the boy for his father's actions."

"We *can* punish him for what he told the Second Chancers. The Canon is clear that discussing the past is cause for immediate Exile," the man says.

"Mr. Stockly, I'm the senior member of the Ten here and must ask you to stand down. You're well aware of the circumstances of Mr. Sundry's pardon. In fact, if you haven't noticed, we have two guests in attendance tonight—my son, Ethan and Ms. Kira Donovan," she says.

"Ah, the well-behaved and obedient son," Mr. Stockly says. "Welcome to both of you," he says, motioning towards us. While we'd been able to disappear into the room's corner prior to the introduction, every eye is on us now and I feel incredibly awkward. I straighten up, but keep hold of Ethan's hand. Who cares what they think. Mr. Stockly scoffs at us and says, "I guess their display is meant to cement Ethan as the choice for Kira's Cleave?"

"Kira and Ethan are close friends who, as you know, were present at the unfortunate circumstances that transpired in this building with the Exilers. They and I are not trying to imply anything," Vienna says. Did she just defend us in front of the remaining Ten and Council?

"Ms. Donovan," Mr. Stockly says. "You are aware of your role as the new mother of Thera? And that the role of father is still up for grabs?" I stand to address him.

"Yes. Though let's be clear. There are two 'fathers of Thera' regardless of whether you choose to acknowledge them both. Ethan and Blake must be equally qualified or I assume you wouldn't have used them to fertilize my eggs before implanting our babies in my friends," I say. I can see Vienna hide a smile at my bluntness.

"Yes, all your offspring will be important to the future of Thera, assuming they are healthy," Mr. Stockly says. "However, you will be required to Cleave one of Ms. Darcton's sons and together be the face of our future. Do you have an opinion?" I see Vienna shoot Mr. Stockly a deathly glare. What does he mean by one of her sons? I thought the only candidates were Blake and Ethan? I know Ethan has no sisters, but for some reason I never asked him about brothers. Of course, I do have an opinion, but I'll hardly share it in an open forum. My only option for staying alive is to pretend to go along with their plans for me and bide my time until I can figure out a way out.

"As I have told Ms. Darcton, I will submit to the will of the Ten and the Council on this matter," I say. "I wasn't aware of any other sons, though. Are there more fathers of my children running around Garden City? On Earth that kind of thing would really be frowned upon." I look to Ethan who appears as confused as I am.

"She hasn't told you?" Mr. Stockly says. Told me what? I shake my head. Vienna stands up and starts to cross the room, shaking her head and wagging her finger. She looks like she wants to hurt him. "Both Blake and Ethan are Ms. Darcton's biological children. After Ethan was born with difficulties, more children were created to ensure a healthy line of Original offspring. Why do you think Ms. Darcton agreed to spare Blake's life without consulting with the rest of the Ten and the Council?"

A full-scale argument breaks out in the Council room. I'm too floored to contribute anything more. Ethan looks extremely pale. Blake is his brother. I will be forced to Cleave one brother over the other, and there's no way that can end with warm and happy feelings in the family.

"I didn't know," Ethan says, his voice hoarse. "I swear it."

"I should have seen it. He has your mother's eyes," I mumble. How could I have missed it? It makes sense. They even have similar facial expressions. "Family reunions could be fun, especially if we invite all forty kids."

Ethan doesn't look amused at my twisted sense of humor. "How can you joke about it?"

"And my options are?" I say, smiling and jabbing him in the ribs. "It's actually kind of funny in a dark comedy kind of way. You and Blake—brothers. Collectively fathering forty of my children."

"I wonder how many other unknown siblings I have," Ethan says. "What if I'd stayed here on Thera and Cleaved one of my sisters by accident? That's some seriously sick stuff." We both chuckle and then return our attention to the escalating fight in the center of the room. It's gotten so intense that security personnel have their guns raised, safeties off, and ready to use if needed.

"At a minimum, I demand you bring Blake Sundry here to address the Council and Ten. He needs to be thoroughly vetted, regardless of your unilateral pardon," shouts Mr. Stockly.

"You are in no position to make demands, Paul," Vienna says.

"Really," he says. "Should we take a vote? I wonder which side would get the most support."

"What on Thera do you think you could accomplish by such an interrogation?" Vienna says. "The Exilers are dead, so understanding their motives and methods will hardly be useful. The situation with the Second Chancers was unfortunate, but we quickly addressed it, and soon Blake will have no access to any of them to repeat the offense."

"You think we won't have threats in the future?" Mr. Stockly says. "If you've convinced yourself of that, then you're clearly not worthy of the position of Senior Ten. I say the boy gets brought forth to answer for his sins. Who's with me?" The crowd applauds, though quiets as Vienna starts typing names into her tablet of those questioning her authority.

"We've had thousands of security detail searching and they can't find the boy, much less produce him to answer to any of you," Vienna says. "As best we know, he's left the city. And if he hasn't, our only hope of finding him is through Kira Donovan, and if she suspects an ounce of harm will befall him, she won't help any of us." I love being talked about as if I'm not in the room. She's right of course. If the deal dies, so does my cooperation.

"I don't care if I have to personally search every cave within twenty miles of Thera. I will find the boy! If Ms. Donovan is the key, I'll be happy to make it clear throughout Thera that Ms. Donovan will suffer if the boy doesn't turn himself in," Mr. Stockly says, sweat pouring from his head and spit ejecting from his mouth.

Ethan grabs me, pushes me behind him, and yells, "Over my dead body."

"And mine," Vienna says.

"That can be arranged if you keep me from finding the boy," Mr. Stockly says.

"How about you stop referring to me as 'the boy'?" a familiar voice says from the entrance to the room. "You want to talk to me? Well, here I am. Have at me. Just leave Kira out of it."

I peek around Ethan to confirm that Blake has indeed entered the room. My heart skips a beat as I realize every gun in the room is now trained on him.

Oh crap.

CHAPTER TWENTY-SIX

Blake

I've been watching the late evening proceedings of the City Heads meeting from the taping room, fulfilling the duties of my stolen identity, Walter Hunt, Grand Council member. I plan to collect data on the cities and leaders to use in Exile or once back on Earth, but I get distracted when I notice Kira cuddled up in Ethan's arms in the corner of the room.

Amidst the snugglefest, a butt-ugly man with a large ego challenges Vienna about me. From what I can gather Vienna Darcton agreed to pardon me. And Kira was somehow involved in this? Seriously? I can't imagine the things she'd have to agree to in order for her to grant me a blanket pardon. But the ugly dude's having no part of it and is accusing Vienna of bias.

Then I hear several things that blow my mind. First, there's some whole deal about a whole lot of Kira's babies being implanted in our Second Chancer friends and both Ethan and me being fathers of them. One of us will be the so-called "Father of Thera." Second, Kira has agreed to be Cleaved to one of Vienna Darcton's sons and *to let The Ten choose for her*. And third, I'm one of the sons. Vienna Darcton's supposedly my mother and Ethan's my half-brother. Gads almighty, help me. Fourth, a good chunk of the people in that room want me dead and are willing to use Kira as bait to trap me into answering for my part in the rebellions—of both the Exilers and the Second Chancers.

I start pacing the small room. Why didn't Kira tell me about the babies and her deal with the devil? She and Ethan look as shocked as the rest of them about Vienna Darcton being my DNA donor. My brother's shielding Kira from Mr. Stockly, the Ten bully. But I know that if the tide turns and Mr. Stockly gains momentum with the Council and other City Heads, that Kira, Ethan and Vienna are not safe.

Time to trust my instinct and hope that Vienna's blood oath with Kira runs thicker than the stream of dissent in that room. I use my passkey to access the conference room.

"How about you stop referring to me as 'the boy'?" I say in a loud voice as I enter. "You want to talk to me? Well, here I am. Have at me. Just leave Kira out of it."

At least a hundred guns shift from Ethan and Kira toward me in an instant. I ignore them and walk down the stairs and towards Vienna Darcton and Mr. Stockly, outstretching my hand to shake theirs. I don't think they were expecting me since they seem to be a little tongue-tied.

"I'm Blake Sundry," I say. "Apparently I'm your *biological* son," to Vienna, and to Mr. Stockly, "I guess I'm your worst nightmare, though I'm confused as to why." I'd never seen Vienna Darcton up close, but I have zero doubt that we share DNA upon close inspection. The eyes. Facial shape.

"You've been elusive," Vienna says. "We've had a lot of people looking for you—for your own protection, of course."

"Of course," I say. "My father and his cohorts take out a chunk of the city, and you're worried about protecting me? I believe that."

"Where were *you* during the attack?" Mr. Stockly asks me.

"I was at headquarters," I respond. "But my only goal was getting Kira out alive. My father took her captive. Thankfully, I ran into Brad Darcton who agreed to try to get her out safely if I created a diversion."

"What diversion?" Vienna and Mr. Stockly say in unison.

"I blew out the glass wall behind my father," I say. "I apologize for the damage, but it was the only thing I could think of."

"Let me get this straight," Vienna says. "You ran into Brad and he told you to create a diversion. You obeyed this, even though your actions resulted in the death of your father?" They both look incredulous about my claims.

"Just ask the security detail that was with him at headquarters. They witnessed our conversation," I say.

"Okay, so even if you're telling the truth about what happened at headquarters… what about the Second Chancers? How do you explain away your actions there?" Mr. Stockly says.

"Sorry about that. It was stupid. I wanted to dish back a fraction of the suffering Tristan and Briella caused Kira. And perhaps I was trying to deflect some of the anger about my part in getting my dad and so many others killed, although I'm not trained as a psychologist so it's hard to know for sure," I say in a voice meant to imitate the school counselor they'd had me see after the explosion at the Goodington's.

Paul Stockly isn't amused. He must think I'm mocking him. The creases in his forehead deepen as his anger increases and voice raises. "Your father killed my Cleave."

"I'm not here to rationalize my father's actions and I'm very sorry for your loss. Obviously I disagreed with my father's tactics or I'd have never helped Brad Darcton. All I can say is that my father felt his cause was just and I can empathize. I grew up with the Exilers and our circumstances were pretty horrible. Eventually my father got my sister and me out and to Earth, but his goal was to bring me back and bring down the Second Chance Institute. He blamed the SCI for my mother's..." I pause for a moment to correct my mistake, "or who I thought to be my mother... her death."

"So you admit you came back here to commit treason against the SCI?" Mr. Stockly says, twisting my words, even if his interpretation is the truth. Albeit a rash decision to enter this room, my intention was to calm the dissension, not further fuel it.

"Please separate my father's intentions for me with my own actions," I say. "I didn't realize until I returned to Thera that my father was working with an extremely militant offshoot of the Exilers. I opposed my father's plans, siding with the Survivalist Exilers, who want peace and coexistence without violence. They are no threat to you."

"Are we really going to listen to this?" Mr. Stockly says to the crowd. "This boy admits coming here to destroy us. I demand justice and I demand it now, even if it requires forcibly removing Vienna Darcton from her post on the Ten."

Within moments, security guards surround Vienna, face outward, and point their weapons at Mr. Stockly. Ethan and Kira both run to act as my human shield, saying the dissenters will have to kill them first to get to me. The guards sympathetic to Mr. Stockly's cause have all three of us in their sights. The two sides shout loud threats to one another.

"This is not your fight," I say to Ethan and Kira. "I can't let you risk your lives to protect me."

"Uh, I've always wanted the opportunity to say this. Shut up, brother," Ethan says, glancing back at me with a sly grin.

"Yeah, shut up, Blake," Kira says from behind me. She grabs my hand and squeezes it tight.

The stalemate continues for several minutes, no one wanting a repeat of the Militants' slaughter, but the threats of it continuing. At its most tense point, and when I've sweated out every bit of liquid from my body thinking I'm a dead man, a third contingent enters the room and I about have a heart attack when I see the people in it.

"What the hell's going on here?" a commanding voice asks. "Everyone lower their weapons now." Both sides are slow to comply, but when they see the masses of new security detail that have entered and plan to execute all of them if necessary, they do so. "So, Sister. Are you going to explain? I got your message about the attack on the city and so we came early," the man says to Vienna Darcton, motioning for her protective security detail to part. I crane my neck to get a closer look at the man, who does resemble my "mother."

But, his sister? How is that possible? The man speaking is California Senator and United States Democratic Presidential frontrunner candidate. He's Vienna's brother? That would make him my uncle. With him are the current United States Secretary of State and a whole host of other people who I learned about in my government class at Carmel Valley High. Are they part of the American delegation due for the second night of the city head's meeting? They are all Daynighters? What the flip? And my dad thought he could take these guys on, the fool.

"Henry," Vienna exclaims. "It's been too long. We have much to discuss."

"I can tell," he says, scanning the room. "Well, don't keep us waiting."

Kira, Ethan and I listen as Vienna dispassionately tells the events of the last week to the American contingent. She doesn't leave anything out, including my role leading up to and during the Militant attack, her deal with Kira to pardon me, what I told the Second Chancers, and particularly, Paul Stockly's demands for my immediate execution and Vienna's removal from the Ten. She allows Paul Stockly to defend his actions and we watch as he backpedals from his harsh stance.

"I see," Henry King says after hearing the whole of it. "Well, let me meet them." He turns around to look our way and then warmly embraces Ethan. "Ethan, so good to see you. About ready to head back to law school and follow in your uncle's footsteps?"

"Yes, sir," Ethan says. "Uncle Henry, let me introduce you to Kira Donovan and Blake Sundry." Kira immediately steps forward to shake his hand.

"It's nice to meet you Senator King," she says. "I'd say I'm surprised to meet you here, but not much shocks me these nights." If she's remotely nervous to meet him, she doesn't show it.

"You are stunning. I can see why my nephew… or should I say *nephews* are so smitten with you," he says to Kira, before turning to me. "And you must be my more notorious nephew, Blake?" He offers his hand.

"I guess so," I say, taking his hand to shake it.

"You have her eyes," Henry says, I assume speaking of Vienna Darcton. "Do you have anything to add to your mother or Mr. Stockly's accounts of Garden City happenings?" he says.

"No. I think your sister… uh, my mother accurately covered things," I say, not willing to give any credence to Mr. Stockly's fantastical take. One of the member's of Henry King's security detail taps Henry's shoulder and whispers something in his ear. Henry nods to him. The man then cocks his weapon, releases the safety, and puts a bullet through Paul Stockly's head. The room silences after a collective gasp.

"Would anyone else like to break protocol, challenge the established line of authority, or fuel further dissension in this room?" Henry says, looking around. No one appears to be taking the bait. "Because my head of security has reviewed the tapes of the last half hour and has a list of those of you who were sympathetic to Paul Stockly's poison. I do believe that those who commit treason are subject to immediate Exile or execution."

Henry directs his head of security to take me into protective custody while my fate is discussed and asks Ethan to watch over Kira.

As we are ushered out of the room I hear "Uncle Henry" say, "Well then, I believe we all have much to confer about. New members of the Ten and Council must be appointed. I want to personally hear each city head's plan to prevent similar attacks from happening worldwide and we have decisions to make on furthering our plans on Earth's soil. Let's get to it. I hope no one was hoping to sleep today, because we're not leaving until every matter is resolved."

"How's solitary confinement treating you?" says my brother, Ethan, who has come to visit, several nights after I'd been sealed in the detention facility. My room's pretty nice considering—other than the mirrored wall which indicates I'm being watched at all times. Home cooked meals. A treadmill and free weights. Comfortable bed.

"It hasn't been all that solitary," I say. "Turns out a lot of people have questions for me. So, how's Kira? She's notably missing off my visitor log." I've had oodles of time with my mother and Henry King, as well as the other remaining member of the Ten and the newly appointed additions. They've been nice enough to let me know that Kira's been staying with Ethan.

"Not by choice, I assure you. Until tonight we've been banned from visiting," he says. "She'll be here soon."

"You are here first to stake your claim, then?" I say. "She's due to Cleave one of us, so I assume you prefer that be you."

"I did see her first," he says, grinning. "But I don't think it's up to me who she ends up with."

"What do you mean you saw her first?" I say. "She didn't even meet you until I went missing during the flash flood."

"Not true," he says. "We met the night of the Goodington party. It was love at first sight for me. She went running off after she caught Tristan and Briella kissing. I tried to catch up to give her a ride home. But then the explosion happened and you carted her off. After, my father banned me from pursuing her until she'd adapted to Theran soil and the Ten could agree on who was her most suitable Cleave."

I pause a moment. So now it all makes sense. Ethan's perfect girl was Kira. The guy Kira spoke of that she'd met at a party who was "perfect"—that was Ethan. She'd known him all along. How shocked she must've been when he showed up again and she learned he was a Darcton. That must've killed the fantasy a bit, although after spending all that time "playing" his girlfriend, she seems to have forgiven him for his bloodline.

"So why did you let me fall for her if you were already head over heels?" I say.

"As I said, I was banned from seeing her until she'd acclimated and met the Second Chancers. The consequences, had I disobeyed, would have been deadly. And, by that time, you two were already spending time in the canyons and the general sentiment was that you'd Cleave 'any time now.' I figured I'd lost my chance," he says, shaking his head. "But then you disappeared and my father ordered me to show her the video of Tristan and Bri and take her home for a break. We got to be good friends."

"That's all?" I say.

"She played along with the whole boyfriend-girlfriend thing while we were back on earth because she had to. She'd never betray you willingly," he says. "She's not like that."

"But you really love her?" I say.

"Yes. I do," he says. "More than you can imagine." Oh, my imagination's been going wild on you and Kira for a while now, so I think I'm all caught up.

"And she loves you?" I ask.

"I hope so, but I don't know. I've never asked her directly. I know she cares for me. She surely loves you. That, she's told me many times," he says.

"So, where does this leave us? Two brothers after the same girl. We've both fathered her children. Not looking like it'll end well," I say, my arms crossed.

"I will abide by whatever she decides," Ethan says. "The choice is hers. I refuse to interfere with her free will."

"That's the thing though. It doesn't sound like she does get to decide. She made some deal with your... our... mother to let the Ten decide who she Cleaves. How could she do that?" I say.

"She did it to save your life. That alone should tell you how much she loves you," he says. He looks jealous, as if she wouldn't do the same for him. I think he underestimates how much Kira cares for him.

"Well, I don't stand a chance given what I've done to the SCI and the fact 'our' mother will clearly favor you over me. Being my egg donor doesn't really create a strong mother-son bond," I say, pacing the room.

"From what I understand, Kira offered to Cleave you on multiple occasions and you *chose* your cause over her," he says. He's right, but I glare at him anyway. "Besides, our mother will do what's best for Thera, not either of her sons. She's not super maternal if you know what I mean. She still has major issues with my 'faulty genes.'" No wonder I have trouble with relationships. Between my mother and my father, you'd think I'd been created by a couple of emotion free robots.

"You have to promise me to treat her right if you Cleave her," I say.

"Likewise to you," Ethan says to me, though it floors me that he hasn't gone running to our mommy to make sure he wins her hand in Cleave. Why would he give in so easily? "Do you love her? Like in the 'she's the only one for me' sense?"

"I don't buy into the whole 'there's only one for me' thing nor do I believe in 'love conquering all or being all'. I've done the love thing before and got burned. But, as much as I'm capable... yeah, I guess I do love her. I just have to keep it all in context. I can't let the entire world go to hell because of it." I surprise myself by admitting this to Ethan. I expect him to tell me that it's not enough. That she deserves better. Because he'd be right. I do love Kira. But, I also love the cause and the people who cared for me in my youth and are suffering as we speak.

He grabs my hand and says, "I may not have asked for it or wanted it, but you are my brother and that means something. Don't ever forget that." I don't know what to say, given I definitely didn't ask for this, so I just nod. We hear a knock and within seconds the door is open and Kira enters. She looks surprised to see Ethan here and it creates an uncomfortable moment where no one knows what to do.

"I'll see you both later," Ethan says. He looks Kira right in the eye and I can see she is guilt-ridden by our triangle. Once the door is closed, she gives me a hug and a lingering kiss on my cheek.

"Hey," she says. "How are you doing?"

"Not too bad for a prisoner," I say.

"What were you thinking? Why didn't you just leave the city?" she asks.

"It's such a nice place and I've gotten rather attached," I joke. "Plus, I wasn't able to find a good bed and breakfast to book outside the Eco barrier." She smiles at that. I have missed her smile; everything about her.

"I'm guessing you have some questions for me," she says, staring down at her feet.

"I think I'm all caught up with the multitude of omissions on your part—the deal you struck, the babies and the like," I say. "But I did find out one new tidbit tonight—that 'perfect' guy you met at the Goodington party was Ethan, wasn't it? And the 'perfect girl' he'd told me about was you."

"I guess. I'm sorry," she says. "I met a handsome, charming stranger at the party. I didn't act on my feelings because I was tied to Tristan and then Ethan disappeared, and I figured him for dead. The more I remembered him, the more perfect he became. That doesn't mean he *is* perfect. That bubble burst long ago."

"Do you love him?" I ask.

"I love you—if I even believe in the institution of love anymore," she says, looking up into my eyes. "That said, I know that being in love doesn't automatically lead to a lifetime of happiness." Everything that's happened has broken her. Or she just doesn't want to admit her feelings for Ethan to me.

"Trust me. Love exists. I love you. Ethan says he loves you," I say. She bites her lip at the mention of Ethan and starts to sway side to side a bit. "And I think you love him."

"Perhaps, but it's not relevant, is it? Tonight, the Ten will determine which one of you I Cleave and when and how I live my life," she says. "They don't care who I'd rather be with."

"You agreed to that," I say, regretting the words as they leave my mouth.

"Yes. And I'd do it again given the same circumstances," she says, a dead serious expression on her face.

"Well, screw the deal. If they Exile me, come with me. We can make our own future," I say. She pauses and sinks her head.

"You know that won't be an option, Blake. As much as I'd love to run away from everything and be with you, I can't leave the people I care about, knowing they won't be safe," she says.

"Even if that means we can't be together?" I say, biting my own lip.

"Even so," she says. "But you can choose to stay and then there's always a chance." She runs the back of her hand down my cheek which sends shivers of desire for her down my spine.

"You want me to stay here and watch while they have you Cleave Ethan?" I say.

"You don't know that's what is going to happen," she says.

"Perhaps that's what you want anyway," I mumble. "You can have pretty little babies together who can grow up to be the 'future of Thera' and who can continue the SCI's grip on the Second Chancers."

"Stop it," she says, fuming. With a whisper she adds, "I had a choice and chose to protect the people I care about. You have a choice. The Ten will have their choice. I don't know if all those things will match or not, but I do know that I'm not giving up about anything. So neither should you. Come here."

She drags me to the corner of the room behind the treadmill—perhaps the only spot in the room shielded from view through the mirror—and she straddles my lap, facing me. To my surprise, she removes her shirt to reveal her shimmery party tube top. The last girl that revealed herself to me in party attire was Bailey and I remember where that led. I still feel a little guilty that I never told Kira what happened.

At first I think that Kira's attempting, yet again, to get me to Cleave her. But that's not the case. In fact, despite her position atop me, she's being a little robotic. She'd never go back on her deal and risk my life. And we both know they won't let us stay "hidden" for long. She points to her stomach where she's drawn an elaborate diagram and instructions in what appears to be... makeup? The picture looks like a bicycle wheel, but when I see what she's written I understand the message she's trying to communicate. Ms. Kira Donovan has discovered the SCI's Achilles heel. When the powers that be banned paper and pencils they forgot that other methods could be used to communicate if necessary.

"Commit it to memory," she whispers as she pretends to nibble on my ear. I gladly oblige, my mind whirring with the implications of what she discovered.

A couple minutes later, the door opens and the security guard informs us we're out of time. She slips back on her shirt and gives me a chaste kiss goodbye.

"I do love you, Blake. I know it's not enough, but don't ever forget that," she says.

I try to stave off the tears until she leaves. Because I fear the security guard is right. The Ten will make sure that our time is up.

When a security guard comes to fetch me at 0200 hours and leads me on a convoluted route to a massive field of solar panels, I'm positive I have a date with a firing squad. At least I'll be dying with Kira's taste on my lips. Instead of finding men with guns, however, I'm surprised to be greeted by my mother and Ted Rosenberg.

"Walk with me," my mother says. Ted's left with the security guard as we stroll between the large panels. "We've come to a decision about you, Blake."

"Firing squad? Hanging?" I say. She chuckles.

"No. Actually, we're giving you a choice," she says.

"I can't wait to hear this," I mumble.

"You can choose to stay in Garden City and assist me in my work at

Headquarters... assuming you agree to pledge strict obedience to all the Theran Canon. Or, if you feel you can't abide by the Canon and put aside your feelings for the Theran government, you can choose to leave Garden City... self-exile, if you will, and the Ten will agree to not pursue you and let you live in peace," she says.

I'm floored. She is seriously offering me a job at the SCI in return for my pledge of loyalty? As her "assistant"? I have trouble believing the Ten will trust me to leave without staging another rebellion. Or what if I leave Thera and out the SCI on Earth? I'm not buying it.

"What is the catch? And what about Kira? Who does she Cleave?" I ask.

"The catch of you staying is that there are still many on the Council and Ten who feel you are guilty of treason, and who may not be your biggest fans here. Your life could be at risk," she says. "The catch of you leaving is that those same people will be constantly leery of what you may do in the future. And could construe any actions you might take... as an act of war against us. You'd have to be very careful to live out your life without any thought of us."

I pause to take it in. What would life be like working with Vienna? Would I be making her coffee? Taking dictation? Having Mommy and Son Sunnight brunch together? I shudder at the thought. Being at the Ten's beck and call doesn't exactly sound like a picnic. Would there be benefits? A passkey to the city models, perhaps? Free rein throughout headquarters? The possibilities are there. But, would the Ten trust me enough to give me any leeway and not shadow me all night, every night? I have to weigh the potential pros with the most certain cons. And the personal assistant option against life in Exile with Doc Daryn and the Survivalists.

"And Kira?" I ask.

"If you decide to stay, the Ten will decide between you and Ethan as a Cleave for Kira by dawn," she says. Her expression is blank. Does that mean she's made up her mind? Will the negative sentiments about me put me out of the running, or will Ethan's faulty DNA kill his chances? They do seem to be all about DNA here, the SCI being busy building a master race of Original-blooded Daynighters, many of whom will be my children.

"Who would you vote for... for her Cleaving?" I ask, to see if I can get a reaction one way or the other. Her expression doesn't change.

"You are both equally qualified. You both love her. I'm torn, as any mother would be between two sons. With Ethan, her long-term future would be with him on Earth. With you, she'd stay on Thera and raise my grandchildren here. I haven't decided either way," she says.

"What do you mean with Ethan she'd be on Earth?" I ask.

"Ethan's attending law school and his path is to follow in my brother's footsteps in the government there. Naturally, his Cleave would be at his side," she says. Yet another thing Kira didn't mention. That means, if I stay, there's a good chance I watch Kira Cleave Ethan and then they both leave to live happily ever after on Earth, while I'm stuck with my mom and her minions. To me, that sounds like worse than living off bugs in Exile. Sheer hell. What if I'm wrong though and I do have a chance with Kira? Can she be the one for me forever? Unbidden, I feel Bailey's ice-cold blue eyes glare at me in my subconscious, reminding me that I'd already failed once.

We've gone in a giant circle and I can see Ted and the security guard up ahead. As we approach them I ask, "Why's Ted Rosenberg here?"

"Because Ted Rosenberg is a true traitor to Thera. He played both sides, trying to set himself up well with the eventual victor. So he's the one who should have a date with the firing squad," she says, loud enough for him to hear.

Apparently Ted's not ready to say goodbye. He makes a run for it, darting between two solar panels. I can hear his hefty breathing as he hikes his heart rate beyond acceptable levels. The security guard dashes after him.

Vienna is chuckling at Ted's flight. "Isn't Ted a little touchy tonight. I wasn't serious about the firing squad. He's headed for Exile."

"That should go well," I say. "I'm sure he's far more hated there than here. I'll go help round him up." I head down a parallel row to try to corner him from the opposite side. I'm sure I can run double his speed without even trying.

I keep light on my feet and listen for his shuffle. He appears to be zigzagging between panels in an effort to hit the outer edge where he'd hope to disappear into the canyon. I make some calculated turns to reach the edge before he does and then slow my pace so I can determine exactly which row to intercept him. His shuffles have slowed. If he's smart, he's stopped to gauge where the guard and I are. Perhaps he'll even climb up into one of the panels to wait us out. There must be ten thousand or more of them in this field, so it'd take forever to check them all, without bringing in every troop in the city.

I slowly crouch down and look through the rows for his feet, betting he's not so smart after all. I'm right as I see him ten feet in, five rows up, trying to blend into the base of a panel. He's probably just catching his breath before making a run for the canyon. Kira would get a kick out of watching Mr. Potatohead try to escape. I can understand why he'd try, but the odds are not with him. Of course, Ted Rosenberg's as arrogant as they come, so he has likely convinced himself it is possible.

In less than twenty-seconds I'm in the row next to him. I slowly and weightlessly inch to the panel in front of him.

"Give it up, Ted," I say. I hear the click of the guard's gun, indicating the guard has him covered on the other side. Rolling towards Ted, I clip his feet and send him barreling backwards.

Between belabored breaths, Ted says, "Vienna's lying. I never betrayed the SCI. It was your father and the Exilers I deceived. That was my job. Brad Darcton assigned it to me." As Ted nervously twitches, I see his chin fat jiggle. I remember how Kira used to joke about using liposuction on Spud's fat chin and wish I was back with her and not here.

"You should be ashamed of yourself on all accounts. I hope you had a good meal tonight, Ted. How do you feel about slop?" I say. He's up on his knees now and begging the security guard. He still thinks he's going to be executed. The SCI, however, will be kinder than my father would have been—my father would have put the bullet through his brain. Ted lured my father and the Militants into the city, knowing they'd be ambushed. Knowing they couldn't win.

"Please, please, please spare my life. I'll tell you everything I know about the Exilers. Everything you need to take them out," he says, whimpering and sweat pouring from his face. "I'll do anything you need. Anything."

Vienna walks up behind him with a second security guard and says, "Shut up, Ted. I said that you *should* face a firing squad, not that you were going to." Ted sucks in a chest full of air and then bows down at her feet. She steps back and says, "Instead, I have a bright orange jumpsuit and nightpack with a night's worth of food. Nathaniel's going to take you outside the city. Good luck, Ted. I hope the Exilers are as forgiving for your trespasses as we've been." I watch as Nathaniel, the security guard, cuffs and blindfolds Ted. Ted's screaming as he's dragged off. Before they get to the edge of the canyon Nathaniel tires of the wailing and uses a piece of duct tape to quiet Ted for the rest of their journey.

Ted probably does deserve Exile. He flagrantly broke dozens of Canon rules with his attempt at being the double-agent. My problem is that there's no due process to the SCI's law. Ted had no trial, no jury of his peers, and no due process. As crappy as the American government can be, democracy still has merit. The SCI assumes that the few know better than the masses. They test their methods on unknowing and unsuspecting Second Chancers. As with any dictatorship, they need to be stopped. I just have to figure out the best way to make that happen with the information Kira gave me.

My mother approaches me. She says, "I need your decision, Blake." I know what I need to do, but it's still hard to do it, as it is any time you have to pick in a lose-lose scenario. As much as my choice sucks, the alternative's unbearable.

CHAPTER TWENTY-SEVEN

Ethan

"You never had a heart defect, Son." Dr. Christo has never been one to mince words, but he's never managed to utter a doozy like this one. He's dressed head to toe in such a dazzling white that it blinds me. I struggle to suck life-giving air into my lungs.

"That's impossible," I finally manage to say.

"Thera's at a critical juncture. The Ten and Council have been decimated, leaving the most extreme in place. It's time you know the truth."

"And you're telling me the truth is that I had a dozen surgeries for a non-existent heart condition?" I ask incredulously.

"It was necessary to make it *appear* that you both had a defect and needed constant medical care. For your protection. And to give me complete, unquestioned access to you."

"*You're* the one who had me locked up for ten years?" I accuse.

He begins to pace back and forth in my living room. Like, Jax, he too has the capability of blocking surveillance, so our conversation is secure.

"The Grand Council and the Ten had lost focus. They were perverting the purposes of the grand design behind Thera and the Second Chancers. I had to take action. At the time, I ran the Assisted Pregnancy lab. Your mother and father had 'won' the lottery and were due. I used your mother's egg, but... fertilized the egg with... I'm your biological father, Ethan. You have both ARB and pure Dark DNT in you. But your parents couldn't know. And the ARB and DNT don't always co-exist well, so I needed to treat you. Hybrids are... rare and exceptional. You have... undeveloped talents."

He lets the news sink in. I sit down on the couch and bury my head in my hands. Brad Darcton, the man presumed dead in the attack on Headquarters, is not my father? Dr. Christo is? Which would make Jax… my brother? I'm some sort of DNA hybrid concocted in a lab?

After a minute taken to get my breathing under control again, I ask, "Why? Why would you do that?"

"You're destined to realign the Ten and Grand Council to their intended purposes. It's almost time to right the wrongs of the Ten. To be trusted by the SCI, you had to be a pure Dark. To be trusted by me and the rest the Arbiters, you needed to have the ARB marker. I trained you from your youth for this purpose." He looks so proud of his accomplishment.

"And if I say no to being your 'sleeper agent' in the SCI?" I ask.

"You won't. You can't," he says.

"Are you threatening me? If so, you're no better father than Brad Darcton was," I say.

"I'm nothing like Brad Darcton. Given what you know about the SCI… what they are doing to the Second Chancers… to the Exilers… to the people you love… Can you turn your back on a chance to fix it?" he asks. He's right. Kira would never forgive me if I had the opportunity to repair that which is broken.

"All those couples are carrying Kira's and my children? What happens when my ARB-marked blood mixes with Kira's?" I ask.

"Not for you to worry about" he says. "You have other concerns. From here on out, things will move quickly. Your Uncle's in town and they are scrambling to fill spots on the Ten and Council. If offered a spot, you'll take it without hesitation. I will advise you as I am able and Jax and I will train you to develop your latent… talents."

"Jax knows?" I ask. "For how long? And what talents?"

"He's always known," he mumbles. "It would be impossible to keep from him. As for talents, it's unclear what you are capable of. We'll have to run tests."

As disturbed as I am by the turn of events, I'm equally intrigued. If I could do a fraction of the things Jax is capable of, it would be amazing. Life changing.

"And, Ethan," Dr. Christo says. "You're to keep this to yourself. *No one* can know. The future of Thera depends on it."

"Hey, bro. I hear a Cleaving *may* be in your future," a very smug Jax says, arriving uninvited and unannounced as always. Kira's been staying with me, but is taking a longer-than-approved shower.

"You bastard," I reply. "You knew about me all along and never breathed a word."

"You," he says, poking me in my chest, "did not have clearance. Besides, all the clues were there. You just failed as detective."

"We're brothers," I say as a statement, still unbelieving. "I seem to be accumulating those lately."

"So I've heard. Half-brothers, though," he corrects. "I'm anticipating a few half-brotherly quarrels in our future."

"Well, then I guess nothing will change," I say. As much as Jax riles me up, it's hard to stay mad at him. "We're always arguing."

"Over trivial things, thus far. Imagine what happens when brothers clash over important things," he muses. What, like Blake and I have been doing over Kira?

"Then we'll have to hope blood runs thicker than hostility," I say, unconvinced that if they Cleave Blake to Kira that I'll be able to get past it and forgive him.

"About that Cleaving… Think they'll pick you?" Jax asks.

"I have no idea. If they don't I'll be in no condition to help you, your father, my Uncle, or anyone else for that matter. I'll find some remote area on Earth and curl up in a ball and wither away."

"Dramatic as always, Ethan. Have you talked to Kira?" he asks.

"She knows how I feel. I can't force her to feel the same," I shrug.

"She does," he says. "She's got a big heart. Big enough to love more than one man utterly and completely."

"Don't remind me," I say. I stuff my hands into my pants pockets and rock back and forth to calm my nerves.

Jax pats me on the back. "Got to run, bro. Kira's done showering and I'd hate to meet her for the first time when she's in… compromising attire. It's almost show time. May the best man win and I think we all know who the best man is." Well, I know Jax always assumes that *he* is the best, but I've got to think that between Blake and me that he'd support me.

"Thanks, Jax."

"Ethan, do you know where my brush is?" Kira yells. I turn around to say goodbye to Jax, but he's already vanished. So, I do the only thing I can. Go to spend what may be my last moments with Kira before the Ten's decision comes down.

We must be willing to let go of the life we have planned, so as to accept the life that is waiting for us.
— *Joseph Campbell*

CHAPTER TWENTY-EIGHT

Kira

The knock comes at 0300 hours. Two armed guards tell us that the Ten has requested Ethan and my presence at Headquarters immediately. We oblige and follow the men. Ethan holds my hand the entire way, and I'm not sure whether this will be the last opportunity to do so or not. Vienna Darcton visited me earlier to tell me Blake would be given a choice to stay or leave and the Ten awaited his decision before choosing my Cleave.

I stress over what Blake decided the entire way to the Headquarters building. How will he use the information I passed to him? I—and now Blake—are in possession of a whopper of a secret. The clues came unwittingly from Brad Darcton. I'm sure he'd be rolling over in his grave if he knew that he'd led me to the information.

Even though I didn't figure it out right away, the key was an offhand comment Brad made the day he showed us the city models. He bragged that the SCI could never be defeated because of the power within a giant, wheel-shaped structure in the model. It helps with "resource allocation and management for the city" he'd said.

The resources are people, the structure—a portal. A mega-portal leading to Earth and every city on Thera. That's how they could have security forces arrive on demand when Exilers attacked. And how the city heads arrived for their meeting. The spokes of the wheels are tunnels—the individual portals. When Ethan and I left Earth we arrived at Earth's mega-portal. The circular room had been paneled, but I'd seen the seams to dozens of doorways.

Without the capabilities of their mega-portal, the SCI would appear weak and scattered. With it, they can transport goods and people quickly from one place to another without the need of airplanes or complex transportation systems. The ships could be used for large shipments and serve as a great decoy, hiding the SCI's true capabilities.

I repeat the million dollar question in my mind. What will Blake do with the information? Will he stay here so that we can formulate a plan to immediately decentralize the SCI government? Or will he choose Exile? Albeit unspoken, we both know our best chance of getting back into the great hall of city models is to stay on good terms with Vienna Darcton.

Ethan and I are screened at the Headquarters door and then separated. I'm taken to a small room where two armed female guards watch over my "care" given by my regular doctor and nurse. They give me a full physical with more shots. I still hate the needles, but since I seem to encounter them nightly, I'm used to the pain. Once the shots and medications are done with, the doctor gives me another full abdominal ultrasound. Are they going to take more eggs so soon, I wonder? I don't ask.

Following my medical checkup, I get moved to a giant dressing room where my escorts ask me to dress in a shimmering gold gown in preparation for my Cleave ceremony. I guess the Ten's wasting no time Cleaving me off now that the decision's been made as to who. Although I'm hardly ready to be Cleaved to anyone and what that entails, I'm ambivalent about the ceremony itself.

I put on the gown. I'd swear it is spun of real gold. Diamond-like gems cover the tight bodice. The skirt's full and imitates flowers and leaves delicately laced together. It fits me perfectly, as though a master craftsman had created it just for me. I feel like a princess about to be crowned queen. Queen in an evil regime, that is.

A kind older lady joins me to do my makeup and hair. When finished I look like the royalty the Therans claim I am, jeweled gold tiara and all. I stare at myself in the mirror. Despite being masked with beauty, this isn't at all how I'd imagined my wedding day as a child. I'm without family or friends. Didn't get to pick my gown, nor is it white to reflect my virtue. The identity of my groom's a secret. There will be no fancy reception.

Forget expectations. Forget what the Ten think they'll be dictating for me tonight. The gown is gorgeous and well beyond anything I'd be able to afford. My Cleave will be my family—with my enthusiasm for that being either real or faked, depending on who they pick. And I don't need a big reception. I can do this. I signal that I'm ready to proceed. I put on my happy face. No one will know the truth. Everyone will think that it's the happiest night of my life.

The guards lead me through a series of passageways and tunnels. Blake told me that Cleaving ceremonies were held in the atrium of Headquarters, but given the massacre that happened there and the destroyed glass mosaic, they must have moved the location.

"Please wait here for your escort," one of the guards says. I nod. We're at a large carved wooden doorway, an anomaly on Thera given the lack of trees. It's stunning, with each of a dozen panels displaying a hand-etched garden scene. After marveling at the craftsmanship on the door, I shift nervously as I await my Cleaving and then I start to pace. What did Blake decide and who did the Ten pick?

I care about both Blake and Ethan. They're both gorgeous, smart and love me. I'm attracted to both.

Considering I will spend a lifetime with my Cleave, I start to ask myself a series of questions. Who will be more honest? The better father? Be more reliable? More fun? Make me laugh? Who'll be more stable? Exciting? Put me first? Us first? Family first? Who'll make me smile when times get tough, which they are bound to? Who will still give me butterflies when we're both old and wrinkly? Which one can look past my flaws? Which one's flaws can I look past? Who'll know what I need and when I need it even before I do? Who has the most substance? Who will I have the most to talk to about? Who's his own man and not a puppet to those around him? Who do I love most? Because, I realize, I do love them both. Unquestionably.

I see Vienna Darcton round the corner to join me.

"You look beautiful, my dear," she says. "You *will* be pleased with both your Cleave and your Cleaving ceremony. I've brought the perfect escort to bring you in. It'll just be another moment." I bite my lip, hoping she's right and disturbed that she just commanded me to be pleased with her selection. The sinking feeling grows. Everything else has gone wrong, so I expect this to as well. In my panic, I can't as much as mutter a reply. Vienna disappears through the door without allowing me so much as a peek inside.

The tears freely flow as my "escort" arrives. He looks confused as to why I'd be crying, but I can't help it. The security guard gives him instructions as to how to walk me into the room.

"Well, pretty lady," my father says, looking healthy, happy and quite alive in a dashing suit with a gold vest. "I guess I'm the lucky guy that gets to take you to meet your Cleave."

"Thank you. I'd like that so much," I say as I wipe my tears. I can't believe Vienna Darcton brought my father here for me. His presence calms my nerves, despite opening a previous wound I'd prefer not remember. Who am I kidding? Remembering what happened to my family at my hands was bound to happen on this night. I slough off the guilt, knowing I must press forward, plastering back on a smile, just as my mother taught me to do.

The security guard opens the door and we're flooded with light as we enter the most spectacular football stadium-sized garden I've ever seen, one I imagine to be like my ancestors enjoyed, and what I assume the artisans portrayed in the Headquarter's atrium mosaic and on the garden doors. Even though it's the middle of the night, the light looks as natural as sunlight, the ceiling like daytime sky—sunny with a smattering of clouds. Chairs have been set up on a central lawn and my schoolmates and my children's surrogate parents are all seated, including my own brother and his Cleave, Leila, and my mother who looks more alive on Thera than she did on Earth. The only thing detracting from perfection is the armed security detail circling the garden.

My father and I walk along sparkling gold stones towards an altar built of stone and I take in the scenery of majestic trees and fragrant flowers of every variety. No groom awaits me, but I see Vienna Darcton motioning someone to come down another path to join us. When I see who it is, I have the epiphany I've been waiting for. I do love both Ethan and Blake—as much as I really know either of them—but I'm not ready to Cleave either of them. Blake's and my relationship has been mired with lies, deceit, and plans beyond our control. Ethan and I have never even had the opportunity to have a real relationship. It looks, however, like I'm going to have that chance.

Ethan's the one walking towards me. The Ten chose him to be my Cleave and if I'm going to be forced into a relationship I'm not ready for, I can't say I'm disappointed.

Ethan's devoted, ready to settle down, and wants to have a long and happy life with me. I've been attracted to him from the moment I met him and still get butterflies when he's near and shockwaves when he touches me. He caters to my every whim and will listen to me talk for hours. We have fun and he makes me laugh. I feel at home when I'm in his arms.

Ethan's positive characteristics don't erase my concerns or give me the illusion that it'll be a "happily ever after" without any work. Ethan's never really opened up. I've asked him on multiple occasions to tell me about his childhood, but he has avoided the subject and makes me wonder what's he hiding. I don't know what makes him tick, what he likes or cares about, or what motivates him. Other than me.

An example—Ethan lived with his Uncle Henry when he moved to Earth. Uncle Henry's been his "mentor." But, Uncle Henry is Senator Henry King, presidential frontrunner. Not only did Ethan never mention this, but I have no idea what Ethan thinks about being forced into politics. Between his parents' and uncle's influence, I don't know whether Ethan's been brainwashed to the point of no return. I'll never be able to fully trust him until he shares his deepest, darkest secrets and thoughts with me.

My biggest fear with regards to Ethan is that he's like the most glorious shell in the sea, but when I look inside the shell is hollow. Or perhaps worse, that his shell is filled with a standard-issue, Ten-approved, Original-blooded clone of the SCI ideal for a human being.

To have the kind of love where I want to be intimate—to give my Cleave everything I have to offer? I need him to bare his heart and soul. Maybe given time we can get there. But I know the Cleaving rules and time's not something we're allowed. I dated Tristan for a full year and never slept with him. So consummating the whole Cleaving thing? Too much, too soon.

I'm not sure I'll ever completely get over Blake. He's made a lot of mistakes. Lied to me. Deceived me. Kept things from me. I realize it's all been to either protect me or to further the Exiler's cause. He cares infinitely more about others than he does about himself and I find that amazing. Blake's exactly what he represents himself to be, flaws and all.

Bottom line—for my sanity, I need to give Ethan my heart and trust that the rest will work out. But, I'm also going to continue to try to figure out a way to take down the SCI, even without Blake's help. Fact is, Blake exercised his choice and he didn't choose me. He chose to leave. He didn't trust me to help him get the job done. So, while he's off with the Exilers, far away from the mega-portal, I'll be here, working on a plan from the inside.

Ethan and I arrive at the altar at the same time and embrace.

"I love you, Kira Donovan," he says, stroking my face and pushing a ringlet aside. "You are, and have been since the moment we met, the only girl for me." He looks incredible dressed in a gold suit with diamond-studded tie to match my bodice.

"And I love you, Ethan Darcton," I say. Joy washes over his face as he hears me tell him I love him. With that one simple statement I've lifted his burdens and worry.

We hurriedly sign the paperwork and then Vienna Darcton announces us as the Mother and Father of New Thera. And then we kiss to loud applause and in that moment, I feel at peace.

We celebrate for hours in the garden and the more time I spend here, the more magical it feels. The garden itself covers twenty acres, per Vienna, and is irrigated by an underground spring that has thousands of tributaries to this garden area, acting as a naturally occurring drip system. I'm astounded by the variety of species of plants and flowers, over twenty thousand, all unique to Thera, in every color of the rainbow. Even the grass area is naturally occurring and has more than a hundred types of grass creating an optical illusion of an image I can't figure out close up and with so many people on it. The fragrance is sweeter and more divine than anything I've ever smelled before.

Ethan steals many moments with me in various secluded spots of the garden. For the first time with him, I don't hold back and I feel longing and desire I never knew I had. I wish I could build a hut on the grass area and live here forever, raising a whole host of children that I birth myself. This place could make me forget about the Ten, the Grand Council, the desert canyons, and cruel undertone of Thera.

I do enjoy the party. Vienna provides a delicious banquet for the guests full of Theran delicacies, my favorite of which is the marinated quellfish, a tube-shaped shellfish caught off shore that tastes like lobster with the texture of a scallop. Some of the girls are having problems with evening sickness so don't partake, but it is still fabulous to spend the time with my friends and family, even those who don't remember me. Tristan and Briella avoid me for a chunk of the time, but finally come to offer their congratulations, perhaps since Ethan left to get us something to drink.

"You got a way cooler Cleaving ceremony than we did," Tristan says. Still competing. "That is a stunning dress."

"We're very happy for you is what Tristan means to say," Briella pipes in. "But I'm a little confused. Where's Blake? How'd you end up Cleaved to Ethan?"

"Blake's gone," I say, trying not to let my voice crack over it. "And Ethan's great. I love him. It's all good."

"Where'd Blake go?" Tristan asks. "And why doesn't anyone ever say goodbye when they leave?"

"He left the city," I say. "And I'm sorry he didn't say goodbye. He must not have had the chance." I didn't get a goodbye either, I think, so once he made his decision, they probably didn't give him that option. Or they did and he chose not to take it and have to explain himself. I just can't talk about Blake any more on my Cleaving day. It's still too fresh and raw.

"Speaking of leaving the city," Vienna Darcton says, inserting herself into our conversation. "I have an important announcement to make. Everyone gather around." She's wired with a microphone and starts to speak.

"Thanks to everyone for joining us on this momentous occasion where we've witnessed the Cleaving of two pure blooded descendants of the Originals. As in the beginning, Dark and Light have been reunited in the same sacred garden at the very altar their ancestors Cleaved," she says, letting the tidbit soak in. A great fable, but I'm not buying that the garden has been here for thousands of years. Given the extreme weather on Thera, how'd they keep the garden alive before they had the technology available to preserve it? How can they prove that the altar was the same one used by the Originals, assuming the Originals even existed as the story was passed down?

"You young Cleaved couples are lucky in that you're carrying Original seed in you, and like any seed, room must be given to grow and flourish. The Original seed must be spread forth across Theran soil. Each couple will henceforth be transferred to another glorious Theran city this night. I compel you to raise these children with great care to be Thera's future leaders. You'll be escorted directly from here to your ships. I wish you great speed and health on your journeys. Please say your farewells and then proceed to the far door where you'll check in and be assigned an escort."

Now that gets a reaction from the crowd as the news takes hold. They're all leaving and being dispersed to different Theran cities, cities they probably didn't even know existed. They line up to say their farewells to me and each other, and promise they'll raise my children well. Ethan holds me upright as I watch my unborn children slip away.

The hardest partings are with Briella and Tristan, who once again hold no memories of our collective past, and with my brother and Leila. I make promises I'll likely never be able to keep about seeing them again.

"It's all good, big sis," Jared says to me in my ear as he hugs me tight.

"Yeah, it's all good," I respond.

The teary farewells behind us, everyone dispersed to the far ends of Thera, Ethan and I return to his home in bright sunlight. Some rather risqué lingerie has been laid out for me on the bed, I'm sure to encourage us to consummate our Cleaving as quickly as possible. How'd this happen again? I'm not even eighteen and I'm Cleaved to a guy I love, but who'll have to leave for his third year of law school shortly after we consummate the deal. I'm terrified.

"We should wait to do this," Ethan says to me, reading my mind. "In fact, my mother insists. She waived the decree for immediate consummation. Our Cleave will stand whether we do or not. She thought we… or you… might need some time to digest everything that's happened and be ready." Maybe my Cleave-in-law's not as bad as I thought. I try not to let my relief be too apparent.

"You'd do that for me?" I ask. My heart's racing. "I love you, Ethan. I really do. But, we haven't even had a chance to date for real… there's so much I still don't know about you. I want to know everything."

"I'd do anything for you; give you anything in my power, so this is nothing," he says, kissing me gently on the lips. He picks up the lingerie and adds with a smirk, "It's not that I don't want this someday. I want you, Kira. But, when we do consummate our Cleave I want you to want it every bit as much as I do."

I nod and ask, "Are you still leaving? For law school?"

"Yes," he says, wrapping his arms around me and burying his head in my neck.

"Can I come?" I ask.

"Unfortunately not. My mother says you have training to complete here on Thera before we can be together on Earth. It's going to kill me to be away from you. I hope you know how much I love you," he says, lifting his head up and reminding me how I'd become smitten early on by his blue eyes and dark lashes. "I'll visit as often as I can."

"How can you leave? I wish you could just defer your last year of law school," I say.

"I wish I could, too," he says. He bites the corner of his lip and looks at me through his curly mess of eyelashes. "Were you disappointed? That it was me and not Blake?" The mention of Blake's name is like a razor to my wrists, which shows on my face.

"I feel terrible about Blake, but no, I am happy it was you. It's still hard though," I say, tears filling my eyes. I don't want to hurt him.

Ethan invites me to lie down next to him on the bed. I melt into his embrace and enjoy his tender kisses and comfort until he falls asleep. For hours, I lay awake, stroking his hair, trying to wrap my head around all the events that have transpired since I agreed to take the SCI Test.

After being left to ourselves for less than twelve hours, we're both escorted, again by armed security detail, to the main city lab. Our doctor greets us and ushers us into a procedure room. Once I'm undressed and in a medical gown, the armed guards join us.

"What's going on?" Ethan asks.

"Now that the two of you are Cleaved, it's time for our Mother and Father of Thera to become literal parents," the doctor says.

"Are you kidding me? We've only been Cleaved a night," Ethan says. The guards draw their weapons, release the safeties and point them at us. That doesn't stop Ethan from continuing his protest. "Why do you feel it necessary to do this by gunpoint? Lab rape's become the norm? Where's my mother? Does she know about this?" Maybe he does have a backbone after all?

"Yes, in fact she ordered it," the doctor says. "Now, the procedure is quite simple and should only take a few minutes." I bite my lip and hold back the tears.

Ethan's not taking the news so well. His protest is making the armed guards more anxious and angry. They push him back onto his chair. One of the men holds his arms and puts him in cuffs while the other puts a gun to his head.

"It's okay, Ethan," I say to him before addressing the doctor. "Please just tell me that it's my own child I'll be carrying."

"Yes," the doctor says. I settle back on the exam table and let the doctor do his bidding. Lab rape indeed. I'll be an eighteen-year-old mother just like my friends. And my Cleave won't even be there to help me with my pregnancy. While he has his head in law reviews, I'll be puking my guts out and getting as fat as an elephant. He probably won't even want me by the time he returns from law school.

When it's all over, the doctor addresses us. "Excellent. That went smoothly, so the embryos should take."

"Embryos?" Ethan and I ask in unison. "There are more than one?"

"There's only about a ninety percent chance they'll both take, but there were two set aside for you," the doctor explains.

"Who's the father?" I ask. "You created embryos using both Ethan and Blake as fathers in that lab of yours."

"I believe there is one from each father," the doctor says. "That's what we'd been requested to implant. You know, in case Ethan's offspring has uh, medical difficulties."

Forget waiting until the pregnancy takes, I lean over the table and puke on the doctor's shoes. He deserves it. If my Cleave-in-law were here, I'd puke on hers as well. The consolation of their perverted act is that I'll be carrying pieces of both the men I love for the next nine months.

Muffled voices awaken me. I freshen up in the bathroom to try to alleviate my puffy eyes. I'd cried myself to sleep. Who's here, I wonder? I slip out of the bedroom, still in my daygown, and towards the hushed conversation happening in the kitchen. Once I hear who is speaking, I delay my entrance.

"Your Uncle Henry wants to see you at Headquarters. Immediately," Vienna says.

"I don't want to leave Kira. She's upset. I'm upset." Ethan says to his mother, "You had no right to impregnate her, much less with babies from two different fathers."

"I have the right to do as I see fit for Thera's future. And, I determined that both brothers deserve to have their progeny born by the Mother of Thera. As the grandmother to these babies, I see it as only fair. Besides, would you deprive Kira children if you're not able to have… healthy children?" she says.

"Do you even know my condition will create unhealthy children? Why do you continue to punish me for something I have zero control over? After all, if my condition is genetic, then blame yourself or my father, not me!" he says. This, I agree with him on. His parent's—and the SCI's—obsession with genetically perfect Original children is Hitler-esque in nature.

"Regardless, we need to ensure that Kira is able to have healthy children," she says.

"Why not let someone else mother and raise Blake's child?" Ethan asks. "Why does Kira have to give birth to *his* baby?" Men. Of course that's what is bothering Ethan at this point. Not that the doctors implanted the babies against my will, but that I'm carrying Blake's child.

"I think you're worrying over nothing. You got the girl, so be happy and deal with it," Vienna says. "It will all work out."

"A line was crossed, Mother. And I won't soon forget or forgive."

Ugh. I decide I'm in no mood for Cleave-in-law time. I quietly return to the bedroom and climb under the covers. The reminder that I've got two embryos implanted in me gets the tears flowing. A few minutes later, Ethan comes in to let me know he needs to run over to Headquarters and will be back soon. He's in shorts and a tank... he must have been planning a workout when his demented mother arrived.

"What's wrong?" he asks upon seeing my tear-stained face.

"Can we talk when you get back?" I say. I need to ask him all the questions swirling through my mind. After the Cleaving, I feel much closer to Ethan, but there's still so much I need to know.

"Oh, Kira. I have to go, but I'll be back as quickly as possible. I love you. We'll work through all of this. I promise," he says. "Trust me."

Ethan leans in and kisses away my tears and then trails his lips to mine. He parts my lips with his tongue and gently, but passionately makes me forget what I was so stressed about. I pull him atop me and return his kisses with enthusiasm. I peel his shirt off so that I can rub his muscular chest and abdomen. We're both on fire and I realize that I want to consummate our Cleaving. I want to be fully his. To indicate I'm ready, I pull off my daygown. His eyes go dark with desire.

"Are you sure?" he asks.

"Yes," I say. "I don't want to wait another minute."

And then a knock at the bedroom door with "Ethan, honey, Uncle Henry is waiting. And, Kira, I made you breakfast," throws a big bucket-o-ice-water on our moment. I scramble to find clothes as Ethan does the same, as I wouldn't put it past that woman to barge in on us.

"I'm so sorry, Kira. I thought she'd left," he says. "You... are amazing. I'll be back soon."

One more passionate kiss, fully clothed, and he's out the door. After breakfast, my Cleave-in-Law sticks around to do dishes and make small talk. About a half hour in, she drops a huge bomb on me.

"Ethan's not coming back," she says. "He doesn't know it yet, but he's returning to school earlier than expected."

"What?" I say, throwing the dishrag on the counter and turning to look at her. "Why?" I need to talk to him and take care of other unfinished business.

"I wanted to make sure you didn't finalize your Cleaving. I don't trust that you could spend twenty-four hours a night for four nights together without doing so," she says. She's right about that. "As Ethan told you, I waived the decree that you had to consummate your Cleaving within twenty-four hours. But, what he doesn't realize is why I did that."

"I'd appreciate it if you told *me* why," I say. I feel a huge lump in my throat. I doubt I'll like her twisted rationale.

"Let's just say that I, as Senior Ten, would prefer to wait until the babies are born before rubber-stamping your Cleaving as a *permanent* thing. If Ethan is unable to father healthy babies, I want the option to revoke the Cleaving, and reassign you to Blake. Because Blake will return, Kira, to take his rightful place as the heir of Thera, whether he realizes it yet or not." *Reassign me?* Like switching Cleaves is no different that changing jobs. Blake would never agree to her terms in a billion years.

I'm flabbergasted at the gall of this woman. There's no end to her evil designs. If I give birth to a defective child my Cleave-in-Law will toss Ethan aside and re-Cleave me to Blake. I have my poker face on. She, of all people, can never know that I hate her with every fiber of my being. I want her to be surprised when, despite Blake being gone, that I find out a way to cripple the SCI's mega-portal myself.

"How could you do that to your own son?" I ask.

"They are both my sons. And you will be thrilled to know that both have seats on the Ten. Henry is discussing this with Ethan right now. Of course, with Ethan at law school and Blake sowing his wild oats in Exile, I'll manage their votes for now. But both will rise to their destiny," she says with a look of satisfaction at her triumph that make me want to take a kitchen cleaver to her. Members of the Ten?

"Neither of them would *ever* agree to that," I say with indignation.

"I'd think you'd be surprised at what people will do when the opportunity for power is dangled in front of them. How well do you really know either of them, Kira? How do you know Ethan hasn't wanted this all along? Or that Blake won't see the opportunity to change the fate of the Exilers and Second Chancers with a seat on the Ten? How much do you know at all about the true purposes behind what the SCI does?" Vienna says as she runs her fingers across the kitchen knives, just daring me to try to get past her for one.

"That's ridiculous. They're not like you," I say, but this time without any oomph behind it. She's right. Depending on how it's presented to them, either one could jump at the opportunity and get sucked right into the institution that stands for everything I despise. But maybe they could get me access to the mega-portal? Gah. Now even I'm getting lured. I mentally slap myself.

"We'll see, won't we? And, Kira, you're not to mention this conversation to Ethan. Ever. Or he dies. Is that clear enough for you? And if that's not enough motivation, please don't forget your other loved ones who are still here on Thera," she says. She'd so easily ignore our previous agreement and would have her own sons killed. Any redeeming value I thought this woman had just disappeared.

This is one time I wish that I'd been raised to know a God. Don't people with faith get through hard things easier? I mean, they can pray or whatever and isn't that supposed to give them some sort of peace? Oh well. Won't do me any good here on this God-forsaken planet, where we're all forbidden to speak to or about God anyway.

"Will I get to see Ethan at all? Or is he simply gone for the next nine months —my entire pregnancy?" I ask. "You didn't let me say goodbye. We had so much to discuss." And do. I think back to how close we came to consummating our Cleave and a jolt of desire hits me hard. Nine months suddenly seems like an eternity.

"I think that if we can come to an understanding about this matter, we'll allow some limited visitation. The terms are simple. One, keep your mouth shut. Two, under no circumstances can you consummate the Cleave before you have my approval. Got it?" she says. Another easy choice. I follow the rules and Ethan, Blake, my parents and brother live.

"I understand and I agree to your terms. So, in the meantime, what do I do? Will I be trained in the 'family business' and as a Daynighter, as promised, or is that on hold, too? Or perhaps you'd like me to sit around and get fat?" I ask.

"At least for the immediate future, you'll be able to proceed with your studies while your pregnancy is monitored. I've arranged for some excellent care… outside Garden City," she says. Like I need a reminder about the pregnancy. I'm in denial and just waiting for some time to myself to have a complete mental breakdown over my situation.

"What?" I say, as I start to hyperventilate a little. If I leave Garden City it will be pretty difficult to figure out a way to take out the mega-portal.

"Yes. We'll leave here shortly to go to the port so that I can drop you off," Vienna says.

"Where am I going?" I ask. "Why would you send me away?"

"It's for your safety, my dear. There's reports of some renewed activity with the Exilers outside Garden City. A few of the Militants escaped and are hoping to convince the other Exilers to join their cause," she says, reaching out to grasp my arm. "You'll be in good hands. I promise. I don't want to take any risks with your life, or those lives you are carrying. You and your children are a target for these people, Kira. They think that if they're able to get to you that they can cause the Theran government harm."

"You think the Exilers would try to kill me?" I ask. "I don't believe that." Not if Blake is with them now. Plus, even if a few Militants escaped, there are over ten thousand decent Exilers who will never join the Militants' cause after hearing from Blake what happened.

"If they get desperate, yes, they could try to kill you. Or kidnap you. Or torture you. Who knows what they are capable of," she says. She's exaggerating to rationalize her actions, but I pretend to be fearful for my own life. I know that Vienna really wants me out of Garden City so that Blake—and Ethan— won't know where I am. That thought does scare me, far more than any threat from a few Militant Exilers.

I follow Vienna's instructions to freshen up and back up my tablet to the central servers. Then, I say goodbye to Ethan's home, a home we shared all of two nights. We take the train to the port, escorted by several armed security detail. The process to get through security takes a good hour, as I'm questioned, fingerprinted, have blood taken, and wait around while they "transfer my files" to my new jurisdiction. I wish I'd eaten a bigger breakfast. It's not like they have vending machines or fast food restaurants here to give me a quick fix. Finally, they let me out of the small, dark interrogation room and Vienna walks me to a large hydrofoil docked at SLOT 5. It looks sleek and modern. I wonder where it was built. It would be so much faster to just take me to the mega-portal, I think, but I'm going to keep that secret to myself.

"I do have some good news for you. There will be some familiar faces on board," Vienna says with a smile. "It's always good to have family with you during a difficult time."

"Family?" I say. "Who?" What distant relatives of hers will she dispatch to keep me in line this time? It's bad enough that my Cleave may be nothing more than a plant.

"You'll join your mother, father, brother and his Cleave for a while. Plus, you'll have your own personal instructor and bodyguard—Jackson Christo. And, as we discussed, Ethan will visit as he is able," she says. I get to be with my family? That's way better news than I'd expected.

"Thank you," I say with enthusiasm and thankfulness. Although I am thankful, and despite her seeming sweet act, I know that she's all evil and always scheming.

"You're welcome," she says. "Ah here he is. Meet Jackson. He will be with you at all times."

"Call me Jax. Pleased to finally meet you, Ms. Darcton," he says with a grin, using my Cleaved name. I grimace a bit as he gives audible confirmation that I have the same last name as my deranged Cleave-in-Law.

As Jax takes me in, I return the favor. His outfit catches my eye first, which hardly seems standard Theran fare. He's fully dressed in glistening white. Pressed white dress shirt, white slacks, belt and loafers. Jax looks to be Ethan's age, has disheveled light blonde hair and what I can only describe as light gold eyes ringed with blue. Equally unique and stunning as Ethan and Blake's eyes, and something I've come to expect on Thera. Jax's skin tone seems unusually golden for the Theran climate, though. Looks like a Nordic god with dimples.

Jax puts a hand on my shoulder and whispers in my ear, "Vienna thinks she has me in her pocket, but I assure you that her pocket has a rather large hole. Trust our interests align and we'll get along famously." I smile widely, liking Jax already. Everything about his demeanor calms me.

"Jax, no flirting with Ethan's Cleave," Vienna admonishes.

"Relax. Ethan and I are the best of friends. More like brothers," Jax says. "You *hardly* have to worry about me. I would *never* disrespect a consummated Cleave." He turns and winks at me. One of Ethan's best friends? Perhaps Jax can fill me in on everything Ethan has failed to.

Vienna looks furious, but shakes her head and returns her attention to me. "If he becomes a problem, let me know immediately. He's rather annoying, but uniquely situated to train and protect you. You can contact me using your new tablet with any issues. It has extra security and requires your fingerprint to access." She hands me the device and I press my index finger as instructed. Vienna continues, "All your data was transferred. I also added a new folder that I think you'll particularly appreciate."

I open a folder marked "Personal" to find pictures of Ethan and Blake. I flip through and can't hold back the tears. Her gesture was not one of kindness. There are pictures of me with each. Pictures of Blake in Headquarters when he's not supposed to be there. Pictures of Ethan watching me from afar. Pictures of my Cleaving ceremony. Pictures of Blake in Exile, donned in orange, which make my heart go crazy. At least I have proof that he left the city alive. That's heartening. Vienna, however, has no heart.

It's clear that Vienna wants me to remember every bit of my love triangle and know that the SCI will always be watching, listening, and controlling. I continue to scroll through and I come across something that gets my blood boiling. A picture of Blake and Bailey Goodington kissing while in party attire. They're in a bathroom with the door closed. You have got to be kidding me. I remember that Bri told me Bailey was all over Blake at the pre-mass Cleaving party, but she or he never mentioned Blake didn't seem to mind her advances. At all. He threw a temper tantrum over my friendship with Ethan when he so readily gave into Bailey? I'm clearly a magnet for lying, cheating losers.

"That's my personal favorite. While you were away and pretending to be Ethan's girlfriend back home, Blake managed to find company of his own. And now that he's *chosen* Exile, he very well may run into her again," Vienna brags. My stomach flip-flops, but I hold a neutral expression.

"So, where am I headed? Which of the cities?" Without understanding the government structure of each, it would be hard for me to pick, but there are definitely cities I saw in scale versions that would be fascinating to visit. Hopefully, my travels will be interesting. It's crucial for my sanity that I find one bright spot in this. Other than being with my family, which will help immensely. I look to Jax, but he just shrugs.

Vienna says, "I think I'll leave that as a surprise for now. Only the ship's pilot and a handful of crew know, for security purposes. I wouldn't want your location getting passed along to the Exilers."

"Okay. Then, how long will it take to get there?" I ask. Can't I know anything?

"Don't worry, Kira. You'll have suitable accommodations on board and the crew will provide you with everything needed," she says, before giving me a kiss on my cheek. I smile and put my hand on her arm. I can pretend to be kind, too.

Of course the SCI will provide "everything needed." They always do. Everything except a certain and stable future.

Vienna turns to leave and I'm left standing with Jax. He nudges me. "Well, m'lady. Are you ready for an adventure?" He leans in to my ear and whispers, "After all we have things to learn, plans to make, governments to overthrow, and lands to conquer. You with me?"

He offers me the crux of his arm and I insert my own arm. "I do believe I am." Then silently, we walk together up the gangway to the ship.

CHAPTER TWENTY-NINE

Blake

She wants my answer. Now. Vienna Darcton is nervously shifting her weight between her two feet as she awaits my decision.

I stand up to face her. "I'm sorry. I have to choose Exile. Although I've gained a much better understanding of the SCI and why they do what they do, I still can't be a part of it." And now that I have what I need to take you down, I'm going to go convince Doc Daryn and the Survivalists that there may be a way to victory over the SCI without violence. Kira and I can't pull it off alone.

"You're sure of your decision? This means Kira will Cleave to Ethan immediately," she says. I wince at the vision of the consummation that pops into my head, but even if I stayed I'm positive the end result would be the same. At least he loves Kira and will keep her safe.

"Yes. I'm sure," I say.

"Very well. Curtis will take you outside the city," she says, motioning to her security guard. I see that he has orange clothing and a backpack prepared for me. "It was nice to have been given a chance to get to know you. I wish you well. Remember to be cautious in your actions. And if ever you change your mind, find Ethan and he can bring you back. Goodbye, Blake." And how do I find Ethan? I guess, reading between the lines, that she is suggesting I use the Exiler-controlled exit portal to return to Earth and find him at law school, which is where he'll shortly be. I'll take her up on that advice. As soon as I have a plan in place and am ready to return.

"I will. Goodbye, Mother," I say. Without as much as a hug, she turns and walks away. I guess it would be too much to allow me to say goodbye to Kira. Then again, how would I explain that I chose to take the information she gave me and bolt, leaving her to Cleave to Ethan?

I'm led out of the solar panels and to a path where two mules packed with supplies await us. I change into my orange attire and put on the backpack. The backpack is at least three times the size of the one they gave Ted and feels like it weighs about a hundred pounds. Curtis blindfolds me, helps me up on one of the mules, and then takes me on what I can tell to be a windy, downward path. Although I have no ability to sense exactly how much time has passed, I'd guess about a half hour, the last ten of which the wind stopped and the environs smelled musty. I realize once my blindfold is removed that we passed over the Eco barrier and nothing happened. They must have deactivated the section we crossed. Why'd it smell so bad?

"The Exiler camp is due north two miles," Curtis says, handing me the reins to the second mule. "You only have a couple hours before sunup, so make haste. And, good luck." He hands me a head lantern and compass, and then turns to leave.

"What about the mules?" I ask.

"What mules?" he says with a grin, before heading back towards the city by foot. My mother's direction to Curtis, I'm sure. She wants me as far away from the city as quickly as possible. Perhaps she does believe my life is in danger. As I watch him approach the Eco barrier I see a ten foot section of ground open. Curtis enters without looking back and I see his head disappear. We traveled under the barrier. That explains the musty smell and lack of wind. The section of barrier closes over him, immediately blending with the surrounding barrier, no seams visible. Amazing. All that work trying to find a way across and the SCI had a way under. They've never had to turn off the barrier to Exile folks or send out security details. I stack some rocks ten yards out to give myself a visual clue as to the location, in case I ever need to find it again.

Time to leave. I have to rack my memories for clues as to the exact route, difficult considering the monotony of the vegetation. Thank goodness for the head lantern and compass. Ten minutes into my journey I hear some moaning and wailing. I follow the sounds until I find Ted Rosenberg curled up into a ball by a Theranberry bush. It looks like Nathaniel didn't give him mules, a head lantern or compass. As much as I'm tempted to leave him there, I don't want his death on my hands.

"Want a ride?" I say, jumping off my mule.

"Blake?" he says, looking up. "Is that you? Please help me." I don't trust him to not steal my supplies and the mules, so I gag him and tie his hands and feet. Then I drape him over my second mule. It won't be a comfortable ride for him, but it's better than dying an ignominious death in the canyons. I feel bad about gagging him, but don't want to listen to his complaints and rationalizations the whole way. I'm in need of peace and solitude to do some thinking.

With luck, I find the Exiler camp as the sun rises. What I find looks nothing like I remember. There are many times more people living in the canyon than when I lived here. Doc appears to be organizing everyone into teams.

"What's going on, Doc?" I ask.

Without fully turning around he says, "We're leaving—at nightfall. There's been a security detail in the area. It's only a matter of time before they come for us. The Militants stole most of our weapons stash, so we're unprepared to properly protect ourselves." Then, finally realizing who I am he adds, "What are *you* doing here, Blake?"

"Shouldn't that be obvious from my bright orange attire?" I say, turning around to show off my jumpsuit. "I'm the newest Garden City Exile. I missed your nasty grain slop so much that I got myself booted."

"Who is that?" he says, pointing to Ted. "What did you do? Highjack a transport team?"

"Nope. I picked up this loser on the way. He was Exiled immediately before me. Doc, meet Ted Rosenberg. He's the guy that betrayed my father and the Militants, and got them all killed," I say. Ted's writhing atop the mule, obviously disturbed that I mentioned his shortcomings.

"Ah yes, I've heard so much about you," Doc says, motioning for one of his men to help Ted off the mule. To his man Doc says, "Dave, take our guest into the cave and get him fed. I'll be there in a moment to have a word with him." Dave, a burly guy who's at least seven feet tall hefts Ted over his shoulder, still gagged and bound, and they disappear into the mouth of the cave.

Doc turns again to me. "So, how'd you get the mules? In all my years, I've never seen an Exiler show up well-stocked before."

"Long story. Let's just say I have a fairy gadsmother in the city," I say. "Shall we see what she gave us?" I open my backpack and the boxes packed on the mules to find food, water, and medicine. And a note from my mother.

"Dear Blake,

I knew there was a very good chance you'd choose Exile over a life in Garden City with no guarantee of Kira by your side. Although I disagree with your choice, you are my son and I have no desire for you to die. I asked Curtis to send you off with supplies that a royal son would deserve and have had a security detail stock a cave nearby the Exiler camp, which should last long enough for you to reconsider your decision.

Fondly,

Vienna"

"I don't think you need to worry about that security detail," I say, handing him the note. "It looks like they were just delivering some supplies for us.

Perhaps we should stay put for a while. We have much to discuss." He lifts his glasses, attached by a chain around his neck, to the bridge of his nose, and reads Vienna Darcton's note.

Upon finishing, he hands the note back to me. "I agree. We do have much to discuss. Why is this woman claiming to be your mother and why would SCI security give us food and medicine? Did you negotiate an agreement with them?"

"Sorry, no. I wasn't really in a position of negotiation before I left." I give him the cliff notes version of what happened since I last saw him, including the story behind Vienna Darcton being my biological mother. Doc's thrilled that I have an "in" with the Ten for peace talks. He's hopeful that he can use Ted to get as much information about the inner workings of the SCI as possible.

I refrain from sharing the information Kira gave me with Doc, for now. Any plan that doesn't involve diplomacy will take a better sales pitch than I've had time to put together. We may want to use the excuse to hold talks with the SCI as a reason to return to the city, while secretly being well prepared to cripple the Theran "transportation" system. Doc excuses himself to go in and talk to Ted. I sit at the edge of the canyon and watch the sun rise over the horizon.

I hope I made the right choice in choosing Exile. In retrospect my decision was pretty rash. I'd been given the opportunity to become an SCI insider. I could have advocated for the Exilers and potentially had access to the city models and portal system. But, the Ten and Council would be watching my every move, expecting me to screw up. And besides, I'm not good at putting on a fake happy face. I'd fail at mock obeisance to Vienna and then I'd just give the Ten further fuel to target me.

As much as I don't want to think about Kira and leaving her behind, I can't help it. She's likely Cleaved to Ethan by now. Picturing them together, consummating their Cleaving, isn't healthy, I decide. I shake my head. My choice is made and I have to live with the consequences. I could have decided differently.

Doc Daryn's return interrupts my thoughts. He asks, "Is your mother a good woman? Will she be open to talks with us?" he asks. "I'm not getting a whole lot out of Ted Rosenberg. He thinks we're going to kill him, so is in there bawling." We both chuckle, knowing that the Survivalists would never execute an Exiler.

"Well, my mother is a member of the Ten of the SCI, so on the one hand, no. Not at all. But, she did right by me by giving us supplies, so I have to hope that there are pockets of good—in both my mother and the rest the leaders of the SCI." What I'm really thinking is that evil that's taken root and left to thrive will eventually overtake and eke out all the good. At the risk of sounding like my father, I think some weeding needs to be done in the Garden. But instead of killing the "weeds" I like the idea of a work camp. That would humble the prima donnas. "Do you really think we can find a diplomatic solution to our problems?"

Doc's wrinkles sink deeper as he crunches his face. He runs his fingers through his long white locks and I see strands of brittle hair fall. Exiler life has taken its toll on Doc. "Perhaps. If they see us as an ally, we may be able to have a positive impact on their policies." He's sticking with his spiel.

"I hope you're right," I say.

"Me, too," he says as he walks back into the cave. I'm concerned. If Earth's history is any indication, dictators don't negotiate. If the talks fail, we will have to consider a more drastic approach. Either way, I'm afraid I'm going to have to return to Garden City.

Perhaps while I'm there on business I'll come across a certain girl who I can't quite get off my mind. Unfortunately, a quite different girl sits down next to me. One that reminds me that Karma remains quite displeased with me.

"Welcome to sooner," Bailey says.

"Shoot. I'd been hoping for later," I mumble. "Much, much later."

She leans in to whisper in my ear. "That's too bad. I know your plans. And I can help."

"How can you help me? Or our cause?" I ask.

"Well, Blake Sundry… As it stands, you have a fraction of the Exilers on board, right? What if you had the Second Chancers on board?"

"I tried that and failed," I say.

"What if you had a Second Chancer who, say, remembered *everything*. One that the SCI let slip through their clutches by way of Exile." My head whips around to her so fast, I pinch a muscle in my neck. She's so close to me that my lips brush hers, leaving me with an annoying tingly sensation.

"You remember?" I say. "For how long?"

"I never forgot. They always say you'll never forget your first…," she says. No way. She *does* have all her memories from before. I suspected, but the implications of the truth have my mind whirring with possibilities.

"Do you remember the transition? How you came through?" I ask.

"Every. Last. Bit," she says as she raises her eyebrows. "People, places, processes. The works."

"What's the catch?" I ask. With Bailey, there's got to be a catch.

"We're partners. Very. Close. Partners. Your daddy's not around to keep you away from me, so I'm thinking we start over," she says as she runs her fingers very seductively across my lips.

"After everything you did to me, you want a do-over?" I ask. Unbelievable.

"Yes. Yes I do," she says. "All that ridiculous drama seems worlds away and lifetimes ago." Touché.

I turn away and take a moment to contemplate whether I can make a deal with the Wicked Witch of Exile. Can I resume our relationship? Her knowledge can tip the scales in my favor. And it's not like I'd be cheating on Kira. She's freaking Cleaved to my brother. They're probably rolling around naked right now. Bailey leans in and puts her head on my shoulder. My body betrays me as it does a little happy dance at her touch, apparently not having forgotten our little incident in the bathroom.

She lifts her head back off my shoulder and I turn to her. She's got her bedroom eyes blazing and is staring at my lips like they're the blue ribbon winner of a decadent chocolate buffet. When she licks her lips and opens them just a fraction in anticipation, all reason goes out the canyon. I'll likely add it to my regrets, but what's one more on such a long list. What happens with the Exilers, is going to have to stay with the Exilers.

"Well, ok then, *partner*. Let's do this," I say as I close the distance and crush my lips to hers.

CHAPTER THIRTY

Ethan

A twenty year old in his third year of law school hardly needs his mom to drop him at school and help him settle, but my mother insisted, she purportedly being worried at how I'll take the separation from Kira. The separation that she forced nights ahead of schedule. I didn't even get to say goodbye. I am livid. By the time I got home from my meeting with Uncle Henry, I found a house full of armed security detail and a mother with a mouth full of excuses. She didn't trust that I'd return to fulfill my law school commitments if I'd had that "extra and unnecessary" time with Kira. The farewells would be too hard on both of us. She called me "selfish" and said, "How could you dare consider doing that to your pregnant Cleave?"

Kira. Beautiful, breathtaking, sexy Kira. I miss her already. Who cares about law school when the love of my life is pregnant with my child? She wanted to consummate our Cleave! Settling in at my desk, I start to pen my thoughts to her with plans to send my letter back with my mother. I have to be careful what I write, knowing that if there's censor-inviting material, the whole thing will be tossed. My cell phone still has the picture of Kira that I took the night of the party and many more I took of the two of us together on our "vacation." I stare at the pictures and consider sneaking back to find her. Unfortunately, my mother won't tell me where on Thera she is.

Everyone thinks they own me. Dr. Christo and the Arbiters with their altruistic plans for restoration of original Theran ideals. The SCI wants my help with world domination and Uncle Henry wants me to become an SCI-owned politician. None of their plans interest me. But I stay obedient to stay alive.

My mother still believes that my non-existent heart condition mars my royal family status, much like a CEO with a few felonies on his or her record would be a problem with the board of directors. Perfectly healthy "Original" progeny means everything to the rulers of Thera. In their minds, all native Therans—those who aren't Second Chancers—should be of pure Original blood. Anything less dilutes their potential power on Earth. Of course, my progeny will be presumed hybrids, like me. Will my ARB marker be as much of a risk to those babies as a heart defect would? Dr. Daddy wouldn't tell me.

My thoughts return to my letter. What I want to write—and what I know Kira wants to hear—concerns my childhood, my real parentage and the vows I've made to keep her safe. But I'm forbidden to discuss my childhood because my "parents" repeatedly broke Canon edicts in my upbringing. Amongst other Exile-worthy violations, they had two prominent heart physicians killed on Earth to get them to Thera for my treatment, even though Daddy Christo took over in the end. It wasn't kosher to risk the SCI being implicated in murder charges over a "defective" Original, but my parents felt their actions were above the law. Taking steps to save my life was as close to an act of love as they've ever shown me. But, it wasn't for me, but to enforce the legitimacy of their seats on the Ten. An unspoken requirement for holding a seat on the Ten is pure Original-blooded posterity.

I can't tell Kira about my ARB-fueled blood, either, or I'd put us both at risk. The SCI wouldn't react kindly to knowing I'm a plant and the Arbiters have taken great lengths to keep their secrets from the Council. So, all I can safely discuss for now is how much I love her. How I'd do anything, everything for her. And how she's the one thing that makes my life worth living.

One day, when I know we aren't being followed or listened to, I'll tell Kira everything. Maybe I can convince my ARB-brother, Jax, to "run interference" so that we can freely talk. Kira deserves to know about me, despite how painful it will be to share. I'll start with my childhood. My loneliness. Fear. Monotony. Emotional abuse. Longing for human interaction. Dreams of escape from my prison. I still yearn for escape. My cell may be larger, but the shackles are heavier than ever. I'm an adult, but have no control over my life. And if I can find something to hold over Daddy Christo, I'm going to get approval to tell Kira about the Arbiters and my presumed duty to them.

Kira saved me from the brink of insanity. Despite my parentage she accepted me. She let me live the childhood I never had with her. For the first time in my life I feel hope for a happy future. I can deal with the rest with her at my side. Or perhaps I can do better than deal—perhaps together we can fight the controlling influences that plague us.

How can I ever describe on paper how much I love Kira? Or how much I'll miss her? How I can't stand being away from her while she's pregnant? How can I tell her that I would do anything in the universe to make her happy? I do my best, but nothing will make up for my not being there.

Once my mother has stocked my apartment, cleaned and dusted like the maternal being she's never been, she's finally ready to depart. I give her my letter to Kira, which she promises to have delivered promptly, although I know the odds are less than fifty-fifty Kira will ever see it.

"I think you're all set, Ethan, so I guess I'll be on my way," she says, kissing me on the cheek.

I grit my teeth. There are so many forms of punishment I could inflict upon my mother, but I'd be killed for any of them. I need to see Kira again, so I choose life. "Thanks for the help, Mom. You really didn't have to do any of that. I'm a big boy now," I say with feigned appreciation.

"It's the least I could do after everything you've done for me and for Thera," she says. "Everything's gone according to plan, thanks to your perfect obedience. The Cleaving is done, the babies are brewing, and thanks to those Militant Exilers, the weeds have been extracted from the Ten and the Grand Council. The Exilers have no idea that they only took out the members we left unsecured that night. Equally important, the seed is set for your brother to make his prodigal return. I think I can speak for your Dad when I say that we're so proud of you." Actually, she hardly speaks for my real father. And, I don't know what planet my mom's from that makes her think her plan or things are perfect. Oh wait, actually I do. The one where the insane people rule.

"Yeah, yeah, yeah, Mom. I'll leave the scheming to you and I think I'll just focus on law school and visiting my beautiful Cleave every moment I can," I say. Perfect cooperation. That's what I vowed to keep Kira safe.

"Don't less us down, Ethan. I expect you to focus and do well. Be top of your class. Nothing less is acceptable for what we have planned for you," she says.

"I know, Mother," I say. "But I refuse to do that at the detriment of my Cleaving with Kira."

"Kira will be fine. In fact, I assigned Jax to be her personal bodyguard and instructor," she says. What the hell? I knew Jax would weasel his way into this somehow. I'm going to kill him. My mother smirks and adds, "She'll be perfectly safe and attended to."

That statement has as much double meaning and little credibility as my Uncle Henry's campaign slogan: "Expect MORE from Henry King. MORE Unity. MORE Service. MORE Security. With NO MORE Taxes." He forgot a few: MORE Lies. MORE Rules. MORE Uniformity. With NO MORE Freedom.

Beware, fellow citizens of Earth. The SCI will soon be controlling a country or city near you. And you won't even see it coming.

Author's note

If you enjoyed this book, please leave a review on Amazon.com and/or Goodreads. Reader reviews help spread the word about new authors and books. I appreciate your support!

As a thank you, for every 25 reviews, I'll release either a bonus for *daynight* (such as sketches of Garden City fashions) or teaser for the next book in the *daynight* series, *arbitrate,* on Facebook and Twitter.

Follow me on Twitter at twitter.com/megan_thomason.

Follow the *daynight* series on Facebook at facebook.com/daynight.series.

My personal blog (where you can sign up for notification of new releases in the series) is at meganthomason.com.

I will be releasing *clean slate complex (a daynight novella)* on April 22, 2013 (Earth Day). *clean slate complex* will explore what The Second Chance is up to on Earth (surely nothing good, no matter how outwardly charitable they seem).

I'd love to hear from you! You can email me at megan@meganthomason.com.

Acknowledgments

Cue the happy dance. This day has been a long time coming. I wrote the first draft of *daynight* in 2009. Rewrote it many times. Still not perfect. Tabled it for a couple years while I worked on other things, and then alas, inspiration hit and a few changes here, there and everywhere and I finally felt happy enough with the results to release it. Well, after enough editing to make many eyes bleed.

There have been so many people who helped and encouraged me along the way. First, I'd like to thank my daughters, Ashley and Breanna. From the time they were in kindergarten, they have had such a huge appetite for reading, I literally could not buy books fast enough to satisfy them. They were thrilled when my husband, Jon Thomason, wrote *Max Xylander and the Island of Zumuruud*. After, when I came up with a new book idea for Jon and he scoffed at the idea of writing a teen romance (not really his thing), my daughters dared me to write *the thin veil*. They gobbled up every chapter that I wrote and when the book was done, Ashley asked me to write the sequel for her birthday, *the thin line*, which I did. A year later, I wrote the conclusion to the trilogy, *thin skin* and then decided to take on a much more ambitious project in my favorite genre, dystopia. Ashley and Breanna, and also my step-daughter Ashley Lyn, have been with me every step of the way, providing commentary, editing, and occasionally threatening my life when they didn't like where things were headed with certain characters. They shared the books with their friends and soon, I had many girls threatening my life :).

A note on editing. I'm a bit of a perfectionist. I've been through *daynight* hundreds, if not thousands of times (on my laptop, phone and iPad, because things jump off the page on smaller screens), and have had three proofreaders go through it. I *hate* finding mistakes. Invariably though, each time I edit, I potentially introduce more errors. So, my apologies if you find a problem and know that I'm cringing right along with you. I've done updates over a single incorrect letter, so email me at megan@meganthomason.com if you find anything.

My husband, Jon, an exceptional writer in his own right, has supported me through thick and thin, also reading and re-reading my books, offering suggestions, and honest criticisms. He also designed the book cover for *daynight,* which I love. When I'm fully entrenched in writing, he puts up with a messy house, less-than-fabulous meals, and a very distracted wife. My kids have patiently endured hearing "Just let me finish this" and "Not now"'s. Is it a bonus that they've all learned to be quite self-sufficient? The honest truth? If I'm not writing, I'm doing another project. My kids tease me incessantly about my projects (sure, the world-class weapons collection might have been a little unnecessary, but at the time it seemed cool. And it will be rather useful come the zombie apocalypse.)

My kids also make the most excellent muses. I feel like I live in a comedy show. Yes, they have been known to have raging debates at the dinner table about the best weapons to use during the zombie apocalypse with guests present (those guests never returned).

A huge shout-out to my friends who graciously agreed to read my books early on... Kelli J., LeAnn R., Marci B., Darlene I, Liz S.... you guys are awesome. My sister... Tara C. And thanks to my kids' friends who also logged some major hours... Rachel P., Jonci R., and Jennifer T.

I find music inspiring and some of the artists who help get me typing include Muse, My Chemical Romance, Imagine Dragons, Owl City, blink-182, The Killers, Fall Out Boy, Ludo, and Neon Trees.

Thanks to the folks who designed and developed Scrivener... they make outlining, organizing notes and research, and writing easy. I'm also grateful to those who created Dropbox, which allows you to open files in Kindle and see your book before it goes live. And a huge shout out to the folks at Amazon and CreateSpace who have transformed the publishing industry.

I'm hard at work on the next installment of the *daynight* series and have other story ideas in the mental works as well.